ALSO BY LEIGH EVANS

The Trouble with Fate

The Thing About Weres

LEIGH EVANS

St. Martin's Paperbacks

THE THING ABOUT WERES

Copyright © 2013 by Leigh Evans.

All rights reserved.

For information address St. Martin's Press, 175 Fifth Avenue, New York, NY 10010.

ISBN: 978-1-250-00641-7

Printed in the United States of America

St. Martin's Paperbacks edition / August 2013

St. Martin's Paperbacks are published by St. Martin's Press, 175 Fifth Avenue, New York, NY 10010.

10 9 8 7 6 5 4 3 2 1

For Mom, forever carried in my heart.

For M. with forever carried in my heart

Acknowledgments

To these people I owe my gratitude:

Deidre Knight—a wonderful person and a hugely supportive agent.

Holly Blanck—my talented, keen-eyed editor, who has lots and lots of patience.

Bella Pagan—my clever UK editor, whose request yielded a prologue I really like.

Angela Zoltners—cheerleader and champion of the missing word.

Rebecca Melson—the friend who's willing to read that first wretched draft.

Sandra Krecisz—this well-loved girl comes up with perfect names.

Stephanie Seebeck DiSandolo & Amanda Seebeck—More names! More love!

Julie Butcher—who listened to me whine. Over and over again.

Victoria Koski—my eagle-eyed friend, who caught so many errors.

My family—last but never least.

On the Tricky Subject of Wishes

I don't know why Weres think the moon's so beautiful. Look at it. The thing's rutted with craters. Not once have I gazed at it and wanted to let loose a wolf howl or break into a melancholy chorus of "Moon River."

Most nights, I refuse to give it more than a brooding glance. Matter of fact, *most* of the time, I make a point of not looking upward. I keep my eyes trained on the life around the pond and the dead air above it.

But sometimes, when my thoughts are muddy and circular—like they are tonight—my gaze will slowly swing upward to a certain star.

Star light, star bright.

If you want to see what I'm waxing poetic about, tilt your chin up and slant your gaze to a few degrees left of the Milky Way. There it is: one twinkle-perfect light. To my eyes, it's not silver or white but a definite blue—a faint copy of the azure that glimmers from Trowbridge's eyes. And even though it sparkles from a blanket of similar lights, to me its glow is far brighter than any other star's.

It stands alone.

Brave. Insolent. Bright.

That makes it unique, and so I claim it as mine. Screw the dudes with the pocket protectors and penchant for Latin. They may have already given that radiant beauty a

double-consonant moniker but I've redubbed that bit of
pretty "Hedi's Star."

The first star I see tonight.

I've never pinned a wish upon my star. Mostly because
I have the sneaking suspicion that Karma's not done with
me yet. And I can't help but worry that no matter how cagily I frame my request, that greedy witch would hear the
naked plea in it, and would immediately begin plotting
something nasty.

And she'd already done a whole bunch of the nasty.

Why? Because Karma's an insatiable bitch.

Which is exactly the type of talk Cordelia loathes hearing. Trowbridge's best friend has several pithy life prompts
she repeats whenever she's convinced I'm in need of some
attitude coaching. "You are the architect of your own life."
(Pinched from Alfred A. Montapert.) "Find your passion
and embrace it!" (Lifted from Oprah.) And her own wry
creation, "Stop brooding, darling, or you'll get lines around
your mouth."

They're relatively new, these buck-up phrases.

At first, back in the day when we were getting accustomed to each other's foibles—basically those early weeks
just after we'd shoved Trowbridge through the Gates of
Merenwyn—my six-foot roommate had been confident
that I'd figure out how to summon the portal.

Uh-huh. That and a dollar bill will get you four bits.

Then one day, she came to the quiet realization that I
wasn't going to summon up the smoke, and the myst, and the
round window to the Fae realm—or maybe better said, she
finally understood that I really couldn't—and she abruptly
dropped the subject of bringing the true Alpha of Creemore home.

That's when Cordelia started focusing on the here and
now, which meant alternately scowling at me with something akin to reluctant affection or holding up her bejew-
eled finger to utter one of those little bon-mots.

And that's when *I* knew.

My new best friend had resigned herself to what she

considered the truth: that Trowbridge wasn't ever going to return home; that Merenwyn had swallowed him just like it had swallowed my twin brother Lexi; and now it was up to the three of them—Cordelia, the ex–drag queen; Harry, a Were who's seen three score and more years; and Biggs, the wolf voted least likely to succeed—to form a protective barrier between me and Trowbridge's pack.

"Look on the bright side, darling, where there's life, there's hope," she says now when she's feeling generous.

But she doesn't look at me when she says it.

Days have run together. Fast forward and we're here—the first night of the Hunter moon, six months and twelve days after I slid my mate through the Gates of Merenwyn. Which was one of the reasons my favorite star and I were having an epic stare-down before I threw in the towel and tried to get some sleep.

Last night, as I lay alone in my bunk bed, listening to the dead branches of the old maple chafe in the wind, I had a mind-blowing epiphany.

Ready? See if you can follow my logic: if there really was such a thing as Karma, then how much of a stretch was it to believe that there's such thing as a benevolent Goddess in the sky? And even more wondrous—what if my Sky Goddess was more powerful than Karma?

Could there really be such a loving deity? One that waits, invisible and Godly, dying to hear your problems? And better yet—what if she could protect me from Karma's whims? What if my Goddess was just waiting to hear me wish upon a star?

On that hazy thought, I drifted off into a dreamless sleep, from which I woke with the sudden, irritating awareness of one additional and painful twist to the previous night's revelation.

Hells-bells, if my logic was sound, then my silence over these last six months wasn't an act of stoic restraint; it was a piece of lame stupidity.

Crap.

So here I am. Sitting cross-legged on Lexi's pirate

stone, slapping at late-season mosquitoes, setting myself up for a fall. On the plus side, I'm solo tonight—nobody's breathing over my shoulder because my would-be protectors believe I'm safe by the fairy pond. The wolves are spooked by it, and the humans don't know about it. Up in the trailer, Cordelia's fussing with her wig. Back at his apartment, Biggs is probably reading some wolf-girl's Facebook timeline. And Harry? Goddess knows what my favorite geezer's doing. Maybe he's oiling his gun.

I'm finally alone. About to pin a wish on a star.

I wish I may, I wish I might.

I clear my throat. "Hey, Star. I'm not sure how this wish-fulfillment thing goes, so I'm going to just work my way toward my request, okay?" *Cover all the bases first. You're not above doing a little groveling to smooth the way.* "I know that it's totally my problem that I can't summon the portal. I accept responsibility all way round on that. And I know if you really want to be pissy, then it's my own fault that I'm in this position. After all, I was the person who pushed Trowbridge through the Gates of Merenwyn—"

Gad, am I turning into one of those wimpy women who tune into Dr. Phil?

"I had no choice," I say, in a harder tone. "It was either that or watch him die."

And I'll never sit helpless again, watching someone die.

"Look, I've been thinking about this a lot. Karma's already taken a big bite out of me. A Were killed my dad, and the Fae executed my mom. The Fae stole my brother too—by force—and dragged him across the portal into Merenwyn, and then . . ." Even now, it's hard to think of it. "They slammed the gates shut. I haven't seen Lexi since."

Unforgivable.

Lexi's got to be alive. Trowbridge, too.

"Maybe it's time for the tide to turn. Maybe you can tell Karma to back off and throw me a bone." I blink hard at the tears gathering, and my star—that round blue diamond—

blurs into something you'd expect to see hovering over a stable, a donkey, and a pregnant virgin.

"I'm not asking for the moon . . ." I feel my lips curve into a weak smile. "So I won't ask you to return Merry, too."

No, I can't do that. She made it home. She's safe now.

My damned throat is so damn raw it hurts to form the words. "So all I'm asking for is . . ."

Oh, Goddess. What if Trowbridge is happier there? What if life is better in Merenwyn? Is that why neither of them have returned home?

I can't shape the words.

I can only silently pray.

Please, Star.

Give me the wish I wish tonight.

Chapter One

Wishing upon a star is a foolish exercise. I'd gone to bed late, after a quiet dinner of two maple-glazed doughnuts and a Kit Kat, followed by a chaser of grape juice.

"I'm dreaming again," I said, feeling miserable and happy all at once.

Because I was, and because it was as good a way as any of saying hello. The alternative was saying "Hello, beautiful," and that was both obvious and repetitive.

On his worst day, my guy is a freakin' work of art.

I know.

I've seen him on his worst day.

Robson Trowbridge stood hip-deep in the Pool of Life, caught in the act of raking his long, curling hair off his forehead. I could waste time wondering why each visit begins the same way—his hand lifted to his brow, his bicep flexed, his abdomen muscles ridged like some lucky girl's washboard—but I won't. It's my dream or his dream or our dream, and it never ends well, so it seems fitting that it begins with him hale and hearty, and so insanely sexy that a girl's heart picks up at the sight of him.

As mine had.

Evidently, art appreciation does that to me.

Blame it on his hair. Except for a few faint silver threads, Trowbridge's mane is as dark as a lump of coal and enviably thick. Though, at present, it was wet, and mostly, so was he. Beads of the Pool of Life's water stood out on the slope of my mate's shoulder—little translucent blips of healing Fae power that paid no heed to gravity—seemingly content to stay there, clinging to his collarbone and the rounded swell of his upper deltoids.

Therein lies one of the inherent problems about being around Trowbridge.

He's so damn beautiful that it's really hard to think in a straight line around him. For instance, when I saw those little beads of water on his hard shoulder, I didn't think "baby needs a towel." Nope. Instead, I imagined myself licking the moisture off.

Sad, the direction my brain slithers when I'm around my mate.

To be honest, I'm not sure if I'm comfortable with the full body flush of sexual desire that nearly levels me when I see him standing there, utterly desirable and absolutely unreachable. I don't trust it. There was no reason to it, no natural progression from first stirrings of attraction to my current level of "wave my panties over my head" lust.

I grew up in the same small Ontario town as he. His house was just on the other side of the pond. As a kid, I'd been the uninspired witness to many Trowbridge sightings. But one day, a few months before puberty, I looked at him, and it was like someone had pressed my sexual identity's switch to on. Bam! Bye-bye, Barbie. Hello, Trowbridge.

Like my body was preset for him, and him alone.

Behind my lover, Merenwyn's forest climbed a series of hills in rolling swells of golden yellow and deep green, providing a scenic foil to Trowbridge's own particular dark beauty. I studied the tree line until my heart settled down, then said with faux calm, "It's cold tonight."

Gorgeous grimaced and pulled his fingers free from his damp locks. "Why does it *always* have to be water? I hate water."

"You know, you look so real in my dreams. Sometimes I think—"

"That you're not dreaming. Well, check the list, Hedi Peacock. Am I wearing any clothing?" Trowbridge ran his hand down his gleaming chest, sliding it along the landscape of all that lovely taut flesh, to disappear under the water. "That's a definite no. Do you know what happens to skin when it stays in water for a long time? Things get shriveled. Important things, like—" He frowned, his hand busy under the water. "God, they feel like stewed prunes."

My mate pulled out his dripping paw, inspected it with a fierce scowl, and gave his hand a savage flick. Droplets of water sprayed—a bullwhip of diamond beads. "Why here? We could have this conversation anywhere else. You *know*—"

"I know. Weres can't swim. You hate water."

He wasn't listening. Instead he was concentrating on dragging his wet mitt across the single dry patch on his pecs—once, twice, and—*ah, there we go*—three times—before he was satisfied that his hand was dry enough to plant on his narrow hip.

Now his chest gleamed in the most distracting way.

"You making any progress on getting these nightmares under control?" he asked.

"This isn't my nightmare."

"Tinker Bell, if this was one of my dreams, you'd be naked and we'd be in bed. *This* is one of your nightmares. I'm standing in the middle of some damn millpond that the Fae consider healing and sacred, without a gun, a knife, or an Uzi. You're under the cherry tree, looking like . . ."

He let his gaze casually roam. First to my mouth, where it lingered on my upper full lip, then slowly down the line of my white throat, from there to the hollow that he'd kissed, and finally to my breast, where it rested for a heated moment or two.

There went his nostrils. Flared as if he could scent me.

"Don't stare at me like that," I whispered, flattening a hand over my stomach.

"Like what?" His hooded eyes glittered.

*As if your gaze were leaving a trail of heat on my skin.
As if I were the sexiest thing you'd ever seen. As if you—*

"You are. You are my fuckin' catnip," he said simply.
"And I'm getting beyond tired of the whole 'look but don't
touch' torture. Come to me, right now. Walk down that hill
and meet me in this goddamn pond."

Eyes the color of the Mediterranean challenged me. Not
the soft warm hue of shoreline shallows—with mellow
hints of turquoise and green—no, more like the saltwater
just past that, where the sea is deep and filled with unexpected currents.

Now, they demanded.

Yes.

I took an unsteady step toward him and then . . . found
myself wobbling, my balance destroyed. I could not move
forward one more inch. My muscles seemed frozen, inca-
pable of the slightest task. No matter how I willed myself,
no matter how I struggled.

With a ragged breath, I retreated. "I can't, Trowbridge.
She won't let me join you."

"I've told you. There is no such thing as Karma. All you
need to—"

"I can't! I cheated her when I pushed you through the
Gates of Merenwyn. This is Karma's revenge. She brings
us together every night, and she won't let me move."

He shook his head once, sharply, in denial. "She doesn't
exist."

"She does."

Anger momentarily tightened his features. Then he assumed control, taking in a long, slow breath. "Okay. We'll
just talk about the weather for a bit. So, is it fall in Creemore yet? All the trees are yellow here." His gaze traveled
as he spoke. A soft hiss of air escaped his lips. "God, I wish
you could see what's behind you."

*I can't. I'm stuck in my head. Just a dreamwalker with-
out a true body, my gaze somehow fastened on you, as if
you were the quavering needle on my compass, watching
you and knowing that I won't be able to—*

"Mannus was right about one thing: this slice of heaven has never met a douchebag with a chain saw. Most of it's virgin forest." His head swiveled left, then right, his brow furrowed. "That's the thing about Merenwyn. The land's whole in this realm. You can taste it—pure and clean—on your tongue. The wind smells—"

"Sweet," I whispered. "It's the magic in the air."

"Maybe. Mostly it smells clean without the humans polluting the place. They smell, and they don't even know it. Their accessories are worse. Their cars, their barbecues, their—"

"You liked driving."

He frowned, as if surprised he'd forgotten that. "Yeah, I did." Then with a light shrug, he pointed to a hill at least a mile in the distance to his left. "There's some whitetails up there. Smell them?" I shook my head to remind him—*I'm only half Were, my little Fae nose isn't as keen as yours, Trowbridge*—but his eyes had become slits, predator sharp; his concentration turned to fix on the quarry in the forest. "One of the bucks is rubbing his antlers against the bark of a tree. Hear it? He's telling all the other bastards to keep out of his way. He's chosen his doe." He listened for a bit, his face rapt. "There's so much game up in those hills."

His nose is perfect. Long and straight. Not misshapen and bleeding.

Trowbridge rubbed his shoulder and stared thoughtfully at the narrow lane that had been cut into the old woods. "How long do we have before the Fae come?"

"They won't come tonight."

He blew some air through his teeth. "They always come. How about giving me a crossbow to fire back at them?"

"I . . ." My voice trailed off.

"Can't or won't," he finished quietly. "That's our basic problem. You keep making decisions without consulting me first."

Not fair, Trowbridge.

The trees behind him swayed, their leaves rustling and parting to reveal the glint of the sinking sun: a yellow-orange ball of fire, as luminous as one of Threall's brightest soul lights.

He lifted his nose to the wind. "Wait . . . something's on the wind."

Not yet, don't let the guards come yet. Just a little longer.

Another inhale, deep enough to flare his nostrils and lift his pecs. "Someone's burning something in the hearth . . . peat? Yeah, I'd say it's peat. Wouldn't it be better to have this conversation beside a cozy, warm fire?"

"You know what burning peat smells like, huh?"

"I'm a figment of your imagination, kid. So, basically, I know everything you know. Hear your thoughts, too." He began a slogging march through the hip-deep water. Six paces to the left, a sharp turn, and eight paces to the right. With each lurching step, the pool's water level rose and fell on the high-water line on his tawny skin. One step and the water was up to his waist, drowning his hands, with the next, it had lapped away, providing a coy glimpse of the soft swell of his ass.

The yearning to touch him began to grow again. Long roots had my desire—like weeds growing between cobblestones.

Trowbridge shook his head. "You know, the only bearable bit in the first twenty pages of *The Highland Warrior's Mistress* was the news that burning peat smells like scorched dirt. One day, I'm going to toss a handful of peat moss on a campfire, just to see if it does. Probably doesn't."

"Why are we talking about this?"

"I'm telling you, I'm well past done with that romance shit. Seriously, who calls his woman 'my sweet wee lassie'?" Water churned behind him in swirling eddies. "The next time you send Biggs to Barrie to satisfy your book binge, let the poor bastard come home with a few thrillers. Lee Child, Robert Crais, maybe an Ian Rankin or two. I don't know how he stands going through the checkout line at Walmart. Why don't you go buy your own books?"

Because you might come back while I'm gone.

"Not going to happen unless you've suddenly remembered the words to summon the portal. How's that going?" He paused in his pacing, his head shifted to one side, his eyes cast down, seemingly intent on something beneath the surface of the water.

Over and over, I've tried. The Gates of Merenwyn are summoned by song. One with very specific lyrics. Which I couldn't remember for the life of me.

When I didn't speak, he sighed, the way men do when they're trying to be patient—through the nose, teeth lightly clenched, jaw hard, impatience a stretched, jagged shadow behind his façade of tolerance. Very softly, too softly, he said, "If I can't find a way home, you're going to have to take your role as Alpha a whole lot more seriously."

"I am taking it seriously. I sign stuff. I—"

"For starters, calling yourself their Alpha-by-proxy is just asking for it. The pack has zero sense of humor about shit like that. Can't you see it's messed up, the way you approach the pack? For us, it's always about status. Who's higher than me, who's lower than me." Water sprayed as my mate swept his arm to demonstrate his point. "You can never let your guard down. You must act, think, and smell like top dog . . . not . . ." He scratched his ear.

A Fae? "I'm doing my best to hold on to your pack but being a leader doesn't come naturally. Until you come home, they'll just have to make do with me. It won't be for much longer anyhow. Sooner or later, I'll find a way to get you home."

"Sooner or later one of them is going to challenge you for leadership," he said.

For a bit, neither of us said anything. Trowbridge swished water through his fingers. I watched a dark smudge in the far distance, winging its way toward us. A bird. Long wings, torpedo-shaped body. Perhaps a duck, but they never flew alone.

"I have my flare," I said.

The bird dipped low, skimming the tree line. An emerald-green cap, a flash of gray and white.

"You have to turn into your wolf, Tink. They have to believe that you are one of them."

"It's a really good flare."

Wings beating furiously, the mallard came in for a landing. It reared back, wings arched, feet thrust forward. A splash and then a long glide. The duck preened its feathers, then paddled sideways to give us a bird glare from its beady eye, before it swam to the end of the pool where the water was murky and the trees hung low.

"Friend of yours?" Trowbridge asked.

I scanned the sky but it was night-gray and heavy, and as far as my gaze could sweep, I could not spot another dark smudge. "Shoo," I said to the mallard. "Go find your mate before winter sets in."

Trowbridge watched the bird, his lips twisted. "Let it go, Hedi."

"Tell me about your life there," I asked softly. "Have you found Lexi yet?"

He shook his head, ever stubborn. "It's moontime there, isn't it?"

"Tomorrow." *Three nights of hell.* "How'd you know?"

"You're more anxious around the full moon. That's when the worst dreams come." Trowbridge's shoulders flexed as he spread his arms wide. He bent his head, his fingers skimming the surface—seemingly poised for a dive.

Don't. Not yet.

Water curled up to his navel and then dipped back. "Have you heard from the NAW yet?"

The letter came this morning. I didn't explain how the air in the trailer had thickened with the sharp spice of Were anxiety after Harry, Cordelia, and Biggs had taken their turns reading it. But then again, in my dreams, I didn't need to.

His wince was the type that happens before a trigger is reluctantly squeezed. And for a second, it was all there. Despair worn down to weary acceptance, fatigue etched into bone weariness—the visual equivalent of a heavy sigh if my Trowbridge was a man given to such things. But he was not. He wiped out the bad and replaced it with a smile that promised hell and havoc. "I have to get out of this pool." My mate started walking toward me, the sound of the churning water loud to my ears. "I'm coming out now. We need to—"

"No!" I closed my eyes. "One thousand, two—"

"Shit! Stop with the counting!"

"Three thousand, four—"

"It's freaking annoying, Hedi," he called, his tone sharp and demanding. "Open your eyes and look at me. I'm good now. There's no scars on my chest or wrists. No silver in my gut. I'm healed."

"Five thousand, six—"

"That's it, I'm coming out of this water right now," he promised, the sound of his splashing progress getting louder, closer.

My eyes popped open. "No! You have to stay in the Pool of Life."

If anything he moved faster. "Dammit, I'm healed!"

"No! Every time you walk out of it, you die!" Acid began rising in my throat.

"I'd rather die on dry land!" he shouted back.

The wind came from nowhere. It whistled through the trees—frost tipped and javelin sharp—and whipped the water into a vengeful chop. It thrashed the trees and shredded their leaves. The remnants came in a whirl, a veritable barrage of dead and broken things; dry whispers of brown, bright flickers of yellow and red. They swirled and danced over my lover's head.

He hunched his shoulders as he batted them away. "Hedi, you're going to blind me with these damn things! I need to see! Chill. I mean it! Close your eyes and think of something else."

I did. I covered my eyes and thought of something easy, but in the landscape of my dreaming mind, the wind still moaned.

"Okay, okay. Shh, sweetheart, I've got you," he whispered in my ear. "Breathe deep. Steady now. It's a dream.

That's all it is." A sigh—I swear I felt his warm breath on my face and the soft press of his lips to the peak of my ear.

"Please, Tink, go back to sleep. Dream of Krispy Kremes and napoleons, not of me."

Strangely obedient, my fist tightened on something soft and giving, perfumed very faintly of Trowbridge. I rubbed my cheek on its cotton softness, but as I wrapped my arms around it, a keening part of me registered the lumpy contours of my pillow.

"Sweet dreams, little one."

Arm shielding my eyes, I rolled over, feeling the sheets catch on my hip.

Gray light in my bedroom. The floor-to-ceiling cabinet holding my clothes and his, reassuringly within arm's reach. *Good. Now wake yourself up, fully. Get out of bed for some water. Go for a pee. Move.* But I didn't. I lay there, drowsy and bereft, hovering on the brink of dread.

You see? I couldn't leave him. I never could.

My eyes closed again all on their own.

In those brief seconds of semiwakefulness, time had passed. Merenwyn's sun had fallen, its golden light given way to the silver shimmer of the stars. Fall had yawned, and trundled off for bed. Gone were the bands of vivid gold, the touch of crimson in the hills. Winter chill was in the air and, save for the firs, the trees in the vista were bare. Viewed from a distance, the horizontal swaths of their gray-taupe trunks and naked branches seemed to be a gray fog wreathing through the vertical spikes of the sharp-tipped evergreens.

Almost like Threall seen from a bird's-eye view, I thought.

The pond was empty, save for the man I could not rescue.

Trowbridge's back was goosefleshed and bluish in the cold. "Back so soon?" he asked, without turning. The muscles on his back pulled and stretched as he folded his arms.

"Karh! Karh!" warned a distant raven.

My mate cocked his ear, and took a step toward the

deep part of the pool. "You should be dreaming of better things than this, Tink." Water crept to his waist as he took another resolute step toward the drop-off. "Why do you do this to yourself? Always come back for the end? Why?"

"I don't want you to die alone."

"You should have checked the fine print of the mating bond. Our destinies will always be connected." His gaze was fixed on the road leading out of the forest. "I told you a Were should never cross the portal. Nothing good's going to come of it."

"I had no choice."

"You did. You could have had the courage to let me go. Instead, you broke the treaty. The Fae will come," he said with a cold certainty that made me feel all kinds of awful.

The Fae have *come. It used to be that I'd meet you every night and now I'm never sure who I'm going to meet in my slumber. Mad-one and some old Fae keep slipping into my dreams. Am I starting to go mad, too? Because that's what mystwalkers do. We lose our marbles.*

Numbly, I watched my lover draw a shape in the water with his hand. A backward *S* curve slid into an upside-down one, as Trowbridge carved a figure eight reclining on its side, infinitely graceful. "I'm tired of this," he murmured softly. "Why does it always have to come down to a fight?"

As I'm tired of it. The welling guilt, the sharp bite of desire, the low swell of longing, the growing acid of fear.

"I'll change into my wolf tomorrow night, Trowbridge. I promise."

But he'd lifted his ear sharply to something only he could hear, and then he quietly asked, his breath misting in the cold air, "What could I say to make you leave now?"

That you're coming home. That you forgive me.

"You ask for the moon, Hedi Peacock." A snowflake fluttered from the sky to land on his shoulder with a frozen kiss. It lay there, a perfect crystal that did not melt. The raven issued another volley of urgent *karhs,* and then, over its sharp cry, came the sound of horses being ridden in haste. I heard the hollow drumming of hooves on hard earth and the long metallic slither of silver swords being drawn.

Trowbridge swiveled his head to look at me. Blue eyes piercing. "These visits have to stop. It just makes things harder. You need to face the fact that I'm never going to find my way back." Then, his jaw hardened. "Now go home, Hedi. Don't watch this."

The sound was getting louder.

All I could hear, those drumming hooves.

The muscles of his neck moved as he swallowed. "It's time for my swim."

My Trowbridge dived into the depths of the Pool of Life, hands pressed like in a prayer, just as the first arrow soared through the air.

Chapter Two

Why do I keep making promises?

"It's easier if you're nude when you do it," Cordelia said.

"What is it with you Werewolves?" I flapped away a mosquito. October in Creemore and the bugs were still hungry. "You're always looking for any excuse to walk around naked."

It was getting dark, but I could still witness her left eyebrow rise into a truly impressive arch. "Do I walk around nude? Have you *ever* seen me without clothes?"

"If anyone had, I'd be three hundred and seventy-five bucks richer," said Biggs from the other side of the cedars.

"Haven't you and your 'bros'"—her throaty voice stretched the word out in one long vowel of dismissal—"anything better to do with your pennies?"

"Hey, Cordelia, inquiring minds want to know."

I knew where this was going. They couldn't say "pass the salt" without sarcasm and disdain hitching a ride on the saltshaker.

All our nerves were shot tonight. Yesterday morning a letter had arrived from Reeve Whitlock, head of the Council of the North American Weres. It had looked innocuous enough. Plain envelope, a Canadian stamp affixed crookedly in the corner. Inside was this piece of news: a formal request from the NAW for our accounts books and notification of a meeting, set for the middle of next week. The prospect of an audit should have produced an eye roll from Cordelia and a heavy sigh from Harry.

Right?

But Harry had said, "It's a smokescreen. They're laying a paper trail down so that they can sew it up neatly later for the Great Council. Whitlock's ironed out whatever problem kept him from sticking his nose into our business and now he's coming for us."

Cordelia had refolded the letter and slid it back into its plain white envelope. Then she'd turned and stared out the dinette window, her carefully painted mouth a long grim slash. "It couldn't have gone on much longer," she said. "We all knew that."

We did?

Six months ago, my aunt Lou had killed Mannus, the former Alpha of Creemore. As crowns for the furry are a matter of lineage and ability, my mate, Robson Trowbridge, had stepped into the position. Well, technically, he'd been shoved into it as he'd been borderline comatose in those desperate moments following his sudden ascension.

I had a choice: save his life or watch his death.

I'm always going to put my money on life.

Anyhow, for the last six months, I'd assumed the role of Alpha-by-proxy, which meant I was "leading" the Weres of Ontario in his absence. Basically the job boiled down to signing stuff. And smiling a lot. And pretending to look like I understood what was going on, when usually I felt about fifteen minutes behind the conversation.

It was hard to keep focused. My brain kept drifting from topic to topic because I hadn't had a good night's sleep in . . . Fae Stars. Eight months? It was bad enough watching Trowbridge die night after night. But now my nightmares pulled me into Threall. And to that room with the old wizard and Mad-one.

Cordelia snapped, "Tell Biggs to keep his eyes straight ahead."

Tetchy, wouldn't you say?

Maybe I should have chosen a place up in the hills to do this, instead of the forgotten part of the cemetery. But only the most intrepid Creemore wolf would willingly put a paw in this portion of the graveyard, because wolves are, on the whole, superstitious, and—get this—scared of anything supernatural. Ghost stories? They wouldn't read them. Hell, R. L. Stine novels are *banned* in the halls of St. Hubert of Liege's School of Learning.

Yup, the pack wasn't much keen on the woo-woo. Even though I've never met a Were who's seen a spook, the entire pack had formed the opinion that their final hunting ground was *infested* with spirits and avoided it like the plague. They wouldn't even take a leak on the cedar shrubs that lined the cemetery and that's when they were dog stupid *and* wolf keen to mark territory.

Yeah, I know. It makes me smile, too.

Truth was, there were only three ghosts as far as I could see. The fussy duet who lived at the newer end of Creemore's St. Luke cemetery kept to themselves, hovering close to the marker of CAROL'S DEARLY BELOVED HUSBAND DWAYNE (1899–1993), while the single spirit who lived in the oldest part—a female ghost who seemed to have a strange fixation on me—always stayed behind the low crumbling stone wall that surrounded her tiny pocket of the cemetery. I'm thinking stalker-ghost was once an outsider, too, because her final resting spot was on the wrong side of the rotting picket fence that once had delineated what was sacred land from that which was not.

What had she been? A suicide?

Whatever she'd been, they'd hated her enough to put two barriers—a fence and a stone wall—around her earthly remains. Seemed unfair. As spirits go, yes, she was a bit of a stalker—snoopy as hell in a very unnerving, focused sort of way—but on the whole, she was quiet, verging on shy. The one time I'd snuck up to say hey, she'd taken off, her shroud wreathing around her in a very cool way. Mostly, she flitted from one end of her corral to the other. She never left it.

That's why we were doing this whole cloak-and-dagger business on this side of the old barrier—the safe side—where there were only five little headstones for five dead babies, and three tall pines, and yeah—one blurry-edged ghost. I considered explaining all this to Cordelia but her teeth were set on presnarl and conversations in the face of that scowl inevitably unraveled. Besides, she'd screwed up her courage to do this here, the one place we could count on not being bothered. Kind of took away from her bragging rights if I told her that the only person watching this besides Biggs was a skittish spook.

"How can I guard you guys if my eyes are straight ahead?" Biggs made a hole in the greenery and grinned through it. He could well be cocky; he was on the other side of the hedge that separated the cemetery from the pack's gathering field. "Someone could sneak up along the cliff path and ambush you."

Cordelia reached for her hoop earring. She could have been getting undressed for the moon-call, but it was equally possible she was getting ready to inflict a course correction on my pack's third.

"No one is going to ambush us," I said, with more optimism than I felt. "Biggs, keep your eyes peeled for any Were who somehow managed to misinterpret my warning not to show up until the moon has completely risen."

"I am."

"Not if you keep spying on what's happening on this side of the hedge."

"A good Were should have eyes and ears on the back of his head," he intoned. "He should sense when a—"

"That wasn't a suggestion, Biggs. That was an order."

There, the Alpha-by-proxy had spoken. *All hail Hedi.*

Biggs subsided behind the screen of cedars. He was the only Were I felt comfortable ordering about. If they were all as simple to control as my friend on the other side of the bush, I'd be—

"Clothing," repeated Cordelia.

It was nippy. Not quite cold enough to frost my breath—

mouth breathing being required because Biggs was smelling kind of funky. Blame it on the moon. On a regular day,
Weres have a distinctive aroma to them—fresh air, woods,
earth, maybe with a touch of fox—but during the three
nights of the full moon their scent turned nose-twitching
raunchy.

Fae don't have a scent.

This is just one of the many distinctions between Fae
and Werewolves. Those born two-natured change at the
moon's call. Fae do not. We make ourselves a cup of cocoa
and go to bed early. We may even clamp a pillow over our
head so that we don't hear all those dog whines and choked
barks escaping from the morphing snouts of the young
cubs who don't know any better. I guess because I'm half
Were I should admit that once in his wolf state, a Werewolf is not the fiend over which picture books dwell and
little children quail. No one in my pack is the type of slath-
ering beast dreamed up by the special-effects department
on a Hollywood lot. Once turned, my Weres actually look
like large wolves. Some of them are pretty, some of them
are sort of ratty looking, but all of them are furry.

Fae are never furry.

And here's a final fact: we don't walk around nude in
public. Did I say that already? Well, let me say it again. We
do not prance around buck naked no matter what stage the
moon is in.

I've got to stop thinking of myself as a Fae.

Cordelia stood tall, her head tipped back, allowing the
moon's light to touch her face with silver fingers that must
have felt damn good, judging by the discreet shudder that
went through her bony frame.

A cool wind whistled through the trees.

My roommate flicked a glance toward the three pines
that anchored the edge of the ridge, and then visibly recen-
tered herself.

"Go away," I mouthed to the glowing shadow flitting
from pine tree to pine tree.

Stalker-ghost melted behind the nearest pine. But half a

second later, her head—nothing more than an indistinct,
wavering bluish blur capped by floating serpent trails of
long hair—popped out from around the trunk.

"Are you paying attention?" said Cordelia, a tetch acidly.

"A hundred percent," I said.

"The more light you let on your skin, the faster you will
change." Cordelia began to unbutton her shirt. For the last
few months, I'd shared a twenty-seven-foot trailer with
her, but this was the first time I'd seen her disrobe. I didn't
want to be able to report on whether or not she had a full
package, even if there was three hundred and seventy-five
bucks riding on it. But she'd offered to show me the ropes.
Or maybe it had been another group decision. I tried to
remember. She cleared her throat and narrowed her eyes at
me, bringing me back from yet another mental detour.

I didn't have any buttons. I hauled my cotton sweater up
and over my head, and then looked for a dry place to place
it. Suppressing a shiver, I bent to drape it over poor little
Samuel's thin, worn marker (1744–1745, BELOVED SON).

"Are you hurrying?" Biggs's voice was strained. "I
don't know how much longer I can hold on."

"He'd bloody well better hold," Cordelia muttered
as she unzipped her skirt. "One of us needs to be in
two-legged form to escort you back to the trailer if this
doesn't work."

Did they really think it had come to that? Unseen danger all around me? Ever since that damn letter arrived, I
couldn't even walk to the compost pile without an escort.

Cordelia was down to her underwear. She had no waist.
None. I could count her ribs under her dead-white skin.
She looked at me steadily, and then her lip twisted into a
lopsided sneer as she reached behind her back for her bra
fastenings.

I partially turned away from her and stared at a tree as
I fumbled with the rest of my clothing. I owed her more
than I could ever repay. The least I could do was grant her
privacy as she shed her adopted sexual identity. As I slid
my jeans down to my ankles, I heard the soft friction of

fabric on skin and out of the corner of my eye I saw something light and lacy land by Cordelia's feet.

A few feet over to my left, beyond the cedar hedge, I could hear Biggs bouncing on the balls of his feet in jittery anticipation. "You'll have to hurry, the Chihuahua is getting anxious," Cordelia said. I shed the rest of my clothing, with the last item—one medium pair of Hanes pink cotton panties—landing on Absolom (1746–1747, LAMB OF GOD). Folding my arms over my chest, I turned back to Cordelia.

She was facing the moon. Her raised arms were outstretched, as if she were trying to embrace it. "You can feel its call inside you," she said in a husky murmur. "The moon will summon your inner wolf. Let its warmth run over your skin. Trust your body. Trust your instincts. Trust the moon." My roommate snapped me a look over her shoulder. "You have to surrender to it, Hedi. You can't go through another moon without showing your other nature. You have to give it to us. Or there—"

"Won't be any 'us,'" I filled in.

"Come hold my hand. Feel it through me."

Sometimes I wondered just who was the minion and who was the Alpha-by-proxy. I tiptoed over, readjusted one arm to cover my boobs, and reluctantly bared my nether regions to reach for the large, well-manicured hand extended my way.

Cordelia lifted our clenched hands to the moon. "Can you feel it?"

I could feel the cold. I could feel the dampness of the ground under my bare feet. I could feel embarrassed and incompetent and all sorts of esteem-lowering thoughts, but I couldn't feel the moon.

"Yup."

"Good." She tipped her head really far back, so far I could see her Adam's apple. "Now, let it happen."

She held my hand tight, even as she started to change, as if, what? As if she could pour a little of her Werewolf essence into me? I felt her skin start to move, courtesy of the bones beginning their stomach-churning, morph-into-a-canine thing. Kind of gross. She pulled me down with her as she fell on her knees.

I slid my hand out of hers, my skin crawling in an all too mortal way at the feel of hers moving under my grip.

A light low moan slipped from her lips, just before she thudded onto her side in her chosen bed of fragrant maple leaves. The tight, well-moisturized skin stretched across her cheekbones began to look like a pot of bubbling cream of chicken soup. *Blip, blip. Blip, blip.* Things were twitching underneath. I'd seen that before, when Trowbridge had started his change. Cordelia's bones started to chitter as they broke and shortened and lengthened and narrowed and did all that horrendous skeleton-shifting stuff they needed to do to accommodate a two-footed being turning into a four-legged creature.

I turned my head away. She'd only just begun if her bones sounded like castanets.

Join them, I told myself. *Be one of them.*

My inner-bitch was restless. She kept pacing inside me and leaking distress into my bloodstream. I heard a whimper. A small whine. I looked around for its source, and then—oh Goddess—realized it was me. That was good, wasn't it? I'd whined. Was the change going to start with my jaw? Was it elongating? I opened my mouth wide— another deep-throated whine slipped out—and tested it, contorting my jaw from its habitual position of just hanging there below my lip waiting for the next cookie to come its way into something more resembling a hungry alligator. I held it like that until my saliva dried on my teeth.

Sea-slurping noises came from Cordelia's bed of leaves.

I am Were.

There, thinking that wasn't half as bad as I thought it would be.

I am Were.

Inside, my inner-bitch grew frantic. She kept bouncing off the ball of Fae magic that sat in my gut beside her, and each time she did, my magic sparked, adding sharp exclamation points of Fae annoyance to the internal writhing that was going on. I pressed both hands flat across the swell of my stomach. Goddess, now that I'd given her full leave to explode, my inner-Were was past mortal logic, past even rudimentary communication with me, her half-bred host. She was all panting "go, go, go" like a pooch who'd spied a squirrel.

"Let's do this without smacking my Fae, okay?" I whispered, darting an anxious glance at Cordelia. "Leave her alone."

"Hedi?" asked Biggs in a strained voice from the other side of the hedge. "Is there trouble?" Two shaking hands parted the shrubbery. The moon was working its mojo on him. His jaw was longer and his mouth a misshapen, stretched thing.

I slapped my hand on his forehead and shoved his heated face back through the cedars. "Stay there!"

"Okay," he mumbled.

My Were did another lunge inside me. This time she hit my ball of Fae head-on, and I experienced the sudden exhilarating leak of its magic into my blood. My mother's gift raced up through my heart, built into a pressure at my throat, divided at my collarbones, and then ran hot, a stream of sizzling glee surging through my veins until it came to my hand where it split into fragments that fattened the ends of my fingertips.

"Crap," I said, flexing my swollen digits. I hadn't accessed my Fae magic once over the summer. No, not because of the threat of payback pain, or even my halfhearted promise to Cordelia to "keep it canned, darling." It was the fear that I would hear my Fae in my head again. Feel her inside me, functioning like a separate entity.

She'd been curiously quiet, too. Not like gone-fishing quiet. More like she'd been drowsing, with one eye open; a dragon trying to figure out if it was worth rousing itself from its warm hearth. I'd felt her faint interest, but she'd been acquiescent.

Now, she was alive in me.

Was she jealous because I'd given my Were full leave?

Wait a minute—was I seeing things differently? I blinked. Yes, things *were* sharper, no longer being admired for their relative shiny qualities. They were being judged, rapid fire, with pitiless eyes—*useful or not*?

Cordelia's wolf yawned.

Thin threads of speculation swirled in my consciousness as my cool gaze lingered over the Were finishing his transformation on his bed of leaves. I found myself looking at him with—what's the word? Objectivity? Acuity? Like a smart person intent on untangling a knot. A conscious being trying to—

Oh Goddess, trying to figure out how to become top dog in Hedi Incorporated.

Magic, magic, mine, crooned a voice inside me.

Aw shit, Fae-me was articulating now.

"Shut up!" I muttered as I probed inward, searching for my Were-bitch, hoping—okay, *beyond* hoping—that she might give her gut-living roomie a good bite on the butt. But no, she didn't come loping to my rescue. Hear-me-howl slunk off and curled herself into a shivering ball low in my belly. "Hey!" I hissed. "You woke her up, you help me deal with this."

"Heeddii," moaned Biggs. "You neeeeed me?"

"No!" My dominant Fae magic sang in my blood, impatient for release. Gone—if there had ever been enough—was the shape-shifting magic I needed to release my inner-Were. I pressed my hands to my belly and felt my muscles tense under their soft layer of padding.

"Come back," I whispered to my wolf. "We'll fight her together. We need to push past this." I ran my hands upward, past the dip of my belly button. Birthed by a Fae, sired by a Were. You'd think I could do both. Shift when the moon called, even as my Fae magic leaked into my bones. Yet it always seemed to go the other way. Fae trying to overwhelm the Were. And now the Merenwynian entity was trying to strong-arm a Stronghold.

Tune the Fae out. Focus on the change.

But there were so many distractions—the aftersmell of

Cordelia's change, and now all around me in a Were cloud, the new scent of her wolf. More like a he, now that she'd shed her perfume-drenched clothing and changed into her wolf form. And Biggs. The shrubbery was no screen against his sharp anxious stink.

But worse was the fear. My damn fear.

It whispered to me. What if my Fae took control of all my functions? Gained the ability to walk? To talk? To kill?

Never again.

I didn't waste time pushing my Fae back into my bowels. I brought the shields down on her with all the fear and desperation I had, and encased her with a layer of my will.

Hold, Hedi. Don't let go.

Then I started counting. Because that's what I do.

By the time I hit forty-two, I was mortal-me again. Just plain, somewhat detached, Hedi Peacock-Stronghold. Looking around me, noting that the scent of flowers had faded to a thin melancholy note, listening to that not-so-helpful internal voice yapping away. *I almost let her out again. What havoc would my Fae have done around all these unsuspecting animals?*

It wouldn't have been pretty.

I stared down into the honey-brown eyes of Cordelia's wolf. Her fur looked damp. I shrugged, and tried to tack a smile on my face. Her head canted to the side. She was very steady on four feet. Her massive sleek white head was just a few inches below mine.

"Still me," I said.

The silver-white wolf woofed in reply. I don't speak wolfish, but still, I got it. A definite "no shit."

"Biggs, shift," I said, getting to my feet. I heard him whine, and then a series of rips, indicating he'd forgone stripping down before his change. It didn't take long. When he'd finished and come to nudge my fingers with his wet snout through the cedars, I said, "I'm sorry, but it's not going to happen. Not ever."

Cordelia barked at me. Sharp. One bark. Just a warning salvo; a reminder that later, if we survived this night, I'd

hear a longer string of human words, which would accu-
mulate into one long-assed speech about perceived threats
and my slacking off in pack responsibilities.

"Once I'm dressed, I'll send the pack off for their
moon-run. Then I'll go straight back to the trailer."

The white wolf stared at me.

"Come on, Cordelia. The pack's not going to hurt me.
It's the guys outside Creemore we have to worry about and
we've got a few days before they come and mess with us."

For the space of another dog pant from Biggs, she considered me—and part of me wondered if she could see the
shadow of my Fae. Then she turned, and streaked through
the Hedi-sized hole in the hedge. A second later, a short
dark wolf erupted out of the dark and gave chase. Biggs
got in one nip to her tail before he shot past her and disappeared over the ridge.

They knew what I had to do next.

I was grateful that I'd been given privacy to do it.

Chapter Three

Crickets would chirp at the end of the world. They wouldn't know better. They'd just keep rasping their back legs together, going about their business, right up to the final cataclysmic jolt.

I felt ancient just listening to their "go us!" chorus.

Somewhere in the last minute or two, the pack had entered the field on the other side of the hedge. I could hear them. Sighing and shivering. Waiting to change. Pawing the grass with the toes of their shoes as if they were racehorses, not Werewolves, as if this were a sprint to the finish tape, not a thing that happened every month.

Some of them had already changed. I could smell their wolves.

Another whine, camouflaged behind a cough and a cupped hand. Soon all of them would be furry. Then they'd expect to be led. Combined, they smelled like one entity, a pack. A family beyond family. Instinct and blood, and what? Would I ever know?

I breathed deep once, twice.

Do it now.

I went down on my haunches to unzip my Nike messenger bag and pull out the bundle wrapped in plastic. Trowbridge's signature scent—woods, grasses, sex, and salt—that indefinable combination of aromas that spoke of him hit me in a wave of longing. I pulled out his clothing, piece by piece. One old running shoe, a battle-scarred T-shirt with a sleeve ripped off, a white shirt with a mysterious stain on it, and his last torn-up pair of jeans. Articles that Bridge had discarded and Cordelia had saved. There was hardly any hint of him left on the items, even though we'd kept them double-wrapped in plastic. I throttled everything down—all those stupid wishes, and equally dim desires—and picked up the jeans.

Holding the waistband in one hand—the little metal snap biting into my palm—and the pant leg in the other, I rubbed his dirty Levi's all along the back of my thighs, across my well-padded butt, and then up the knobs of my spine to my neck. I abraded the skin there, making sure that whatever scent molecule lingered in the denim's weave was transferred to my nape, before I scrunched the pants into a ball, which I dragged hurriedly and ruthlessly over my breasts and belly.

This was always a nasty part, the moment when my Were felt Bridge's essence on my skin. She uncurled from her miserable huddle and stretched like an abused dog on the receiving end of a long, tender scratch.

Were mates usually smell something like each other. Not exact copies, thank the powers that be—because it would suck to be a Were-bitch that smelled like a guy— but a new signature aroma, one with scent tones from both of them. I'd been scentless, thanks to my Fae heritage, all my life. After shoving my mate through the portal's maw, I'd luxuriated in the novelty of smelling like Trowbridge. Foolishly, I'd thought it would be permanent, but that delicious olfactory brew of woods, and wild, and grasses, and *Trowbridge* had gone down the trailer's rust-stained shower drain just five hours later. Now I smell like a bar of Dove.

I put all his stuff back in the messenger bag then picked up my shirt off Samuel, my bra and panties off Absolom, and rescued my pants from Prudence.

I turned to pick up the Royal Amulet.

He wasn't there.

His Nastiness should have been there, right where I left him, on top of baby Jasper's grave marker, but he wasn't. *Had he fallen off?* I squinted in the half light. There was no ball of gold glittering among the pine needles and sparse tufts of grass.

I'd kept my promise to Merry to care for the Royal Amulet as if he were as precious to me as Trowbridge. I'd found a rowboat and plucked His Royal Nastiness off his lily pad. And for the first couple of days he'd been easy to take care of, because at first, he'd been mostly dead. But as fate would have it, he'd thrown a few intermittent sparks of light from the depths of his blue stone so I—feeling very Dudley Do-Right—had made it my daily ritual to offer him a variety of shrubs and deciduous trees to suck the sap out of. It had been touch and go for a month or more, but he'd made a full recovery over time and eventually had developed a personality. Not a good one, but a soul of sorts. The sullen type. Permanently set on rebellion with intermittent fits of entitlement.

He'd pissed me off so much I'd renamed him Ralph.

In the faint hope of a cease-fire, I'd explained to him, "This isn't some war flick. You're not a POW and I'm not your captor. I'm doing the best I can for you." How had Ralph rewarded me? With simmering silence and night-time stealth attacks. Sneaky juvenile stuff. Pinches and scratches. And, might I add, completely at odds with his behavior during the day. Then, he seemed happy enough to peacefully coexist and hang from my neck. Either because he liked to be in the know about pack business, or more likely, and as I was just beginning to fully understand, he used that time to minutely sip from my essence.

"An amulet will die, and its soul along with it, if you don't take care of it," Mum had said. The last thing she'd done before setting a ward on my cupboard was to place Merry around my neck. "Keep her safe."

She should have said, "Goddess, keep all of us safe." Because in one night, the Fae had executed her, a Were had killed my dad, and my twin brother had been forcibly taken across the portal into Merenwyn.

My skin goosefleshed as I craned my head and studied the trees. The Royal Amulet hadn't had enough time to climb one, had he? "Marco," I coaxed with false sweetness.

I twisted to look behind myself.

Huh. You don't see that every day.

Casperella crouched close to the ground on her side of the stone wall, a huddled shape of fluttering fabric and twisting hair. That was both unusual and noteworthy because to this point stalker-spook had basically been the hummingbird of ghosts. Flit, flit, flit. From one end of her enclosure to the other. Usually, spectacularly spectral—all shroud and serpent hair doing the swirling, obscuring thing around her vague glowing outline. Inner lit, just a bit, like the TV tube after you've held your thumb down on the power button. Face rarely glimpsed, and even then, it was little more than a rounded blur with dead gray eyes.

But she had grown two things: intent and a stubby, semitransparent arm that was straining to reach for the baby-fist-sized ball of gold at the base of a nearby tree.

Hello, Ralph.

Ever hungry, the Royal Pest must have morphed into a sphere, and used gravity to roll down a hillock hoping to hit that sturdy maple. But, Karma being the bitch she was, he'd missed and landed by a pine instead.

Ralph turns his nose up at evergreens; they turn his blue stone a tad greenish.

"Hey," I said. "You don't want to touch him."

Casperella's head rolled in my direction. A glimpse of a black eye, a flat bleak slash for her mouth. I scratched at the mosquito bite on my arm, frowning. Was he in any danger? As I contemplated, the Royal Pain in the Ass reverted to his default shape; a round gold pendant, Celtic in appearance, lots of openwork, flattened bands of gold in four trinity knots surrounding an icy blue jewel that was big enough to make any self-respecting rapper's heart go pitty-pat. He casually propped himself against the pine tree, his necklace of Fae gold in a lazy loop near his feet. "Who, me?" his body language screamed. "I'm harmless."

The little imposter.

I shook out my panties. Practically speaking, this situation couldn't be counted as reckless endangerment. Casperella was a twisting shadow of rags who'd sprouted an arm devoid of a hand. (Can we spell *i-n-c-o-r-p-o-r-e-a-l*?) He was a solid Fae amulet loitering under a pine a good five feet beyond that.

Thieving required fingers. Light ones.

And opportunity.

Also, I think it probably helps if you were born with smarts. The type of cool, calculating common sense that allows you to look ahead in the future, and ask yourself, "Do I really need this? Or do I just want it?"

Because hindsight is a bitch who never knows when to call it a day.

I was fumbling with the hooks of my bra thinking how much I missed stealing when Casperella gave a massive shudder that made all her floaty bits snap in the air. Interesting. I adjusted the girls, watchful as the blob at the end of the arm struggled to morph into something that resembled a hand. Apparently growing mitts required a whole-body effort. She contracted with a sharp inhale—yeah, yeah, I know that's impossible, but that's what it looked like—that flattened her tattered shroud into a long sheet of ragged edges. Then, with a soundless sigh, she exhaled.

Must add that to my rule book. Ghosts remember how to breathe.

Pop! A hand formed—if that's what you could call a thumb and flipper of melded fingers. Unlovely, but adequate, I guess, if you're a spook thinking of pinching a pretty piece of something sparkly.

"You should stop and think about this," I warned. "He's nice to look at, but he's got a temper."

Oblivious to my tidbit of wisdom, Casperella added a

little more ghost juice to her Pilates and succeeded in extending herself until she was an inhuman U-shape curved over her stone barricade. Her flipper-fingers chewed the dirt in an effort to get to Mr. Sparkle.

It looked painful.

Was it worth telling her that all the stuff that spoke to her worst instincts—his loops of Fae gold, his intricately cut jewel, his long, glittering diamond-cut chain—amounted to nothing more than glitzy ornamentation? The real deal was the rice-sized shadow in the center of the blue topaz.

That was the mind and soul of the Royal Amulet.

I'm thinking he was an Asrai before he'd been imprisoned in the jewel set in the middle of the pendant, because that's what Merry had been. She'd recognized him, and I figured then and still did now, that like recognizes like. My amulet friend had fought for the jerk's life, just as I had fought for Trowbridge's.

You don't do that shit unless you have a reason.

Some evenings, before I put Ralph to bed in his brand-new terrarium, I hold him up to the moonlight with a pair of tongs, and speculate whether he'd ever been Merry's lover.

Hey, it could have happened.

Back in the day, he'd had legs, arms, a head, and in his case, probably a dick. I know because I checked. The day after I rescued him, I'd borrowed a magnifying glass from the librarian's drawer, duct-taped his chain to the dinette's table, and studied the dark smudge in the center of that near-perfect stone. I'd arrived at the firm conviction that the imprisoned sentient being was male; it was something about the way he stood, like a toy soldier with one little sticklike appendage out—I'm thinking his arm, not his dick, in case you're wondering—as if he'd raised it to ward off the magic, but the curse had struck first, and now he was frozen, his hand forever poised to halt the evil speeding toward him.

His Royal Nastiness was probably an enchanted prince.

Oh, put away your hankie. It's just as possible that he could be a dumb Asrai peasant who got too close to a Fae bent on mischief. Possibly that's why he dislikes me—he was cursed by one of my kind to live eternity in a hunk of blue stone. Or maybe it's because of my Were—its hot blood is disappointingly thin in terms of required Fae magic.

Whatever. If he was the fair lost prince of the Asrais it would explain his sense of entitlement. How many people had a "the" in front of their names? It had to mess with your head. Keeping half an eye on Casperella's flipper-paws progress, I picked up my socks. *The Alpha.* That worked. *The Alpha-by-proxy.* Weak. *The Fae.* A tad non-specific because I was the only Fae—well, half Fae—on this side of the portal. *The Mystwalker.* If the pack knew what that meant they'd be horrified, given how they felt about the supernatural. I imagined bringing it up in casual conversation. "Hey, do you know I use *my mind* to travel to a different realm? Uh-huh, sure can. And you know what I can do while I'm there? I can sort through a Fae's memories like they're a deck of playing cards. Rearrange them, too, if I felt like it."

Yeah, that would go down well.

I flicked a glance over to the Royal Asshat as I slid the white cotton anklet over my heel. His reaction was covert, but I recognized his interest in the ghost. Where once there had been slack in his chain, now there was an indefinable tension.

"You've got a whole bunch of Napoleon syndrome going on tonight," I told him. In response, the Royal Amulet flashed a blip of light twice—a piece of communication I'd witnessed enough times to recognize as an insolent FU.

"Nice language." But the oak tree shivered behind me, and I did, too.

He set out a lure: a string of white blips brightened the dim gloom under the tree. White blip (see me sparkle), white blip (ain't I pretty), white blip (uh-huh, I'm so damn fine).

Fascinating. He was coaxing her closer. But why?

What was the worst that could happen if I allowed them to interact? Could he drain her dry of whatever supernatural essence she had? I tried to imagine Ralph with more attitude, which almost immediately led to the thought of me standing in front of Merry with an apologetic expression, explaining how I watched disaster unfold while I fumbled with my socks.

No, thank you.

"Hey, Boo," I said. "Beat it."

She didn't even turn her little Medusa head my way. Her mincing hand inched forward.

Annoying.

Plan B. Remove Ralph from danger. I plunged my hand into my bag. *Where are my tongs?* The damn messenger bag was crammed full of stuff. Trowbridge's shoe. A soft leather pouch attached to a pool of golden chain. An almost empty roll of duct tape. *Crap, crap, crap. Where are they?* My fingers delved past the empty coin purse. Brushed against a romance novel with the cover torn off. Hit the bottom seam of the bag where the orphaned Skittles lolled. Did a hurried and rough exploration of its contours.

And came up tongs-empty.

When he was in a pissy mood, tongs were kind of essential amulet-handling equipment. I popped the red Skittle in my mouth, and sucked on it for a soothing half second, considering my options. You know when you know something bad is going to happen and you just can't figure out how, or why? A certainty of impending doom corkscrewed through me. But even as a little voice said to me, *Perhaps you should take a brief moment right now for a spot of reflection,* I'd already swung my messenger bag at Casperella. Because in my book, that's what you do.

You act. You don't think.

I charged.

The messenger bag was a twelve-inch nylon rectangle, heavy enough to make my shoulder ache. Theoretically, it should have batted her smoke right to the nearest ashtray.

It didn't.

On impact, she half turned toward me, her head arched and tilted sideways in an all too mortal WTF as my messenger bag sliced through her fluttering shroud. It made dust rags out of her garment, and then, curiously, its momentum slowed markedly, too.

Not something you see every day: a ghost with a Nike shoulder bag planted in her middle. She seemed to buckle over it, and then she heaved—the way a cat does before it throws up a hairball—and my bag broke through her, curved in a sharp arc, and walloped me hard enough on my naked thigh to make me spit out my Skittle.

To top it off, she'd graced my messenger bag with a thin layer of her ectoplasmic goo.

Why are people always messing with my stuff?

As my foot sliced through her and she became a Rorschach test around me, I realized something interesting and potentially important. Casperella was not smoke. In fact, she was more like dark ink. I registered this, and my automatic *ewww,* as something liquid-cool and syrup-thick started sliding down my throat.

How can something that smells that good feel so bad inside? While I choked and spasmed to cough her up, she reassembled the rest of her inky bits and dove for the amulet, in a graceful, arched column. Like the St. Louis Arch, except dark and planted over a crumbling stone wall.

Without a sound, she enveloped him.

No, no, no.

I threw myself into the stream of her and got in a couple of flailing ink-smearing bitch slaps, but soon found myself sinking to the ground. Because, as it turns out, the burden of a writhing body of ink can be soul-wearying.

Her sadness weighted my limbs.

"Home," I heard her say in my head. "Let me go home."

The slightly foreign cadence to her voice threw a chill down my ribs. And with that, I forgot all about protecting Ralph. And the gathering Weres. Even the damn letter that sat under the bowl of oranges on the dinette table. The

accent was unmistakable. I'd grown up listening to it, first
with my mum then with my aunt Lou.

Oh, sweet heavens, I thought, clawing for air. *Casperella's not a Were.*

She's a Fae.

The ghost from Merenwyn was over me, fluid and in-
tangible. I felt like I was drowning under the smothering
blanket of her. Picking up flickers of thought and broken
bits of a life once lived.

So tired.

A blip of light shone in the murky ink. White, sharp.

Followed by a sparkling flash of gold.

Ralph had unwound his trinity knots into rapiers and
gone all Three Musketeers. His blades flashed. They may
have been thin and short but they were made of Fae gold—
stronger than titanium—and were thus neither as soft nor
as fragile as mortal precious metal. Also, and more importantly, they weren't being wielded by a lily-livered popin-
jay. Merry's boyfriend was lightning fast, using one rapier
to thrust and slash, the other to cut and slash. He really must
have been a prince once upon a time, back in the day when
they wore feathers in their hats and swordplay was a way
of life, because the arc of each slashing cut was precise in
a way that bespoke long hours of training.

Casperella surged back in retreat, a contorted, whirling
whisper of smoke and ink. I caught a glimpse of her eye,
black and tragic. An open mouth and a pale thin jaw. I
could feel her yearning for home like a sad song in my
heart.

"Enough, Ralph," I said.

Unappeased, Merry's lover sprang up, a veritable Jack
in the Box of doom, and jabbed both swords into her
throat.

Casperella moaned one word. Low, piteously.

And then she broke into fragments of ink. The blue-
gray droplets hung in the air, impervious to gravity. Another groan, this time from the wind sawing through the
oak tree on the other side of the picket fence. And then,

slowly, in a way that kind of hurt me, I watched those floating bits of ghost turn the color of ash.

October's breeze breathed through them and they were gone.

I rolled and reached for Ralph. He swung his rapiers my way, ready to slit my wrists.

"Don't even think about it."

He retracted his blades and hopped on my palm. I snatched up my bag, abandoned my running shoes, and then I dove again, this time for the hole in the cedar hedge.

"Mystwalker."

Had she really called me Mystwalker?

THE THING ABOUT WEIRS

Chapter Four

The Hedi-sized gap in the line of cedar shrubs guarding the boneyard hadn't been there in the spring, but after I'd realized it was faster to take the footpath along the ridge around the pond than use the public road to the Trowbridge land, I'd gone to the local Home Depot and liberated an electric hedger. Ralph and I blew through that aperture like a watermelon seed through wet, pursed lips.

The air eddied around me. Were-fragrant.

Casperella's a Fae.

"You ready?" called Harry from the crest of the little hill. My second was tall, really tall, and would have stood out in a crowd even if he weren't playing school monitor to a bunch of morphing Werewolves. Long, white, shoulder-length hair, hooded eyes. Slow to talk.

For instance, he could have said, "So, you couldn't change into your wolf?"

But he didn't.

Sweat glistened on his forehead. "I can hold off long enough to see you back to the trailer."

I gave him a Starbucks smile. "Then who'd lead them on the run?"

"You're right." His forehead pleated as he lifted his brows in wry agreement. "Watch out, though. Some of the brethren have come for the Hunter moon run." Harry's voice grew muffled as he pulled off his denim shirt. "Their energy has changed the feel of the pack."

Oh joy. Dog whines greeted me as I walked down the incline toward the wolves milling about in the green dip of flat field between one hill and the other. Most of those assembled turned at my approach. Some briefly, others whipping their heads back and forth between me, and the line of trees, with the same keyed-up excitement a dog displays for his leash and master. A few spared me so brief a glance, so indifferent, it almost bordered on a challenge. And some—the happy-go-lucky ones—occupied their time by either licking things they'd wish they hadn't in the morning, or just standing, visibly trembling, their gaze everywhere except on me.

I didn't need to stop and count to know I was way up on eyeballs.

Maybe eighty pairs of eyes swung in my direction as I came to a stop by Cordelia. There she was—the only white wolf in a huge patchwork gathering of buffs, grays, and browns. Untouched by them. Sitting distant, aloof. I resisted the urge to run my fingers through her white fur and maybe steal a little of her aplomb.

Concentrate, I told myself. *Try to exude confidence.* Or failing that, strive to look balanced and centered. Most importantly, ignore that which cannot be ignored: the presence of my personal Fae, now sitting bolt upright near my spine. Aware. Awake. Like she'd swallowed five cans of Red Bull without pausing to wipe her mouth.

Talk about lousy timing.

The Hunter moon is recognized as an opportunity for representatives of the smaller packs to join their Creemore brethren, so that they can socialize and put forward whatever petitions they feel need to be answered. But mostly they come to party and look for a mate. At the end of the last run of the change, they buy a couple of cases of Creemore Springs beer and head home the next day with a hangover and some happy memories.

But these visitors weren't just coming to socialize.

They were coming to see if all the back-fence talk was true. That the mate of the missing Alpha couldn't actually change into her wolf. That she was round, and small, and young looking. That she didn't have the right smell to her because she was part Fae.

They'd come to sniff out the truth.

Goddess, if they could smell my Fae . . .

Rumors had spread about me. I don't know how. Within an hour of Ralph's Great Lily Pad Rescue, Harry had suggested that I put a gag order on the pack. So, as the Alpha's proxy, I'd banned any mention of our pack business or Trowbridge's ascension on all methods of communication—no phone calls, letters, e-mails, text messages, or forum messages. Not even a tweet. Nothing at all sent to the outside world about the interesting state of affairs of the Ontario pack.

But there are other ways of saying things without actually moving your lips, aren't there? Raised eyebrows and expressive hands. Lips pursed when a certain question is posed. Some silences are more condemning than a crowd of chanting protestors.

Acceptance of Bridge's rightful ascension—and as his mate, mine—wasn't limited to the approval of the assembled pack. Weres have been in this realm for a long, long time. Long enough to form affiliations and associations. Long enough to breed that dreaded plague known as the political body. The hierarchy is simple. The wolves of North America fall under the aegis of the Council of North American Weres, who in turn genuflect to the Great Council of Weres.

As our immediate concern was the NAW, a letter had been carefully crafted to its leader, Reeve Whitlock, containing several carefully worded statements of fact.

Item one: Robson Trowbridge, once a rogue suspected of murdering his wife and family, had been exonerated by the truths revealed before the death of the last Alpha—his uncle Mannus Trowbridge. As is required by Pack Law, Robson Trowbridge's right to the crown was undisputed,

as several pack members were there to witness his Alpha-
flare and the subsequent flare from his chosen mate. (See
attached witness statements by Cordelia LaRue, Harry
Windcombe, and Russell Biggs).

Item two: Robson Trowbridge is recuperating from se-
vere wounds inflicted on him during the ascension. His
mate is acting in his stead until such time as he is ready to
resume his duties.

This letter, the placement of each comma and period
argued at length over our dinette table, was a fluid piece of
chicanery, because the devil was in the things *not* said. No
mention of the mating deception, no hint of my Fae blood.
Not a peep to indicate that Bridge's recovery was taking
place in a freakin' different *realm*. Nothing whatsoever
revealed that could connect me to the person who actually
killed the old Alpha.

Under normal conditions, sending an "everything's fine
over here" letter would have been a joke. The NAW would
have sent someone up here posthaste to do their own investigation, and very likely our heads would have ended
up on a pike beside Mannus's. What saved us was the fact
that Reeve Whitlock was in a pissing contest with the Great
Council.

No one outside of the inner circle knew exactly what
the issue was, though the common consensus was that it
was far more significant than the usual snarlfests about territory disputes or implied disrespect. Harry had tried to
winkle out the facts from his sources, but all he'd been
able to unearth was the rumor that the Great Council had
hired forensic accountants to study the NAW's coffers.

Oooh, death by audit. Scary.

Whatever, Whitlock's problems had been a bonus for
us. We'd been given a rubber-stamp approval for the change
in leadership—at least for the interim. "But when they
come, there won't be any long-drawn-out inquiry," Harry
had said back in May. "If the Council's investigator thinks
the line of ascension was in any way shady . . ."

And, oh Goddess, had it been twisted.

Without the full help of the pack we'll never be able to pull the wool over the Council's eyes, when they come to investigate. Now, a thread of dread tightened around me. Even I couldn't ignore the obvious. I may have taped the pack members' mouths shut and rapped their texting fingers, but that cloak of silence was becoming as threadbare as Cordelia's favorite housecoat.

Harry was right. If the pack energy had been a visible aura it would have been a purple cloud of something nasty. In the perhaps ten seconds it took me to recollect our problems with the NAW, a fight broke out. One of the visiting wolves snapped the air in frustration, stirring the aggression of another, who chose to respond by turning to mount one of the Creemore wolves. Well, no self-respecting, Maple Leaf–loving Were would stand for that. With a snarl, the offended wolf pivoted and lunged, jaws agape.

"Stop!" I yelled.

It was like I hollered "Go!" instead. In the blink of an eye, the two-dog spat became a tail-bristling, teeth-baring, three-dog tussle as another wolf leaped into the fray. Before the fight instinct swept through the ranks, Harry barreled through the pack, cutting through the milling wolves like a hot knife through butter. He leaped—all one hundred and fifty pounds of graying fur and stringy muscle— bringing down one wolf who broke away with a yelp. Then, he spun for the next. They postured for a second. Noses crinkled, napes bristling. The other wolf was younger by decades, and leaner in a way that spoke of sly strength.

Cordelia's paws did a prelunge cha-cha.

Time to flare, time to flare.

Not for the first time, I wished flaring really were as easy as pulling a bunny out of a hat. It's more complicated than that. First, you need to be stirred by a strong feeling. Fear, love, hatred, pain . . .

Quickly, I pulled up Trowbridge's face—sharp cheekbones and long curly black hair—and was rewarded by an almost immediate burn in my eyes. *Almost there.* I thought about his scent, wrapping around me, slipping along my skin, filling in my pores. *Yes.* I could feel the throb of the green comets spinning around my dark pupils. *And now, for the presto!* I remembered the moment I'd shoved his limp body into the Gates of Merenwyn. How his fingers had twitched as the portal's suction had pulled him deeper into its maw.

And I flared.

Light—green-blue and electric—spilled from my eyes. Need a visual? Think Superman. Perhaps a little more diffused. His gaze is a pulsing beam complete with vibrating sound effects, right? Mine's cone shaped and silent. Also, unlike the Man of Steel, I've never really found my talent particularly useful. It can't do cool stuff like melt something into a puddle of metal, or lift a tank. Okay, come to think of it, my flare is nothing like Superman's.

Bottom line, my light amounts to the pack's music—its touch soothed the savage breast. Or more literally, their savage *beasts.*

I swept my gaze over the transfixed pack. The younger ones lifted their heads to my caress, as if it were a blessing from their favorite rock star. The rest did a collective canine shudder of pleasure. Yup, puppy Prozac, that's what my talent amounts to. I kept it moving, touching briefly on furry flanks, skimming tips of pointed ears. Never focusing directly, never landing too long on one spot. The trick was to wash their bodies with the gentle touch of my soothing blue-green light.

Harry limped toward the woods.

"The moon is calling you," I said, in pretty much the same soft but firm tone my mum used to say, "Time for bed."

From the head of the trail, Harry issued an imperative bark. The wolves turned and funneled toward the path, tails lifted, tongues peeping through happy lips.

Hurry up. My eyes are burning.

This was the point they all were supposed to melt into the trees to chase a few rabbits and run down an unfortunate deer. Instead, they inexplicably lingered, a logjam of wolves near the mouth of the forest. Jostling each other. Milling about. Anticipation crackled in the air, the way it might before the hunt master lifts the lid on the fox's cage.

"Animals," I heard my Fae murmur.

My Fae is talking in my head again.

Oh Fae Stars, shut up.

Because we had problems. The pack wasn't melting into the woods. Safely out of the range of my flare, the energy that had fouled the mood earlier started to percolate again. Golden eyes turned back toward the near-empty field, their feral attention centered on the group of four wolves who stood in a tight shoulder-to-shoulder wedge. George Danvers was in the lead. He lifted his snout, and let a little lip show.

Oh no he didn't.

"The moon is calling you," I said more firmly.

A low growl, from deep in his throat.

Oh yes he did.

Up until then, I'd never been frightened around the pack. Well, not since the first night when I watched them back up the trailer on the Stronghold ridge. And though, over the last six months, I'd intuited an evolution of emotions from them—curiosity, unease, distaste, and more recently, faint flashes of cloaked dislike—the slow diminishment of their good opinion hadn't really impacted me. My feelings had been simple. They exist, I exist. We try to exist together as we wait for Trowbridge to return.

Until now.

The first faint stirring of real fear trailed icy fingers down the knobs of my spine and poked a hooked nail at my shivering Were. *No help from my inner-bitch.* Hoping to crank up the wattage on my flare, I pulled up a memory— one that I usually tried to stifle—of Dawn Danvers, the girl I dispatched to doggy heaven six months ago. Not of her face as she lost her life—that was a thing of my nightmares. Instead, I thought of the way she wanted to hurt me and mine. Of the anger and naked aggression in her face as she stalked over to where I held my lover braced in my arms. And how I'd grimly vowed, "None will hurt this man."

The recall of it stirred my own aggression, perhaps a little better than I anticipated. My flare sharpened, no longer a gentle hand smoothing their pelts. Claws extruded. Languid strokes turned into a heavy hand pressing on those who dared to challenge.

"*Yes,*" hissed my Fae.

Danvers's muzzle crinkled but he stood firm under my censure, stiff-legged in front of his wolf brethren. *Submit.* Despite a few growls of disapproval from the watching pack, I didn't dare soften my focus. I kept my angry eyes resting on that group until they trembled and every last one of them sank to their bellies, including the oh-so-aggressive George.

Mutiny quelled. I released a bit of the inner heat and let my cooling gaze drift over them, waiting until their scents joined into one collective aroma of forest and wild, then I let my flare peter out, softly, like the last flicker of a blue flame before the fire turned into a spiraling wisp of gray smoke.

Turns out, my relief was premature.

No sooner had my light dribbled away than George rolled upright. He stood, feet firmly planted, his eyes steady on my own watering ones. Tail fat, and quivering. From where I stood, the thought bubble over his head either read "Chew" or possibly "I shall rend the Fae-bitch's flesh into itty-bitty pieces."

Whoops.

George charged.

It was instinctive. I've looked back at it over and over again, and it's always come down to that. As the old wolf with more balls than brains streaked for me, three things happened relatively simultaneously.

My Were screamed "Danger!", my Fae magic hissed "Murder!", and my right hand sprang out. Without pausing, without asking, without even waiting to be told, the essence of my Fae self streamed from fingertips in a long coil of fluorescent green. Before Cordelia or Harry could run interference, it surged across the field and intercepted George Danvers with a bitch-slap of purely epic Fae proportions.

The impact lifted the brown and buff wolf off his feet. Back legs pedaling, he dangled some five feet in the air, held aloft by my invisible rope of magic.

"Detach!"

My Fae serpent of doom gave one last squeeze then tossed the wolf. Old George did an undignified tuck and roll in mid-space then landed on his left flank in the clover with a high piercing whine.

Amazing how fast an old wolf can move when motivated. He scrambled onto all four paws then tore across the field toward the safety of his brethren, followed by his wife, his son, and some other wolf whose identity I never did nail down.

Oh crap.

As far as the pack could tell, I'd just *willed* the old wolf into midair. They couldn't see my magic, now arched over my head like a green serpent poised to strike.

Well, that's not completely true. Cordelia could see it.

And of course half-bred me.

Oh, and Ralph, who chose that moment—oh thank you, Karma—to stick his head out of my cleavage. Glowing like a lit emergency flare, my would-be protector uncoiled a rope of gold and held it up menacingly, a mash-up of the Three Musketeers meeting Spaceballs.

So much for "stay low."

The field emptied fairly quickly after that. I'm not sure if Cordelia even needed to herd some strays toward the path. Or if Harry had to stand jaws open in a snarl, pink gums showing above his sharp, fanged teeth, as they rushed past him. And absolutely, Biggs snapping at George's back leg was completely over the top.

The last two to exit the gathering place were the Scawens wolves. The older female was delicately boned and more cream than the usual black, brown, and buff coloration of the average Creemore Were. The younger female was fairly sturdy. Rachel Scawens said something to her daughter. I don't understand that nonverbal stuff, so to me it was a pantomime—nibble, nibble, nip, shoulder check, snuffle throat. Petra Scawens articulated a reply, which sounded almost like a sluggish car turning over in winter.

Then the two of them hung a left—so closely pressed together they seemed to be a six-legged dog—for the woods. Just before they slid into the forest's welcoming shadows, Rachel Scawens's wolf face turned to look at me.

"You are Fae," her eyes said.

Then Trowbridge's sister spun away.

Sometimes I needed to stand on the Stronghold point and stare at the fairy pond below. Usually, it calmed me. The Creemore pond was pastoral and pungent in summer, bird-busy and weed-sweet in fall.

It would be nice to say that I left my heart down by the pond's pebble-strewn banks, but that's just some dumb perversion of an old geezer song. I still had my heart, tucked away where it should be, under a layer of fat, inside a cage of bone, nestled near all the other organs I needed to survive.

But I had left part of me there.

My fingers found the pointed peak of my left ear. I stroked its tip, watching a white moth dance dizzily over the top of the cocklebur thicket near the water's edge, willing my heart to stop its anxious pounding.

I think I screwed up.

"Whatever you do, keep your Fae canned." That's the first thing Cordelia had told me six months ago when we'd stood together outside the trailer and watched the last of the pack's well-wishers leave.

My heart wouldn't settle. It kept drumming away inside me as if I'd just completed a triathlon with a fifty-pound weight strapped to my back. Watching the mallard family perform figure eights around the bullrushes wasn't relieving its frantic thump-thump one bit.

*I'm like a pressure cooker, filled to capacity and for-
gotten. Now I'm rocking on the back burner. Sooner or
later, I'm going to blow, spewing bits of Were and Fae all
over the pack.*

That would be bad.

I inhaled slowly, fighting for calm.

Back in spring, the fairy pond had been bisected in the
middle by a pine log. Lily pads had grown in its northern
end and only the lower half, near the beach on which my
pirate rock held court, had been open water. But one night
a couple of weeks ago—a night where a raging Goddess
had lit up the sky with her thunder strikes—someone had
pulled the log from the pond and left it up by the culvert on
the road. They'd poured a half gallon of kerosene on it, but
after all those years spent pickling in the fetid water, it
hadn't done much except smolder. I'd sent Biggs and Harry
to track the vandals down, but they'd come back to report
that the torrential rains had rinsed away the perpetrator's
scent signatures.

No one owned up to doing it. Nobody squealed.

Pack solidarity, you've got to love it, right?

I belonged here and yet I didn't. These tree-covered hills,
these grassy fields, this pine-scented air; they all felt so familiar to me. If I kept my eyes shut and didn't take in the
whole picture, I could pretend that the old path leading from
the Stronghold side was the same mud-slick one my twin
Lexi and I had flown down on our bikes when we were eight,
grinning at each other and shrieking at the top of our lungs
as our tires hit the little puddle near the end. I could remember how the water would shoot up, half translucent, half
muddy, leaving a wake behind us as significant as any boat
launch's inaugural spray, and how we'd crowed at this visual
statement of our superiority. Because in those days, in our
naïve arrogance, we'd assumed the splatter trail of mud that
flattened grasses on either side of the trail *was* a statement.
We had passed through and left evidence of our passage. Of
course, in our triumph, we inevitably forgot that the bottom
of one Creemore hill usually led to the start of another.

Not all fairy tales ended happily.

As witness Casperella's final resting place—the edge of the bad part of St. Luke's cemetery, surrounded by the crumbling ruins of a freakin' stone wall.

Goddess, is that where the pack buries Faes?

"Wakey, wakey," I said to the entity within me. She'd been feigning sleep, possibly tuning into the turn of my thoughts. But I'd felt her, dragon-ready, in my belly. Alert and interested. Pumped, as it were.

"Go," I said.

Given release, she ran up my chest, gave my heart a big enough kick to make it skip a beat, and then surged to my shoulders and down my arms. A squeeze through the wrists and then she funneled a stream of Fae magic to the end of each of my fingers.

Then she waited. Patently obedient. Wholly gleeful.

I pointed my magic-hot hand to a broken branch that clung to the cliff. "Attach." A line of green magic leaped from my fingertips, sizzled through the air, and landed with a soft kiss on a twisted branch. I raised my hand, and with that upward movement the piece of maple lifted, my magic a strong-armed extension for my will.

My Fae talent could not be faulted. It did exactly what I asked, transporting the stick across the open water to where I pointed and then lowering it, so gently, so tenderly, onto the bank of the pond.

She meekly waited for the final order.

"Detach." The cables of magic slipped free from their burden. They hovered, a fat fluorescent cable, faintly undulating, perhaps expecting me to call them back. I stared at the green light extruding from my fingertips, and then imagined a pair of scissors cutting each strand away, severing me from my talent. Snip, snip, snip, cut close to the quick. Hide all her traces. Make her disappear.

"Cut," I said.

Instantly, the tether between me and my line of Fae magic broke. The floating string of magic rolled back on itself and formed a fat, green, translucent ball, bobbing slightly on a current of air. I watched, curious as to what it would do next, now that it had been given freedom.

Nothing, apparently. It hovered there, glimmering in the moon's silver light, unreal as Tinker Bell's fairy wings, alive as the dragonfly that had just zipped past it.

Busy as a hive. As inherently evil as . . . Oh hell. As me.

"Disappear," I said flatly.

A moment of hesitation then poof, the ball of Fae-me broke apart into a starburst pattern of hundreds of brilliant bits of green. The sparks lingered in the air—dying remnants of a fire that refused to be quenched—before they slowly faded.

They'd find their way back to me, each and every spark. That's when the full measure of payback pain would come. Those of Fae blood can't use magic in this world without expecting to pay the price. My fingers were already fat and swollen. Painless now, but that soon would change.

A bit of a wind lifted the hair at the nape of my neck and sent shivers through the trees.

The air above the pond was motionless.

I had maybe fifteen minutes before the first wave of pain hit.

Of the trailer's two bedrooms, mine was the one with the bunk beds and the washed-out teal curtains that vaguely coordinated with the pink, green, and blue floral print on the comforters. No pictures. Nothing shiny or bright. At some point in its history, some DIY enthusiast had inexpertly faux-painted the walls.

I stood in front of my closet, puzzling over the state of my hand. My fingers *should* have been swollen, blistered, and hurting like I'd slammed them in a car door. I'd been home puttering around the trailer for well over twenty minutes. But my mitts were feeling, on the whole, pretty close to normal. Maybe a little tender, but not too bad. I tilted them toward the light. Four straight fingers, a thumb with a hangnail, and a palm with a fate line that puzzled me. Normal. Pale flesh, completely unmarked by the fever blisters of payback pain.

"I love your skin," Trowbridge had said back in May.

It was a damn good thing he'd fixated on that, as the rest of me wasn't going to win any rhinestone crowns. My hair had grown to the middle of my shoulder blades and then, for no particular reason, had refused to sprout another inch. In terms of color, volume, and texture, it is, respectively, brown with a hint of chestnut highlights, depressingly limp, and baby fine. My full upper lip earned more than one or two speculative glances from the male members of the pack, but that thread of sexual desire usually died as soon as their gaze traveled upward. In the comfort of their furry worldview, there are only two appropriate eye-color choices: amber-brown or blue. Mine are a clear, light green, as pale as the sunlit crest on one of those big, rolling ocean waves that hurtle toward the shore. For the record—and I am so fond of debunking myths—my irises aren't translucent. A Werewolf might notice that if they studied them, but few had ever demonstrated the courage to outstare me, and so they missed the flecks of blue and yellow swimming in that peridot sea.

See? It's surprisingly easy to give a Were the willies. Pale eyes instead of predictable brown or blue. Pale skin instead of sun-kissed tones. A little bit of magic and a Fae pendant, and you've got the hair on the nape of their necks standing at attention like some dumbass sentry outside the gates of Buckingham Palace.

With a sigh that would have made Cordelia proud, I walked into the bathroom and turned on the taps. I stared at my reflection as I waited for the water to run cold. *Gad, what a sight.* The whites of my eyes were pink. *What had stalker-ghost looked like before she turned into stalker-ghost?* I wet the facecloth under the weak stream of water dribbling out of the faucet and pressed it against my aching lids.

Better.

Blindly, I felt my way back into my bedroom. Questions swirled. Had the wolves killed Casperella? Perhaps they'd met a strange Fae wandering in their world, gone all wolf-territorial, and then buried the body to hide the crime? Is that why her grave is surrounded by a stone wall?

I dropped the facecloth into the laundry basket then stood naked by my narrow bed, contemplating my pillow. *Tonight requires more comfort than the nightie Biggs brought back from Barrie.* Trowbridge's scent teased my nostrils and pebbled my nipples as I smoothed his age-soft T-shirt down over my hips.

Or had Casperella lived among them and somehow managed to offend the wrong person?

My stomach let out a gurgle. Stress did that to me. All the nausea meds in the world couldn't fix my gut turmoil as well as a hit of pure sugar did.

Screw it. I went for my stash. Two Cherry Blossoms (three if I counted the one I'd left on the kitchen counter), two Kit Kats, and a bag of stale M&M's. A moment later, the Kit Kat lay nested in my palm, wrapped in its cheery red paper, promising me the sweet crunch of satisfaction, a twelve-second sugar high, and a prompt collapse into sleep.

Good enough.

Wake up.
  You've been dream-napped.
  Wake up.

"I never took part in treason," hissed the girl with the long blond hair. She stood by a window set in an arched framework of stone. Past her shoulder, the view could best be summed up as pastoral. Merenwyn's fields were impossibly green, dotted with a small herd of shaggy cows with really wide, long curved horns. *Pretty.* In the distance, the silhouettes of two trees so close together that their trunks seemed to be one.

How can Mad-one tug me into her dreams?

She didn't live in my world. She didn't share a bedroom wall with me. I'd reviewed every moment of my visit to

Threall, and I'm sure we'd never exchanged anything that could serve as an anchor, or a talisman. And yet, increasingly, I found myself being tugged back to this small cluttered room that screamed wizard's snuggery.

I would have thought Mad-one too proud to let me witness her final hour in Merenwyn.

The Mystwalker looked very much the way she did in Threall—the same long nose, the same blue gown. But to my eyes, there were a few distinct differences. Her expression was tense. Her fingers were twisting at her waist in agitation.

Animated and anxious: two words I wouldn't have used for the Mystwalker.

"I am blameless," she told the old man in a low urgent voice. "I should not be asked to bear your punishment as my own. I knew nothing of your daughter's love affair. I was ignorant of the potion you created for—"

The fraying sleeve of the old man's robe slid to his elbow as he held up a single gnarled finger in a timeless shut-thee-up. Frowning fiercely, he funneled all his attention on the tome in front of him while Mad-one worried the tasseled end of her belt. After another string of words he lifted his head in satisfaction to watch sparks dance above the leather-bound manuscript. Then, I heard a distinct hiss—sounding awfully like a tire going flat—and as I watched the bright glitters of light faded, one by one.

"I have set the wards," he said grimly, closing the book.

"Master," she began again.

"It was rash to interrupt me, Tyrean."

"I must speak before it is too late to do so." Her voice was placating but anger had flushed her cheeks. "I have been your obedient servant since the day I was brought to the castle. Never have I shirked my duties. I have never pleaded fear when asked to travel to Threall—even when I was sick with worry that I would not succeed in finding my way home. And this is my reward? What you ask of me—" A look of desperation tightened her patrician features. "To stay in Threall forever? To guard your soul forever? Why am I being punished so? Within the space of three suns, I won't remember how to return to Merenwyn."

"I am sorry, child." But he looked more hard willed than sympathetic.

"I beg of you," Mad-one whispered. "Do not do this. Do not demand this of me. I am—"

"Your service will *not* be forever, Tyrean."

Her control broke and the next stream of words came out rushed and shrill. "I am not a knave. Your sentence will be the Sleep of Forever!"

The Old Mage aligned the book's edges so that it sat centered on the lectern before he slid off his stool. "Fate will deliver to me a nalera," he said. "Once she has pledged her fealty, you will be released from service."

"Admit that it is over," she cried. "Let me finish my life here."

He shook his head and this time his expression was genuinely sad. "You should never have allowed your feelings for Simeon to grow—it has made you so vulnerable to attack. Your foolish heart has made it impossible for me to leave you here, a weapon that can be used against me." The Old Mage's mouth tightened. "Before you judge me as heartless, consider carefully the fact that I could kill you now and remove that threat forever."

"You won't," she said coldly. "Because you need a protector in Threall."

He studied her for a beat. "True."

"What will stop Helzekiel from destroying your body? While you slumber, it is as defenseless against—"

"I have friends among the Inner Circle who will ensure that no unnatural harm will befall my sleeping body should it come to that." He fiddled with the quill lying beside the heavy tome. "Child, it has taken me this much loss to understand the damage I have done. I cannot take back the conjure that tore the sun out of the Pool of Life, any more than I can undo the war that followed. But as long as I live, both in soul and body, my wards will last. It will be a testament to our endurance. We must hold in Threall until the next true Mage of Merenwyn is born . . . It is he who should benefit from my Book of Spells, not a man with questionable skills and unlimited ambition. Helzekiel's lust for power is not tempered by compassion. Ruin will follow when there are no more constraints against his greed for magic."

Mad-one's eyes filled, but she did not cry.

"You know I speak the truth. You know he already demands to be known as the Black Mage among his circle." The wizard walked to the door, then paused to say quietly, "Simeon has vowed to take your body to a place of safety and guard it at the price of his own."

It was the arrow of pain she never saw sailing toward her. "You asked my lover to watch over my body as it slowly decays?" she said in quiet horror. "To pass milk-sopped bread between my slack lips?"

The Old Mage's expression softened into true regret. "We have all suffered and will continue to suffer. Would it help to remember that your sacrifice will protect the world in which your lover lives?"

Not a whole lot, judging from the pain on Mad-one's face.

He heaved a sigh and ran his hands through his thinning white hair. "Now, I must leave you to face my jury."

"It is not a jury, Old Mage," Mad-one hissed. "You will walk through those doors and never return."

He turned to give her a hard look. "And you have five minutes with your lover before you must return to Threall."

Wake up now.

Wake up before Simeon enters the room.

Chapter Five

"What?" called Cordelia.

"I didn't say anything," I mumbled. The rest of my sleep had been uninterrupted by dreams but filled with anxiety. I'd woken up every couple of hours, heart pounding, a growing conviction in my Fae bones that I was on the brink of something. I'd felt anxious and off balance all day—my fretfulness made worse by the fact that the pack always needed a day to recover from their moon run. That included Cordelia. Being quiet as a mouse in a house just so she could get her beauty rest had left me feeling a tad peeved.

Now it was late afternoon. I needed something more substantial to eat than a few Kit Kats.

"It's those bloody motorcycles, they're playing bloody havoc with my hearing," she complained. "I can't wait for fall to be over. All those stupid tourists with their loud bikes. Idiots. Reliving their childhoods."

I couldn't hear a thing.

"The shower's yours now if you want it," she said. A drawer opened and closed in her bedroom. "I called Harry. He and Biggs should be here soon for our usual premoon-run strategizing. Sign those papers for Harry, will you? And eat something. Something that will carry you longer than two hours. Oh, and the pack leader from Kenora is insisting on a private audience with you. Which means—"

"Dodge him." I flipped the document over to the SIGN HERE flag and did just that.

Our fridge had milk, eggs, the remains of Cordelia's hunk of roast beef in a plastic container—so raw it said "moo"—a thick block of cheddar cheese, and a leg of lamb waiting to be undercooked. I went down on one knee and looked at the bottom shelf. Cold cuts in yet another plastic container. Butter. A loaf of bread. Inside the vegetable crisper were some root vegetables. There was nothing decent to eat.

Blood had pooled at the bottom of the plate of meat. For a second I just stood there, letting the fridge air chill my bare feet, thinking, *Predators, each and every one of them.* In the door were a liter of Diet Coke, Cordelia's supply of hormones, and an unopened silver tin of Ralph's maple syrup. Numbly, I picked up the can and used my hip to close the door.

It would serve for an early supper.

The movement of the refrigerator door had stirred the air.

My nostrils flared. *Stranger danger.* I followed the current of Were perfume to the doorway, where a draft of air constantly leaked between the insulation and doorjamb. A deep inhale. *Uh-huh. That's an unfamiliar scent signature.*

I twisted to look through the dinette area's window.

A strange guy was sitting in one of our white plastic garden chairs, gaze fixed on our twenty-seven-foot trailer. He'd taken sitting into a whole new slumped category, folding his arms over his chest, and balancing his butt on the very edge of his seat. Around thirty. Wiry. A study in black, from his neatly trimmed hair to his dark graphic T-shirt. Wearing a hooded sweatshirt, unzipped, under a battered leather jacket. A leather belt with a silver-toned buckle. Black-rimmed glasses—*on a Were?*—very übercool and NYC ugly. And then, there was that *thing* on top of his head.

A fedora.

In Creemore.

Something about the way he lolled in the chair made

me think of a rattler sunning itself, waiting for some bare ankle to pass by. I called to Cordelia, "What was the name of that guy from Kenora?"

She cleared her throat. "What?"

"The pack leader from Kenora behind on his tithes— the guy you said wanted to speak with me. What's his name?" I tucked my hair behind my ear as I bent to give the Were in Black another thorough inspection through the dust-specked window. I don't know what I expected from a Kenora wolf, but I knew it wasn't urban chic. More like plaids, and white T-shirts, and maybe jeans with rips that had been earned versus designed.

Were in Black crossed his arms and lifted his chin in my direction. Not in a slow "hey" manner, more in a "yeah, I see you looking at me" way.

She paused brushing her wig to think, then said, "It was a stupid name. It reminded me of the drink my dear mama used to get blotto on it. Gin and . . . Collins. Tom Collins."

I narrowed my eyes at him. "Well, it's cocktail hour on the patio. Tom Collins is sitting in one of our chairs, watching our front door." I brought the blinds down, and then, for good measure, swiveled the wand until the slats were closed.

Try ogling me through that, Fur-boy.

"Damn," said Cordelia. A drawer opened and shut in the master bedroom as I used a can opener to pierce a hole in the top of the syrup tin. I found a saucer. And a napkin— Cordelia had managed to instill some table manners. I poured a good measure of syrup into the saucer as I sat down at the banquette.

"Use a spoon," said Cordelia, suddenly appearing over my shoulder. I got a snootful of Chanel as she leaned over to haul the blinds back up. She'd put on one of her neutral outfits. Beige pants, beige top.

Checking out Tom Collins had been enough to lure her out of her room without her usual dash of bright carmine-red lipstick. She needed a shave. I twirled my finger in the saucer of syrup until it was coated, then I stuck it in my mouth. "He's just waiting for us," I mumbled, sucking on my digit. The guy from Kenora smiled slightly.

"That's not Tom Collins," Cordelia murmured. She made a minute adjustment to her red wig.

"Huh?" And that's as far as I got, because those motorcycles that had been annoying Cordelia got close enough for even my ears to note them. One—no, two—bike engines throttled down for the turn at the end of our private road. Fae Stars, it was a veritable convoy. The old rusted mailbox listed on its post as the first motorcycle rumbled past it. Harry's truck followed. Then another vehicle, and beyond that, two more, followed by another motorcycle.

Cordelia's eyes were the same arctic blue, but they were now bleak. "Your hair's a mess," she said. And then she touched me—something hardly anyone did—gently pulling at the sides of my loose ponytail, so that the tips of my pointed Fae ears were hidden. The bikes came into the yard, their engines loud, abrasive. Under the cover of their noise, she said, "If you haven't as yet killed that poor little bitch inside you, now's the time to bring her out."

I stared at her, completely flummoxed.

"I've been watching you slowly throttle your Were for months and I'm tired of it. We need you to be you again. Be that girl who had the courage to take over a wolf pack."

"I am that girl."

"No," she said sadly. "You're not anymore."

The guy on the BMW pulled up near the Were in Black. Motorcycle guy pulled off his helmet. He was tall, like the Creemore Weres, but broad, with a gut that spoke of beer and bratwurst—not lean like one of Trowbridge's people. According to my book, Weres smelled like forests and were uniformly lean muscled. They didn't smell rank as a fox's lair and look like they spoke in double negatives.

Barely moving her lips, Cordelia whispered one final instruction. I gave her a quick frown.

The afternoon sun glinted off Harry's silver hair as he exited his trunk. A second later Biggs got out from the

passenger side. They stood with their backs to us—uneven
bookends, the older man head and shoulders taller than the
younger—both eyeing the guy in the lawn chair.

Harry scratched the back of his neck, and then turned
his head toward our window. He winked at me. His sleeve
was torn. There was blood on his faded denim shirt and at
the corner of his mouth.

I could barely smell the copper of it over the stink of
Biggs's fear.

"Cordelia, what's—" She shushed me, and motioned
for me to hide Ralph. I slid out of the banquette and tucked
him inside my shirt all in one fairly smooth motion. She
nodded to me—like she had before we slid Bridge through
the portal. *We are in serious trouble*, I thought, as she took
a steadying breath and opened the door.

Then she stood aside, in a deferential manner I'd only
seen her use once before.

My stomach gave a squeeze. *Are you listening, Hedi?
Danger.* I reached for the Cherry Blossom on the counter
before I sidled through the door.

The Were in Black waited until everyone's eyes were on
him and then got up from his lawn chair. He strolled over
to the bottom of my steps, passing Biggs and Harry without even acknowledging them. "I've come for an audience
with Robson Trowbridge," he said.

I could scent the tension radiating from Cordelia. Glibly,
I pulled out our stock answer. "He doesn't take private
meetings."

"Now why's that?" Mr. Snoopy had parentheses beside
his wide mouth.

"He's recuperating."

"Still?" His brown eyes examined me through his glasses.
"It's been six months."

"He was badly injured during—"

"Silver, wasn't it?" He gestured to his belly. "In the
stomach, I heard. That would take some recuperating."

"Who told you that?"

"It's occurred to me, Ms. Peacock . . . It is Ms. Peacock?"

At my numb nod, he pointed to the trailer. "I'm not going to find him inside, am I? Here or in his home." He held up a hand. "Don't bother lying. I've checked. He's not in the Alpha's home. The only thing left of him in that house is a whole lot of blood. Old blood. He hasn't returned to that house or that room since the night of his alleged ascension." His face got hard. "You want to tell me what the hell is going on?"

Behind him, Harry gave me an imperceptible shake of his head.

"Who are you?" I asked.

"I was sent here under the authority of the Council of North American Weres to investigate the death of Mannus Trowbridge and the subsequent Alpha ascension of his nephew, Robson Trowbridge, and to verify whether or not the Treaty of Brelland was willfully broken by one Hedi Peacock, née Helen Stronghold. This morning I discussed the results of my preliminary investigations with the Council, and I have been since authorized to place you under arrest until your trial at sunset, in approximately one hour. Your jury will be me and the members of your pack."

"You can't do that. We have done nothing—"

"At that time, Hedi Peacock, you will answer to the following charges." He pulled out a piece of paper. "Your involvement in the murders of Mannus Trowbridge, Stuart Scawens, and Dawn Danvers. Your fraudulent representation as cherished mate of the deceased Robson Trowbridge as well as your assumption of his title."

"I don't want Trowbridge's title. I'm just trying to hold the pack together until—"

"And finally," he said, talking over me once again. "The most serious charge. Conspiracy and treason."

"Conspiracy?" I squeaked.

"That's generally what they call it when you pretend to play for one team, but really play for another. Did you really think you could send an Alpha into the Fae world without us finding out about it?"

Oh . . . My brain froze, stuck between "oh" and "crap."

For the life of me, I couldn't come up with a single glib lie. The spot where I should have inserted a plausible rebuttal stretched, and stretched, and then it was gone. Bye-bye. Behind me now. Opportunity had presented itself, taken a bow, and left.

Cordelia cleared her throat. "Do something!" her icy blue eyes insisted.

Okay, I thought somewhat slowly. *I'll use my flare like I did last night and that will buy us some time, and . . .* That's what you do, right? When the thinking part of you stutters to a halt, and you can't brainstorm your way out of a problem? You head for your automatic defense weapons. *I'll hit them with my magic!*

I gave Cordelia a faint nod.

Then the NAW's man chose to do that *thing*—that wordless, incredibly insulting *thing.*

In front of everyone, he blew out a short burst of air through his nose. Derision streamed out of his nostrils, twin fingers of contempt flicked insolently at me. My reaction was all wolf. I *felt* his mockery as if it were a missile aimed at me. Bullet shaped, fin tailed. Coming straight for me.

It hit, right there, mid-chest.

For a very quick count of three, I gazed at the approximate point of impact.

When I looked up again, my defense had flipped to offense. *Oh yeah, go ahead and smile, you smug bastard. I'm going to give it to you—the full dominant light of an awesomely pissed-off fairy—and you, my friend, are going to drop to your knees.*

I gave my opponent a slow smile, knowing that I had plenty of rage to fuel the fire of a truly awesome flare—six months of suppressed anger, half a year of growing disillusionment, 195 days of tamping down the Fae inside me.

Puppy, we're going to make you piddle your pants.

I looked within, ready to tap into my magic.

And within.

And, oh sweet stars in heaven—*within.* My paw tightened over my Cherry Blossom, as sudden comprehension rolled over me. *That's* what mortal-me had been ignoring all day. Sunrise should have found me sitting at the dinette—hand submerged in a bowl of ice water—listening to the chatter of grackles as I willed my wounds to heal. But that hadn't happened, had it? The ball of magic inside my gut should have been rigid, swollen with aggression, ready to take on any Were who dared to doubt her malevolence, but instead the essence of my Fae felt curiously soft, and frighteningly empty.

I wasn't hungry, I was void.

Where was all my magic? Why hadn't she come back to me? What remained of my handy ball of magic felt as soft as a month-old helium balloon. I gave it a squeeze. I was down to residue. The rest—that big sphere of green fire that I'd walked away from with such disdain—had not returned to me in the night.

"Yes, that's what I've been trying to tell you," growled my Were. "We're not right! We're . . ."

Running on empty. *Not good.* I squeezed what was left of my Fae talent, hopeful of wringing out a little juice for the much-needed flare.

It obliged, kind of.

A brief burn in my eyes, a buildup of expectation, and then . . . three, tiny, inconsequential spits of green fire; the type of impotent spark one might expect from a used-up lighter.

"Oh shit," muttered Cordelia.

More of a misfire, really, I thought in dismay. A lot like my miniflares before I found My One True Thing.

"Boys, put on your glasses," said the Were in Black, sounding bored. His goons whipped out dark-rimmed glasses identical to his, and put them on. "If that's all she's got, I don't think we have anything to worry about, but we may as well be armed. The Council paid the coven a good chunk of change for these things. Guaranteed protection against any strong flare." The NAW's main man thought that was funny, he did. His shoulders shook, before he remembered his role as a professional goon and reined in his amusement. With firmer lips, and a voice deepened to reflect the gravitas of the moment, the Were in Black said, "The following people have also been charged: Harry Windcombe, Russell Biggs, and Frank Evers."

Frank Evers? I flicked a WTF at Cordelia.

He nodded toward the west where the sun was beginning to follow a downward arch toward the western, ragged line of trees. "You've got an hour until you meet all your jury. Full restraints, boys. Gag and bind 'em."

"Who *are* you?" I asked.

He opened the door on Harry's truck, and then with one foot on the running board, smiled. "They call me Knox."

And that's how Plan B ended. With a hiss of air from my lungs, my early dinner waiting for me on the dinette's table, and the stiff edges of the yellow Cherry Blossom box cutting into my sweating palm.

Chapter Six

This house will be the death of me. For all its gabled grandeur, the Trowbridges' cream-colored Victorian looked abandoned. One of the shrubs under the bay window was leafless. The portion of the front lawn that hadn't gone to seed had given way to weed. A memory came unbidden: *Bridge, eighteen and shirtless, pushing the lawn mower around his home. Headphones on. MP3 player jammed in the front pocket of his faded cut-off jeans.*

I should have asked Biggs to look after it better but I couldn't stand the thought of anyone walking through the rooms. It was not a place for the curious. It was the place of my deepest hurt.

That's where I'd lost another part of me.

The hour had passed achingly slowly. Knox's minions had let me sit and stew in silence while they'd passed the time watching one of those television shows featuring a new mom, a boyfriend, and a paternity test. At the end of the program (the paternity test proved negative), the beefier of Knox's minions had blindfolded me with a dirty red bandana while the ferret-faced one had riffled through our mail.

Just to make conversation, I'd said to Fatso, "I thought all Weres were lean."

"Shut up." It hadn't been a cordial response, but then

again, we weren't destined to be friends, Fatso and I. After my observation, he'd taken care to make sure my blindfold was tied tight enough to make my eyes pound and my head feel like it was in a vise.

That's when it had occurred to me, admittedly a little late, that my personal understanding of Weres might have been woefully limited, because bowlegged Fatso was living proof that not all Fur-boys were clever, tall, and lean. Who knew? I'd thought all wolves looked like the Creemore Weres—long-distance runners versus weightlifters.

I'd been wrong.

As they drove me to my inquisition, managing to hit every pothole on the rutted dirt road, I kept mentally playing that Bobbie McGee song. Not the whole song, because I don't know the whole song. I know most of the melody and fragments of the lyrics because Cordelia's head is crammed with old songs, like the one about Bobbie McGee and his dirty red bandana—a tune she'd taken to singing as she scrubbed at the lime deposits around the trailer's chronically leaking taps. Here was another truth: while facing bad guys is tough, facing them without your friends is tougher. All of a sudden, I was so keenly aware of *everything*. I was busted flat—in the wrong car, on the wrong road, traveling to the wrong place, without the comfort of my personal Bobbie McGee, Cordelia.

They'd hustled her and the boys into the open bed of Harry's truck and driven them away not long after Knox got into his truck. Her last comment to me had been uttered while she stood beside me on the trailer's meager front steps, the delivery pitched low. She'd meant it for my ears only, and she delivered it in a tone of grim certainty, as if she'd looked into the future and figured out all the options and likelihoods, and had done so in one quick flutter of her fake black lashes.

"When the chance comes, don't wait for us," she said. "Run."

I'd worried over that suggestion all the way to the Trowbridge place. Puzzled over the gap between who she thought

I was and who I thought I was, as Knox's goons shoved me down to the floor in the back, and told me to "stay." And oddly, for someone who found living by rules difficult, I'd done just that—I hadn't tried to get up, or kick anyone, or hissed anything nasty to Ralph when he chose to burrow into the cup of my bra. I'd been silent—thoughtful even—quietly taking advantage of the rough nap of the carpet to rub the blindfold as high as my left eyebrow as I tried to figure out who, what, and why.

I needed to *see*.

A minor rebellion. Fat-guy had yanked me out of the truck before I'd worked myself free of the blindfold, and when I'd lifted my hands to tug it away, Knox's voice had come out of nowhere. "Leave it!"

Oh really? Enough.

But before I could do what I meant to—yank that damn thing off and toss it in Knox's face—Fatso had pinned my arms behind me. Mutiny quelled.

Still, my efforts in the truck had won me a spy hole if you will. Light glimmered through the tiny crack over my left cheekbone. The sky was not yet black. Gray-blue in the west, indigo blue where the moon hung low in the sky. If I tilted my head, I could see well enough to note that there were a lot of cars illegally parked on the Alpha's front lawn.

So, the pack was already here. Waiting.

My Were paced. Back and forth, forth and back. On every circuit, she brushed the spot where my Fae talent usually lolled, and each time she did she uttered another rumble of deep distress. We—Hedi Incorporated—weren't firing on our usual three cylinders, she told me. We weren't *we* anymore.

Well, tell me something I didn't know. My gut felt hollow without the reassuring weight of my Fae bobbing inside me. But it occurred to me, right then, that if I kept listening to my Were unravel, I would soon be leaking her despair through my skin, making me, in effect, as obvious a snack choice as meat-on-a-stick.

I need to stop listening to my Were.

Knox led us through the backyard. "This way," he said for the benefit of his guards, as he veered off for the worn trail. The light was dim in the woods. No one talked. The urge to make a dash for it was almost overpowering, but the fat guard Knox had appointed as my personal companion never loosened his grip on my arm. And besides, I don't do that anymore.

That's the thing I don't do, Cordelia. Hadn't you noticed? I don't run anymore.

The old Hedi would have; the new and improved version couldn't. Not after seeing Trowbridge take my beating. And yet, had it changed anything? Here I was, right back to where I'd been six months ago, future looking grim, being shoved down a trail through the woods by someone who really, really didn't like me.

Fine time to develop a moral code.

"Hurry up." The beefy goon was a mountain of a man, given to double negatives. Fat and stupid; Fatso's life had to be a bitch.

Remember to use that against him.

I bowed my head, and under the guise of complete submission, used the time to experiment with a combination of grimaces and forehead pleats. By the time we emerged from the trees into the gathering place, I'd eyebrow-shrugged my blindfold up so that it sat crookedly over the bridge of my nose. Fat and stupid hadn't noticed. But I felt a tiny smidgen of hope. I was getting closer to full vision. Left eye open and recording the sights as I trudged to my destiny. Right eye operating at fifty percent capacity, which was both good and bad. I wasn't totally blind, but I had an obvious weak spot—and Weres love those—and I knew if anyone were looking for a chink in the old Fae armor, they'd come in from my right.

Keep to the truth. You're holding the pack together until Bridge comes back. Don't embroider. Don't lie. Don't give the NAW anything they haven't asked for.

The pasture was full of Weres still in human form, most of them clustered in the open area in the middle.

Goddess, where is Cordelia? When the pack saw me, being led, partially blindfolded, toward them—dinner on the hoof, as it were—all talk ceased for a beat, and then picked up again. Lots of murmurs with individual words indistinct in the stew of conversation.

The combined scent of those assembled was enough to choke a sewer rat: a nose-twitching layer of the sharp spicy musk in the night air; body level, thick as soup, as pleasant as day-old sweat. It didn't seem to bother them, but then again, they were in that place between human and not. They may have appeared mortal, but their body language had subtly altered, as if their minds were already infected by the moon's glow, and their brain cells were changing, mutating well before their muscles.

A few of them weren't even looking at me. They were looking upward.

Bastards.

I tilted my head way back. Above me, the man in the moon was laughing, mouth wide open. His celestial vehicle was still on its ascent, an imperfect circle above the ragged tree line. He knew what would happen in the next twenty minutes. The youngest would change first—while the moon was low and the sky was indigo blue—and the oldest would hold off until the night sky was a black canvas for the stars and moon. It was a sign of strength—who had the guts to act the most indifferent to the moon's song?

Usually, Cordelia and Harry made it a point to be the last to change. Harry because he was older than dirt and naturally dominant, while Cordelia held out because she was too proud to bend, too insecure and remote to want to join the pack in their communal let's-get-doggy strip-a-thon. Biggs would inevitably change earlier than he should, given his rank. But he was younger than the other two, and his hold on his prestigious rank was not a natural extension of his inner toughness—his rank had been bestowed on him. A gift from me, who remembered him charging down the hill, gun held in his hands. Enforced by Harry. Tolerated by Cordelia (providing she could bitch and snipe to me

about the poor wisdom of letting a Chihuahua be part of
the inner circle). Our divisions and fault lines we'd tried to
keep private. We'd made an effort to appear four strong.

That will make four on the run.

I started mapping out potential escape routes.

The pack's customary moon-run gathering place was
enclosed by a horseshoe of trees—woods to the north and
east and the cemetery's living fence of evergreens to the
west. The open part of the shoe was south, right on the
edge of the cliff that overlooked the pond—one of many
lookout points found along the ridge on the Trowbridge land,
almost as if the first Alpha had decided danger would come
from there, not the woods.

My head swiveled as we crossed the old cow pasture.
Forget the woods. I was too slow. Cordelia could outrun me
in a pencil skirt and a pair of stilettos in the bush, never
mind a wolf. Nor did the pond offer much hope—I'd never
get my Were friends to willingly leap off a cliff into pond
water. I hadn't met a Were yet who could swim.

The cemetery was the ticket.

I looked over my shoulder. Predictably, my personal
Casperella had drifted to the gap in the cedar hedge to
watch me. But this time, she wasn't coyly half hidden by a
tree. Nor—for the first time in memory—was she mostly
translucent. In the passage of a few hours, she'd grown a
body. A darn firm one. If I hadn't known she was a spook,
she might have passed as one of those supermodels with
foreign names that frown fiercely from the covers of Ital-
ian fashion magazines.

She stood in the open space I'd carved in the cedar
hedge last spring; her long hair floating around her triangular face; the gauzy material on her robes streaming behind her like she was standing in front of her own personal
wind machine. Glowing. I could pick out the details of her
face—expressive eyes, soft chin—and her clothing. What
I'd taken for a shroud was really a very tattered pearl-gray
gown.

Hauntingly lovely fit her.

There was definitely an anticipatory quality to the way she was watching me. Had she gotten a memo from the Goddess above? *"Dear Jane Doe, please meet Hedi Peacock-Stronghold at the Pearly Gates at moonrise and escort her to her final resting place."*

Oh hell, no.

And then she did something I hadn't expected, and really, at that point, my imagination was wide open to suggestion. She made a quick sudden gesture with her white hands, as if she were squeezing the air between her hands, or maybe not that, maybe more like she was trying to contain something. And *then* . . . oh my word . . . bits of green light started to glimmer in the space between those cupped hands. Just tiny little sparkles. She bent her head and frowned over them, and then appeared to put more elbow grease into whatever she was doing. Something started to take shape. The glitter bits glowed brightly and then—bam!—well, not bam, but in my head, a definite wham-bam, because with a sudden burst of brilliance, the pieces of light coalesced into one sphere of green Fae magic—a damn near duplicate of the ball of light I'd disintegrated the night before.

She dropped her hands. My rejected Fae magic rose on its own accord—a rather beautiful and deadly sphere—until it found a place of comfort, a foot beyond her shoulder. And there it stayed, lofting in the wind like a well-tethered, miniature air balloon.

"Fae Stars," I breathed. That's how she got her body back. She'd stolen my fairy mojo. "That's mine!"

"Shut up," said my guard.

"I need that!" I hollered to Casperella.

She tilted her head in inquiry—*is that gnat speaking to me?*—and turned toward the pond. My magic bobbed behind her.

"Give it back!" I yelled.

"Save it for the trial," Fatso said.

She'd stopped within feet of the cliff. Maybe because she'd reached the edge of the crumbling stone wall, or maybe because she was rightfully afraid of my ire. That was my magic, and I intended to whistle it back home.

Some of the pack moved toward me—more in the way of "hey, it's a car wreck, let's gawk," than to offer any support—and I lost sight of her for a few seconds as they made a ring around me. "Move aside," Fatso said. He planted his meaty palm on my shoulder blades and began to push me through them.

Most did, except the freakishly tall guy that works the cash register at Cash Corners. He chose to stand his ground, planting his daddy long legs so that I either needed to move out of his way or bounce off him. *Really?* I faked a stumble, and delivered a knee in the general direction of his belt buckle. He collapsed over his nether regions with a surprised and pained "wuff."

That cheered me up a little.

I went to meet my judge and jury with a faint smile, chin up. Okay, maybe I did turn around and give the wheezing Cash Corners jerk an FU smirk. And perhaps I did slant one last-ditch "call 911" appeal toward one of the marginally kinder bitches. But for the most part, I cut my way through the pack like a stoic Joan of Arc, heading for her funeral pyre. Hell, I was freakin' Marie Antoinette with her nose turned up at the peasants.

I am a Stronghold.

The Danvers bitch's eyes widened as I favored her with a toothy smile.

Then the last of the crowd parted.

For a second, my left eye didn't believe what it was seeing.

A trio of battered Weres—Cordelia, Harry, and Biggs— were tightly bound to three adjacent sugar maple trees by a series of chains and padlocks. *They'll die trying to change into their wolves, chained so tightly like that. There'll be no room for the transformation.* Already, Biggs looked the worst of the lot—the slump of his shoulders radiated more resignation than his bloody lip. Harry's battered face was set, his dark eyes shrewd. No one had righted Cordelia's wig, but her spine was beauty-pageant straight. The only trace of blood I spotted on her was across the knuckles of her bruise-mottled hand, but then again, there's only so much detail you can take in when you're got a red and white bandana obscuring part of your vision.

But I'd seen enough.

I'd led them to this: with every decision I'd deferred to Cordelia's wisdom, with every dispute I'd asked Harry to solve, with every social occasion I'd dodged and sent Biggs to instead.

As lightbulb moments went, it was a little dim and a whole lot late.

My Were-bitch whined as the teenager closest to Harry let out a groan and sank to his knees. A young Were pulled off his T-shirt and lifted his head to the moon. Still human, he snapped his mortal white teeth in the air.

My fingers itched for some magic.

"They're stronger than us," my wolf moaned. "They don't like us. They've never liked us."

Goddess, Cordelia was right, I thought, listening to my inner-bitch's whimpers. *I'm* not *the girl I was.*

I need to find her again. I need to mend her.

Come back, magic-mine.

The murmur of conversation dried up on cue as Knox held up his hand for attention. Those most happy about my change in fortunes had pushed their way to the front of the throng. I studied their stony faces. It was easy to read the Scawens and Danvers families; for them the dice had long tumbled down the green felt.

It was much harder to judge the mind-sets of those who milled behind them because the magnetic lure of the moon had left them all with the focus of a junkie overdue for his fix. *Is there any leeway in the verdict? Any way I could talk them out of hurting my friends, too?* Hard to tell. Their attention bounced from me, to Knox, to that rising silver orb; the same sequence playing over and over in a restless shuffle. A teenager yipped and was quickly shushed by a sweating adult.

"We are gathered here," began Knox. He'd removed his hat, losing his cool factor. Now it appeared he was working on emphasizing the wolf hidden within. My accuser either brushed his hair to amplify his feral qualities or it grew that way—from his widow's peak, it rose into a ridge that ran down his skull to the base of his neck.

The Royal Amulet tensed against my breast as a trickle of sweat rolled down between my boobs. I'd expected a longer preamble from Knox, maybe a little back history about who he was and what gave him the right to chain up my friends and bring me forward to this kangaroo court, but after a relatively short intro, the Council's boy pulled a bunch of papers out of his back pocket. He thumbed up his glasses. "Though you are known as Hedi Peacock," he said, "your name is actually Helen Stronghold. You are the get of a denounced Were and his Fae whore."

"My mother was mated to my father, and I have not tried to hide who I am—"

"Until six months ago, you were presumed dead or to be—" He paused, and then dropped the Fae-bomb. "In *Merenwyn*."

The crowd did the obligatory mutter.

"Not true." I cast a searing glance toward my magic. "I've never been out of Ontario." *Magic, return to me. Come back to me now.* Casperella's head reared back. Did she hear my silent plea? With cool deliberation, she lifted her hand to the sphere above her. At her touch, my magic ball sparked. A few glittering bits of it swarmed out of the sphere, did a quick circuit, and then dived back into the melee of magic.

Oh yeah? I took a chance, and used real words and a forceful tone. "Magic-mine, return to me. Right now, right here."

Knox did that thing with his nose again. "Go ahead and say your prayers," he murmured, flipping to the second page. "The Council's charges are as follows. The accused, Hedi Peacock-Stronghold, conspired to end a century-long peace held between the Weres and Fae by sending an Alpha into the Fae realm through the forbidden portal."

He took a breath, and then said in grave tones that didn't jibe with his ensemble, "This action constituted a deliberate violation of terms set by the Treaty of Brelland—an agreement that has kept the peace between our realm and the Fae's for some hundred years. The consequences of this are real and significant—her actions have put the welfare of all Weres in peril."

The pack inhaled in feigned shock. Two-faced terriers. It was common knowledge among the wolves of Creemore that the portal to the Fae realm had opened up long enough for Cordelia and me to shoot Bridge past its gates. But now they had to look like it was all news to them, didn't they? No one wants to be considered an accomplice to a Fae conspirator.

Guess they are afraid they'll end up chained to a tree.

"Additionally, she is held accountable for the homicides of Mannus Trowbridge, Stuart Scawens, Dawn Danvers, and Robson Trowbridge. Covering up their deaths cost the pack, and the NAW, significant dollars."

More rumbles from the pratless pack.

I searched for a comeback to the NAW's charges—something brilliant along the lines of Winston Churchill—but my word pile was as low as my Were. So, I said the obvious. "I'm innocent."

"She murdered my daughter!" screeched Lucy Danvers.

Well, besides that.

"She's bad luck! Nothing has gone well since she's been here." I swiveled my head to pick out the lout who'd said that, but the Hedi-hater had melted back into the crowd—clearly a stealth accuser, unlike Rachel Scawens and her daughter, Petra, who were standing near the front of the pack, their body language screaming "Burn her."

"I will eat your flesh," Rachel's eyes promised.

And I hope you choke on it.

Knox scoffed. "Are you saying that you're not a Fae spy? That you weren't sent here to make it look like one of us deliberately broke the treaty?"

"I am *not* a spy!" I tore my gaze from the Scawenses and pinned Knox with my one-eyed glare. "Robson Trowbridge is *not* dead and I *am* his mate. In his absence, I have looked after this pack. This whole—" I would have thrown up my hands, but the guy behind me had me pinned fairly well, so I did an aggressive move with my chin. "Come-to-Jesus intervention is bullshit. I'm working for the pack, not against it. At any point in time over the last six months have I tried to run? Have I done anything threatening or hurtful to you people?"

A soccer-mum Were shrieked, "You have been waiting for your people to come!"

"I have been waiting for my mate to return," I hurled back. I matched my vehemence with a really savage head toss, which finally—*finally*—popped my blindfold off my brow. It sat on the top of my head, an ugly crown of red cotton. But now I could see everything: hatred, confusion, a smidge of ambivalence, aggression, mixed with a whole bunch of moon lust.

"From Merenwyn!" someone screeched at the back. "We all know why she sent him there."

"Kill her!"

I gave the ball of green hovering over Casperella a swift (but very earnest) look of entreaty. *Come home,* I implored. *I'm sorry I sent you away.*

"Wait," someone yelled, as he shoved his way through. "Stop!"

I groped for the insurance broker's name. John? Jason?

Nameless skinny guy demanded, "Who's going to lead the pack of Creemore if she's torn apart by our wolves? No males of age have shown the gift of blue light."

They couldn't just shoot me?

"The Council has investigated the situation." Knox stuffed the papers into his back pocket. "That is true. No male—"

"Or female," interjected Rachel, with a significant glance at her daughter, Petra.

"So far no one in your pack—male or female—has shown any definitive ability to flare."

"As yet," said Rachel firmly.

Knox paused to give her a glare that should have melted her. "The NAW knows that there are quite a few young Weres—male or female—who have the right lineage. Which leaves your pack in a problem, should you decide that this"—he ladled on some scorn—"Alpha-by-proxy is guilty of these charges. In that case, the NAW will step in and appoint a Regent."

Slowly, the insurance guy asked, "And this Regent . . . Would he be chosen from our pack?"

"No." Knox's eyes gleamed behind his glasses. "I was sent here to fulfill that responsibility. When I left, the NAW was not sure how many of the charges leveled in the letter of complaint were accurate, but now, looking at the evidence—"

"What letter of complaint?" asked the insurance guy.

"What evidence!" I howled.

"I don't believe he was ever mated to her," Rachel insisted.

"It's easy enough to prove." Knox's brown eyes were calm and nerveless, shielded as they were behind the magic-coated lenses of his glasses. "If she's truly mated to your Alpha, she will bear his scent, correct?" He pulled something out of his back pocket—black, plastic—a box cutter? *No, not that, it's too . . .* I blinked as he hit a button and a knife blade flicked out.

A switchblade. I took a half step back—but really, there's only so far you can retreat when you have a tub of lard behind you.

What is Knox going to do with that knife? Peel my skin off?

The thought flashed—it would be a good time to turn into Buffy. Maybe lean back against Fatso, lift my legs, and deliver a Jackie Chan double kick into Knox's tight gut.

But you don't absorb that type of stuff watching reality TV or reading historical romances; you learn that in a dojo. Since I'd spent ten years either gazing out of an apartment window or reading yet another bodice ripper boosted from the bookstore, it wasn't part of my first-response options. Instead, I did what felt natural. I cringed—shoulders hunched, chin tucked into my neck—as the knife-happy Were stepped forward for the kill.

Try not to cry out.

Knox sketched a smile, victorious and black hearted, and caught my chin with his fingers, forcing it to lift until we were nose to nose. His gaze roved over my face and then his brows knitted together. He visibly stiffened, intent—like a wolf's sudden interest in a limping elk—on the heavy gold chain around my neck.

"She wears a fairy amulet." He reached for the necklace around my neck.

Someone howled into the night. Eerily animal-like though not as yet changed.

"You don't want to do that." I sketched a taunting smile.

Knox ignored me, and started hauling the Royal Amulet upward: an extraction that turned out to be a little more difficult than he might have imagined because Ralph didn't want to leave the valley of the boobs. Not that way, anyhow. Not because some dumbass wolf was yanking his chain. Furious—as anyone could see by the purple bleats of indignation throbbing from the center of his stone—he rappelled up his chain in a superblur, shortening it behind him as he did—don't ask me how he did that, but I can tell you that Merry used to do the same weird maneuver when she was trying out different looks—until he'd morphed from a twenty-inch necklace to a too-tight choker. Then, with a savagery to match the most feral wolf, he went for the Were in Black's fingers.

Chomp. Knox's mouth dropped open, and he took a quick step backward, which gave my amulet all the time he needed to burrow back under my T-shirt. Once under its meager cover, Ralph tore down his chain—*zing!*—swung over to my boob, and scuttled for cover inside my bra cup.

Knox snapped to Fatso, "Hold her tight!"

My heart began to beat like a cornered bunny's as the Were in Black reached for the sleeve of my T-shirt. Grimly, Knox funneled his thumb underneath the fabric and kept going—his ragged nail scoring a line of pain along my bicep and shoulder—until he'd pleated the fabric all the way to my neck. The shirt dug into the back of my neck as he pulled the wad of jersey taut.

He lifted the knife then paused.

He's teasing me with it. I registered that and, absurdly, that the skin over Knox's flared nostrils was potted with big pores and that—*oh look at that*—moonlight can make a silver blade gleam in a deadly and beautiful way. My belly tensed as he pointed the tip at my shoulder. *It's going to hurt, it's going to—*

It didn't.

Because it wasn't my Fae blood he wanted—not right away, not yet. First he wanted me to curve my tail in shame. His sharp, moon-bright blade sliced through the T-shirt's bunched material before I even had time to finish the thought, *Oh my Goddess, he's really going to stick me with that thing.* My shirt fell apart. At least the right side of my bodice did. It flopped down like it was the bib of a pair of overalls, folding over itself, exposing my shoulder and a good part of bra.

Someone laughed.

My skin goosefleshed, since it was, as I'd said before, a particularly cold night—not because I was twenty-two years old and it was becoming painfully evident that next year, when my birthday passed, it would remain uncelebrated, but because the air suddenly felt frigid, as if death were passing its fingers over me, pinching me to see if I was done yet.

People keep wanting to kill me. Why is that?

Poor Ralph didn't know where to go. There was no

place to hide, because with another fabric fold and a quick slash of Knox's blade, there went the other side. Two more slashes and my shirt wasn't a shirt anymore. The shredded garment slid down to my hips, paused at the curve of my ass long enough to sign the separation papers, and then split in two. One tattered scrap ghosted down the back of my legs, hell-bent on kissing the earth. The other, Knox held aloft, speared on the tip of his shiny blade.

"Let those who doubt her guilt smell this," he said, offering my white flag of shame to Rachel Scawens. "She doesn't carry Trowbridge's scent on her skin like a true mate should. She has to wear his clothing to fake you out. Test it! His signature is there, but it's old. Didn't anyone notice that? What did she do? Conjure up your obedience? Cast a spell on the pack? Mislead you through her magic?"

Rachel brought the scrap of fabric up to her sharp little snout with both hands, closed her eyes, and inhaled. She kept it there, for one long second, and then her lids lifted. A dark hope—the type that hones cruelty until it's dagger sharp—had swelled in her heart during that deep breath. Without comment, she passed the shredded bit of Trowbridge's shirt to her daughter, and then stalked toward me, hips swinging. Her face was alight, no longer pulled down by gravity and sorrow. She leaned in, took a long, insulting sniff. "She has no scent of her own!"

The cheering ranks opened up for Rachel Scawens. She accepted the scrap of T-shirt from her daughter, and held the shredded T-shirt over her head as she walked deep into the throng. As Weres go, she was only moderately tall. Her head disappeared as they clustered closer. I heard her shout, "Smell it!"

The hair went up on my nape as one of the pack unleashed a howl.

It turned into a wolf mob. They crowded her, pushing at each other in a frenzy of eagerness to have their turn at the prize. Their humanity—that thin veneer over what they really were—fell. From deep within their midst, I heard her yell, "It's my brother's shirt! See, it belongs to Robbie!"

She must have tossed it up high—I saw it flutter in the air—and someone caught it and tossed it again, and then it became a game, my white flag of shame flying over the heads of the gathered pack.

"The Fae will come!" a man bellowed.

"Chain her to the tree!" someone else yelled.

I spun my head toward Cordelia—her mouth was open, she was shouting something to me. Biggs's head was doubled over his chains; he was visibly writhing in pain. Harry's head was thrown back, the tendons on his neck strained.

"Let them go," I said to Knox. "They're not part of this."

"Too late," he said.

"Magic, come to me!" I screamed.

Knox nodded to Rachel, and Fatso gave me a shove in the mob's direction. It was like tipping a fox out of her cage at the start of a hunt. Five or six of Trowbridge's pack rushed me. I flailed out blindly, and then gasped as Lucy Danvers's elbow caught my head. Stunned, I found myself being lifted by a group of angry pack members. My body was turned, and I was carried facedown—my head spinning—right over to the old oak tree.

"Cover her eyes," someone hissed. Hard hands pinned me to the tree as another's stinking shirt was thrown over my head. *They still think I have a flare.* I heard the clink of the chain, and then someone went around and around the tree with it, like a reveler circling a maypole, painfully binding me to the tree at three points; once around my hips, another loop cutting into my waist, and the final spot a hard pressure across the top of my chest.

It was hard to breathe again. *This is how Bridge must have felt.*

"She is your Alpha's mate," Harry yelled. "She doesn't—" His voice broke off into a sudden grunt.

Some bitch with filthy paws was trying to secure the shirt covering my head. I caught a bewildering mix of scents: the female's breath on my cheek as she fumbled to tuck the ends around my chin, Knox's dominance, the pungent spice of Weres on the brink of surrendering to the moon's call. I heard a snick of lock and felt its cold weight added to the steel that bound me.

My inner-Were was cringing, remembering the last time such aggression flowed.

Enough. Me and my wolf were chained to a freakin' old oak tree.

And they think I have a flare.

With a snarl that would have put any Were to shame, I whipped my head away from the woman's ministrations. The woman—works in the post office, eats a lot of Slim Jims— reached out for my face again, her intention obvious.

I didn't have all my magic, but I had rage, and I had a morsel of flare left in me. It wouldn't last long; I'd better make the best use of it. I summoned it. No preburn itch in the eyes, no slow buildup. Bam. *Here I come.* Green light poured hot from my eyes. Post office lady stared back at me, her gaze nailed like a deer staring at the feathers of the oncoming arrow. From the back of her throat came a high-pitched whine.

"Release me, right now," I said. "Or I will—"

I heard it first—dribble, dribble, dribble, splat—in concert with something warm and wet soaking my shoes. And sue me, but if someone peed on your foot, you'd break your gaze, too—*is that pee on my foot?*—just to check it out. Which is when post office bitch spun away with a shriek, and pushed past the others in a panic. "Come back here!" I followed with my glare until her tight little ass disappeared into the woods.

The one bitch I could have controlled and I let her go free.

I had to hurry; already the younger ones were beginning to change. A girl shucked her dress off and lifted her face to the sky. The teenager beside her was fighting with his zipper. Behind them another puppy was already on his side on the ground, his legs jerking.

Once they became a wolf pack, they'd circle my tree and attack me from behind. I gritted my teeth against the bite of the chains as I tried to twist my hands free from my bindings.

"You," I yelled to one of the cheerleaders in the front. "Come here!"

My intended target fell to her knees with a faint moan, and held her hands up to the sky as if she were at a revival meeting, as her face started to ripple. She wasn't a kid, succumbing to the moon. She was an adult. Goddess, Biggs would be changing.

"Cordelia!" I screamed.

"Run!" she screamed back. But I couldn't. Couldn't she see that? I was bound like her, surrounded like her. Her voice had changed to a man's—strained and forceful, as she fought her transformation. I lunged and squirmed, but there was no give to the chains that pinned me to my tree—steel as thick as my baby finger held me captive.

"I am the mate of your Alpha. Release me!" I let my fading flare drift over those still upright, freezing them in the act of pulling off their clothing. "Free my second and my friends. Right now!"

The hair went up on my nape when another wolf howled. One of the braver young wolves—probably a freakin' Scawens second cousin—darted toward me. "Back," I shouted. He stalled, mid-charge. "Get back!" He lowered his body, but his hackles were raised. His tail was down, but his snout was wrinkled.

My flare spat, flickered, and sputtered out. I closed my eyes briefly, feeling the itch and burn of my abused eyelids. How long would it be before the wolf attacked? A minute? Thirty seconds?

A question left unanswered, because that's when Casperella began to sing.

Chapter Seven

Ghost-girl's mouth was open and from her lips came music so poignant it sounded like one of the Goddesses had come down to earth and decided to serenade us. So liltingly—well, hauntingly—I almost didn't recognize the melody, until she broke into what I'd always deemed "the chorus."

The Weres stopped in their tracks, heads cocked.

She knows the portal song.

Faes don't just go abracadabra, or pull a device out of their pocket and hit the button to summon the Gates to Merenwyn. They have to use their voice to call to the portal, and because they're all Middle Earth, and have a tendency to add a bit of decoration to even the simplest thing, the portal summons wasn't just a string of words in their language. It was, Goddess-curse-it, a song.

She stood behind her tumbled wall, singing the call to the portal the way I'd never heard it sung before. Not even by Lou at the height of her power. This was in tune. With sweet passion and longing. With a voice that probably made the angels knuckle their eyes and weep.

She knew *all* the words.

The pack could hear her, even if they couldn't see her. One of the wolves growled, but that threatening throat rumble turned into a whine through his snout. His distress call was picked up by another. Those already changed into their wolf form were the worst affected: they whimpered and milled about yipping. The Weres still in the agonizing throes of their metamorphosis heard the group anxiety and contributed some guttural moans. The old geezers still holding out in their pissing contests with the moon had conceded to the point they were getting naked with hunched shoulders and sucked-in bellies. Even Knox's two buddies were shedding their clothing.

"Mother of God, protect us," cried the waitress from the hotel.

Asses jiggled as they ran full out for the safety of the trees, leaving only those who couldn't or wouldn't follow. My writhing trio of friends, Casperella, me, and Knox, who was backing away with one hand fumbling for something inside his jacket. And, somewhat surprisingly, a fully clothed Petra Scawens. Unlike the other members of her family, she didn't seem particularly shaken by the green sphere or the spook rendition of "Come to Me, My Portal."

If anything, curiosity was the biggest emotion playing over her features.

Fatso had left his clothes ten feet away. He'd done what most of the Weres did—piled his wallet and watch under the tent of his overturned shoes.

The keys were there.

Biggs was howling.

"They are your pack. This is wrong and you know it," I implored Petra. "The keys are in Fatso's pants pocket. Please let Cordelia and the boys go."

She chewed her lip, and then, I knew—in the firming of her features—she'd made a decision. With ruthless speed, she tracked down Fatso's teepee of clothing. A shoe went flying as she made a grab for his bulky jeans. She jammed her hand deep in the denim's pockets.

Out came the keys.

Oh Goddess, the misshapen thing pinned to Biggs's tree was moaning, its jerking leg was part man, part dog; its toes were tipped with claws. Cordelia's back was bowed, her face melted. Harry was panting, but holding on by a thread.

Once committed, Petra was fast. She sprinted across the field to Biggs, stuck the key in the lock, and turned it. And then it was quick work—she tossed the lock, undid the chains, and stepped away. The thing that was once Biggs dropped to the ground, still moaning. Next she moved to Cordelia's tree. Then to Harry's. When she was finished, Petra Scawens dropped the keys to the ground and walked away, shedding her clothing as she did.

What am I, chopped liver?

"Are you guys okay?" I called. "Answer me!"

I heard a grunt—Harry's?—from their direction.

Casperella was already at that little dip and dive at the end of a long stream of Merenwynian that I could never decode because the end of one word ran into the next.

Hurry up, I willed.

The scent came first.

Flowers. Freesias, to be exact.

A howl was quickly stifled from the woods.

I strained to listen. Yes. There. A rippling noise coming from the pond, as if water were being agitated. Above the pond, the air seemed to thicken, and then a mist was born. Faint, white, and transparent. It began to thicken in density and color, turning from just a hint of fog into a stream of white vapor that rotated in a circle above the surface of the agitated water. The empty hollow of the circle was filled out as the vapor swelled in size. Denser now and different in color, too.

It will turn to pink and then deep purple.

My heart started to pound in my chest as the vapor blushed. An uneven blush, I realized, looking down at it. Purple blotches, blooming like anemones in the stream of white-pink fog. They began to multiply, changing the hue of the rotating air from soft pink to amethyst.

Bring the fireflies next, please, oh please, my Goddess. Bring the fireflies next.

A bright, tiny spark of gold light. There. Just a quick blip. Then another and another. Here. There. Bright stars of iridescence splintering the dark plum-colored mass of swirling air. I watched them, waiting for the next step where the lights would grow in number, until the whole swirling purple mass would appear pinpricked with starlight.

Casperella's face split into a smile. She held a glowing palm up to the sphere—for all the world like Mariah when she was aiming for that top note—not quite touching, but close enough that I fancied I could see a faint electrical stream between her and that ball of my Fae magic.

She hit a high note.

And then everything seemed to happen all at once.

The thing she called—the portal to Merenwyn—responded to her song and her magic. The purpled air began to swirl, the lights to multiply, and then she threw out her other hand—as if she were the telegraph pole between two long stretched wires of communication—and with a flash of light, the magenta mass consumed the fireflies, and the air turned violet-pink in hue.

Rapidly, so fast that later I couldn't be sure how long it took, the vortex changed in aspect. No longer a whirlpool, it separated and redefined itself until it was now a stage of sorts. A back wall of violet smoke surrounded by two billowing columns of fog and a lazy, wreathing floor of mist.

I stopped breathing.

I think everyone did. The frogs on their lily pads. The shivering wolves in the woods. Even the dark birds perched in the old elm fell silent. Not a single wing adjustment among the flock of them.

Her song finished.

There were just three final words for her to say. She'd called the portal—it'd returned to the exact spot it had disappeared from half a year ago. At the midpoint of the oval pond, hovering a good ten feet above the surface of the water. Now all she had to do was utter the short command that would make the gates materialize. I knew two thirds of it. It was just that very last word that I could never duplicate. That *heuh* sound the Merenwyn Fae make with their palate was beyond the curl of my tongue.

But for the record, she didn't sing those final three words. I *know* she didn't say them.

Because I was shocked when—unbidden—the backdrop of mist started to curl in a clockwise fashion, and then clear in the middle, disappearing like the mist on your bathroom mirror when you held a blow dryer to it . . . from impenetrable to thinning, from thinning to frustratingly coy blotches of barely perceptible shapes, and from that, to a crystal-clear fifteen-foot round window.

A picture window into another realm.

Through it, I saw the field of Merenwyn, its grasses still long and green in eternal summer. The sky was blue. Why was it always daylight in Merenwyn? The Pool of Life shimmered down in the valley below. Dazzlingly pure, enough to make me close my eyes in pleasure. At the sound of chiming bells, I opened them, in time to catch a blur of movement inside the gates' picture window. Two men were running up the hill full bore, shoulder to shoulder, with a little brown wolf keeping pace by their heels.

One dark haired, one blond. Both tall.

They'd been bound together, wrist to wrist. It should have made them awkward, but no, they ran smoothly, their legs in perfect harmony. The blond was fully dressed; from his toes—knee-high, glossy boots—to the natty bowler hat rammed on his head. But the other man . . . he was a wild, bearded warrior with long dreadlocks of dark hair. He wore nothing but a pair of tattered pants. The sun gleamed off his bare chest. His free hand gripped a rough rope that served as a leash for the wolf-mutt beside him.

My heart started slamming into my chest. I knew. Even if his scowling features weren't distinct. Even if his dark hair was improbably long and Rastafarian.

I *knew.*

He'd found a way home. He'd come back to me—when I had all but given up. My left knee went out in relief and joy, and I sagged momentarily against my chains.

Trowbridge, Trowbridge.

They didn't pause to calculate or reconnoiter the portal

area. Without breaking stride, as one, the three leaped. Their images were frozen inside through the gates' picture window for an instant. The Fae, to whom my mate was bound, had leaped with his head down, his free hand tight on the brim of his hat. My mate's body was strained, tied between the Fae and the tug of the wolf's leash. His face was taut, set in a fierce snarl. The little brown wolf's body was extended, front paws up to its chest, its tail a plume behind it.

And then I blinked, or the image shattered, and they plunged through the veil between this world and Merenwyn. Trowbridge landed hard, and braked harder—the misty floor billowed upward as the little wolf landed right by his heels. It went skidding toward the edge, to be pulled up short by the rope around its neck.

But the guy with the bowler hat didn't know that they had only a four-foot landing pad, or that Trowbridge would stop suddenly and brace himself. His feet kept going, but his arm didn't. His reaction to having his shoulder almost wrenched from its socket was a stream of fluid, fierce, and incomprehensible Merenwynian curses. He half spun toward Trowbridge, his free arm lifted.

Trowbridge bared his teeth into a triumphant sneer.

Mine.

Violence simmered between them, until the little brown wolf gave an anxious yawn, and tugged at its leash. They stalked over to the edge, and for a moment, stood, refugees from Merenwyn inspecting the lily pads. My mate's forehead creased—I could almost see him thinking, where's the freakin' log?—and then he lifted his nose high to scent the air. His body tensed as he caught the smell of the pack.

I'd have sold my soul to have a scent signature of my own at that moment. Hell, I'd have signed on for another bruising engagement with Karma just to watch his face break into joy when he caught my scent.

The wolf snuffled at the fog and sneezed.

Screw it.

"Trowbridge," I called.

All three heads snapped upward, though I only really cared about one.

One cherished face.

A hundred quick impressions. His cheekbones seemed more pronounced and his curls were no longer finger-soft. They'd grown into long unkempt spirals of fuzzy hair that covered his face and blanketed the swell of his shoulders. One dense ringlet dangled by his eye, before he flung it out of his vision with a feral flick of his head.

He had some beard thing going on, too, that I wasn't overly keen on.

As a matter of fact, in no way did he match the man who visited me in my dreams . . . and yet . . . you could strip Trowbridge down to a pair of rough trousers, you could daub him with mud, you could cover his lower face with a straggly beard, and he'd still be a work of art. My body would always recognize him—it was already tightening with anticipation.

My Trowbridge. Here. Finally, mine again.

Come to me.

Free me.

Across the mist, across the pond, across the gap of time and experience, our gazes caught and held. Sparks started to turn in a lazy circuit in his eyes. Little nameless comets with white-blue tails spun until his eyes glowed, and emitted a wide fanning beam of Trowbridge blue. There is no other way to describe it—it was a hue even deeper in tone than the waters of the Mediterranean.

My heart—that poor organ that'd had such a workout over the last ten minutes—started to do another impetuous quickstep in my chest. I reached for an answering flare. Willed a spark to turn. Felt the burn.

His flare waited for mine. A test . . . Oh shit. A test.

Tears welled, blurring my vision.

I'm out of juice.

The flare in his sputtered out and died.

Trowbridge measured the distance, rapidly evaluating the number of feet he'd have to leap to get to me. Then, he looked down at the murky water. Grim turned to something fouler.

"They pulled the log out last month," I called helpfully.

"Why are you tied to a tree?"

"It's a long story."

My true love shot me a hurried look that could be best described as enigmatic. He went back to frowning at the water. I probed inside myself, hopeful that I'd find a little something not used up so I could return a belated flare.

Nothing, I'm dry.

The Fae's bowler hat sat low on his head, tilted so that it brushed the ear that sported the long dangly earring. He said something to Trowbridge in my mother's tongue, to which my mate snapped, "You're on my land now. We speak English here."

The Fae was about thirty, maybe thirty-five, with a long nose and a spill of blond hair that fell to his waist. With a tight frown, he noted, "The Black Mage's men are expert trackers. We can't linger here."

"I don't intend to," said Trowbridge. "We're going to make a leap for it."

"Across the water?" The Fae had a light accent.

"No, we're going up there," said my nonswimming boyfriend, with a toss of his head toward me and my tree.

Disbelief crossed the Fae's face as he examined the cliff's crumbling handholds. His gaze roved the gathering place. Not much to see, really. Knox backing away from the cliff. A mostly empty field—from that angle it was doubtful the Fae could see Cordelia, Biggs, and Harry going through their change near the edge of the forest. A few mounds of clothing and a few clumps of shoes, all placed strategically far from any bush or tree. His gaze lit on me and indifferently moved on. Which was damn well annoying—*hello, over here, chained to a freakin' tree*—but it was clear my damsel-in-distress situation wasn't half as fascinating as Casperella. The Fae took in her ghostly awesomeness with the squint-eyed approval of a trophy wife looking at a pair of Jimmy Choos.

"Move back, we'll need a running start," said Trowbridge. "We'll go on three."

The Fae pursed his lips as Trowbridge crouched to slip the rope from the wolf's neck. "I can bring the portal closer."

"How?"

The blond gave a fleeting sidelong glance at the golden chain binding his wrist to Trowbridge's. "I'll need my arms free," he said.

"Not going to happen," said Trowbridge.

"As you wish," Bowler-hat said with a cocky smile. He lifted his free hand and flicked his fingers—a mirror of the way I do—in the direction of the glowing green sphere above Casperella's shoulder.

His magic hit mine with a hiss.

Trowbridge's head snapped back in surprise. He fought for control, and then said in a thick voice, "What is that—"

"You taste Fae magic through my skin, wolf. Nothing more." The Fae with the hat, and the balls the size of melons, said to my mate, "If you cannot bear the feel of it on your flesh, you should release me."

"You're not in Merenwyn anymore," Trowbridge growled. "You take orders from me now, Shadow."

Bowler-hat retorted, "And *you* are not in Merenwyn anymore, Son of Lukynae. Call your pack. Show me that your leadership skills here are equal to those you claim in my realm."

White teeth flashed. "I don't need to tell the wolves of Creemore that I'm home. In a few minutes, every one of them will have caught my scent and know that Robson Trowbridge is back."

The Fae grew stiller than a mouse facing a stout lady with a sturdy broom. "Trowbridge?"

"Robson Trowbridge, son of Jacob, grandson of Stephen. Last of a long line of Alphas."

Bowler-hat offered his traveling companion his profile as he half turned toward the Stronghold ridge. He had a long nose. A little pucker appeared at his lip as he eyed the silver outline of the trailer. Then, his mouth firmed. He looked over his shoulder toward the gates then spared the full moon a quick, sharp glance. "Will you be able to hold against the call of the moon?"

"I will hold," Trowbridge said through his teeth.

"If you change while I am bound to you, I will use this magic to smite you."

My guy lifted his lips, and growled, "Not before I smite you."

Trowbridge said "smite"?

"There's no time for argument," said the blond. "Know that I could kill you with the magic I have seething in my hands. I could, but have not. Consider that. Perhaps I mean no ill to Robson Trowbridge and the Weres of Creemore."

He returned his attention to Casperella and my magic. A glittering bead of green swelled at the point of contact on the sphere bobbing above her shoulder. The Fae squeezed his eyes shut, his expression fierce as he concentrated. The hole widened, and then magic bits began to stream out of the ball in a thin, supple line of green fluorescence.

Who the hell is this guy? It didn't surprise me that I couldn't see his magic—that was just an inherent fact about the Fae gift; you can only see the visual proof of your own talent—but the realization that *he* could see mine well enough to steal it was downright shocking.

Thief.

"No!" Casperella cried out, heartfelt and pathetic.

Without remorse or hesitation, the Fae drained the ball until it was nothing but an empty sheath that turned itself inside out, before it, too, disappeared into the end of the rope of magic. At that, my friendly ghost dropped her hands and issued a faint moan. Casperella's expression was tired, tragic, and angered all in one as she melted in front of us, thinning from a three-dimensional corporeal shape to something far more translucent. A moment later, her gray dress turned back into a shroud, her face became a blur of white, and then, with a final, silent sigh, she disappeared altogether.

The Fae rolled his neck and with one fluid wrist flick of his right hand he sent a bullwhip of magic streaking toward me. I let out a high-pitched screech and turned my head away.

Thud!

Gad, I flinched from my own magic. Eyes squeezed shut, I waited for the pain. I had been dodging hurt all night; the odds were against me that he would miss. After the lapse of what probably had been two seconds, I whispered, "Four thousand." *It wouldn't have hurt me, would it?* "Five thousand." I waited for my hands to heat, my skin to blister.

"Six thousand."

No payback misery. No dizzy swelling of Fae inside me. No discomfort at all, actually, other than the fact that Ralph had chosen to burrow out from under my hair, and was using a loose hank of it to rappel to the top of my head. His little golden feet bit into my scalp as I cautiously lifted my cheek.

Huh.

"Who *is* he?" I said in awestruck tones to Ralph.

A long cable of *my* magic was now wrapped around the trunk of the maple to my left.

The little brown wolf nudged Trowbridge's knee and issued a whine of distress. Bowler-hat bent his head—why? To pray? To focus? Then with a deep inhale, he began winding my magic around his hand like a rope, over and over his knuckles, winching the Fae portal—all wreathing mist and purple-pink lights—across the pond with every rotation of his large fist.

Geez, this thieving Fae hadn't needed to use any verbal commands like "Attach" or "Stick" or even a "Go get 'em, Tiger." My *full-blooded* Fae mum had needed phrases to inform her magic of her wishes. "Dance," she'd say to the water in the pond. And it would dance.

This was some Fae, for all his dandified ways.

"Hurry," said Trowbridge.

Knox tried to ghost past me, intent on making an exit

before the Alpha of Creemore gave him an ass-thumping. Which just ticked me. "My mate's back," I called out to his retreating back. "He's going to kick your bony ass."

It happened so quickly. Knox was there, halfway to his getaway, and then he was back—right in front of me—close enough that I could have licked the sweat off his upper lip. Ralph tensed on my head, as I shrank against my tree. "You really are mates."

I lifted a proud chin. "Told you so."

The NAW's man leaned in closer. What? To whisper an insult? Then his shoulder flexed as he punched me in the gut.

It hurt.

"If I wasn't tied up at the moment," I said through my teeth, "I'd make you pay for that. Guess I'll have to leave it up to Trowbridge to make you sorry."

"I don't think so," he said, with a savage smile. "If you die, he will, too. Checkmate, bitch."

Checkmate? For a few seconds, I didn't feel any major pain—my brain wasn't registering my body's cry. Instead, I wasted two seconds puzzling over "checkmate" and another couple taking in a lungful of air to scream, "Trowbridge!"

Knox sprinted across the field, his focus on the path that led in the opposite direction of all those dangerous wolves waiting in the forest, away from the threat of the angry mate, and the strange Fae. He ran, all out, for the front of the house where his truck was waiting.

He ran for his life a little late, I thought with savage satisfaction.

Knox shouldn't have flown across that field—he must have known better than to run from another wolf—but his arrogance had made him think he was bulletproof. Stupid and shortsighted. In the time Knox had rustled enough bile to punch a girl—*one tied to a freakin' tree*—and flee, the portal had landed with its cargo. The little brown wolf perceived game sprinting toward escape, scented in that way that spoke of wounds and weakness. It had four legs, Knox had two; it wasn't an even race. It flew after her quarry, leash whipping behind it. Its teeth caught the fabric of his jeans. The Were pivoted, leg kicking out, ready to hurt. It dodged, and then suddenly—spine twisting, jaws open—spun back at him. Snap. Its jaws clamped down on his arm.

Take that, Were in Black.

But he flung it off like it was a kid whining for attention and the little brown wolf became the little brown *flying* wolf. Its body cut through the air. It hit the ground with a spine-rattling jolt and a pathetic yelp.

Trowbridge and the Fae went thundering past me—*nice of you all to stop by*—my mate's long ropes of hair flying behind him, the blond's a sheaf of wheat, as they tore across the field. Halfway across the pasture, the gold chain twined around their wrists fell away. The portal travelers matched momentum for a few more ground-eating strides before the Fae realized he was no longer bound and stopped running.

My man kept going, two hundred pounds of male in hot pursuit.

Knox made it into the tree line near the start of the path, but then he stopped, knee-deep in the vegetation, to shout, "I'm from the NAW!"

"I don't care," Trowbridge snarled. "You stink of sun potion and my mate's blood."

"You can't touch me." And then Knox—perhaps realizing that he couldn't outrun Trowbridge—did the dumbest thing.

He tried to stare down a true Alpha.

I saw Trowbridge's back stiffen, and the muscles on his neck tightened. What transpired between them—what exchange of power and submission flew between them before Knox turned to run again—I'll never know.

I'm feeling odd.

I lost my distance vision between one blink and another. The hurt in my belly was blossoming and unpleasantly—almost urgently—heating.

No, I really don't feel right.

The stomach blow was hurting beyond all reason, as if Knox's punch had been the match set to a pile of dry kindling ready to burn in my belly. Worse than heartburn. Its flames were growing; its burn spread outward.

Pain. Down there. Below my boobs. I bent my head. *Goddess, Goddess, Goddess!* There was a handle sticking out of my gut. My breath caught in my chest—frozen between an inhale and an exhale—as I tried to reconcile myself to the sight. *That can't be good. You can't live with a knife in your gut. I want it out. Somebody's got to take it out.*

"Help," I said, in a faint voice. I swallowed—the knife jerked—and called again, but this time far louder. "Help!"

Tiny feet tap-danced on my scalp. A prickle of gold at my hairline, and Ralph dived off my head, zip-lining down to the end of his rope of gold to inspect the damage. A second before, I'd wanted someone—anyone—to pull it from my body, but now I was filled with fear. Fear that the slightest brush of touch would cause terrible pain. *Don't touch it,* I thought, seesawing with fright. Instead, he swung below my bra—a bleat of red in the center of his amulet flashing like a cop's gotcha lights—and then he hung, oddly still, studying the black handle that trembled with each of my shallow breaths. Something warm and wet trickled down my stomach.

Fae smell like flowers when they bleed. Sweet peas were in bloom as my blood leaked from a terrible, horrible hole.

My Were howled inside me.

Someone's got to pull the knife out.

I opened my mouth to say that. As I did, I heard a scream, guttural and harsh, coming from the house. *Was it me? No. I didn't scream. Not even when Knox pushed that thing into me. Not me. Someone else.* It didn't matter who it was. Life had narrowed. To this tree. This pendant. That knife. *Oh Goddess, look at the knife go up and down as I breathe.*

I was burning up, turning into a candle of pain, wordless in its flame.

Ralph eased himself down to my skin. *Too close to the bad spot. Move away from it!* The Royal Amulet shifted quickly to find a better place, one right over my racing heart, and then he slowly lowered his pendant to my chest until his core was pressed flat to my skin. Prism colors swirled inside his stone.

He was trying to heal me, just as Merry used to.

A little late, but I love you anyhow, Ralph.

A shadow moved just beyond the edge of our narrow, dark world. *Trowbridge?* Fear fluttered at my throat as the wrong man stepped close. Long blond hair, not black. A dandy's hat, a clean-shaven jaw.

Not my mate.

The Fae's eyes were shadowed by his bowler, his mouth pulled into a pensive frown. His long white fingers reached for the blade— *Don't touch that knife.* I sucked in a ragged breath and opened my lips to beg, to entreat, to plead. Anything to stop him from touching the handle. The blade. My wound. But forming words had become complicated so suddenly. My tongue was heavy, my throat too dry. *I'm so helpless.* Arms bound to my side, bad thing in belly, Fae all around me. No Trowbridge. No Merry. Just my new best friend Ralph and this cold, strange Fae.

I want Trowbridge.

Another mewl of distress. My head sagged.

I couldn't run, I couldn't talk, I couldn't plead, I couldn't fight.

Terror-pain spread with each thump of my frightened heart. I cringed as the Fae touched my wound—so lightly, so carefully—and shuddered as I saw my blood staining his fingers. Liquid and still thin enough to drip down the back of his hand and curl around his hairless wrist. Then to my keening, quivering horror, he lifted a wet index to his nose and sniffed that wretched finger oh so delicately.

That's my blood on your hands. My Fae blood—

His Goddess-cursed hand was moving again, but this

time his fingers were reaching for my face. There was no escape from them. My chin was too heavy. I hurt too much. The blade, the fear, and Ralph, all of it was too great a burden. *I want Trowbridge.*

I slumped into my chains.

The Fae lifted my heavy head and parted my hair. He teased one sweaty hank off my cheek, and pursed his lips as his cool gaze roved my face.

Don't hurt me.

Whoosh. Suddenly, the Fae was swiped sideways, gone in a blur as Trowbridge shoved him aside. Grunts. Smack of flesh on flesh. More grunts.

Hurting here.

"Let me help her!"

"Keep away from her!" A growl. *Trowbridge?* "She is mine."

I moaned when someone—something?—hit my calf hard.

A flash of green fire. A furious roar.

That's my *magic.*

A wolf growling, snarling, snapping.

"Back, Anu!" cried the Fae. Another flash of green, followed by a yelp sharp and high. "Stop it! Calm yourself."

"Get away from her!"

"You're under the influence of the moon. Think beyond your anger." A thud, followed by an unintelligible roar of outrage. "Stop struggling!" shouted the Fae. "The blade is silver; the wound is fatal. I must act immediately."

Fatal? I struggled to form words to make an objection.

"She needs sun potion," said the Fae. "I can't hold you aloft and tend to her. Give me this boon, and I will give you one of equal weight."

A furious growl. "I have no cause to trust a Fae!"

"You must. It is a mortal wound," the Fae shouted. "You know it is!"

Stop saying that.

"She belongs to me!" shouted my mate. "Do not touch her with your filthy hands, or by God I will tear your throat out, deal or no deal."

"You have a choice, Son of Lukynae." The Fae pleaded, "Let me save her. For all the . . ."

The green fire went out.

Magic-mine? Come home . . .

I waited. A second? A minute? Four? Five? But magic-mine didn't return to me. The night was dark again, lit only by the moon and stars, not the green fire of the thing I'd dismissed so coldly just twelve hours ago. Just me, and Ralph, and the silver knife—its handle shallowly bobbing, very slowly, up and down, up and down . . . My Were was stumbling, too; hurting terribly, as if the blade had not only pierced my skin, but torn through her pelt, through her ribs and sinew to pierce her heart.

Where's Trowbridge?

A clink of metal. A grunt. Two hands held me upright as another tore the chains from me. Then I was in his arms. The right man touched my face, cupped my jaw, and lifted it. Dark hair, dark brows pulled together. A glimmer of blue eyes. A glimpse of high cheekbone. His scent wrapped around me.

Yes.

Finally, the right man.

"What did you do?" he asked brokenly.

I did nothing. Except wait for you.

"Oh God, look at her." A voice as raw as the wound in my belly. "Tink, you hold on, you hear? You hold on."

I wanted to keep my eyes open, so that his eyes would be the last thing I saw, but I felt myself starting to drift. No longer held by any chains, no longer hurting. Warm arms cradled me. How many nights had I dreamed of being held so? A deep, strong heart beat under my ear. How many hours had I spent remembering the warmth of his body, the scent of him, entwined around me, comforting as his embrace?

My lids fell, and I fell, too. Inside myself.

It's not so terrible, not really. Not if he is here, holding me.

I am loved.

"Come on, sweetheart. Come on."

I am loved.

"Move away," the Fae said quietly.

"No! Give me the juice. I will do it." My mate's loving fingers were hurtful now, thumbs digging into the soft flesh of my cheek. Prying open my jaw. Something metal clicks against my teeth. My tongue investigates it. Round and smooth. The edge of a cup.

"Drink it, sweetheart. Please." A low voice. Rumble soft.

I'm so tired.

"I swear to God, Hedi. I have gone through hell to come back home. You will not die in my arms. Do you hear me? You will drink this."

Cold liquid floods my mouth.

Tasteless, and yet somehow potent. My tongue, which had felt so thick, now tingles.

"Swallow it." Hard command in his voice. The water tastes like spring water, but purer and sweeter than any that came in a plastic bottle. I feel panic as it clogs my throat. *I'm choking on it.* I spluttered it up, and then gasped air, precious air. Water leaked from the corners of my mouth.

"No!" Another squeeze of my jaw, another mouthful poured between my chattering teeth. "You've got to drink it all. You have to. I promise that you'll feel better."

A hand massaged my neck. My throat flexed, struggling to get the hurtful ball of wet past the knot.

"Please." His tone softened. "Do it for me."

I forced it down.

But I didn't feel any better.

"On the next mouthful, I'll slowly pull the blade out of her," said the other man.

Don't let the Fae touch it.

"More, Hedi," said Trowbridge harshly again, pressing the cup back to my lips. Another cool flood into my mouth. Something tugs at me, pulls at me. I swallow, chest hurting. The liquid cools my throat, then my gullet. As it swims down into my core, I struggle to focus on his eyes. To see past the ropes of hair, the black whiskers.

Blue comets, blue fire.

Mine.

And then . . . a wave of warmth . . . and I was no longer hurting. The raging fire in my center was cooling, easing, being pushed away by something that wasn't seething hot, but warm as my mum's hand on my brow. Soothing as someone stroking the pointed tip of my ear.

"Don't you dare leave me. If I could hold out this long, you will find the strength to fight this . . . You understand?" He gave me a little shake. "You won't leave me. Don't you dare do it. You hear me? You will fight this!"

The juice took the fire, the misery, the pain, and carried them away on some tide to some other continent, while I lay on the warm beach of this one, feeling so . . .

Content.

Such a simple word. My legs felt pleasurably heavy, weighted for sleep, ready for slumber. Even my Were felt drowsy and serene. The thought came to me that maybe I wasn't being healed, but I was being carried to that land that you never, ever, thought existed.

A place where nothing hurt.

And bad things had no teeth.

I was loved.

Heaven.

Chapter Eight

So, here's a good rule: if you're teetering on the brink of death, the one word you do not want to think, breathe, or hazily imagine, is "heaven." Because if you close your eyes—and truly you can't help but do so when you're so profoundly tired—you may find yourself opening them in a realm not your own.

For a few moments, I was muddled. Where was I? Obviously, I wasn't in Creemore anymore. No scent of Were wrapped around me. No arms holding me painfully tight. I knew myself to be alone . . . I could practically feel the silence pressing down on me.

No, no, no.

This was so wrong on so many levels. Not only was I too young to die, but—come on, for fuck's sake—Trowbridge and I had finally been reunited. This was when the good times were supposed to roll. *This* was to be the moment when my real life began.

Oh, that incredible bitch.

Karma had given me one sweet, brief taste of my heart's desire then promptly pushed me into heaven. Though, come to think of it—this sure didn't feel like paradise. Wasn't I supposed to be met by a family member, or at the very least, some messenger holding a sign that read WELCOME TO CLOUD NINE? Besides, the ground felt solid underneath me . . . and surely heaven wouldn't smell like wet earth, and rain and——

Fire.

Shit. As in brimstone and hellfire?

Well, that was a game changer. I lay there, eyes closed, thinking in terms of moral audits; my balance sheet kind of sucked. I stole, though not from the pack. I lied, but then again, who didn't? And yeah, I did kill Dawn Danvers. But . . . she really, really deserved it. Didn't that give me a get-out-of-jail pass?

Enough stalling. Open your eyes and say hello to the guy with the pitchfork.

Cautiously, I slit open my eyes and was treated to a microview of brilliant green moss.

Oh thank Goddess, I'm not in hell.

A stream of blue-gray smoke slipped past my sightline, undulated over the verdant, textured surface with a harem girl's teasing touch, then slid under the scraggly undercarriage of the overgrown hawthorn hedge. There it played for a moment or two, ever the teasing will-o'-the-wisp, flitting between twisted branches, until it grew bored, and melted into the playground of the wild woods beyond the hedge.

Unbelievable. I'd found myself thinking "heaven" and ended up in Threall? Exactly what part of my subconscious paired those two thoughts together?

Close your eyes, and will yourself back to Creemore. Right now.

I focused on Trowbridge because that's what worked last time I wanted to zap myself back to the realm of chili burgers and cell phones. But I couldn't seem to call up his face. Whenever I tried, my brain got hazy, as if something—someone?—had pulled me here and was reluctant to let go.

My presence had been demanded.

By whom? To witness what?

I took stock.

It seemed that I'd landed in exactly the same place as

on my first visit to the realm between realms—on the right-hand side of the clearing of land, my head turned toward a hawthorn hedge, my body within feet of the roots of the dying black walnut tree. The ground under me was spongy and unpleasantly wet. *That's new, too.* Tentatively, I flattened my paw on the damp moss and watched with a small frown as a miniature puddle of brown water formed under it.

Odder and odder.

Water squelched as I rolled to my knees. For a moment I felt unbalanced, my sense of equilibrium rolling like the bubble inside a tilted level. I don't know where my Were goes when I travel to Threall, but when we pull into the station, the spot near my spine where she usually curls is absolutely empty. And it was a given that I'd arrive in the land of myst without an amulet. But this time—unlike last time—I was without my Fae, as well.

I was . . . just me.

Hedi Peacock-Stronghold, stripped of her add-alongs.

At last. Hadn't I always just wanted to be me? Good old unadorned and simplified me? No longer a complex stew? Seeing the world through my own perceptions?

I felt so much lighter without them.

Lonelier, too.

I swallowed and breathed through my mouth until the sensation of loss passed.

My gaze moved past the ruddy red balls of light buried deep inside the hedge beside me, up beyond the ragged tops of the hawthorns, upward and beyond, to the very top of the ancient trees—

Aw, there they are.

Mine.

Hundreds of soul balls, high up in the overcast sky, each one lovingly cradled by the boughs of its proud tree. Lit from within—some shining so brightly they made my fingers itch—protected from harm by their thin vellum-soft skins. Oh Goddess, the heart-stirring beauty of them. Even now in Threall's daylight, they glowed. A hundred variations of yellow, pink-blushed primroses, and heavy golds, sun-pure lemons and tawny topazes, lime-fresh citrons and orange-tinted umbers. And here and there, balls with imperfect colors; their surfaces streaked with shadows of red, suggestions of eggplant, soft whispers of forest green.

Darker souls.

But even so—

Still mine.

I pivoted to look the other way and shrieked as the ground fell out from beneath me. My head snapped back, my knee twisted, and downward I tumbled, arms flailing, mouth wide open.

It was a short plunge, overall, and I landed with an oomph on something soft.

The foxhole had three things at the bottom of it. A great deal of churned-up earth—loose, and quite fine. A foot of water—muddy, and very cold. And one mystwalker— immobile, and quite possibly . . . dead.

I'd landed draped across Mad-one's body.

Immediately, I was assailed by a bitch-storm of broken visuals, all jumbled together, with no sense of pattern or time sequence. Two fireballs exploding in a shower of sparks and cinders in the night sky. Rain, gentle and soft. The Old Mage with his lips pulled back, his teeth clenched against some terrible agony. A fast-moving dark shadow skulking along the length of the hawthorns. A black walnut tree, the red light in the center of its purplish soul light flickering before a fresh shower of fireballs arced into the air toward her. A little girl, well turned out in her best pinafore, her hair pulled back, the rakes of a comb still evident in her hair.

Simeon, tall and fair.

Simeon.

All delivered so fast, it made my stomach want to hurl.

And feelings, too. Fae Stars. So much emotion. An intense explosion of surprise, anger, and hatred. Then fear—oh, a whole bunch of that—followed by a sickening wave of weak despair. Hissing with shock, I scrambled off her then scuttled up the mud-slick incline for the surface. There I froze, half in, half out of Mad-one's foxhole.

The top of a nearby stump was hearth to a clump of smoking moss.

What had happened to Threall?

War? It sure looked like it. The formerly lush and semi-tranquil landscape was a ruin of rutted bomb craters and scattered tree branches—all of it fanning outward from the healthier of the two black walnuts that held court at the edge of Threall's world. Anger grew inside my belly as my gaze roamed. Whatever had occurred during my absence, the souls of Threall had endured at least two casualties beyond the loss of the former Mystwalker of Threall. Signs were everywhere: a long sheaf of moss swinging from the root ball of a fallen beech; the crushed remains of a flat-tened hawthorn. An empty soul ball, with its skin torn and its contents spilled, reproached me as it flapped against a spar of elm thrust into the damp earth.

It's just a hawthorn. And an old tree.

And yet, sorrow brushed me with dry fingers.

Souls had been killed.

Two of mine.

There it was again—the same feeling that had assailed me the first time I'd visited Threall. An inexplicable feeling that this world was mine, and everything in it—the souls, this mossy terrain, these trees—was my Goddess-given duty to protect.

It scared me.

Focus, I told myself. *Will yourself back to Creemore.*

Except focusing was suddenly incredibly difficult to do. I was positively flooded with an inexplicable feeling of possessiveness. If I left, who was going to protect those souls?

I flicked a resentful glance to my left, to the beech un-der whose leafy canopy Mad-one usually lolled about with her mandolin. The Mystwalker's favorite tree had taken at least one direct hit, judging by the hole in its foliage, and the wattle fence built to protect it had been torn asunder. Her overturned silk chaise sported a burn spot in the shape of a bull's-eye on its back.

She never even saw it coming.

My gaze swept the area, searching for a shadow that didn't belong, then moved to the line of hawthorns. Soul lights glowered inside their thorny embrace, but nothing or nobody popped out with a gotcha "Boo!"

Still, someone had to be responsible for all this destruction.

I twisted around to inspect the other end of the pasture, where two hulking black walnuts served as sentries to the end of Threall's world. The trees were of equal height, but other than that, they were as dissimilar as they could be; the most obvious difference being the smug and rude health of the one on the left versus the one-wheeze-away-from-adios-my-friends of the walnut tree supporting the Old Mage's essence.

Because that pathetic, leaf-denuded relic was host to the old man.

I knew that as clearly as I knew Trowbridge was meant for me. Last time I'd been in Threall, I'd found myself clinging like a limpet to one of the dying tree's wind-chapped boughs, and I'd heard him. Inside my head.

Without a word of a lie, I'd *heard* him. Speaking directly to me. Sounding old and wise. That day, I'd thought him a mixture of Gandalf and the Wizard of Oz. Kindly. Paternal. Now, I knew better. I'd spent too many slumbers watching Mad-one's last hour in Merenwyn to be fooled by the bonhomie in his voice.

Bottom line, kindly men don't make good mages.

And yet . . .

Over the last six months, Threall's soft wind had further ravaged the Old Mage's black walnut, stripping off its bark, beating its topmost branches into bleached, frayed splinters, and the remaining signs of life had been reduced to a few whippet-thin branches that boasted a few handfuls of leaves. His sagging soul ball drooped from its tether; its rich hues had faded from their glowing brilliance into a watercolor blur of dead golds and toothless reds.

I should have been unmoved at the sight. An arrogant man was finally meeting his inevitable end. But I wasn't. Sorrow, that's what flooded me at the sight of that languishing soul. An ancient sorrow—not a fresh pain—deep inside me, down in my gut where my Fae usually lived.

A great man is dying, I thought.

Even I recognized the awesome weird buried in that comment.

Look away. The sight of his tree is muddling your mind and stirring something buried inside you.

It took a force of will to tear my gaze away, but I did it, and that creeping instinct to genuflect to the dying black walnut disappeared the moment my attention turned to all that empty blue between the two black walnuts.

Fear—it's the ultimate mind-wipe.

You couldn't look down that sky-blue end of the clearing without thinking about falling. Not a "whoops!" pratfall, but a long, screaming, arm-flailing, endless plummet. Here's the thing about Threall. It isn't round like the earth. It's flat. Past those hulking brutes, where Threall's landscape should have continued to undulate in an endless vista of rolling hills, winding trails, and ancient trees, there was nothing *but* a vast blue sky.

Well, that, and the portal to Merenwyn.

There it was, fifty feet from the crumbling edge of the world, a white plume that rushed straight up toward Merenwyn, which could be defined as paradise or hell, depending on what blood flowed through your veins.

I'd seen Mad-one blow a soul across that void.

And I'd seen the portal eat it.

With one gulp.

This is a war zone, and I'm without a weapon.

I gave the terrain within arm's reach a quick visual sweep in search of a suitable bat. There were plenty of choices out *there*, where the tree lay shattered, presumably the result of some unseen assailant who could still be lurking, but there wasn't anything handy, just waiting for me to casually pick up. Only clods of earth, brittle leaves, shreds of torn souls, and damp moss.

Nothing within reach.

I lifted my right hand, prepared to summon my Fae magic, then remembered that I'd left her by the fairy pond in Creemore. *Well played, Karma.* I really could have used my talent at that moment.

I wanted to go home, and to do that I needed to close my eyes and concentrate, but . . . there was a bad guy out there, somewhere. He or she could be watching me right now. Waiting to pounce, or to blow me helplessly into the wild blue yonder just past those trees.

I can't close my eyes, not without a weapon.

My gaze flicked to the body slumped at the bottom of the foxhole. The Mystwalker of Threall was the picture of a battlefield corpse, lying in a semifetal position, one arm protectively curled over her middle, the other stretched out as if she'd made an aborted effort to climb out of her grave before she'd drawn her last breath. Her lids were at half-mast; her eyes milky. Evidently—as witnessed by the death grip she had on a sturdy oak branch—her sunny personality had persisted right up to the last. The back of her hand was swollen, and red; the knuckles fat with yellow blisters; her fingertips familiarly sooty.

Mad-one had suffered from payback pain, just like me.

She doesn't need that bat anymore, I thought, staring at the cudgel.

But was she really dead?

She looked it.

Her chest wasn't moving . . . and a clod of earth lay temptingly near my hand. "Hey, Mad-one," I said, picking it up. When she didn't rouse, I tossed it at her. The missile of dirt hit her cheek and then rolled to the spot between the cleft of her nose and her upper lip. She didn't surge to her feet with a blood-curdling screech.

She lay inert.

Yup. Dead.

I blew air out of my cheeks, considering my options, then with a mental shrug, I reached for the piece of oak clutched tight in her cold dead hand and gave it a tug. My first jerk on Mad-one's billy club made her arm move in a way that brought the contents of my stomach lurching to the base of my throat. Girding myself—*don't puke, don't puke*—I reached for her hand, prepared to break those curled digits, one by one, if I couldn't peel them from the bat.

"You are one stubborn corpse," I hissed, using my nail as a lever to prise Mad-one's finger open. I loathed touching her because those jagged pictures had disappeared, and now I was tapping into her final thought stream. And as it turns out, you don't really want to know what the dearly departed were thinking before the Mack truck turned them into a one-dimensional science experiment.

Primarily because it makes them seem oh-so-mortal.

Mad-one's emotions had seesawed between despair (I'm losing) and hatred (equally divided between the shadow that kept lobbing fireballs at her and the *other* black walnut), and her line of thinking had been simple and repetitive. It went sort of like this: "I'm so tired . . . Here comes the devil's spawn again . . . Help me, Goddess . . . I'm so tired."

Annoying. I didn't want to feel another crumb of pity for the Mystwalker. After all, last time I'd visited her realm, she'd tried to nail me with a fireball, and that was kind of unforgivable. But despite myself, I felt bad. Tyrean had been conscripted into an eternal life of duty in Threall, and she'd met her end alone in a muddy foxhole, fighting in the dark, knowing herself to be losing.

Who deserves a fate like that?

I gave the hedges another quick, harried glance, then returned to the job of separating Mad-one from her billy club. But as I did, I puzzled over her memories. The hatred she felt for the healthier of the two black walnuts was quite concentrated. And when her weary eyes rested on its twisted branches, she didn't think, *Tree*, she thought, *The Black Mage*.

So, Helzekiel's host was the sprawling specimen with a twisted trunk and powerful, thick limbs? Yeah, I could see that. The soul ball glowering from its leafy embrace screamed ambition gone bad—it was the mottled purple-brown hue of an overripe eggplant and was lit from within by a red glowering light.

Geez. Tim Burton would go to town with that tree.

A diverting thought that I shelved for later because Mad-one's middle finger had reluctantly lifted and her improvised cudgel was finally mine.

Unfortunately, the instant I began lowering my lids to conjure up memories of home and hearth and Trowbridge, the one thing I'd counted on *not* happening, happened. Mad-one's slack mouth opened for a ragged inhale, her dead eyes shifted from unfocused to alive and vengeful, and in less time than it took me to squeak "Crap!" she'd transformed from an insensate corpse to a bloodthirsty assassin.

"You!" she hissed, as her hands scrabbled for my throat. We toppled back into the mud in an awkward sprawl. And once again, the moment her flesh met mine, I found myself dog-paddling up her thought stream.

The Mystwalker of Threall really, really wanted to kill me.

Get in line, whackjob.

"Get off me!" I shouted, giving her a good shove with my free hand.

Luck was with me because Mad-one had the strength of an exhausted kitten. Her hands slid from my neck, and she flopped back into an exhausted half recline. Okay. My blood may be sweet, but I'm not. I looked at her and smiled. Just slightly.

Last time we'd been face-to-face, she'd been the perfect example of the cold, aristocratic Fae. Long blond hair, brown eyes, faint patrician sneer. Pretty dress. This time she was ass-deep in the muck, elbows planted deep in the faintly foul-smelling guck, looking like she'd been dragged backward through the hedgerows.

Karma had thrown me a dog-chewed bone.

"You touched me!" she hissed in shock as she clumsily moved to her knees. "You looked through my memories."

"I fell on you. The touching part was accidental."

"Liar." Deep disgust laced her voice. "I can feel the traces of your visit inside my mind." Judging from the way her face was squinched up, signs of me were the equivalent of a slimy snail trail. Her gaze fell to the cudgel in my hand. "So it has come to this," she said with fatalistic calm. "The Black Mage has sent you for the final kill." She shook her head. "Killing me will not kill the Old Mage. He is stronger than you think."

"I told you before, I don't know any Black Mage."

Her lips curved into a sad half smile as she looked over my shoulder down toward the other end of the clearing where the big old beech tree stood, a battered specimen, amidst the ruin of what used to be a wattle fence. "It is over, Simeon," she said, in much the same tone that Davy Crockett might have used to say, "Boys, we're out of ammunition."

Mad-one's face tightened. A deep inhale then she gave me a fatalistic nod and slowly closed her eyes. She stayed like that, spine ramrod straight, swaying slightly on her knees, her face set in stoic lines of courage.

Did she really think I was planning on a spot of mystwalker bashing?

Goddess, the Fae are bloodthirsty creatures.

Well, we're all entitled to our Joan of Arc moments. I let her fully experience the complete satisfaction of being courageous in the face of certain death. About six seconds later, her heroism turned to irritation.

"Do it!" she said testily.

I gave her a shrug. "You are seriously annoying, and I'm never going to forget that you tried to turn me into a roman candle the last time I was here, but from what I can see, today you're about as much a threat to me as a june bug."

She stared at me. "Verily, you speak strangely."

"Ditto." The mud made a wet sucking noise as I shifted my weight onto my other knee. "Why did you drag me here?"

Her eyebrows rose in scorn as she gave me a thorough once-over. "Does your master not provide you with clothing?"

I bit down on the urge to suck in my belly and cross my arms over my blood-smeared bra. "Unlike you, I don't have a 'master.' Also, unlike you, I'm not the slacker who allowed Threall to go to hell in a handbasket. What happened here?"

But Mad-one's head had slowly tilted during my little speech, uneasily and eerily similar to a robin spotting a juicy worm. "No master?" she murmured to herself. "Can it be the creature is unbound?" She leaned toward me, her eyes narrowed into speculative slits. "Answer me truthfully. Have you taken the Oath of the Mystwalker? Are you unbound?"

There's an oath?

When I didn't immediately say, "Verily, I am so bound," Mad-one eyes widened in a way that made me feel like I was the last jar of peanut butter in the food pantry.

"Look, *Tyrean,* let's cut to the chase," I snapped. "You've got to stop dragging me into your dreams, okay? I'm done. No more dreams. I'm sorry the old guy gave you a raw deal. And yup, I believe you probably didn't have anything to do with whatever treasonable act led to your mage being sentenced to the Sleep Before Death. But I can't change what happened, and I want the dreams to stop."

Her mouth fell open.

"Also, dragging me to Threall against my will? That ends right now." I jabbed the cudgel in her direction in a quasi-threatening manner. "You just screwed up a really big moment for me in my own realm."

Real anger flushed her cheeks. "Do you think I would *ever* beckon one such as you to my dreams? I am not a knave—"

"Newsflash. You do it all the time. Same dream, right

down to the same dialogue. You're standing by a window. The Old Mage tells you that you must spend eternity protecting him and the wards over his Book of Spells. You tell him that you don't want to. It ends with . . ."

Somewhere in there, Mad-one had detached. As my words trailed off, she stared unseeingly at a piece of parchment fluttering from the broken spear of a nearby tree stump, her forehead creased.

"I cannot sense her presence in my memory of that," she mused out loud. "And yet how else could she know? There were none to witness our conversation. Even Simeon, waiting in the next room, could not hear us through the wards placed on the door . . ." The penny dropped and the puzzlement cleared from her expression. "It is my mage's memory." A look of absolute joy and relief softened her features as she gazed at the dying black walnut tree. "At last. He has found her. Finally he has chosen his nalera."

She lifted her small chin skyward.

"Thank you, Goddess," she said shakily. "Thank you for delivering this wretch to us."

"That's it, I'm going home now."

"You cannot leave Threall," she said harshly. "You are the chosen one. In all the eternity I have served, there has never been another so well suited to my mage's needs. You are not of our world. You are unbound. You are young and strong."

I swear it was like trying to say good-bye to a telemarketer.

"And you, my friend, have been chatting with trees too long."

"It is your destiny!"

Then, just when I was leaning away from her, worry bubbling—*Goddess, how am I going to think of all those things that are my talismans for home, Trowbridge, Cordelia, and Ralph, how can I do that with Miss Loony Tunes scaring the crap out of me with her destiny rant—* the strangest thing happened in a day positively bursting with the extraordinarily odd and peculiar.

One second the Mystwalker of Threall was slopping toward me through the mud, her clawed hand stretching toward me, her face animated with zeal, and in the next . . . between one rapid thump-thump of my heart . . . her face blurred into a pale, white smear.

The smell of earth and fire and rain disappeared.

And so did the fear.

I heard Trowbridge's voice coming from a great distance: "Another mouthful. Come on, sweetheart, swallow it. You're almost there."

So real. So urgent.

Couldn't see him. Couldn't feel him.

But as I strained to listen to his hoarse call, the blue mysts swallowed the Mad Mystwalker. And then I was no longer bogged down in mud. I felt adrift in the dense fog . . . my body a little ship bobbing in the soft swell of a lake that knew no rough winds.

Feeling languid and happy. Knowing that the sun and the warmth were just through that next patch of fog. All I had to do was steer for home. And that I could do. Hell, I had a rudder, and compass with a true north needle, if you will.

I'm happy. I'm finally happy again.

All that guilt and sadness that had weighed me down. All those wretched doubts and pathetic fears that had fluttered around me these last six horrible months. They were nothing more than gray moths. I pursed my lips and blew them away.

Clear skies ahead. Trim your sails for home, Hedi.

Search for the connection to your real body again. Recall the heat of his body. The pressure of his arms. Fae Stars. Think of the man on whom you've staked your future.

Listen for him. Hear him.

He's there, in the real world, holding you. Calling your name.

He's your One True Thing, isn't he?

The fog is thinning. Almost there . . . Damn, damn,

damn. I can almost smell home . . . It's just there . . . obscured by that bluish haze . . . a maddening stubborn veil over what I want.

Why can't Trowbridge hear me?

Because you're broken.

No I'm not. It's just . . . my voice has gotten so small.

Then make yourself bigger. Remember home and your true body. Imagine it all, every little detail. You're in Creemore. On a field. Feel the grass prickling through your jeans. The pain in your belly. The slick warm heat of your blood.

Remember who you are.

That's easy. I'm Hedi. Mate to an Alpha. Sister to a twin. Friend to an amulet . . . and a six-foot mother hen . . .

No. Those are the people you love. Who is Hedi?

She's the girl who left her magic by a fairy pond and her wolf in a field littered with discarded clothing.

You need to go home to find them. And when you get there, you need to glue yourself back together. Because this is wrong. This feeling you keep trying to push away—like you're jagged and broken, a mirror cracked.

And FYI? No one can choose your destiny.

Right. No one can. I won't let them.

Oh . . . there he is . . .

"Sweetheart, drink it. Don't fight me, dammit. DRINK!"

Chapter Nine

"Let her go. You must! It is beyond reason to expect you to hold against the moon's call much longer."

"I will hold," rumbled Trowbridge. "She'll come around soon."

Working on it. But I was toasty warm and heavenly safe. Back on terra firma, where there were no Mad-ones, no scary trees, no soul balls glowing in the sky. My boat had pulled into shore, and now I just felt contentment. Lazy, bone-melting happiness. Like being in your bed and knowing that you don't really have to get up. It's a holiday. Or a Sunday. Mortal-me, she-bitch-me, and Fae-is-me—the three us were having a lie-in. There was no alarm clock dinging in our ear. No ex–drag queen rapping her knuckles on our door, telling us to "get up before you turn into a mattress."

No worries, no fear.

Goddess, I felt freakin' wonderful. Downright joyful.

My mate and I were together again. And for the time being, I didn't give a rat's ass about the niggling details . . . like how the portal opened, and who the Fae was, and why Trowbridge looked so different from my dreams. I began to hum, feeling one with this world, and all the little furry creatures in it.

"She's singing." The Fae's voice softened with amusement. "The sun potion affects some that way."

*Damn right I am. I am so absolutely in perfect unity
with myself and the universe—uh-oh.* An intrusion of mild
dismay. Trowbridge's skin was twitching under my cheek.
His skin felt damp, too. Sweat? His scent was sharper than
I remembered. Spiked with testosterone.

"Hedi," rasped my mate. "Wake up."

"Your claws will pierce her skin," said the Fae. "Release
her. Pass her to me."

Don't you dare.

"She is mine," Trowbridge growled. "Do your job. Close
the portal."

I would have rewarded my man with a loving gaze, but
my lids felt like all seven dwarves were sitting on them.
Instead, I idly wondered why I knew—in a flash of deep
intuition—that the Fae greeted that information with shock,
and was struggling not to show it.

"By what right do you call her 'mine'?" demanded the
Fae. "She is not of your pack."

"*She* is my mate," Trowbridge said simply.

I am his mate. Happiness made my heart swell. Every
medicine cabinet should come equipped with a silver flask
filled with Fae juice. The unbearable heat in my gut was
completely gone.

In its place . . . this wondrous sense of well-being.

"You lie, Robson Trowbridge," snarled Bowler-hat.
"Her skin does not carry your scent."

Shut the hell up.

Trowbridge's arms tensed. "She is part Fae, she has no
scent."

"No friends in the pack, either, it would seem," the kill-
joy continued. "One of your kind plunged a knife into her
belly, while the others left her to die. A true Alpha would
never leave his mate in such mortal danger."

"Stay out of my business," rumbled Trowbridge. "Close
the fucking portal, right now."

"Give her to me," said the Fae. "I will take her to safety."

At that, I uttered a mewl of distress, and felt perverse
comfort when Trowbridge's grip tightened almost painfully.

Could there be anything better? His chest against my cheek. The smell of him—a heaven-sent musk cloud around me.

"You won't travel an inch in my territory without my permission," my mate said. "And if you don't shut those gates right now, I'm going to—"

"Your 'territory'?" mocked the Fae. "Your wolves have not come out to greet their Alpha. They tremble in the woods."

"They can wait," grated Trowbridge.

"For what? For a sweet reconciliation with your mate? You are no longer of this world, Son of Lukynae. Tender words will not change you back to what you once were. The moon is demanding that you transform, and transform you will. Then you shall become the beast and she will know you for the animal that you are. Perhaps she'll be frightened, sickened by—"

"You better hope I can meet their challenge or have you forgotten what you will lose?" Trowbridge asked.

A pause.

Then the Fae said in a hard voice, "You need to display—"

"I know what I need to do!" Trowbridge snarled.

"Then do it. I have risked much to come here," the Fae hissed. "I will not have everything lost because you are too stubborn to yield to the moon. A challenge has been issued. You must meet it."

"When I'm sure she's healed," he said, in a low, fierce voice. A prickle of nails as Trowbridge slid his hand across my ribs.

"Don't," I whined, curling against his chest. But my mate persisted, tenderly pushing away the leg I'd brought up to protect my belly. "Shh, sweetheart," he murmured as his fingers examined the place where once a knife had bobbed.

I summoned up the effort to dislodge Grumpy, Dopey, and Sleepy, and failed. Whined a bit instead, high through my nose, as my own paw tried to feebly swat his away.

"That's it, Hedi," said Trowbridge. "That's more like you. Fight me."

I don't want to fight you. I want you to hold me and promise me that you'll never let me go.

"We have no time for this. Give her another mouthful of the sun potion," said the Fae. "She cannot lie like prey on the ground."

The silver flask was offered once more, and I accepted, possibly a little too enthusiastically, because the good stuff was jerked away before I could suckle more than a tablespoon of it.

"Open your eyes, Tink," said my mate.

I did and found myself looking upward into Trowbridge's face. *Don't worry, I'm fine,* I wanted to tell him. *Even if you're not.* I knew my emotions were dulled, and blunted—contentment was grudgingly slow to make room for dismay—but I recognized that. He wasn't fine. Black whiskers crawled up his gaunt cheeks. Beneath his tired eyes, purple shadows darkened the skin.

Goddess, he's suffering or he has suffered.

Under the cool light offered by the moon, I could see again.

But I didn't want to. Not like this. Not with the clamor of unwanted emotions and sudden terrifying perceptions overwhelming that blank peacefulness. I searched for that pink comfort I'd felt just seconds before, and felt a petulant peevishness that it was gone. Shamed, my eyes slanted away. *Don't think about those bruises beneath his eyes.* I essayed speech and came up with a croak. "Trowbridge?"

Firm lips pressed against my brow. I lifted my hand to draw his head closer to mine—*kisses are a very good thing*—but my fingers got entangled in the rope curtain of his dreads. The sound of their dry rasp filled me with a strange foreboding.

My hand fell.

"The first taste is lightning in a bottle," mused the Fae. "She'll never find that joy again."

"There will be no other time." Trowbridge's breath warmed my ear.

"A wolf believes himself qualified to make choices for a Fae?"

"Not only can a Were make the right choices, but he can command," retorted Trowbridge. "For the last time, close the portal."

Good luck with that. I rolled my head to watch.

Bowler-hat shrugged and made a chopping motion. And just like that—with one indolent wave—*my* magic parted from the tree to which it had been tethered. I thought it would fly back to me—even lifted a weak paw to welcome it home—but it flew over to the fog-shrouded portal; there it floated, an unsecured strand of fairy seaweed, no ocean bed for its roots.

Seriously, never piss off your magic.

The Fae eyed it with something akin to boredom. He tapped two fingers downward in that same annoyingly lazy fashion. And then the whole damned writhing, searching cable of magic exploded. *Exactly* like last night, when I'd told my magic to go to hell. Myriad bits of green fluorescence glittered above the smoky ground.

Not so fun to feel all discombobulated and direction-less, is it, magic-mine?

"Sy'ehella," the Fae said.

Bells chimed as the Gates of Merenwyn closed.

My magic glittered in the evening, a hive of fairy bees. I opened my mouth, thought to say something, and decided against it. It seemed to me I'd said enough.

However, magic-mine took my open mouth as an invitation.

She dove past my tonsils, slid down my gullet in a choking ball of pressure, and then—thump! She filled that damn near empty magic space inside my gut with some Fae vim and vigor, claiming her spot near the tail of my spine without so much as a murmur of apology.

My inner-bitch wagged her tail in greeting, then hunkered down again.

I could feel them inside me once more.

The Fae alive. My Were beside her, ears pricked forward. We were whole again.

There was supposed to be a long, tender moment there.

I didn't get it.

Trowbridge's embrace—so solid, so welcoming, so right—turned inexplicably stiff.

He hadn't seen my magic return to me, had he? That wasn't part of the mate thing, was it? That might have looked a tad ugly.

I tested my mouth and discovered that I could speak, and so I filled in the awkward moment with what seemed to me a reasonable request. "Get me out of here, Trowbridge. Before those wolves come back."

Uh-huh, in hindsight, I might have chosen my words more carefully.

If he'd felt stiff before that statement, he became rigid after it. Thoughtfully, I wiped a droplet of Trowbridge's sweat off my cheek—*hey, my fingers are working again*—and rolled my head toward My One True Thing's chin.

Aw hell.

Dreads and beards can make any man dangerous looking. Moonlight might amplify that perceived threat. But at that moment, Trowbridge was staring down his long nose at me in a way that felt both foreign and oddly menacing.

This is not going well.

Blue comets started playing a halfhearted game of tag around his pupils. Usually a lovely sight, that prelude to an Alpha's flare, except now blue fire illuminated his face, and I could see well enough to perceive the fact that his features weren't shaped in aching joy at the sight of me. They were set in a grim, faintly pained cast that appeared semipermanent, and his brow was—*oh wonderful*—visibly shifting. My mate was a breath away from his transformation into his Were.

"You're"—I made a hazy circle near my own temple—"turning wolf."

And maybe I did wince with ill-disguised disgust, because at that precise moment, the bone in his cheek chose to move, and it was both ugly and fascinating to watch his skin roll, crest, and then recede back to resemble something reasonably normal.

"Shit," I said, for want of a better word, as my inner-bitch moaned in disbelief.

I'm a card-carrying Trowbridge interpreter and have a mental catalogue of every expression his handsome countenance had ever assumed in my presence. I'd privately labeled them: cool curiosity. Covert lust. Simmering annoyance. Devastating tenderness. Pussy-melting possessiveness. Combustible passion.

By golly, to be scrupulously fair, I'd even kept a file on some of his less cozy displays of emotion—forced patience, annoying arrogance, bullheaded maleness, and perverse stubbornness.

I'd thought I'd seen them all—including, more than once, evidence of true love in his eyes.

But at that moment, I didn't know how to read him—never mind the fact that he was on the cusp of turning into his Were.

Dismay coiled inside me: a fat, hungry worm hidden in the apple core. Had I imagined the depths of his feelings for me? Had I wanted to be loved so badly that I'd tinted every one of our shared dreams with soft, seashell-pink fantasies of forever after?

My cheeks grew hot.

"I want to sit up," I said in a little voice.

He allowed me to slide free of the comforting band of his arms, though he didn't entirely relinquish his hold on me. When I made a weak attempt to crawl a couple feet away, he used gentle pressure to keep me there, sitting cross-legged between the cradle of his hard thighs.

There are worse places to be.

I could have leaned back against his damp chest, if I'd wanted to. Flattened my palm over his heart, and checked for a beat. He had a streak of blood near his hairline.

Knox, I thought broodingly.

Add another dollop of guilt to my felony list.

That's when the little brown wolf from Merenwyn let loose a low, menacing growl, and began to slink toward me, its amber eyes flicking between my mate and me in a way that might have unnerved me if I hadn't spent six months holding a pack at bay.

This pissed-off fairy has had a day, *puppy.*

Behold the wrath of my flare.

"Don't," warned Trowbridge, before I could summon a spark. The light that had lit his face dimmed. "Don't ever use your flare against a wolf. I've seen that, and it's never good."

I said, my heart twisting, "That's bullshit, Trowbridge. Your father used his Alpha flare to control his pack."

"My father was a Were." His tone was implacable. "He had the right to use it on his kin."

This time, I gasped.

The little brown wolf crept forward, nose crinkled.

"Anu!" Trowbridge said sharply, before breaking into a long string of Merenwynian, directed at the wolf eyeing me like I was the last hamburger on the grill.

Yes, I know. I should have thought, *What's with that wolf?* or better yet, *Who the hell IS that wolf?* My inner-bitch certainly was suddenly on alert.

But my mind swirled over yet another puzzle.

Impossible, I thought, horror filling me.

In the space of a summer, Trowbridge had learned to speak my mother's tongue. I'm not referring to the use of a few Fae curse words; I'm talking about fluid language skills. Verbs, and nouns, and maybe an adjective or two thrown in for good measure. I couldn't tell what he was saying—I'd never managed to pick up the Fae language other than that freakish time in Threall when I became temporarily fluent in Merenwynian. But I'm thinking Trowbridge had issued a "cease and desist" order, because the little brown wolf's ears flattened, and it paused, mid-stalk, hackles raised in a line of outrage, nape to rigid tail.

What was I? A language idiot? Trowbridge spent half a year in the Fae world and suddenly he's fluent in a language I could never get my tongue around after twelve years of listening to my mum? Was it really that easy to pick up the language?

Goddess, did he think I'd deliberately kept him trapped in Merenwyn?

I gave the tip of my pointed ear a stroke or two and felt no comfort.

My One True Thing made a sharp "sit" gesture with his fist. The canine looked at it with something akin to frustration, issued a noise that sounded uncannily like a peeved Wookie, then lowered its ass to a choice patch of Creemore's clover.

The remnants of my pink glow of happiness were eroding faster than a wad of cotton candy ground between two molars. "What happened here?" Trowbridge asked.

Good question.

He flicked a dread over his shoulder. "Why did someone try to kill you?"

"Not someone. A Were," I said flatly.

"Why?" he asked grimly.

"Because the NAW came." I tilted my head toward the woods. "Knox—the guy you dispatched—I take it he *is* dead?"

Trowbridge nodded.

"He was sent here to investigate claims that . . ." I floundered for a second, realizing that I was edging myself into turbulent waters and, Goddess curse it, I was already at sea without a life vest. "I was accused of breaking the treaty, and what you saw was the end result of a trial by my 'peers.'"

"Why didn't you claim your status as my mate?" he demanded.

Oh crap. The treaty and the mate question—two things I really wanted to avoid in the first few minutes of our fragile reconciliation—delivered in a one-two bitch-slap. "It must have slipped my mind," I said, sarcasm dripping.

I know. I should have saved being a smartass for later, but it was so wrong . . . every bit of it. The Fae watching us with his head tilted in deep calculation; the pack listening in from the bushes; the little brown wolf shifting on its haunches yearning for leave to attack. None of it fit my script. I'd imagined my mate walking across the field toward me, top button undone on his blue cambric shirt. When his gaze fixed on mine—I usually got choked up at this part—his features would crease into an expression of deep tenderness, bordering on aching joy. Yup. That's what I'd been anticipating.

I gave myself an inward kick and struggled to stand. He helped me up.

"This isn't the homecoming I had planned for you," I muttered.

Trowbridge's eyes narrowed. "Considering I had to find my own way back home, I imagine it wasn't."

Low blow.

His nostrils flared. "Why wouldn't the pack support you?"

For a second, I gazed up at him, feeling like I was on that portal again, the ground beneath me breaking into pieces. What had happened to my dream-guy?

Gone.

I looked back down at my knitted fingers. They were visibly swelling, payback pain's itch finally starting to bother. My gaze skittered away from them, studied a blade of broken grass, found no enlightenment, and then twitched back toward the jaw of the man who stood between me and the rest of the world. It was slick with perspiration, patchy with a rough beard. My gaze dipped. His neck was ringed by something that looked like a heavy callus and—I squinted—underneath that, a few vertebrae were moving.

He wanted the truth?

"Because it was easier to throw me under the bus," I said slowly. "Because it was simpler to let the NAW think I killed Mannus, and Dawn, and Stuart, and . . ." I gave him my own bitter smile. "You—the lost heir to the Alpha crown. Because they found me wanting as an Alpha-by-proxy. Because I don't carry your scent. Because I can't change into a wolf. Because I fucking well eat cookies."

Trowbridge's hands—*look at that, they're tipped with curved talons*—tightened at his hips, and he took a deep breath, like he was afraid he was going to bust apart and both of us would be drenched in an explosion of after-birth, and gore, and all that other flying crap that just might hurt, like anger, disappointment, and the ugly cruds of once-perfect dreams.

"Because I'm not, nor ever will be, one of them," I finished.

Silence greeted that prediction—a little broken quiet moment where the unexpected void between us grew and grew.

It was almost a relief when the shrubbery shivered.

A black wolf emerged from the woods. One of the Danvers, but I couldn't be sure which. Then another wolf—this one buff and brown—slid out from the shadows. It chose a place behind the black wolf, the quality of its personal challenge made murky by the way its head was lowered. Crickets fell silent as two more Creemore wolves crept out from the cover of the forest.

"And hello, Karma," I murmured.

"I'm waiting to see your pack greet you, Alpha of Creemore," taunted Bowler-hat.

Trouble-making poseur. I hated the Fae's clothing: his pants were indecently tight and his high boots spoke of guys that really, really like their laced cuffs and duchesses. Plus, I loathed how he'd angled his bowler over his left ear, convinced he'd done it to highlight the long fall of yellow hair that spilled over his other shoulder. And finally, I totally despised the way he appeared prosperous, while my guy looked like he'd been rolled in a dark alley by a hooker named Bess.

"Piss off," I mouthed to the Fae, and then felt taken aback when his wide mouth stretched into an approving smile.

Trowbridge studied the wolves quietly, then turned back to me.

When I didn't volunteer to step up toward him, he moved close to me, obliterating my personal space, until all I could see was a broad expanse of well-muscled chest, half covered by ugly dead ropes of hair. I heard him sigh over my head. Then he bent his neck until we were relatively nose to nose.

Do not roll into a ball of boo-hoo.

"I have to make this short—" he began.

"Why?" I said with admirable coolness. "What is so pressing that—"

Trowbridge covered my mouth. Not hard. But gently—surprisingly so—two knuckles on the top of the swell of my upper lip, fingers curled so that the points of his talons were sheathed. "Don't talk," he said in a rough whisper. "For once, Tink, please don't talk."

For a second, everything in me tensed, ready to pull back a fist and hit him, because there was a savage ache inside my breast and I wanted him to hurt as much as I, and then—thank you, Goddess—my wits registered the tremble of his fingers. And with that, my heart started slamming inside my chest—fast, like an ocean-skimming bird that's finally found land.

This is not the touch of a detached man.

Silently, his knuckles brushed the contour of my upper lip in a way that was familiar and unsettling. His gaze was fixed on my mouth as if it were something he yearned to possess.

Damn him.

For half a year, I'd watched him die over and over again. For 196 days I'd hated myself for my inability to bring him home. Never had I felt so incompetent, so guilty, so tightly caught in the grip of Karma's curse. I'd rethought every moment of that terrible night and wondered how I could have changed the outcome.

Spring had melted away. Summer had flared and died. And I had longed for him.

"Trowbridge?" I whispered.

His brows pulled together again—but this time the way a hard man does when he's trying to hold back his emotions. So very briefly, the shutters rose. For a heartbeat, I saw yearning in his eyes. The awful type. The sort of pain that had been given enough time to erode from an intense burn into a worn, chronic ache. Past grief, past resentment, past bargaining. Resigned. Unwilling to believe or hope.

"Life keeps kicking us in the ass, doesn't it?" he murmured, shaking his head. "Don't run, Hedi. Whatever you think you understand tonight—I can explain. Just promise me you'll wait. Give me time to tell you things you need to know. All the other stuff, we'll figure out, somehow." A rueful smile. "We've come this far."

Oh Trowbridge.

The shutters slammed shut, and his expression became hard again. "The Fae is known as the Black Mage's Shadow," he said. "He has no morals, no ethics. He is responsible for the near genocide of a race of Weres. He'll lie and charm and steal to get what he wants. He will try to play to your emotions. Don't listen. He will ask you to help him escape. Don't do it. He has to stay here—I'll leave you some guards. Say nothing, agree to nothing, do *nothing* he asks—" He sent an angry look up at the moon. "I wish I had more time. Promise me. No matter what is revealed tonight, promise you won't leave with him."

"Why would I—"

Another pressure of fingers sent a shudder of sensation straight down my spine. "Lives depend on you. Vow to me that you won't do anything to ease his escape. He must not be allowed to reopen the gates. Your word. I want you to give me your word."

And there it was. The one thing guaranteed to superglue Hedi's heels to the ground. Give me your word. No other man would ask me for it and actually believe I could be held accountable to it.

Redemption.

"You have it," I said, feeling tears well.

He rubbed a talon-tipped thumb along the line of my jaw. "I never thought I'd see you again," he said roughly, his eyes soft. "Go to my house, Tink, and wait, okay?"

His hand drifted to the back of my head, a prelude to the soft kiss he placed, just beneath my ear, right where my skin was tenderest, and my blood surged.

Kiss me. Make us whole.

My One True Thing whispered, "Don't get mad." Then he swiped Ralph right off my neck. Snatched him off me, *that fast*. Before I could splutter, "You thieving swine!," he'd turned, and placed the Royal Amulet around the little brown wolf from Merenwyn.

Chapter Ten

"Hedi—stop," Trowbridge said, capturing my fist in his. "I can't go face the pack with a Fae amulet dangling from my neck, and I can't leave the Royal Amulet in your care."

Unspeakable fury. "I have taken care of that—"

"The Shadow will try to charm it off you," he said grimly. "He knows the words to summon the portal and with the amulet—"

"I am not some—"

"I have no time!" he said through his teeth.

Which was true, because Ralph was done. Totally fed up with being jerked around. He began to slowly shorten his noose—taking more time than required, because His Royal Nastiness was all about the big statement, and he not only wanted to choke something, he wanted the mortals who insulted him to note his intent.

Quickly Trowbridge inserted his mitt inside the narrowing gap. "Can this amulet understand language?"

"Yes," I snapped.

"The Fae wants to take you to the Black Mage," Trowbridge said to Ralph, talking fast. "It's probably the true reason he lured me back through the gates."

Lured? True reason?

"The wolf you're trying to choke is a Raha'ell." That seemed to mean something to the Royal Amulet, because he loosened his choke hold enough to let Anu, beast of Merenwyn and general ass-licker, heave a grateful pant. "You know their reputation," Trowbridge continued. "If I tell it to protect you, it will, with its life."

Bowler-hat inquired in a bored voice, "Do you really think I need an amulet to open the Safe Passage?"

To which Trowbridge said, "Yeah, I do."

Ralph chose fur over Fae. His chain lengthened in a blur of gold, until he swung, all princely and brightly jeweled, from the neck of the little brown wolf.

"Traitor," I mouthed.

Another wolf crept out of the woods, and then, behind that one, more.

Trowbridge gave me one last regretful look, then he stood. His fingers fumbled with the rough twine ties—*seriously, twine?*—of his trousers, as he strolled to the dead center of the old cow pasture. Once there, he turned to face me and, one more time, to impart something to me with his eyes.

I did the same.

He exhaled, and shook his head in reproof. Then, "Just wait for me."

What the hell did he think I'd been doing?

He dropped the twine, and his trousers slipped down his lean legs to puddle at his bare feet. With typical Were lack of respect for modesty, he coolly stepped out of them, and stood, proud, naked, and tall. A wolf whined as he tilted up his jaw to the moon's silver glow. He made a noise between a grunt and a hum—the same happy *mmph* he moaned when my hands found the right spot on his body—then fell to his knees in a slow, controlled glide.

But as soon as cartilage met turf, he began to change.

From man to wolf.

From that which I almost recognized to that to which I'd never been formally introduced.

It takes—I know, I've timed it—anywhere between five to fifteen minutes for a Were to shed his mortal hide. It took Bridge less than a breathless forty-five seconds.

When it was done, his wolf lay on its side for another ten seconds, panting lightly, then it rolled to its feet. It was, in the monochrome of night, all shades of white and gray. Its face was lean and angular, with darkly rimmed tilted eyes set in a white mask. Its legs were long, ending in ludicrously large fat paws.

By any bitch's standard, Trowbridge-the-wolf was a handsome fellow.

The gray wolf stepped away from the remnants of his change, and performed an all-body shake, before he turned—just a little bit—to slant a sideways glance toward the woods.

"Stay very still." The Fae peeled off his backpack. "Everything depends on the next five minutes."

I spared Bowler Boy a look of pure annoyance, then turned back to watch the show.

Not a dog whine was wrested from the wolves casting judgment from the forest. Indifferent to them and patently uncaring of the Danvers coterie, Trowbridge spent a minute or two investigating the shoes and clothing dotting the landscape. When he reached the pile that Fatso had hurriedly abandoned, he lifted his leg.

I flinched as the Fae retrieved a stiletto from his boot. Silver. Long. *Cold-blooded killer,* I thought uneasily. And then I wondered, just how valued was I, if my mate had no qualms about leaving me unprotected?

Those are the type of questions that make my stomach hurt.

I will not show fear. But part of me kept my peripheral vision on Bowler-hat, while the other prodded my Fae. *Are you with me?* I silently asked. *Or are you still enamored of the Fae that left you tethered to a tree?*

I felt the promise of her revenge warm my belly.

Trowbridge wandered over to where Cordelia and the boys were finishing their transformation—a difficult process for all three because the transitions were complicated by their need to heal—but he didn't greet them, probably because the change was a private thing. The hair bristled on his back and shoulders as he spent some time sorting out the scents still clinging to their chains. With a huff of disgust, he stalked away from them, stiff-legged.

Then, a short run to work out the kinks. Past the Danvers wolf. A turn to chase something I couldn't see—a moth perhaps—before his cantering pursuit softened into a lazy lope along the edge of the forest. His head whipped between the scents trapped in the grasses and those that rode a current of Were-fragrant air. With supreme indifference to watchers in the shadows, he trotted to the center of the field. There he stood, almost as if saying, "Take a good long look, boys. I'm back."

The Danvers wolf's lip curled to display fang. He stalked toward Trowbridge's gray wolf, hostility evident in his raised tail.

Trowbridge's ears flicked slightly forward, but that was the extent of his show. His wolf stood steady, confident. No growl. Just a confident display of dominance. Topped, of course, by the unearthly Trowbridge light growing from the power of all those comets spinning faster and faster around his dark pupils. The black wolf froze. Then Trowbridge did what he had bade me never to do.

He flared for the wolves.

Trowbridge light, blue and electric, shone from his eyes.

Alpha strong.

Alpha pure.

The Danvers male fought it, of course—he was after all a sodding *Danvers*. Papa George growled, and lifted his lip, and bristled like an outraged porcupine, but he was facing a searchlight of blue.

Some part of him—deep in his black heart—wanted to fall on his belly, to bow to this other wolf. Maybe even needed it, too.

It's imprinted in their DNA—either lead or follow.

Trowbridge's stand was an utterly strange and wonderful display of power and confidence. Dominance through magic, will, and birthright. There was no anger in it, no obvious urge to hurt or frighten.

In three pitiful seconds, the challenger went from a hackles-raised stalk to an ingratiating cringe. Body lowered, ears back, tail doing a hopeful wag, he approached his Alpha.

Hopeful. That I'd never seen. When I'd fixed the Danvers wolf with my light, he'd been resentful under my power, biding time for the moment of his release.

Trowbridge's wolf stood easy as the black wolf licked his Alpha's mouth, calm as the others cautiously approached. He let out a bark, which meant what? Welcome? All's right with the world? Immediately, the sharp stink of their anxiety eased, and another layer of scent overlaid the one melting away . . . happy excitement. Relief as if the six months before had all been a bad dream. Their joy was heartfelt—finally, a leader—punctuated by happy yips, much tail wagging, and some oddly touching gambols of pure happiness.

During it all, their Alpha stood steady and calm, head high, mouth slightly open, accepting his due.

A few canine heads turned my way.

Trowbridge's wolf growled a low warning to the rabble, before he loped over to me. Tail up, jaws open in a grin. Before I had a chance to hold him off, he claimed me with a paw. His massive face came in for a nuzzle. A long tongue licking away the tear that had dried on my jaw. I don't know why it softened me. His tongue was rough, and he'd been around fish at some point in his recent history. But it did. I felt . . . like he was breaking ground for me, letting me in, and each pungent dog kiss amounted to a public declaration, This is my mate.

Still, I mumbled, "I'm not a dog."

But his fur was thick and each strand glistened, silver-tipped under the benevolent moon. And my wolf . . . oh my wolf. She was up on all four feet and she was trembling. My Fae rolled her eyes as I threaded my fingers through his dense pelt.

Trowbridge-the-wolf made a noise that I took as one of deep approval.

I leaned my head against his throat to better hear its rumble.

A moment of welling peacefulness, broken in two, when from our left, the little brown wolf uttered a yip—a canine's "Hey!"—as it began running in our direction. One hundred sixty-four amber eyes turned toward the interloper.

I'm getting really tired of that dog.

One of the bulkier wolves broke from the group and began to slink toward the outsider, his hackles raised. Trowbridge's wolf pivoted—his claw raking my thigh—to let loose *another* fearsome growl.

Everybody froze.

Except for the little brown wolf barreling toward its Alpha, all happy, happy, anxious to play with the big dogs. Theoretically, it should have turned into a meal-on-paws right then and there. I lifted my head to watch the inevitable bloodbath. Creemore Weres don't like—

The pack parted for it like the Red Sea.

Unchallenged, the little wolf careened forward, ears pricked forward.

Ooof. It barreled into us—an eighty-pound cannonball—and I went sprawling. I pushed my hair off my face in time to watch Trowbridge's wolf engage in a regrettably brief show of fang and fur. Just when I was hoping it'd set itself up for a well-deserved ass-whipping. Happiness unquenched by its Alpha's reproof, it folded, right down to its belly, mouth open in a grin, limbs acquiescent under his heavy paw. Then, sweetly whimpering, it licked the rim of his black lips. It even dared to teeth him slightly, before ducking down, and glancing mischievously at the Alpha with its head turned at an angle.

It did it again. Just in case I didn't get it.

I'm slow, but not *that* slow.

Nor was my inner-bitch. Her tail stiffened into a fat broom of aggression as my eyes narrowed to slits. Together, in absolute harmony of thought, we watched Anu's performance.

Lick, lick. Tail wag. Followed by a sly glance in my direction.

Blame the healing potion; it had made me a little fuzzy headed. Blame my expectations; they'd rendered me reality resistant. Consequently, I'd missed a few important details about that little brown wolf. Vital stuff like, *IT* was much smaller and lighter than the male beside it. *IT* had dainty paws and an elegant clever little face.

IT was female.

She darted forward and shoulder-bumped him again.

Trowbridge's wolf rumbled a light growl at the female's daring, nothing much to the rebuke, in terms of stuff I'd witnessed among wolves. Really, for a canine, it amounted to nothing more than the equivalent of a lazy "shh." But for me—the girl who'd waited six long months for *her* man—it was the hold-the-presses, here-it-comes, all-time shitty "shh" of incoming heartache.

Trowbridge's wolf barked. He lifted his snout up to the freakin' moon and irritation welled in me. Was he avoiding the accusation in my eyes? Turning his head to worship that freakin' silver orb over our heads?

The little bitch made a noise—not quite a bark, but something more . . . intimate . . . that stiffened my spine. Her scent—oh crap, I wasn't getting a scent from her.

Just Trowbridge's.

Only mates smell like each other. My mate bond to Trowbridge didn't stick?

My eyes darted back to his, probing for an answer, but he'd gone dog on me. A wave of his personal scent hit my nose. Sharper than I remembered. It used to have a warm earth undertone. But still, woods and Trowbridge and fur, and . . . something else. Oh Goddess, it wasn't part of her essence, was it? It was on my skin, at my throat.

I looked past him to the little brown she-wolf.

She found Trowbridge's scent on Fatso's cowboy boots, gave a happy woof, and squatted.

"Who's the bitch?" I said through lips that suddenly felt numb.

* * *

I could feel the wolves' anticipation, hoping perhaps that I'd do something more than sit there on my butt, curiously frozen as what was left of my fragmented heart splintered beyond all recognition. Some of them watched with calculation, some with an obvious impatience to get all this mate business dealt with—after all, there was a moon shining down from the star-dappled sky. But worse (and I was not sure why it felt more horrible) I was aware of another set of eyes studying me from under the brim of a bowler hat. I could feel the Shadow's gaze—burning and insistent—on my turned head, as heavy as the weight of a hand resting on the nape of my neck.

It felt odd and somehow familiar.

Somehow sympathetic.

I almost turned toward it, but Trowbridge's gray wolf issued an inarticulate noise from the back of his throat, which apparently meant something to every other living thing in that pasture, but little to me. What was it? Dog shorthand for a command of "sit"?

Oh hell no.

"Stay there!" yelled Bowler-hat as I lurched unsteadily to my feet.

Six months, I'd waited. Thinking he was waiting, too.

My retreat was a blind blunder in the wrong direction, and then . . . thud. A heavy paw hit me between the shoulder blades, and down I went. I rolled away, once, twice—okay, *three* times—and the gray wolf followed my rotations with his paw—jab, jab, like I was a delicate salmon treat flopping on the riverbank.

"Stop that!" I shrieked, striking out in fury. I was flailing, legs kicking out, arms thrashing, and when my fist connected with his black nose I felt savage satisfaction. It felt good, but not enough. Not *nearly* enough. Before I could do it again—his wolf reacted, so feral and fast that my brain didn't have a chance to form the thought "oh, shit" before I found myself underneath one hundred and ninety pounds of fur and muscle, trapped between the brackets of his legs.

I stared up into a full set of canine teeth. Very sharp, slightly curving teeth. Pink gums. Black lips set in a grimace.

Tears burned my eyes.

I'm not stupid. There was only one reasonable check box on my list of options at that moment. So, I played dead, and it wasn't too much of a stretch. I was a corpse, except cold rage blinded my eyes, and black, biting hurt gnawed at my insides.

He'd tricked me. He'd asked for my word—promise me you'll stay—knowing, *knowing* that I would give it. *Knowing* the moment I caught the scent of him stamped over that little brown wolf I would yearn for the right to break it.

I don't share mates.

Trowbridge's wolf removed his paw from my chest, though he continued to straddle me, head up proudly, like some snout-to-the-breeze statue the pigeons use for target practice. One of his back claws dug into my thigh.

I welcomed the pain of it.

Distance, I wanted—no—I *needed* distance.

Not the fake and fleeting, fuzzy pink detachment I'd experienced when I swallowed a few mouthfuls of that Fae go-go juice. No, the real type. The permanent kind. Involving miles and screw-you declarations. Even if I could hear his heart. Right over my head. Steady, a little faster than usual. Beating from inside his massive canine chest that was covered with a deep thicket of coarse gray fur.

He dipped his head. Blue eyes—icier and less forgiving than his mortal ones—examined me.

It was six months, I condemned him with my eyes. *Six lousy months.*

You found my replacement that fast?

At the count of eighteen of the longest seconds of my life, he stepped neatly off me and allowed me to sit up. Stiffly, I rolled up to my knees. From there, I stood, slowly, because my sense of gravity was off—my inner-bitch was careening inside me—and somewhat carefully, because payback pain sent a louder message of retribution to my hands. They felt fatter, hotter. I curled them into claws. They would throb in earnest soon.

"Dissension in the ranks so soon?" Bowler-hat drawled, plucking a piece of dog hair off his pants leg. The gray wolf didn't bark anything in reply—hell, even the crickets had lost their voices in the sudden oppressive silence. I shifted my glance toward the Fae—today was all about shifts: eye shifts, direction shifts, fortune shifts, relationship shifts—preferring to look at him than cast my gaze toward Trowbridge's wolf.

Watching the Fae's mouth, I understood that Trowbridge's wolf and the Fae were in the grip of a silent, nasty conversation.

It seemed that whole telepathic thing wasn't limited to dogs.

The Fae flinched, and then said sharply, "That would be impossible. You have not fulfilled your part of the bargain."

Trowbridge had made a bargain, had he? With a "cold-blooded," murderous Fae?

I ran my thumb gently over the blister forming on the tip of my index finger, thinking about escape scenarios. *I'd need money or a credit card. And a car. A fast one.* While I plotted, the standoff between Fae and wolf stretched, until one of the ravens watching from the tall pines grew tired of the impasse, and broke the tension with a sharp caw.

The Fae sighed and removed his hat, sliding it into the curve of his elbow. "There. I am hatless. Are you satisfied?" His lip curved, and he insolently added something in Merenwynian.

Trowbridge's wolf bristled. The bitch beside him groomed her paw.

But the Fae turned to me and bowed.

And then, I got that feeling you get before a thought is fully formed—that wait-a-minute, here-it-comes prickle. Now that he'd doffed his chapeau, I could see him fairly well. Not perfectly—moonlight will never show details as

clearly as a good old hundred-watt bulb—but well enough.
The hat was a shield, I thought. Without it, he looked curiously vulnerable. His hair was strange, shorn to the skin
on one side of his head, the other side covered by a long
fall of sun-bleached hair. And his face seemed longer. His
nose had been broken once and not properly reset.

But it was the expectant quality in his eyes—deceptively
sleepy, tilted up at the edges—that scratched at a scab almost healed.

"I will fulfill my part of our agreement once you've
proven to me that they accept you in mortal skin," he said,
turning his head slightly toward Trowbridge. "Think
twice. If you kill me, no one wins. Those most in need will
never find their way to the Safe Passage."

I don't know what the Shadow said after that. My gaze
clung to his long, wide mouth, fixated on the way his lip
puckered at the corners. Then he rolled his neck, as if he
were getting ready to do something really dangerous.

Oh heavenly stars.

Bowler-hat glanced back at me, and our gazes locked.

The final, axis-spinning shift.

Once the Fae had been thin—too much so, a slender-
ness born of nervous energy, and high expectations, as if
he burned off food faster than he could eat it. Like he
yearned to move fast enough to outrun the restlessness that
was always part of him. That was gone. Now he was solid
the way men get when they mature. Still lean legged, but
the upper part of his torso was well developed, his neck no
longer sapling thin.

He was so damn old.

How is that possible?

My Were turned around inside me in an anxious circle,
and with each restless circuit, she brushed her flank against
my Fae, who kept sending sparks of malicious glee up my
spine. I wanted to tell them both to buzz off—for once just
leave me the hell alone—this day had been a day beyond
all days.

My world kept reeling.

I'd like to faint, I thought, resting the back of my wrist hard against my churning gut. *If only I was the fainting sort.*

He was still handsome in a battered-beauty sort of way. But then I'd always suspected he'd taken the lion's share in the looks category, hadn't I? Hell, he'd always been a thief—sucking the good genes right out of the womb we shared. He got the courage I lacked. The gift of gab that I longed for. The brightness and light of my mother, mixed with an adventurous streak that was, perhaps, his alone.

The other half of me.

Once, half of my soul.

My brother, my twin.

Chapter Eleven

Trowbridge's wolf leaned his dog head into my personal space and gave me a look. Don't ask me what it meant. I was beyond decoding canine body language, and no one, not one damn flea-infested mangy one of them, had given me a copy of *Visible Pooch Cues for You: What They Mean, and How to Deal.*

"Don't you have places to be?" I asked, darting another disbelieving glance at my twin.

If a dog could huff, he did. Then he turned his muzzle up to the night sky and howled.

As howls go, it was *the* trumpet call.

Long ago, when I was just a little Fae-mutt asleep in my bed, I'd heard a similar bay. A song to the moon. A ring-out to the clan. "Come," it said. "Run with me." Trowbridge's wolf did it again—a true Alpha calling to his pack—and the response from the gathered kin was fervid. Yips, yaps. You didn't have to be a canine to recognize their joy. He trotted through the center of the pack, and those closest to his passage sank low onto their front legs and tried to lick his muzzle as he passed.

The king is passing. Kneel.

He gave them no heed. Head high, ears forward, he trotted to where Cordelia and the boys waited. Gave homage to their loyalty with a thorough inspection of their snouts, their necks, and their wounds. A conversation—probably telepathic—occurred.

A chuff of agreement from Harry and a slower one from Biggs. The two of them came over close to where I sat and settled. Backs turned to the pack. Gazes fixed on the Fae.

Lexi's guards, or perhaps mine.

Hurt curdled my stomach, barely appeased by the fact that the little brown wolf was next to receive a set of orders. She slunk over to join Harry and Biggs, tail drooping, Ralph a glimmer of gold about her throat.

Yawned and sat.

Three guards then.

My One True Thing turned and gave another piercing howl—one that said, "You and me, moon, let's get it on"—and then, the natural-born Alpha of Creemore, my grade-school crush, and the ghost that I had carried in my heart for the last six months turned for the woods. He stopped one shrub in. Directed to me *another* piercing command . . . This one I had no trouble interpreting, a furred promise for "I shall return," before he melted into the forest.

I watched, feet numb, mouth flat, heart—well, Goddess knows where that was, I was hardly conscious of the loss of its usually comforting thump—as the rest of his newly claimed pack fought for rank and file. Nipping and snapping, growling and yelping, each one struggling to be first, or second, or perhaps third to follow his exalted ass down the trail. Rachel Scawens won second place. Then another jostle and a yelp, and a stiff-tailed wolf—they all looked the same to me—secured third best. The middle ranks sorted out their relative positions. Some of those discussions were downright ugly, all fangs and crinkled snouts, throat growls and yips.

I was conscious of Lexi standing behind me, watching me watch them. I felt . . . uncomfortable. Suddenly shy. I didn't know what to do, except sit there, with my hands resting on my thighs, palms upward and fingers throbbing; my brain was curiously numb.

Cordelia's white wolf was the last. By choice, I knew. She made a whine of distress, her gaze flitting back over her shoulder to the brother I knew stood nearby, and then back to the path down which the pack had disappeared.

Yes, Cordelia, our boyfriend's back.

"It's all right," I told her, lifting my shoulders. "He won't hurt me. Go now."

I watched, head turned, until Cordelia's white tail was swallowed by the forest's dark. And then the air was quiet, until the ravens spread their wings and left.

I wanted to break the silence that was stretching wire thin between my twin and me—to call out his name or to send him a thought picture—because he was walking toward me, and he needed to stop. *Don't come any closer. Just stay where you are so I can inspect you for changes first. You're a stranger to me, you shouldn't be, but you are.* Still, he kept coming, eating up the ground between us, and I knew that I had only seconds to reconcile myself to this—*this* Shadow of a boy that had filled my memories with laughter and light.

Why hadn't I recognized him?

Even though he'd donned his hat again there were obvious similarities between the brother I lost and the man crossing the field, if I'd only known to look for them. Lexi had grown tall, but then again, that should have been expected; my twin had always favored my father's side over Mum's. And lean—of course, *he'd* get the Were-lean gene. Then there was his jaw. I'd always thought the rest of his face would eventually grow into it, but, very obviously, it hadn't. It was, as it had always been and likely always would be, the most dominant of his features; triangular and a little too long, finishing with a stubborn, solid chin—an upside-down pyramid with the top shorn off.

Who could miss a jaw like that?

But where was the wide Joker smile? The irrepressible, "I'll do it first" twinkle in his green eyes? The man wearing a carefully blank expression—and he *was* a man, this

Fae who'd long since shot past his twenty-second birthday—
wasn't the same kid who used to send me thought pictures
during Ms. Webster's history class.

A game changer, that's what the Shadow was.

In one sweep, he'd destroyed the series of images I'd
created in my head to comfort me when I felt my most
twinless and alone: my brother at thirteen, a year after
he'd been stolen away by the Fae, looking much as he had
at twelve, except perhaps cleaner and better dressed; my
twin at seventeen, his hair a little darker, his face filled
out, sending a wink to a blushing female. Gone. All those
imaginary head shots I'd created, envisioning him growing in tandem beside me, changing from a restless grey-
hound into something more languid and refined, perhaps
an aristocratic Fae.

I'd been wrong. This was no nobleman.

The Shadow walked toward me, hip first—a street
fighter balanced on the balls of his feet—until the gap between us could be bridged easily if either of us had the
courage to reach out and touch the other.

Leather and sandalwood teased my nose. He'd affected
a perfume, a deliberately cultured one. "They smell like
dogs," my twin used to gripe. "I'm glad we have no scent."
Not Lexi, not Lexi, not Lexi.

I studied the fawn stitching on his black boots, not yet
ready to speak, turning words over in my head. Bad ones.
Genocide. Manipulator. Thief. Liar. And he must have felt
it, too—that distance, that perplexing turn on the map of
reconciliations—because my brother didn't choose to embrace me. Instead, he sank down onto the backs of his
booted heels, then slid his suspenders off his shoulders,
and pulled off his shirt.

"Here," he said gruffly.

"Thanks." I accepted the garment awkwardly. It was
dove colored with an indistinct paisley design. Lustrous
small gray buttons mocked my swollen hands. "It's too
nice. I'll ruin it," I said with a nod toward my midriff. "I'm
a little . . ." My voice fell off. "Bloody" would be the best

description. It was everywhere, coating my stomach, staining my bra, smearing my arms, graffitiing my jeans.

Don't faint.

"Don't mind that," he said softly. "You're fully healed beneath it."

But I couldn't tear my gaze from the red smears. My brain shut down—there'd been too many axis shifts in one short night—and for a bit, all I could smell was the scent of my own blood, sweet and floral like crushed sweet peas.

"Hell," he chided, and when I didn't respond—*who calls me Hell anymore?*—he touched my head. Just once. Very lightly. But a spark shot between us, and it startled me out of that blank place I'd sunk into.

"No one calls me Helen anymore," I told him. "It's Hedi now."

"The sun potion heals wounds, even almost mortal ones, if given in time." Then the man Trowbridge had labeled bankrupt of kindness tentatively stretched out a hand, and held it in the air between us, a fragile bridge hoping to span a turbulent sea.

Permission to touch? his eyes asked.

They're greener than mine. I'd forgotten that.

He took my silence for approval. "Stay still," he ordered, leaning on one knee to squeegee the gross stuff off my belly. "See? Nothing there. All healed."

I bent my head. Smooth, unmarred skin. No hole. No gash.

He sat back on his heels, resting his arm on his knee. His hand was large, long fingered, big knuckles like Dad's. Not pretty. Capable. Smeared with my blood. "Raise your arms," he ordered. *My brother talks with a Merenwynian accent now.* I lifted, and held them like that, curiously obedient, as he threaded arms through sleeves, and head through hole.

Gently, he eased the gray shirt down to my hips.

I shook my head. "It's ruined."

"Not a problem." A glimmer of a smile. "It's not mine."

"Then whose is it?"

But he didn't answer, because his expression had grown tight again, and . . . *frightening.* "Give me the name of the beast who hurt your hands."

"No one *did* this to me," I said, thinking guys with wide mouths can flatten them awfully fast. "It's just payback pain. It always happens after I use my talent. When my magic returns to me—by the way, that was *my* magic you pinched—my hands do this." I held up one flaming paw. "It's only temporary. It'll blister, and then eventually heal, if I give it enough time."

"Payback pain," he repeated in an odd voice, stretching his fingers.

"You don't get payback pain?" *Why not?*

"Not the type that hurts my hands," he said, with a bittersweet smile at the moon. "You don't change into one of them, then?"

"No. I can't transform into a wolf," I said flatly. *Can you?*

Look at me, Lexi.

A small animal plucked up its courage and waddled for deeper cover. Leaves rustled, a twig cracked. He twisted toward the sound, nostrils flaring.

"Raccoon," I said. "Creemore is overrun with them."

"Possum," he murmured, still staring at the dark forest. "Your nose was never as strong as mine."

"Who says?" I responded instinctively.

"Your brother does." Just as quickly, he'd fallen back into the old rhythm, finishing the volley as he'd done back in the day when he'd been only a few minutes older and two inches taller than me—with both eyebrows raised, as if to say, "You challenging me, shrimp?"

And there it was. My brother's left eyebrow had always been lazier than the right. The sight of his right brow lifted slightly higher than its twin scored a sharp nail over the glacier holding my heart hostage.

Love welled.

"Hey," I said, wishing my hands weren't hot and swollen fat so that I could do something, anything, with them—fold them over my heart or maybe touch that long sweep of wheat-colored hair—to show him, to tell him—

Now I recognize you.

"Welcome home, Lexi," I said softly.

He blinked before allowing a wonderful, big huge Lexi grin—his mouth so wide that his top teeth gleamed—to warm his face. "You haven't grown much, runt."

"You said I'd never pass five feet." I grinned back. "You were wrong."

"How so?"

"I'm five two. Three, if I wear shoes."

"And you consider that grown?" My brother's smile faded, and his voice grew serious. "Hell, how old are you?"

"I turned twenty-two in August," I said softly.

That was . . . a blow. A long, dead interval passed before Lexi'd collected himself enough to speak. "Eleven years? That's all it's been?"

Ten and a half, I thought, resisting the urge to correct him. "We don't look like twins anymore," I whispered. *You look so old, Lexi.*

A muscle flexed in his jaw. With a rough nod, "No, not anymore."

"How long have *you* been gone?"

"The Fae don't count years," he said tonelessly. "But it seems time passes faster there than here." He looked over to the Stronghold ridge, and asked, "Mum and Dad?"

"They both died the night the Fae took you across the portal. Dad first."

He nodded as if he'd known, and I reached for him, but that made him abruptly lift his arm as if to cast a spell or maybe to ward off something—a blow? A curse? "Sorry," he bit out. "I don't like being touched anymore."

Were you ever that keen on it?

My brother bent his head and raked the ground until he turned up a twig. This he turned into a tool to draw a furrow in the hard earth. "Tell me. All of it."

"The portal came—no one called it from this side of the gates—but Mum could feel it coming. 'It's on my skin,' she said to Dad. He took his gun down to the pond and was waiting for the wolf when it leaped through."

"What type of wolf?" Lexi drew another line parallel to the first he'd scored.

"One of ours. A Creemore wolf named Mannus. Do you remember him? He was Trowbridge's uncle?" He didn't. So I told him about Mannus, and how he'd feigned love for our Fae aunt, and how she'd made the mistake of bringing him over into the Fae realm.

"Dad held the shotgun on him, and said that he'd have to bring him to the Alpha. But the wolf turned on him, they fought, right near our pirate rock." *In the mud, while I watched.* "Mannus got away, but he'd wounded Dad so badly—"

"How?"

"Dad's stomach was torn open. His throat mangled."

Lexi drew a horizontal line across the two lines he'd already made in the earth. "Where was Mum?"

"Still in the house. Trying to cast protection wards on the windows and doors."

His hand stilled. "She knew the Fae were coming."

"Yes, she knew, and she was desperate to get the protection up before they arrived." I worried my lip, watching him rework the lines. Slash, slash, slash. Now the diagram looked like the setup for a game of tic-tac-toe. "We got Daddy into the house, and she had a moment to seal the doors against them, but . . ." *Her face had been white with fear.* "They broke through her wards like they were . . . tissue paper. It took two kicks to break down the door, and then . . . they were in the kitchen."

"Mum had time to put you in our hidey-hole."

That's what we'd called it back then. Not a hole, but an old kitchen cupboard—the type you hung on a wall and put soup tureens in. Cream paint worn off near the handles and the hinges to expose the pine beneath it. Double doors. A side for each twin. But yes, our mother had pushed me into it first. "I was handy. She was going for you next. She was calling for you—screaming your name."

"Back then I was a sound sleeper," he said, spinning the stick to drill a hole in the earth to make a jagged hole in the center of one of the boxes he'd drawn.

And I'd been a light one.

His stick moved to the next hole. "The pack didn't come in time to save the house?"

"Only Trowbridge came."

The twig broke and he cursed in Merenwynian. Sharp. Hard.

"Don't," I said. "It was my fault."

His gaze jerked to mine.

"She told me, 'Go get your brother.' But I didn't. I followed Dad down to the pond instead." I lifted my hands helplessly, unable to tear my eyes off that single pitted hole in the middle of the hashwork of lines. "I didn't understand, I didn't think. I was curious and . . . It's *my* fault that you weren't warned. All mine." I swallowed, miserable. "I'm sorry, Lexi. I'm so sorry. If I could take it back . . ."

He searched my face before he shifted to extract a silver flask from his pocket. Expression shuttered, he uncapped it, and brought its mouth to his. His throat flexed as he swallowed.

"I missed you, Lexi," I whispered. *Did you miss me?*

He took another swig from his flask.

"Is that the stuff that healed me?" I asked in a little voice.

He nodded.

My hands throbbed. "What magic is in it?"

He slanted his gaze toward my blistering mitts, then gave the flask a thoughtful look. A sharp, short inhale through his nose, before he poured a small measure into the cap of the flask and gave it to me. "Only a sip," he said. "It's too easy to start liking it too much."

"And that would be a problem?"

He gave me a wink. "For some." Then my twin tucked the flask back into his satchel and stood. The corner of his mouth pulled downward as he stared at the pond below. "That boulder there—is that where it happened?"

"Yes."

"And the apparition," he said, with a nod to the cemetery. "Does she have a story?"

"Casperella's not much for conversation," I replied. "Mostly, she shadows—" I stumbled, and chose a better word. "Watches me from the cliff while I stand by the pond."

A finger rubbed the corner of my twin's mouth, before he nodded to himself. "She was probably there all the time when we were kids. We were just too young to see her."

"I guess." Seeing spooks started around puberty—around when my magic came in.

I hunched my shoulders against a sudden chill. *Now what?* I wondered. I didn't want to go back to the Trowbridge house. There were memories there that I didn't have sufficient courage to face. Especially after tonight, when my nerves felt flayed. And I didn't want to stay there sitting Apache-style on the same damp ground on which I'd lost and gained and lost again. New memories were attached to this field, some of which I wasn't sure if I'd ever reconcile myself to.

Biggs let out a look-at-me whine, which the little brown bitch ignored.

"I wonder what Harry's searching for?" I asked, my tone wonderfully indifferent. The old wolf limped across the field, favoring his paw, nose snuffling the turf.

"Not looking, hunting," Lexi corrected, his eyes narrowed. "Never forget that they are animals and are driven by the instinct to hunt."

It worried me, the way Harry hobbled, and suddenly my heart hurt almost as much as my fingers and head. I whispered, "Who's the mutt Trowbridge brought back?"

Lexi's gaze flicked to the she-bitch, and then to the ground. He toed aside a clump of sheep sorrel. "A servant in the Great Hall."

"No, I mean who is she *to him*?"

"How would I know? The Son of Lukynae is not fond of conversation." He adjusted his satchel more comfortably on his shoulder.

"Why do you call him that?"

But he'd turned to eye the Trowbridge property with an expression of dismissal. "Look at the size of the trees ... they're saplings compared to those in Merenwyn." Then, with deceptive laziness, "Tell me, what is Robson Trowbridge to you?"

That I couldn't—wouldn't—even try to answer. When I made a tsk of irritation, he slanted me a familiar big-brother smile. "How are the hands?"

I flexed my fingers. "Much better."

He nodded in satisfaction as long hair fell in a slow, golden glittering sweep. *Like wheat in the field,* I thought, watching him slide it back behind his ear—ah, for crap's sake, his jeweled ear. "You've gotten awfully girly," I said glumly.

A snort of laughter. "I went native," he said. "Count yourself lucky, you should see what some of the women of the Court wear."

I have. Mad-one's gown is blue and jeweled.

"I need to empty my backpack," he said. "Shall we go home?"

Trowbridge had asked me to wait in his house—now I gave that request the nanosecond of reflection it deserved before I lifted my chin and pointed to the silver bug on the opposite ridge. "The house burned to the ground. That's home now."

He scowled. "That's the best they could come up with?"

"I don't need much." *Where did you live? In a castle?*

"Through the cemetery?"

I stood. "It's the fastest way."

A wry smile. "And expedience is always preferred."

I smiled with relief. There it was. An echo of the old impatient Lexi, always appreciative of the fastest way to get the job done.

"You do this part," he used to say.

"Why?"

"Because it's faster that way, dummy."

Then Lexi said, his tone somewhat goading, "Wolves, feel free to follow us."

Biggs's wolf rose to his feet, his head whipping back between the she-bitch and Harry. Some communication passed between the three of them. Harry stayed, while Biggs and the bitch took a position on either flank.

"Sorry," I mouthed to my friends. Harry uttered a huff then lowered his head once more to the turf.

"Home," Lexi repeated. Then—because he was at least a decade and twelve minutes older—he strode away.

And me? I did what I'd always done.

I hurried to catch up.

Some things remained the same. Lexi led the way, and when faced with the fork in the path, he unhesitatingly turned left. And yet? Time waits for no man—no woman, either. I'd learned to keep my gaze fixed on the homely shape of the trailer as I passed the ruins of our old house, but my brother stopped short.

"I'll give you some time," I said, knowing he needed to grieve in privacy. "You'll find me in the trailer. You hungry?"

No reply.

I turned on the lights in the sitting room and left the door open, hoping he'd follow when he was ready. Then I had a three-minute shower. The clothing that was mine I bundled into a wad and shoved into the garbage. My brother's purloined shirt got a soak in the bathroom sink. Hurriedly, I threw on some clean clothes. Then, six swipes of the comb through my hair, and a little daub of Cordelia's face cream, and I was ready as I'd ever be.

What to feed the prodigal son? I wondered, staring at the contents of the fridge. The Fae had hummingbird's tastes. Maple syrup and honey. Everything—except themselves— sugared and sweet. I brought out the syrup and then, in afterthought, the last of my Tim Horton Timbits.

I've got a thousand questions.

But here's the thing. If the boy existed inside the man, then I knew from experience that it was a waste of time peppering him with questions. He'd shut down. And it would be a slow, spiraling route toward the answers.

I'm tired. And so is he. We have time.

Smiling, I set the doughnut holes on the dinette table, along with the tin of syrup, bowls, and spoons, then worried over my choice. When we were growing up, my twin had been the one to make a fist pump at the sight of a thick wedge of steak. Maybe meat would be better? I rubbed the peak of my ear, trying to decide, and leaned to look through the window.

My brother stood with his back to me, his arms limp.

Come on, Lexi. Move away from it. You won't find any answers in the rubble of our old life.

He'd need comfort, once he was ready.

I should cheer him up with a thought picture.

It's the way my twin and I had talked when we didn't want other ears to listen in. It had been how we'd comforted and amused each other. It was the one time that I could count on Lexi not to tease me, because to a Fae, a thought picture is a sacred thing, used with love.

I hadn't received one like that since the spring of seventh grade.

I sank down onto the seat, remembering.

Ms. James was an odd duck, even for an unmarried Were-bitch, as witnessed by the fact she seated everyone in the class alphabetically. Didn't matter if you were myopic or short. It wasn't terrible; I could have made my peace with trying to see the board past Terry Stewart's high ponytail, because the next person on the list was my brother, John Alexander Stronghold. He sat right behind me and it wasn't a stretch to say he had my back. But two weeks later, Ms. James proved herself a Fae-hating witch by yanking me out of the *S*'s and shoving me into the *G–J* row. According to her, I kept looking out of the window, and that was a problem.

My new seat sucked.

I had a jock in front of me, and a jerk behind me, and true to form, J&J spent the next eight and a half months making me miserable. One afternoon in late May, when the classroom stank to high heaven of wet sneakers and sweaty Weres, Jock said something Were-witty about my lineage to the Jerk.

What had they said?

I lined up the spoons, trying to remember what exact bon mot had sent me over the edge. Something, something, what? Deep in thought, I folded two napkins, just the way Cordelia liked them, and tucked them under the bowls.

A low growl from outside yanked me back to the present.

Lexi was on the move. He slipped off his leather bag and glanced up at the sky, then walked over to where Mum's garden used to be. Anu, the wonder-bitch, issued another warning rumble, which he totally ignored. But then again, Lexi never did pay much attention to what others thought—at least not visibly.

It must be wonderful to be like that.

Biggs's wolf turned his shaggy head toward my window.

"It's okay," I mouthed. Trowbridge wouldn't have left that bag on him if he had anything of worth in it. I don't know how I knew that, but I did.

Back in Ms. James's class I would have given anything to be as opinion resistant as my brother. The day of the Big Insult, I'd sat there—telling myself to hold on, don't give them the satisfaction—all the while knowing I was teetering on the brink of a rage.

And then Lexi sent me a mental nudge.

How to describe it? You know when you've forgotten something but you don't know what it is? You're heading toward the car, keys in your hand, and suddenly a thought comes to your mind directly from your unconscious—out of the blue, completely unbidden. *You're missing something.* You know that feeling? That's like a nudge. Except, for Fae, that tentative tap comes from someone else's mind, not your own. And you feel it, physically, like the touch of someone's shoulder giving yours an affectionate bump.

Soft, tentative. A light lean versus a heavy push.

Lexi's nudge had been well timed. I'd opened my mind (all you have do is to allow that searching blankness to extend) in invitation.

A slip, a slide, and he was in.

Ta-da!

My brother's thought picture—the first in what I knew would be a series—was as clear as if I were squinting through a View-Master. His debut image was of the Jock stripped down to his tighty-whities followed by a close-up of a bottle of flea shampoo, succeeded by a snapshot of a garden hose—I'd started smirking by that point—then, an old-fashioned galvanized tub.

My twin waited a beat or so to raise my anticipation before he offered me his pièce de résistance. It was a doozy— all the visual elements combined—a picture of the same Were, no longer smutty and smug, sitting bowlegged in a tiny tin bath, his head lathered with flea soap, a stream of tears streaking his flushed cheeks.

Okay, it was crude. But it worked.

I broke into a guffaw that made Ms. James drop her chalk.

Smiling in recollection, I glanced out of the window then bolted upright.

"Wolf," Lexi threatened. "I will wear your pelt."

The deep rumble coming from the lanky old wolf's chest spoke of no good things coming to pass. Head lowered, shoulders stiff, Harry stood his ground. Biggs flanked him, hackles raised.

"It belongs to my family," snarled Lexi. "Drop it. Now." And then, proving that he truly was my twin, he flared. Green, just like me. A little weaker in terms of intensity—I didn't see any of the three wolves prostrate themselves under *its* light—but maybe he hadn't put his all into it.

"Calm down," I soothed as I walked toward them.

"Harry's part of my inner circle, like Cordelia. He doesn't expect to be challenged while on Stronghold land."

"He is not my friend," gritted out Lexi. "And I'm a Stronghold, which makes this my land, too."

"No one is challenging your right as a Stronghold," I said. "But Harry's *my* friend and he's welcome here."

Lexi's back stiffened. Then, with a deliberation that I'd spend some time thinking about later, he turned, and gave me a dose of my own medicine. Green light washed over me and just about bowled me over. *Sit, bow, crawl,* it said to me. Oh Goddess, the urge to go on my belly was almost overwhelming. I locked my knees. With a sneer, I asked, "You done now?"

His flare flickered out.

With a sigh, I sank to one knee, and leaned toward my former second-in-command. "What is it, Harry? What have you got?"

The old wolf gave my brother one last "any time" growl before limping his way over toward me. A string—no, not a string, a gold chain—hung looped from his black-rimmed lips.

I tilted my head, hope stirring.

Please let it be her. Please.

Harry stopped, lowered his head, and placed what he carried so gently in his mouth with exquisite care onto the ground.

It was many things—this lovely object that gleamed so wetly.

It was magic and valuable beyond words—a pendant, smaller than Ralph, made of amber and Fae gold.

And once, she'd been my only friend.

Chapter Twelve

"Merry, you came back." My whisper broke in two; no, three; no, four pieces—one for each word; a broken shard of one big fat crock of misery with a piece for my friend, and one for me. Another for the hope I'd held in my heart that she'd find a way to end the curse that kept her imprisoned in that hunk of amber, and the last for the future that we were going to live after this miserable night was done.

Because she'd come back when she should have stayed in Merenwyn with her own kind. Not here among wolves and humans. Not returned to the care of someone who didn't have anything to offer her. No hope, no sweet life, no promise of anything except the same old miserable Hedi mess-up.

A wink of red glowed from within her amber belly. Warm red, the kind that spoke of love and comfort.

That's what Trowbridge had told Harry before he left on the run, "Go find Merry."

Biting my lip, I opened my palm.

Waited.

If Merry came back to me—it would be for me. Not because I demanded it. Not because I reached for her. It would be her choice. No more greedy fingers.

She'd be my equal.

I forced my mouth into the shape of an indifferent smile

and held it there. But I am greedy, and sometimes, horribly needy, so I let my watering eyes feast on the sight of her. Before I sent her across the void she'd been brutalized by my aunt, but it seems that she, too, had found a measure of healing in Merenwyn. Her Fae gold seemed to glow, and the entwined ivy vines set around her amber stone had been recast. Each leaf was daintier—definitely smaller—and each one appeared vastly more articulated and accurately rendered than before; graduating from her old, flat, grade-school-artist version of an ivy leaf to something distinctly five lobed and well shaped, detailed enough for me to see a fanwork of veins running from the heart point near the base to the end of each fine tip.

She'd gone from dime-store workmanship to the type of jeweled artistry that belonged in a store that I'd never have the courage or the money to walk into. I peered into the heart of her pendant to the place where my true friend lived. She was an Asrai, like Ralph, bewitched like him, and shrunk until she was little more than a smudge of something dark in the interior of a semiprecious stone. Cursed to stay in a prison by Lou.

Merenwyn had been good for her. Even her amber stone appeared to have undergone an upgrade in the look-at-glorious-me sweepstakes. It seemed more polished, more lustrous.

Why, Merry? Why come back? Couldn't anyone be found over there to break the curse that keeps you imprisoned? You'll never find it here. I have no mages, no Book of Spells, no inside knowledge. No matter what Cordelia says, I'm still very much me.

Maybe that's what she was looking at, inhaling the lack of differences—the depressing same-old, same-old sight of me on my knees, shoeless, with hair a mess—and maybe, just maybe, she was wondering exactly the same damn thing.

Should she really have braved the winds of the portal for this?

My feet had fallen to sleep under my rump. A wink of

orange from her heart, as if she could read my thoughts and enjoyed the joke.

"I kept my promise, you know," I whispered. "I've worn the Royal Amulet every day. I've fed that miserable sod and kept him clean and dry. I didn't smash him against the wall when he tried to choke me a week ago . . . *in my sleep*," I emphasized, just to make sure she understood how difficult the job had been. "I've renamed him. Unless you've got a better name for him, I've been calling him Ralph." I chewed the inside of my lip. "I know you expected to see me wearing him, and I have. Really. But Trowbridge put him around the neck of that guard-bitch over there—if I hadn't been woozy at the time, I would have seen it coming and fought him off. Tomorrow morning, when Trowbridge is human again, I'll get Ralph back. I promise you. I'll . . ."

My voiced dwindled to nothing.

And then, my friend chose me.

An unfurling of vines, a quick readjustment of her Fae gold, and she was as I knew her. A stick figure with two legs, and two arms, fashioned of ivy and impudent spunk, marching across the battlefield that separated us, trailing a golden rope of chain behind her. She marched right up into the crater of my cupped paw and straight back into my heart.

I bit down on a whimper as I fumbled to place her over my head.

My brother closed the door to the trailer with a violent tug, which could have caused real damage to Biggs's lupine snout if his wolf hadn't been nimble enough to jerk back in time.

"You're embarrassing me," I hissed to my twin. "Those are my friends out there. They've been good to me. I don't know how I could have gotten through these last months—"

His head very slowly turned my way, and his gaze fell on Merry, hanging from my neck, and for some reason, I got that feeling again—like I should cover her up and be afraid—and that annoyed me and deflated the general esprit de corps, so I muttered, "Stop it."

"Stop what?" he asked, with a thread of challenge in his voice.

Geesh. He's sounding as territorial as a Were. Merry scuttled up to my shoulder and gave a bleat of orange-yellow. "Looking like that," I said, a tad snappishly.

Lexi's gaze roved, swiftly assessing the cheap oak cabinets, the stained carpeting, the narrow curtains with their fussy little tiebacks. "And that is?"

"Like you're a cowboy in a wanted poster wearing a bowler. It's already weird enough. The long hair, and—" I blew some air out of my nose. "Like right now. You're doing it again. Stop being so . . ."

He walked down the short corridor toward Cordelia's room. Three seconds spared on examining it from the doorway, before he turned, wiping his nose. "What?" he said.

Calculating and scary looking. Different. But everything was different for him here, wasn't it? And he hadn't had ten years to get used to it, or a friend like Merry. "Forget it." I shrugged, forcing my amulet to tighten her grip on my bra strap.

My brother's eyes were greener when they rested on Merry.

I'm not sharing. Not Merry. "Why don't you put down your knapsack and relax? I put out some food."

He nodded, but I recognized the onset of trouble in the set of his shoulders as he brushed past me to head for the other end of home-sweet-home.

Yup. Trouble.

There was a frozen quality to the way he stood staring into my bedroom, oddly similar to the way I sometimes stared at the numbers on the bathroom scale.

I stifled a sigh. *Who dressed him?* If that was what they wore in the Fae realm, somebody better send a fashion rescue team to Merenwyn, stat. Unlike Mad-one's vaguely

medieval garment, there wasn't even a trace of Middle
Earth in my brother's clothes. His couture was a bastard-
ized blend of sixties pop culture—I was forming a definite
hatred for his hat—and swashbuckler movies. And it was
devoid of color. Everything was either gray, or white, or
black.

A muscle worked in his jaw.

I sucked in my cheeks and opened the fridge. "You
want anything to drink? I've got some Coke, and there's
some apple juice left."

"Do you have anything stronger?" he asked, disappearing into my room.

"No, I don't." Cordelia didn't drink. Worrying my lip, I
poured two glasses of Coke and replaced the bottle in the
fridge. *What the hell is he doing in there?* There wasn't
that much to look at. My room was small and regrettably
short of sparkly things. The only personal touches were my
books—oh crap, he wasn't thumbing through my books,
was he? I grimaced at the thought. Some of them naturally
fell open to the racy sections.

"Hey," I said. "Why don't you come back into the living
room?"

A beat later he did, offering me a fleeting, cool smile—
one that felt as authentic as a diplomat's—before saying, "I
need to use your sink. Have you got any shampoo?"

"I left hot water in the tank." I squeezed in my stomach as
he passed me. *He sucks up more space than Cordelia.* "Why
don't you take a shower?"

"I don't need one now." Lexi placed his knapsack beside the sink and frowned at the kitchen's nickel tap and
faucet.

"I used up a whole bottle of Cordelia's clear nail polish
covering the areas where the finish had worn down," I told
him, recognizing his concern. "There's not much iron in
the steel. You won't feel a thing."

He gave me an approving smile and set to unwinding
the string wrapped around the closure on his knapsack. The
bag was large and made of supple black leather, with an

embellished design on the front. Before he lifted the flap, he muttered something.

Then I felt a shock. Just a little one. A tiny zap.

"What was that?" I asked.

A flash of pure devilment—possibly mixed with a soupçon of pride—lit Lexi's face and made him appear, if not young, then younger. I smiled at him and asked, with a naughty-naughty voice, "Spill. What did you just do?"

"I used my talent to break the ward on the bag," he said, giving me a lopsided grin that melted my heart. "I can see magic, and if I can see it—"

"You can steal it," I said, with wonderment. "That's how you nicked my magic."

"It's what I do. Not another Fae in Merenwyn can see magic like I can. "

A stench filled the room.

"Fae Stars!" I pressed my hand to my nose, then gasped as the bag flexed. "What have you got in that bag?"

"Shh," he muttered. "Don't scare her."

"You traveled through the Gates of Merenwyn with a living creature tucked in your knapsack?" I said, awed.

"No, I *leaped* through the portal with the Black Mage's bag," he said with a grin. The flap lifted, and a nose twitched, scenting the air. Flesh pink, small. "His ferret, Steellya, just happened to be inside it."

The Black Mage. The hair stood up on the back of my neck at the way he said that name so casually. "Have you given any thought to what happens if her owner decides to follow you and reclaim his personal property?"

"He'd need an amulet to do that." Lexi cradled the ferret in his arms. An inquisitive face—white muzzle, black ring around the eyes, highlighted by another band of white—tilted sideways to examine me. "And she smells because she hasn't been bathed."

"He keeps a ferret in his bag? Who keeps a ferret in his bag?"

Lexi's expression grew harsh. "The bag's an improvement on her usual quarters. A little cage, filled with soiled straw. Never enough water or food. Rest easy, Steellya," he said, putting the plug in the sink. "Let me wash that filth off you."

"Cordelia's going to have a fit," I murmured, watching him squeeze a dollop of detergent into the filling sink. "What does the Black Mage do with a ferret?"

"She can squirm into places that Fae can't. Is Cordelia the animal whose scent fouled the bedroom back there?" he asked, in a neutral enough voice.

I felt my spine stiffen.

Then he cast me a glance over his shoulder and softened me with another authentic Lexi smile. "Thanks for putting the food out, runt. But do you have any hot dogs? You wouldn't believe how I used to dream about those."

Which is how I found myself kneeling in front of our tiny refrigerator, pawing through the cold-cut drawer looking for hot dogs while listening to my brother's husky, soothing murmur as he bathed the Black Mage's ferret in the sink that Cordelia daily scoured with a soft scrub brush and a little bleach.

A familiar feeling—Lexi and I breaking a couple of rules.

With a wash of tenderness, I remembered again the last thought picture Lexi had ever sent me—the one with the flea-shampoo-doused Were in the tin bath—and without pausing to think twice, I gave my brother a mental nudge, thinking he'd enjoy the symmetry.

It was just a little one. Nothing really in terms of nudges.

I'd even call it tentative.

Terror—that's what he poured into me in return. Sick, twisting dark fear. The type that makes your heart suddenly lurch into your throat. That fills you with panic. *Oh Goddess! Is this the inside of my brother's head?* I screamed, hands covering my ears in protection. But from what? It was in me! An asp of horror, slithering and brushing against good memories and bad. Leaving a slime trail of utter ruin in—

And then it stopped.

"Shit," cursed Lexi. "I didn't mean it—"

"Get away from me!" I recoiled from him, my elbow up to shield my face.

"Hell," he said brokenly. "It's been trained into me. One of the first things you learn in the Fae realm is to fight back when someone tries to touch your mind."

"What's happened to you? You're nothing like Lexi!"

"I am," he said, sinking to his knees beside me. Then softer, "I *am* Lexi."

The fridge door hit the cabinet as I scuttled out of his reach. "Trowbridge called you the Black Mage's Shadow. He said you were responsible for genocide! Against Weres! That you were a cold-blooded killer—"

"Hell," the Fae murmured, shaking his head. "Don't believe everything you heard from the wolf."

"No! My brother didn't hate being touched. My twin wouldn't have pulled away from me. My Lexi would never have sent a thought picture like that. Ever! You put that, that—" I stumbled for the right word. "Sickening shit in my head."

"I'm sorry, I'm so—"

"You slammed the door on Biggs and made sure he heard you say, 'Dogs don't belong in a house!' You don't want my food, but you keep looking at Merry as if you want to steal her off me. You wear your *hat* in my home. You're . . ."

And then . . . my words dried up.

Because in that spate of accusations Lexi finally found his way to protest. He pulled off his hat and held it against his chest as if it were a shield he didn't want to drop, before he laid it on the floor. Then . . . he just stayed there. Waiting for my verdict. Immobile, his face carefully shuttered, his body language broadcasting acceptance of whatever came next. Or maybe, something even worse than that. Not acceptance so much as weary resignation.

Lexi, Lexi.

Merry was hot against my chest. A wolf was howling

outside, while another threw himself against the flimsy
trailer door. I knew all that. Dimly, I recorded all those
things. Warnings and calls to arms. But all I could do was
stare at his uncovered head, feeling my horror and confusion and rage slide away like the leftovers on a dinner plate
being tipped into the garbage.

"Who tattooed that obscenity on you?" I whispered.

At first glance, the mark on his skin looked like a paw
print. Obviously intended to be a wolf's, based on the
shape and claws. Not quite half the size of one of Harry's
prints, but pretty damn close. Turned sideways, so the tips
of its claws looked as if they were stretching for the peaked
tip of my brother's ear. That alone would have been insulting, but it was the detail inked inside the five pads that really squeezed my stomach.

A wolf's face had been worked into the paw print, and
the ink mixed with magic, so that the buffs and blacks, the
greens and beiges would never fade. Forevermore, my
brother's skull would thus be adorned: above the peaked
tip of his ear, a lupine face poised with predatory anticipation, frozen in ink—black nostrils, black fur, smiling
lips—forever caged within the track of the wolf.

"This is good," he said, spearing another piece of roast
beef and putting it into his mouth.

My brother has a hard time looking me in the eye, I
thought, watching his eyes flick away from mine. And he
ate too fast, but then he always had. Gobbling down food
as if it, too, were territory and he was in a hurry to go back
and stake his claim to more.

It was quiet in our home.

In the way of most families in the midst of a horrible,
soul-tearing fight, we'd hit pause, because that's what you
do when you have a two-ton rogue elephant in your living
room. You hit that stop button, because admitting you have
a pachyderm problem implies an obligation to do something about it. You start worrying that getting it out of the
house might involve painful demolition. You start thinking

about the ugliness of walls torn down to studs and the cost of reconstruction. Maybe, given the alternative, you could live with an elephant in your home after all.

Time out? my gaze had asked of my twin after he'd doffed his hat.

Absolutely, he'd nodded gruffly, a flush tinting his cheekbones.

So, first, we'd taken care of outside business. My brother rescued the utensil crockery from the ferret's exploration, and I went to placate Harry—who'd broken through the door—before he huffed and puffed and blew the whole trailer down.

Harry, being Harry, was not inclined to being fluffed off, without a thorough inspection of the premises and my person. Once finished with that, he stopped, and eyed the ferret askance. "It's why I screamed," I lied to him. "I didn't expect a ferret to come out of his bag."

It's a good thing a wolf can't raise an eyebrow and drawl, "Bullshit."

Merry had sparked a red blip when the ferret in question chose that moment to overturn a mug on the counter.

"The ferret's not prey," my brother had announced, sealing his silver flask. He wiped his lip with two fingers, and took a deliberate step in front of the animal. "Touch the ferret and I'll take you out, wolf"—that's what his body language told Harry.

I'd smothered a smile at that.

My brother, Lexi, the Ferret Defender of the Free World.

Harry had curled his lip at my twin. Then he'd given me one more weighted glance before he'd limped out of our twenty-seven-foot home on wheels. Lexi had picked up the door, and fitted it back more or less in place. When that was done, he'd leaned against the wall and filled in a bit of dead airtime by tying knots in a strip of sealant. Finally, he'd said tautly, "My master, the Black Mage. He ordered this . . . decorative touch."

"Master?" My hand had gone to Merry. "Was he the

same Fae who stole you away the night Mum and Dad died?" She'd curled a tendril of ivy around my thumb.

"Yes," he'd said simply, as if that reply were the answer to all the questions, the key to all the things I didn't understand.

I remembered that Fae. Long rectangular face. Too much jaw. High wide forehead. Hooded eyes, their blue hue leached to something that chilled. The cold one. "Rose of the House of DeLoren, you've broken the Treaty of Brelland, and allowed one of the unclean to bathe in our sacred pool. According to the laws of Merenwyn and the Treaty of Brelland, your life is forfeit," he'd said in a voice that sounded flat and bored. As if death and cruelty were just another job-sheet task he'd initialed. Then the cold Fae had examined my brother as if he were livestock. "I'll take him as payment."

For what?

For my mother's sin of loving a Were? For my aunt's folly of trusting a bad man?

"You've been staring at it for five minutes. Stop it," Lexi murmured now.

Hard not to. One side of Lexi's head was shaved clean, and under the kitchen light his white skin gleamed, an obscene and horrible contrast to the other side of his head, where a heavy mane of wheat-ripe hair fell. Lexi had told me that it was kept so by the Black Mage's command, in order to better display the tattoo inked above my brother's ear.

"Now will you tell me about your life in Merenwyn?"

"Not yet."

Mouth pulled down in a faint half frown, my twin studied Anu-the-wonder-bitch through the window. She, in turn, was favoring us with a piercing, unstinting stare. *It's unnerving, the way she doesn't blink.* The little brown wolf sat alone, ears pointed toward us, Ralph's chain half buried in her fur.

"Can she understand English?" I asked Lexi.

"No," he replied. "She speaks Merenwynian and wolf,

and that is all. But I expect she will learn it quickly. She seemed adept enough at Court."

"I hate her." The words, venom-dripped, gushed out of me. Flushing, I looked down at my plate. Shreds of a paper napkin formed a haystack by it. "Why did you let him bring her?" I asked in a low voice.

"She would have been abused in Merenwyn. This is where she belongs."

Gee, thanks, Lexi.

"You really are bonded to him, then?" he asked.

"We said the words, but—" I lifted my shoulders and let them drop. "But technically, Trowbridge may have been semiconscious when he said his part."

Lexi picked at something on his arm. "If I asked you now, would you leave here? Tonight? Right now?"

"Stay, I can explain." That's what My One True Thing said.

For once, you better say the right thing, Trowbridge.

I lifted Merry off my neck, placing her near her own saucer of maple syrup, which earned me the display of a double pulse of golden light. "What is the Safe Passage?" I asked, hoping to change the subject.

"It's supposedly a secret portal from this world to the Fae's." Lexi stared broodingly at Merry. "One that was never closed and wasn't keyed to reject Were blood."

"Do you know where it is?" I pulled Merry and saucer closer to me.

"That's what I told Trowbridge."

"Then . . ." Hurt welled and my voice broke when I asked, "If you knew its location, why didn't you come home?" I watched him, hoping for a cue, a reason, an explanation—Goddess, curse it, I'd have taken a lie. "If your life was bad, why didn't you just come back?"

He rubbed his face with both of his hands, then muttered into his palms, "Who said my life was bad?"

"Does every half-breed wear a tattoo like that?"

My brother lifted his gaze to mine. "I didn't know how to summon any portal until a few days ago. And I needed an amulet." He leaned forward, eyes demanding that I understand. "For once, the stars aligned for me. I found a record of the song. I couldn't believe my eyes. I turned the page, and there it was. Music. Lyrics. Everything I needed. Then the Son of Lukynae—"

"You mean Trowbridge."

"I mean the wolf whom the Raha'ells have elevated to some sort of mythic hero status." He sniffed and wiped his nose. "The Court considers your mate as big a threat to its race as we are to his."

"Trowbridge."

"The one and only." My brother could nod and shake his head at the same time. "He might have one or two problems reintegrating with the Creemore Weres tomorrow. He's lost his veneer of civilization. His wolves may have regrets in the morning. Maybe even now, as we speak."

He's out on a run with them. Alone, with only Cordelia for backup.

"Tell me more about the Raha'ells," I said sharply.

"Of the three packs of Merenwyn Weres, they are the fiercest. I'd never venture into the woods they claim as their territory without a full company of my men. The Raha'ells know no pain. No fear. And they heal—too fast. You have to get them . . ." He stopped, perhaps belatedly realizing that he was dropping bombs like a foulmouthed hooker at a Tupperware party.

Lexi braced his hands on the table to stand. "I need a pick-me-up."

"You just had one," I said automatically. But my brain was busy. *My brother has men. He hunts wolves.* And he kept flicking hooded glances at Merry.

I put her back around my neck, stomach tightening.

Lexi picked up the shreds of my paper napkin and balled them in his fist. "In Merenwyn they keep the maple syrup and honey in beautiful pottery, and it's served with much ceremony. Each diner has his own servant, and they pour your choice into your wine goblet."

And for fun, they tattoo half-breeds.

"I used to watch them eat at the long table and tell my belly to be quiet." On his way to the kitchen, Lexi checked on the ferret, who'd inexplicably chosen to go back into the mage's bag for a snooze. "She's curled up in a ball around my other shirt." Anger flattened his mouth. "He's worked her for days. Never letting her rest."

"They kept you hungry?" I repeated, in a hushed voice. *My brother, my twin.*

Chapter Thirteen

"Every servant is a little hungry." Lexi opened a couple of cabinets before he found the garbage. Then, tossing in my handful of napkin confetti, he added, "The morning I discovered that I could see magic, I knew I finally had something worth bargaining with." He shook his head. "I practiced on the sly at first. And discovered that I could steal it, too—but that's not as useful as you might expect. I can't hold it for long. Eventually it always seeps out of me."

His black fitted undershirt pulled free of his belt as he arched his back in an enormous stretch. "Magic has a scent to me. I can track it using my nose, and once I'm close enough to it, I can see it—if I clear my eyes of all distraction, I can see its shine."

I thought about that for a second, making circles in the bottom of my own bowl with my syrup-drenched piece of bread. "Wouldn't admitting that have been dangerous?"

"To anyone else but the Black Mage, yes." Cradling the knapsack like a baby, Lexi eased carefully back down on the seat. "But he was quick to realize that my gift could warn him of danger. I could warn him of *any* danger. In less time than it takes to birth a king, I went from eating kitchen scraps to eating at the long table."

In Threall, a sinister red heart winked from the interior

of the Black Mage's deep purple soul light. "Did the Black Mage raise you? Take care of you?"

"I didn't need anyone to raise me after that first week in Merenwyn."

"What did you do for him?"

A quick shrug of the shoulders. "Whatever he ordered me to do." Then he knuckled his lip, and looked away. "Recently, most of my time has been spent working on the Old Mage's Book of Spells."

Fae Stars. To hear the book mentioned so casually, in this realm. I wiped my syrup-sticky fingers on a napkin, sorely tempted to tell Lexi that I'd seen the heavy tome with my own eyes. Instead, I feigned ignorance.

"Who is the Old Mage?"

Lexi snaked a careful hand into the bag. "Shh, rest easy, rest easy, I just need to get my—" He winced, and then carefully pulled out his reserve of the Fae go-go juice. "From what I've heard, the Old Mage was the last of the truly great wizards before he got himself into trouble and ended up with the choice of either putting himself into an eternal coma—the Sleep Before Death—or being buried in the ground to his neck."

"What exactly did he do?"

In reply, Lexi held up his silver flask. "He created this and it led to civil war."

"Sun potion led to war?"

"It changed everything in Merenwyn," said Lexi as he unscrewed the cap and placed it by his plate. "Before the old man found a way to extract the magic of the sun from the Pool of Life, the wolves in the Fae realm kept to their packs, their own territories, and their own kind. They were, in many respects, more animal than man."

"That seems harsh." I watched my twin fold a piece of salami and eat it in one gulp.

Lexi shrugged and swallowed. "Not if you take into consideration the fact that there are more full moons in the Fae realm and that Weres there spend a lot more time as wolves than the packs do here." He paused to take an appreciative sniff of the contents of his flask as if it were a very fine spirit, not a nearly colorless liquid. "Then the Old Mage's daughter fell in love with the leader of the Raha'ells, and she bore him a son named Lukynae. Elorna lasted ten winters, maybe twelve, among them and then she came back with her child. No one knew where exactly she'd been—the Old Mage had come up with a story rationalizing her absence that most of the Court had swallowed. When she pleaded for his help to hide her son's birthright, he went into his den and came out months later with the spell for sun potion."

I'll bet good money that my brother doesn't know that the edge of the Old Mage's sleeve is more frayed on his right wrist than his left.

"To the Royal Court, a wolf amounts to a subspecies," he continued, oblivious. "But with just one measure of this stuff, taken before a full moon, a Were can ignore the call of the moon. He doesn't have to transform into his wolf . . . and his secret can remain a secret."

"But a Were needs to release his wolf."

"Not true. In my world—" He caught himself and rephrased it. "Today in Merenwyn, few Weres answer the moon's call."

Lexi's mouth turned down as he stared at the flask in his hand. "Lukynae was the first to be offered the choice to hide his wolf. He could have continued taking his sun potion before every full moon, and no one would have known who or what he was."

"But Lukynae chose to release his wolf."

"Even ten years among the Raha'ells was enough to leave its imprint. When Lukynae grew up, he stole the spell and left the Court, and suddenly, the Fae could no longer count on trapping wolves during full moons. And worse, tribes that had previously acted as separate packs began functioning as one rebel group led by a man called Lukynae."

Lexi lifted a shoulder. "Eventually the Royal Court discovered the Old Mage's treason. They appropriated his spell for sun potion—which created a new class of servants—and sentenced him to the Sleep Before Death."

"Servants? You're confusing me. I got the impression that the Raha'ells lived in the hills."

"You know that after the war between the Fae and the wolves of Merenwyn, a treaty was signed."

"Yes, the Treaty of Brelland. All but one pack of wolves signed it and accepted exile to this realm. Which confuses the hell out of me because you keep talking about three packs."

"The Kuskadors chose to remain and submit to subjugation to the Fae rather than accept exile. They were tied too closely to their farms to leave."

"Then what is this about the Raha'ells—"

"Most of them were captured and exiled with Lukynae. But some escaped before the net fell and took to the hills. They've bred over time. There are not a lot of them, but there are enough to be a nuisance." A bitter smile narrowed his mouth. "They're rebels, and they must be hunted to the ground."

He lifted the flask, his gaze on Anu. "She was raised as a Kuskador house servant."

"You drink a lot of that stuff."

"No more than I need." My brother's body tensed up, anticipation poised for the moment, then he tilted back his head and swallowed. A pause to savor it. "Anyhow, the old man hasn't got much longer. I've seen his body." Lexi's eyes fluttered closed for a moment, then he continued, his voice dreamy. "They keep what's left of the Old Mage in a special room in one of the older wings of the castle. His bed is high on a dais, and the bedding's made from the finest silk." A ghost of frown. "He's got long white hair and his eyes are half open—that gave me a scare when I entered the room. The old man's in some sort of coma. If he was aware of me, he didn't show it. I waved my hand in front of his face and he didn't even blink." Lexi absently rubbed his jaw, using the backs of his fingers. One long stroke, then another.

Lexi had found his own way to self-soothe.

He looked at me with drugged dismay. "I wouldn't want to live like that. Neither alive nor dead. He's lost most of his toes and fingers. They look like they've been chewed on by rats."

I pushed the bread around the bottom of my plate, sopping up the syrup, while thinking about wind-nibbled trees in Threall.

My brother wiped his mouth. "It's made my job easier."

"How?"

"Before he went to his sleep, the Old Mage put protection spells on every page of his spell book."

Yes, and he forced a young mystwalker to serve his life sentence with him.

"Those wards make tinkering with his incantations dangerous and reading them next to impossible," said Lexi. "And it's made me practically indispensable to the Black Mage. I'm custom-made for his needs—the thief who can see magic." He flexed his hand, a self-mocking expression twisting his features. "The Old Mage is on his last legs. And once he's gone, all the wards he placed on the book will crumble." Lexi rubbed his chest, smiling with eyes that suddenly looked content and slumberous. "It must have pleased the Old Mage to imagine his spells blowing up in his assistant's face—I heard that they didn't get along. Too bad he couldn't live forever."

"But you're working on the book," I said slowly.

Lexi's head bobbed languidly. *Crap, he's wasted.*

"I can see the lock right on the page—as if the magic were layered over it like a gossamer veil," he said slowly, pride swelling in his voice. "All I have to do is figure out how to lift it free. I study the edges, figure how thick it is, and then I steal it. My talent gives the Black Mage total access to whatever is on the page. With me by his side, he looked powerful." An ugly smile. "But now, his true colors will show."

Helzekiel's ambition and greed?

Lexi's gaze was heavy-lidded, his eyes glazed. It both-

ered me to see him like that. Yeah, he'd just come home.
He had a right to celebrate in his own way. But I didn't like
it. Even if part of me wondered if being tanked on sun potion was any worse than some of the local boys getting together for a case of Creemore Springs beer.

My twin slumped a little lower into his chair.

I pretended to be preoccupied with sopping up every
drizzle of syrup while my mind spun around the answer to
that puzzler. Casually, I asked, "You feeling better now?"

"The buzz doesn't last anymore." Lexi frowned at the
moon, then reached for the cord to the blinds. "Not like it
used to, anyhow."

"There are no other amulets over in Merenwyn that
will open a portal, right? Right, Lexi?" I watched him
fumble with the sides of the carefully pressed curtains.
"Stop tugging them like that. All you have to do is unhook
the tieback."

Lexi gave up on the curtains and threw back his head in
a huge yawn.

"Only one that I know of and it's held in the Royal
Vault. The Queen's crown jewels have less protection," he
said. "My mage's going to be shit out of luck because his
spell-catcher has flown away, and the Old Mage's Book of
Spells is going to crumble to dust before he reasons out
how to break the wards on the page he wants."

Don't call him your mage.

My brother's eyes drooped to half-mast, but still, I knew
his gaze was fixed on my hands, as I carefully cleaned off
Merry with a napkin. A thought came to me, and I froze.

"Lexi," I said. "What page?"

"Huh?"

"You said the page he wants—is there a page about
amulets?"

He favored me with a slow smile. "Amulets, and portals, and everything else."

"The Safe Passage, too?"

"You ask a lot of questions, runt," he said, studying the
ferret.

*What would happen if the Black Mage were able to lift
those wards? Would he come here? Would he*—"Lexi,
there's no way he could lift the ward off the page without
you?"

"He'd be risking destroying it." He flipped his hair back
over his shoulder with a languor that set my teeth on edge
and then stretched his arms along the back of the seat.
"The Black Mage's time is coming. No matter what he
thinks. I don't care how many mystwalkers he discovers."

He leaned his head back. Two minutes from passing
out.

"He's training mystwalkers?" I asked casually as Merry
shifted inside my blouse.

A slow nod. "He's always so optimistic when he finds
one . . ."

"How many are there in Merenwyn?" When he didn't
answer, I kicked him and yelled, "Lexi!"

He stirred and favored me with a heavy frown. "Stop
shouting."

I repeated my question.

"They're all dead except for the one he's training now.
And that never goes well." He yawned. "It makes him look
bad, you know? The Old Mage was really good at training
his mystwalkers." Then, with a contented sigh, "He's so
fucked."

"How?" Tension set my teeth to the ragged edge of my
thumbnail.

"The Court hasn't got a seasoned mystwalker and his
apprentices keep dying on him." He rubbed his chin on his
shoulder, then looked at me with a sly smile. "And now,
he's having a hard time finding new recruits. Every time
he hears about some kid who walks in dreams, he sends
me out, but most of the time, it turns out to be nothing. Just
some villager starting a false rumor. Maybe the talent for
it is dying out among the Fae." He shook his head. "Good
riddance. No one should be able to fuck with your mind
like that."

I tore off my nail and spat it out. "How does he train them?"

"I don't want to talk about them anymore," he mumbled.

"Just—" I reached over and gave him a prod. "Answer that last question."

"Mind exercises." Lexi tried to rub his nose, and missed. "The hard part isn't teaching them to cut their soul free from their body—it's getting them to return home. He sends them to Threall and they never come back."

Lexi's eyes drifted shut.

My mouth opened and then slowly closed.

Four hours later, I found myself in my bed, listening to Lexi search for a comfortable position in the bunk over my head. He'd taken a long nap on that narrow dinette seat— mouth open, neck bent awkwardly—and had roused only when I scolded the ferret for key theft. After rescuing his new pet, he'd wandered down to the bathroom. There, he'd stayed in the shower until the hot-water tank was dry and the ferret had knocked over every single thing on the counter. Then I'd heard the medicine cabinet open and close, the drawers slide open, my brush (or for that matter, possibly Cordelia's) clatter in the sink.

And all the time I'd tracked the sounds of his snooping, I marveled that he was here, alternated with worrying about his reliance on the happy juice and the curl of his lip when he'd spoken about mystwalkers.

I'd wanted to blurt out, "I'm one! I'm a mystwalker."

But I hadn't because I kept thinking about the look of disgust on his face and the expression of fear on my mum's when she'd begged me not to tell anyone I was a mystwalker. "*Not anyone. Not even your brother,*" she'd warned me.

And now my mystwalker-hating brother was above me—he'd come out of the shower wearing the pants he'd worn before and a braid, fastened with one of Cordelia's expensive hair elastics. I'd been right about the muscles. My brother's upper body bordered on the impossible. A whole bunch of "ceps"—bi, tri, whatever—had been added onto his former stick-boy body.

He got ab, and I got flab.

I couldn't find a good position in bed, either. A worry festered in me that he'd fall asleep before me, and somehow, I'd end up pulled into one of his dreams. That concern wasn't a new one—I used to dread being dream-napped every night back when we slept in adjoining bedrooms, and then there had been a thin wall between us. And now there was only a mattress between us. Not even a wall. Worse was this stark fear—what if he turned around and asked, "What are you doing in my dream?"

And finally, of course, there was the other issue—the Trowbridge-scented bitch outside. I had two problems with the little brown wolf. Problem one: I wanted to kill her. Problem two: my instincts—usually guaranteed to lead me into trouble—were preaching caution. Yeah, yeah. I know romantic hogwash can hijack a girl's intelligence and innate caution.

But let's not forget I'm part Were.

My wolf was talking to me. *Stay*, she kept repeating. *Stay*.

Sometimes you have to listen to your inner-bitch. Besides, there was a part of me (a huge, honkin' part) that totally wanted the pink, heart-shaped box of chocolates. It kept going back to that moment when Trowbridge's shaking fingers were pressed against my lips.

Impossible to resist dwelling on the tremor in his hands. The conflict in his eyes.

Wait until tomorrow for the explanation.

There has *to be one.*

I sighed as my twin sat up. Again. Thunk. *Yeah, the ceiling is exactly where it was the last time you hit it.* "Totally-undecipherable-string-of-Merenwynian-curse-words!" he exclaimed. Another whack of the pillow, another shake of its polyester fill. Another thump as his body collapsed back down.

I shouldn't have let him have that shower. Especially not with the ferret. He came back out of the bathroom more alert, smelling of shampoo, and somehow, indefinably Lexi again. Now the ferret was out cold, curled into a ball in a nest of one of Cordelia's sweaters by his feet. It smelled of lemon and oranges, too.

"Lexi," I whispered. "You know Mum loved you as much as me, right?"

Worry and trouble curled around me.

Silence from my brother. A quiet, thoughtful, pregnant one broken only by the sound of a cap being unscrewed. I listened to my brother swallow another mouthful, before he sealed the flask again. He lay back with a sigh. Then I smelled something different over the various layers in the room. A faint tendril of scent—woods and ferns. I inhaled sharply, trying to pinpoint it.

It was nice, whatever it was.

"Hell," said my brother.

"Yeah?"

"Be careful with Trowbridge in the morning. They gave him sun potion for the moon before last. He wasn't able to change into his wolf, and the urge to be a wolf, to run under the moon . . . Once it's thwarted like that . . ."

I strained my ears. Did he sigh?

"The need builds up inside the beast. When it's finally allowed release, it has a hard time sinking back down inside the man. Trowbridge will still be feral in the morning. Even if he stands on two feet, not four."

Great.

"Lexi?"

"Yeah?"

"Whatever happened to the original Lukynae?"

"He was captured and tried. Since they didn't want him to become a martyr, they sent him into exile."

I struggled to remember what Mum had told us about

the Weres in Merenwyn. Then I gasped, and said, "Do you mean—"

"Yes. They sent Lukynae to this realm. Which is why the Raha'ells call Trowbridge—"

"The Son of Lukynae."

"Now go to sleep, runt," he murmured. "I'll keep watch."

I knew it.

I knew it, I knew it, I *knew* it.

I should have guarded myself from sleep. Pinched my arm when my lids felt heavy. Squirmed out of my sleeping bag and taken a cold shower. Maybe bounced up my sugar level with a liter of Coke and a Kit Kat. Too late. I could feel that strangeness, that sense of being inside a foreign skin. My eyes were open, but the things I saw, the way my gaze roved and held—that's not the way I look at the world. Not the way I examine a place, an object, a scene. I'd been dream-napped, caught in the web of a drowsing Fae's memory.

But not, I thought, Mad-one's—or the Old Mage's. That nightmare always played to its miserable end in the same room.

The trees are huge, massive. Merenwyn, then. But whose dream? Not Lexi's. I remember sharing his dreams from his perspective—his lens view was always tighter, focused on something with the intent to seize. Not this searching, frantic hip-hop from one focal point to another.

Whose eyes am I seeing through?

Concentrate. Listen. See. Dark woods through the slats of a wooden fence. *Not a fence,* I realized as he or she tilted their head. *A pen.* With wooden bars for walls, a dirt floor, and stars and a moon for a ceiling. The Fae stared at the latter for a long time—it was a brilliant yellow-orange, and so full and close it felt like it was going to fall and smother us with its weight.

I hate the moon.

Then the Fae pivoted, small fists still curved around the bars.

A girl, I thought. Small fingers. Slightly chapped. Nails chewed down to the quick.

"Merciful Goddess," I heard her whisper, "don't let them eat my body before I'm dead." Her gaze roamed, offering me a glimpse of an elaborate grandstand—the type you see in period movies, where knights tilt lances and ladies favor them with secret smiles. Behind that, a palisade. Many smooth pine trunks, stripped of bark, aligned vertically. The fence of wood went as far as she could see—too tall to scale.

She's in a pen within a pen.

The girl swung her head, and I realized that she was not alone in her cage. A large male lay facedown, unmoving and half hidden by shadow. His calves were muscled swells below the tattered edge of his trousers, and his torso—though striped with blood—was well developed.

He's been lashed.

She watched him for a count of three, then turned back to press her forehead to the bars. Her breath rasped in and out of her chest. I studied the woods as she did and was rewarded for my vigilance when a shadow parted itself from a tree. And then I understood, before a howl pierced the night, exactly what she feared.

Wolves. Lots of them. More than twenty, less than fifty.

One of them broke from the cover of the trees and loped along the forest's edge, ears pricked forward, nose lifted to scent the wind. He stopped and turned. A flash of amber eyes telegraphed a predator's message: "I know you're there. Soon."

I want to wake up now.

There was no horn. No general call. Just the clattering of swords and the drum of feet. The guards lined themselves up in front of the grandstand's lowest tier then stood at attention, their weapons crossed over their chests.

The fine ladies of the Court entered on the cue of laughter. They mounted the stairs, filing into the seating on the second tier. All of them wore light gray cloaks of the same material and weight. The girl's gaze—and thus mine—clung to one woman whose beauty was carefully cultivated. Uncomfortable under our scrutiny, the lady glanced at the empty seat beside her and then took particular interest in the arrangement of her sleeve.

She will not rescue you.

Next, the men. Again, wearing cloaks. *Why?* They filled the topmost tier by order of seating. Most wore a look of haughty privilege, but it was the fifth man who caused a chill to run along my spine. *How well this realm fits him.* The Black Mage's hands were long, and white, and when they rested on the arms of his chair, they hung over the edge slightly curled, like the talons of a hawk as it cruised the sky looking for defenseless prey.

He has such pitiless eyes.

Our gaze moved along the rest, indifferent, searching for—

Lexi.

My brother stood aside from the rest, on a landing between the first and second tiers. Wearing the same bowler hat and boots. No cloak. His expression blank, neither filled with anticipation nor boredom. Beside him, a lever. Our gaze moved from it to follow the pulleys, the hemp rope, the line strung between the grandstand and our pen.

A male moan, low in the throat, from behind us. We spun—so fast, the bars a passing blur—as the man in our pen rolled onto his back. His foot scraped the earth, his leg bent at the knee.

Carefully—oh so slowly—we bent.

Our glance flitted anxiously between him and the dirt floor. A quick impression of small white hands—fluttering like frightened doves—searching, patting, feeling the ground for—ah! A small rock. She folded it in her fist.

"Merciful Goddess," I heard her murmur. "Please let my aim be true."

I woke from the dream with a gasp, heart hammering against the walls of my chest. Merry warmed against my breast.

"You okay?" Lexi asked. "Bad dream?"

I thought of the pen within the pen and my brother standing beside a lever. Whose dream had I been in? One of my own? Created by my anxieties? "Yes, I had a nightmare. Did I wake you?"

"No," he said. "I've been thinking about a way out of all this."

What did he mean by that?

Out of what? He was home. Trowbridge was home.

"Get some sleep," he added. "I'll stay awake."

I rolled to my side. Merry stiffened in the cup of my bra and then went limp. I placed a cold hand over her. She issued up a spark of warmth, the comfort of which made my eyelids feel heavy. But despite it, my brother and I were both half awake when the trailer's door creaked open an hour later.

Chapter Fourteen

"What in God's name has been done to my front door?" Cordelia asked, each word a miniature iceberg in the sea of her cold wrath.

"Not now, woman," grumbled Harry. "Move back for the Alpha."

Anticipation held the air captive in my chest, told my heart to get ready, get ready. *Please, Trowbridge, find the right thing to say. Just this once. Make me believe that we can work this out.*

Crash! Door met floor.

My eyes flew open as his hero leap into my trailer ended in a four-pawed skid. *That can't be right,* I thought, tilting my head. Nails clicked on linoleum as My One True Thing made his way past my kitchen. *Oh Goddess. Karma must be clutching her sides, bent over for a belly laugh. He hadn't changed back into his human form at morning light? For the rest of my life, I'll be buying dog chow. Making sure he's had his shots. Picking up—*

Another dip of the trailer, as another set of claws entered my home.

The bitch was with him? In *my* home? My hands tightened into fists on my pillow. Trowbridge's scent was sharper than ever, woods, wild, and him—that thing I could never find a name for that always stirred me right down at gut level, and perhaps a little below that, as well. It floated down the short corridor toward me. *You, me, us,* it said, seeping under my bedroom door, speaking of destiny, and futures, and all of that stuff that I couldn't stand to think about—not *now* with Anu's stench slyly slithering in the wake of his. I squirreled deep into my sleeping bag until there was nothing above its open mouth but my tangled rope of hair. Yet still—*still*—a finger of his scent tunneled through the zipper's teeth to touch my skin, soft as a kiss. A film of him was on my hair, an invisible lick of him on my flushed cheek.

A pause. *What's he waiting for?* I peeked through the slit in my bag. *Ah, the bedroom door.* That shouldn't represent a problem. Look what he did to the last one.

Hurry up, Balto. Come rescue me.

A long, impatient scratch down the faux-wood panel. The handle turned and— Bang! My bedroom door swung back with a thud on my closet.

Lo, the citadel has been breached.

The king of the Creemore wolfpack entered my boudoir slowly. I resealed my eyes and made like I was invisible. Just part of the mattress. A lump of something that should not be disturbed. Unless, of course, you were planning on placing a paw on the chest of said lump and pledging your eternal undying love with a heartfelt howl.

Dog breath warmed my face. Yup. Right through the sleeping bag. "Let me out, let me out, let me out," whined my inner-Were, doing a bum-wiggle inside my belly.

An impatient huff in my ear. Almost immediately echoed by a feminine dog whine.

Fuck you and Toto, too.

"Who's the bitch?" I asked through a double layer of poly-loft fill and nylon.

He didn't answer—maybe because he was all Alpha-furry and *a freakin' wolf*—and instead began a rude inventory of my aromatic history with his wet nose. Snuffle, snuffle down at my legs, pausing at my crotch. *Hell, no.* I curled myself into a protective ball. A double sniff over my hip, zeroing in on the exact place bruised by the chains. A huff, as he followed my curved form upward, pausing at the dip for my waist, and then over for a tour of the area where my boobs spilled above my tightly crossed arms. He spent some time there, during which sister-wolf paced inside me, leaking ho-hormones.

"He's still feral," said my Lexi, from the bunk above me. "Don't make any sudden moves near him."

Crap. As dream reunions go, this one was about as successful as the 2010 Spice Girls World Tour. I had a bitch in my house and it wasn't me. My brother was up in the cheap seats, critiquing my every move. My mate was panting-hot and happy to see me, but—I cringed as Trowbridge's wolf inhaled a little too sharply, and sneezed out a few billion dust mites—that happy thought was offset by the fact he was going to need a dog license.

My mate rubbed his muzzle against my mattress.

Not another word, Lexi.

Then the Alpha of Creemore did something sort of . . . nice, and I forgot all about my twin, and a smidgen about the bitch that waited in the hall. The big gray wolf pushed his nose through the open mouth of my sleeping bag and tunneled his snout toward me. His soft, warm nose nuzzled the nape of my neck. Rather sweetly for a savage, wild, and feral thing. And he kept doing it, until the instinct to bop him on his black nose turned to something boneless and accepting. Oh Fae Stars . . . worse than accepting. I hunched my shoulders as my jubilant inner-wolf sent oh-yum sparkles of happiness up my spine.

The bunk over my head creaked.

"All you have to do is ask, and I'll clear this room," said my brother. "Let me deal with him."

Oh, for a magic wand. I slit my eyes open a fraction. Trowbridge's gaze was fixed on Lexi in a way that spelled war. His rigid tail fat and quivering. With a sigh, I slid my hand free from my safe cocoon to touch his pelt and said (in what I still maintain to this day was a nice, soft, pacifying whisper), "This would work better if you weren't a wolf."

At the sound of my voice, Anu-the-mate-stealer poked her canine head through my door. I sat up fast and snapped, "What is *that* bitch doing in my room?" Possibly it was my tone, or the way I heaved myself upward—whatever. My distress jarred the exhausted ferret back to life with a start and a squeak of alarm. Look, as squeaks go, it was *tiny*. Nothing more than a ferret's version of WTF?

But that, as they say, was that.

Wolf-girl leaped for the little animal, jaws stretched like a bear trap. Then it was a blur—a Marx Brothers scene of utter chaos—as my brother shot off his bunk, hands out reaching for an interception, and the ferret ran for its life.

Enough. I pulled the covers back over my head.

Well, as it happens, Trowbridge didn't give a rat's ass about his bitch, my brother, or the freakin' ferret. He cut to the chase, because he's an Alpha at heart, and always will be. Without a warning huff or a "pardon me," he grabbed a mouthful of sleeping bag and hauled me and it right off my bed. Thud! I gasped as hip and elbow met linoleum then winced as someone—I'm thinking it was Lexi—stepped on my hair. Didn't stop my guy. With dogged determination, he kept right on backing up out of the room, hauling Hedi-and-bag down the hall, around the bend in the wall for the kitchen—ouch—past the debris left by the shattered door—ow, ow, ow—and right out of the trailer.

And that's how Trowbridge coaxed his mate from the safety of her silver bug.

I fought with the zipper but I could only wriggle one arm free.

"Hey!" I yelled. "Knock it off!"

Either his wolf's linguistic skills were limited or he didn't take well to commands when he was on four paws. The Alpha of Creemore kept going, ruthlessly dragging me and my red sleeping bag right across the dirt scrubland Cordelia had taken to calling our front yard, then around the big old dead tree that me and Lexi used to climb, and finally down the path leading to the pond.

How sweet. He was carrying me home. Kind of like a newspaper from the end of the driveway or a bone dug up from the neighbor's garden.

Not so fast, Lassie. I saw a thick root and grabbed it.

The big, gray wolf kept going, tail high.

So did the sleeping bag.

A quick twisting moment later, I was shucked free of it.

Forehead resting on my extended arm, I took stock. My inner-bitch's ho-hormones were flooding me with feral heat, and frankly, it was making my stomach puke-queasy. Beyond that, there was definitely going to be a bruise on my hip (the corner of the kitchen cabinet), another on my right butt cheek (top step), and one high up on my shoulder (bottom step). Also, a graze on my ribs (friction from the bag's zipper), and a small patch of road rash on the inside of my forearm (inflicted when we hit that smudge of gravel).

On the other hand, I was no longer being dragged willy-nilly down the garden path.

Merry squirmed her way out from the crush of my cleavage to find a lookout perch on my shoulder blade. Her little ivy feet prickled my back when a series of urgent, excited barks and hoarse shouts erupted from the inside of the trailer.

"No!" yelled my brother.

I listened with half an ear to the sharp crack of crockery, soon followed by a hailstorm of small thuds, pretty much on top of each other.

That had to be the bowl of oranges.

"Leave the ferret!" shouted Lexi from our home. "Ow! You little—"

"Hey, she's just curious!" hollered Biggs over the barking. "She's not going to—"

Another crash.

And that was either the toaster or the kettle.

"Get that animal out of the house!" roared Cordelia.

Some mornings should come with big, fat, round, red reset buttons.

"Rolling," I informed Merry before I did just that. She

scrambled then held on to a pinch of jersey as I did a quick pelvic tilt to adjust my wadded-up T-shirt. Then we lay there, squinting against the brightness of the rising sun, listening to things break.

What was that old saying? Come the morning, all shall be well?

Ha, ha, and ha.

I raised myself up onto an elbow.

Trowbridge-the-wolf was busy nosing my empty sleeping bag as if it were a scent catalogue of my naughty dalliances.

At my huff of total disbelief, he turned.

Last night, in the dim gloom of the moonlit field, it had been difficult to get a sense of just how relatively large an animal his wolf was. But now as he approached me, Alpha-proud, massive head lifted in inquiry, the waist-high weeds lining the path seemed to shrink in size.

My wolf, moaned my inner-Were.

Oh shut up.

His scent investigation of my person started with my foot.

I pushed myself into a sitting position because Hedi Peacock-Stronghold had some things she needed to say. "Trowbridge," I began, with remarkable civility considering he was sniffing my instep like it was an item on an exotic menu that he was as yet undecided about.

"Trowbridge!" I repeated.

This time, the gray wolf responded to his name with a piece of canine articulation that could have meant anything from "nice pedicure" to "I'll pencil in a chat for sometime later next week." Then, quite uncaring of my affronted glare, he resumed his ruthless examination of my body.

Snuffle, snuffle, snuffle.

I leaned to the right and then to the left in an effort to avoid it. But it didn't matter how I squirmed or pushed at him, his big, inquisitive nose still nuzzled my hair, dampened my T-shirt, and found the pulse at the side of my throat.

He was, after all, an *Alpha* male.

"Enough!" I said, sharper than I meant to. "We need to talk. One paw means yes, two paws means no, okay?"

Blue eyes, rimmed with black, studied me.

As I gazed into them, doubt—like cold water on bare toes—washed over me. Those eyes were almost the same hue as those of the guy whom I'd shoved through the portal, but within their icy depths, there was no warming spark of recognition, no comet of light brightening that sea of azure. Whoever—whatever—lived behind those eyes was not precisely Trowbridge. And from the looks of it, that half-wild entity was as perplexed about me as I was about it.

Eight hours with a tail had changed the balance of who he was.

"Trowbridge? You in there?" I asked. "Can you understand me?"

Nothing. No paw lifted in greeting. No head tilt of inquiry.

Mine, whined my Were, impatient with my fumbling.

I drew up my knees and clasped them to my chest while I considered this new spin on the Hedi Wheel of Disaster. The sun was shining and I had a wolf for a mate. His paw was larger than my hand. Dried blood had caked the fur on his muzzle and powerful chest. And he far outweighed me—not surprising when one took into account the fact that he was a solid wall of fur and muscle.

"It's going to be a bitch to search your coat for ticks," I muttered, feeling grim.

And that's when the sleeping volcano inside me started spewing ash and fireballs.

As far as my inner-bitch was concerned, my off-the-cuff comment was tantamount to the squirrel perched on the fence; the cat sunning itself on her front steps; the Yorkie terrier taking a piss on her shrubbery.

She was *done*.

Too many months she'd sat in my gut, being jostled by my Fae, kept belly-low by my constant checks and counterchecks. Too long she'd waited for the return of what had been promised her. Trowbridge's wolf was hers—to claim, to protect, to fight for—and no one, including me, was going to stop her from trying to do so.

With a howl of pain that hurt my heart, she tore into me, attacking me from the inside in a flurry of frantic pawing. *Let me out!* She fought—claws slashing—utterly heedless of the damage she was inflicting to our shields.

Let me out!

I bowed over my belly, fighting to contain her.

Want to run! Want to be! Want, want, want . . .

Trowbridge placed a heavy paw on my thigh.

I looked up at him, my eyes flooding. *Don't you see? She's tearing me apart.*

She's mine, the wolf's cool gaze replied.

I hurt. She hurt. We hurt.

Then again, so briefly, I saw a flash of the big picture—all nicely assembled and coherent—slide by me. I'd struggled to grab on to it for months—no, not months, years—and there it was, shooting past me, the diagram to my life, the snapshot of my problems.

But it went by so quickly; I didn't have time to grab it with both hands. All I got was the barest fragment of the whole truth. And I wished, oh, how I wished, I hadn't. In a bitter moment of utter clarity, I saw the thing I didn't want to see. The picture viewed from the other side—and from that viewpoint, the self-restraint that I'd so heroically forced on myself no longer looked like self-discipline; it looked like self-loathing.

A cruelty.

To her. To me.

Even my Fae recognized it. "Release her," she said. "Else we will break apart."

And so we did. Mortal-me and Fae-me stepped back, and we let the animal within us run free.

Yes! Sister-wolf cried, shaking loose the strangling choke collar. Her essence surged through us, and with it came her emotions. Not muted. Not dampened. The purest of pleasures—canine joy—rose in our chest. Happiness—skin-singing happiness, so pure, so unadulterated, so free. It suspended my breath.

No side thoughts. No doubts. No pauses for logic tests. Just him and her. *At last, at last.*

To touch. To smell. To taste.

Our arms looped around the neck of her beloved wolf, our face pressed itself deep inside his thick, dense pelt, and we knew a happiness that had been denied for too, too long.

Woods, and pine, and sex, and yes—a little bit of blood from the kill.

She knew him to be strong.

She knew him to be hers.

And all was simple and good.

I don't know how long it went on—the stroking of his fur, the inarticulate murmurs of contentment coming from my throat, the rumbles from his, the sense of homecoming that I siphoned from my Were.

But here's a sad fact; sweet things will always dissolve under a hot tongue. In this case, Lexi's. I hadn't noticed that the turmoil inside my silver home had stopped. Or that our wolves' tender reunion was being watched and judged.

"That is a wolf, not your mate." Lexi pushed back his bowler.

Tell me something I don't know.

But I uncoiled my arm from the gray wolf's neck. He gave me a chuff. Which meant more to Anu than me—she began stalking toward me, nape bristling, but Harry checked her with his knee. "No," he said in English. And quite surprisingly, she stopped. Right there, between Biggs and Harry.

I dragged my fingers lightly through Trowbridge's pelt.

"Will he stay like this?"

"No." Lexi stroked his ferret pet. "He'll change when he's ready."

"When will that be?"

My twin turned to gaze at the Trowbridge ridge. "He'll wait till he's home."

THE THING ABOUT WEASE

"No," Lexy spoke for Ferret put. "That'll change when he's ready."

"When will that be?"

My twin turned to peer at the looming cage door. "It'll wait like a hound.

Chapter Fifteen

The Trowbridge house was an old brick Victorian, every ninety-degree angle on the building embellished with a curlicue of wood. Six months isn't long, but it's long enough to make a house appear well and truly abandoned. Paint had begun peeling off its exterior, revealing the yellow brick beneath it, and the grass was mostly of the crab variety.

Something smelled bad.

Trowbridge's four paws were planted on the porch, his impatience telegraphed in his stance. His wolf uttered a sharp, reproving bark at the door. I tried its handle. "It's locked." My stomach twisted at the rank smell seeping through the cracks in the door. "I don't have the key. Does anyone have the—"

"I can send Biggs to the camper to fetch it," Cordelia broke in.

A low, warning rumble from the gray wolf.

"Wait, there's a spare." Biggs lifted a white hanging planter down from its hook, and dug his fingers into the soil around the petrified geranium. "It used to be just—" A couple of cigarette butts fell and rolled down the slanting porch. "Got it," he said.

I stood aside to let Biggs fit the key to the lock, only to

find myself shoved forward by Trowbridge's impatient snout. "Give it to me," I said.

The instant the door swung wide, the stench slapped me hard—a horrible invisible cloud of it—hamburger meat gone bad. Trowbridge's wolf entered first, nose wrinkled, lips curled. Hand covering my nose, I took a step in.

"The light switch is on your left," muttered Biggs.

My hand grazed the wall. Light from the single, weak bulb illuminated the hallway, but didn't penetrate the gloom beyond it. Biggs strode over to the bay windows to yank aside the living room's heavy curtains. The bay windows were reluctant to open, but he and Cordelia forced them up, one by one. That helped, adding light and airflow where there was none before, but not in the way I needed. What I *needed* was for it all to be gone. The foul smell of the dried blood—so strong, so putrid—completely scrubbed out of the air. The shadows banished, or at least tamed. My gaze saw too many of them: a gray mass behind the battered easy chair, a collection of ghouls beyond the overturned table. They waited for Trowbridge and me, memories from that nightmarish spring night that had somehow taken spectral shape.

Goddess, I'd told Biggs to seal the house, but I'd forgotten, hadn't I?

The blood. The gore.

I should have come back and cleaned it myself. Sanitized the room, been brave enough to personally exorcise the ghosts with bleach and paint before the door was sealed from curious eyes.

Part of me rued that, as Trowbridge's wolf padded over to the fireplace. Framed in his father's hearth, he lifted his heavy head up high and let out a howl.

Long, deep, mournful—the call of an Alpha.

My Were flooded mortal-me with sensation. Pleasurable, but not loopy canine joy. This felt raw, and intense, and somehow primordial. It poured into me, almost sexual in feel, but instead of coming from my loins, it came from

her truest core—and its thrill flooded outward, a warm
rush that smothered all the other senses.

The Alpha of Creemore's call to his pack trailed off.

The reply to his summons came the moment Trowbridge lowered his muzzle. One of the Weres waiting outside let out a howl, and almost immediately after that a
female added a long sorrowful note. High and clear, almost a whine. Then another and another. So many voices.
So many individual messages woven into one hymn to
brotherhood.

Tears glazed my eyes as Trowbridge's pack sang him
all the way through his transformation from wolf to man,
their vocalization both mournful and meaningful.

The sound of the gathered pack howling in the daylight
should have made my skin crawl.

But it didn't.

Instead of horror, there was deep comfort; the relief
you get when a terrible pain is finally lifted from you.

Until last summer I'd never been within spitting distance
of a wolf as he reverted back into a biped. Yes, my father
was a Werewolf. But he was also a loving dad, who was
very strict about certain things. "Lock the door behind
me," he'd repeat to my mum as he left for his moon-run.
"Don't open it until I can tell you what day it is." That type
of caution sticks with you. Still, curiosity had chewed at
me. One morning, not long into my tenure as Alpha-in-
residence, I'd crouched behind a spy hole in the cemetery
hedge and watched a wolf turn into a man. Later, Cordelia
had cornered me in the trailer. "There are things you need
to understand," she'd said sternly, her arms folded over her
chest. "Emotionally, it's easier to turn from a person into a
wolf, than to change from a wolf back to a person. We're not
completely human in those minutes following our transformation. What you did this morning was criminally stupid."

"I can hurt you," her eyes had said.

The Alpha of Creemore lay curled on the dusty floor.
Two arms. Two legs. No tail.

Silence fell, and grew.

"Hell, back out of the room as quietly as possible," murmured my brother. I ignored him, staying exactly where I was. Plastered to the inside wall of the living room, heels pressed hard against the baseboards, palms pressed flat.

I couldn't have moved. Not from fear—I'd never been afraid of Trowbridge.

From anticipation.

I didn't give a rat's ass if he wasn't precisely human for the next few minutes. I'd take what I could get, though as I stared at my mate on the floor, part of me wondered what exactly that was. I'd sent a man named Robson Trowbridge through the Gates of Merenwyn. Prior to that, his wolf, though an essential part of him, had only shown itself to me in flashes, like brief glimpses of the red lining on a dark winter coat. But over the space of a night, the fabric of my mate's soul had been turned inside out. I could still see his canine nature in the feral spark of his mortal eyes, in the tilt of his head, in the flare of his nostrils.

I could see other things, too.

Morning light is harsh and unforgiving. *Goddess, he's so old.* Was that fair? Perhaps not. Weres age a trifle slower than humans. Compared to a normal person, I'd hazard a guess that he could pass for his early thirties. But the brackets beside his wide mouth were deeper. And he seemed . . . harder. Leaner. All his former pretty-boy features had been rasped away, until he was bone and sinew. And his eyes—they were set so deeply they were almost sunken. Looking at him, you couldn't help but wonder, what measure of suffering made him so harshly beautiful?

He's suffered . . . But going to Merenwyn was supposed to fix that.

Trowbridge turned his head to study the corner of the room.

The wooden chair they'd bound him to was still there, sitting upright by the overturned table. *Trowbridge's arm secured to the table by silver chains, his mouth bloody, his nose broken. "Don't you do it, Hedi! Don't you tell them!"*

Cold fall air streamed through the bay windows.

My mate was horribly still. He took his time as he gazed at the tableau before him. The chair. The table. The footprints—once bright red, now rusty brown—that circled the chair. Then he slowly spun to face us, and as he did, his dreadlocks rustled and stirred the perfume of deep anger seeping from his skin.

My gaze skittered away, suddenly ashamed, landing on the faded chintz of the easy chair, the dust obscuring the family portrait in the corroded brass frame, and then because—dammit, I'd never been able to tear my eyes from his scorching flame—my eyes flitted back to inventory the rest of the changes. His fisted hand offered no clue to how well his right paw had healed. But the other wounds he'd been given that terrible night—one across each thigh, one high across his chest, one on each wrist—had faded, their scars now invisible. The same couldn't be said of his belly wound—the long thin one, in the seam of which they'd placed a filigree chain. The flesh there had knitted itself back together, but roughly. Where the silver had sunk into his belly, the scar was thick and uneven.

White, too. The type of silvery paleness that's a gift of time's passage.

Just how much time has passed for him?

He'd always been lean, and still could be called so, because his new physique carried nary an ounce of fat. Over the passage of 196 days on my calendar, he'd widened the way a man does over the course of a decade. His shoulders were bulkier, his pecs were like two hillocks of hard clay on top of a rippling ridge of abdominal muscles. Fae Stars, even his navel had been put on a reducing diet. For the life of me, I couldn't recall it looking like that—a shallow divot stretched over a taut belly of muscle. The only thing I recognized on his new and improved body was that vein running down his hip. I followed that familiar road map until my gaze picked up the thin, narrow trail of dark hair just a smidge south of that, and then I followed it like a road traveler following an infallible GPS device, all the way to the darker nest of curls, where his—

Mine, mine, murmured my Were in deep approval.

My cheeks grew hot. My gaze darted back to his face.

Wild man's eyes. A little flicker of one single blue comet did a quick half turn around his dark pupil and then flickered out. He stared at me, with an expression I could only define as a look of distrust.

"Trowbridge?" I said in a little voice.

His brows knitted, then he started across the room, but so very, very slowly and deliberately. One foot placed directly in front of the other. An odd gait—as if he were walking a tightrope—head lowered just the fraction needed to stir fright and trepidation, eyes steady on the target of me.

Sex. The man oozed it. That, and suppressed violence.

His scent reached for me first, as it always had. Stretching out for me, before his hand ever met my flesh, to prepare the way, to brush my skin with invisible, silken fingers. *"Hello, sweetheart. It's me."* That's how I remember it. Soft and light. Teasing. I'd replayed the sensation of it on my skin many a night as I lay in my bunk bed, running my own hand along my hairless arm, trying to reconstruct that wonderful sensation when his scent wrapped itself around me. But the unexpected rawness of it now on my skin was a far cry from my memories. It felt far more solid, as if his personal signature had been cooked over a high heat until it was thick as syrup. Potent, too, with a sexual heat so very different from the coaxing, tender element that I'd marked as Trowbridge's. This essence of him didn't have time for sweet whispers of seduction. It was arrogant and sure of itself. No flattery. No pretty words.

It hit me with the brute force of a linebacker, and my lady parts responded in an unexpectedly sharp contraction of desire. *Well, isn't that just dandy,* I thought, woozily straightening as it wove me into its foreign embrace. *Score one for his team.*

Yes, his eyes replied. And for a second, in the brief curl of his wide mouth and the gleam in his eye, I saw the ghost of the man I'd shoved through the portal. But that faded away all too soon, as this new Trowbridge tilted his head back to inhale deeply.

Again, his nostrils flared.

It felt rude—that intimate assessment of my fuckability in front of others—and in reaction, I clamped my knees together, trying to contain the scent of my desire. My mate paused, mid-step, eyeing my resistance as if he were surprised, and then he began to stalk toward me again, chin up, cheekbones highlighted by the morning light spilling from the window, inhaling my essence without my permission. He came to a full stop in front of me, an arm's reach away. Cocked his head to the side, and just studied my face for a bit. His gaze roamed. My hair. My face. My boobs.

One hot look was all it took for my nipples to bead and my breasts to swell.

His neck moved as he swallowed.

"Don't look directly into his eyes," I heard my brother say, "He's still under the influence of the moon and part wolf."

Seriously, shut up, Lexi.

Trowbridge took a step forward—claiming my personal space as his territory—to prop his arm on the wall above my head. Fuzzy ropes of hair tickled my cheek as he bent his head. I heard him inhale slowly through his nose.

I don't carry your scent anymore.

But I was becoming . . . fragrant. I was wet, and positively aching.

So, there are *two* situations when a Fae exudes her own aroma. Never noticed that before. But then again, I only feel this way around Trowbridge, and usually if he's naked, I am, too. And then it's impossible to separate scents.

There are just the two of us, mixed together into one identity of heat, and flame, and passion.

"Hell." I slanted my eyes to my left. Lexi held out a hand. "Slide away. Come to me, and I will protect you."

Smack. Trowbridge flattened his left hand on the wall between us.

Well, I guess that would be a no. I stood there, trapped in the cradle of his body, quietly luxuriating in the warmth radiating from his arm. Trowbridge's scent wrapped itself around me, now spiced by the musk of his arousal. *Is this what violence and sex smells like? When it's been welded onto the surface of a man?*

I liked it.

Trowbridge had always been an insanely sensual visual feast . . . but now? All the civility had been stripped from him, and what was left was raw male power.

Who knew. I was a back-to-basics girl.

Like for instance—his arm. It was dusted with hair, a little dirty from the grime he'd picked up on the floor during his change, and well, not to overwork a theme, really freakin' well muscled.

My vagina clenched like the buttocks of a cheerleader doing an aerial rah-rah. And suddenly, I was damn glad for the support of the wall because it was fifty-fifty that one of my knees was going to give out.

"Come *now*," said my twin.

Like hell I will.

From the moment my hormones started cranking out the girl pheromones, my inner-Were, my mortal heart, my very DNA—whatever you want to call the sum of my want for Trowbridge—had recognized him as mine. And now here he was. His body arched over mine. His cock full and heavy, its blunt head teasing the folds of the loose cotton T-shirt I wore.

His T-shirt, come to think of it.

"I don't need protection from him," I told my brother, my gaze clinging to Trowbridge's parted lips.

"You don't know what he is," hissed Lexi.

"But I know *who* he is," I said, touching my Trowbridge's face. Oh, I recognized him. He was there, under all that wolf and tangled hair, buried deep. A muscle tensed under my finger as I stroked his skin. "He's Robbie Trowbridge, son of the Alpha of Creemore. He lived in a big yellow house, he drove a Jeep, and he was the most popular guy at St. Hubert's."

The fanwork of lines at the corner of his eyes tightened.

"Some nights, he'd go sit under the tree on the lookout, and play his guitar. He thought he was alone, but he wasn't." A spark of a blue comet circled his pupils. I softened my voice, seducing him close with a low whisper, until his mouth was mere inches from mine. So close.

Kiss me, Trowbridge. Kiss me.

"I was there. Whenever I heard that guitar, I'd sneak out of the house and go find myself a hiding spot near the lookout on our ridge, so that I could listen to Robbie Trowbridge play. Sometimes, he'd play for a couple of hours. But other nights he'd only get halfway through a song before he stopped playing. Then he'd just sit there and stare up at the stars. I used to wonder what he was thinking. Even after I was back to my own bed, I'd ask myself, what was Robbie Trowbridge thinking when he looked up into the sky?"

My words were coaxing him closer, tugging the man hidden inside the wolf nearer, but it wasn't enough. I'd waited so long. Hoped for so much.

Mine, mine, mine, crooned my wolf.

"Trowbridge, what did you see in the stars?" I asked, daring to cup his face.

The wolf wavered, reluctant to step back.

Then, because I play dirty, I did what I knew I must. I dropped every barrier I had, and flared the way I'd done the first time for him. For him, for us, I showed him all of me—what I am, what I should be, what I could be—through the pure light spilling from my eyes. *Did you try to forget me?* my flare asked. *I will never let you.* He made the smallest inhale, and then the beast was gone. My Trowbridge flared back and gifted me with a beautiful electric-blue light—fire hot, soul bright.

Our two separate flares flashed across a battlefield not of our making.

Evermore, you are mine.

For a moment—how long it was I'll never be able to define—there was no Trowbridge electric blue, nor Hedi fluorescent green. Our individual flares merged into one, and the room that I remembered as being red turned into the warm blue-green of a sea that knew no turmoil, no current, no wind.

Evermore, I am yours.

My flare flickered out on the heels of that vow. His held for another half beat, then it, too, faded. "There you are," I murmured, looking into his tired eyes. "There's my Trowbridge."

That won me a smile. Slow and small.

I did that, I thought, cupping his face. *I made him smile again.*

"I knew you watched me play my guitar." His voice was rough. "I knew you were there hiding in those bushes."

I shook my head. "Impossible. I was quiet as a mouse."

My mate pressed his forehead to mine. "I could smell you."

"I don't have a scent," I whispered back.

He thumbed away my tear. "Tell that to some other Were."

Such a sweet thing, his touch. I leaned into it—and that's when I hit a brain skid. *It can't be.* Mentally, I did that thing you do when you're trying to figure out left from right. "Trowbridge," I said, with awe. "Your hand."

With a faint smile, he raised his fist. And then slowly, one by one, he unfolded his digits. A rounded nub close to his palm for his pinkie. A diminished ring finger, cut down to the first knuckle. A pause . . . and then he unfurled a completely and beautifully whole FU finger.

I'd seen Stuart Scawens lean into the blade and sever it from his hand.

Right in this room. Just over six months ago.

My gaze flew to his. "How?" I whispered, touching it with wonder. For a reply, he did that thing men do when they don't know the answer—a tilt of their head, a flex of their neck, that upward swing of their jaw.

So mortal. So man. So Trowbridge.

"I don't know." A slow smile as he spread his fingers. "When I turned into my human form, it was like this. I couldn't figure out if the stuff that happened in this room was a dream." He shook his head. "It got all messed up in my head. But it did happen, didn't it?" His head started to turn to that corner again, and I caught it and kept it safe in the cage of my hands.

"Don't," I said.

"You look the same," he said in a hushed voice, laying his palm on my cheek. "*Exactly* the same." Three fingers tunneled into my hair to cup the back of my head.

"Is that a good thing?" I asked, as he pulled me closer.

My mate answered by using his thumb to gently tilt up my chin. "A very good thing," he said, his cheeks flushed, his eyes glittering. "It's like you walked out of one of my dreams." He stroked my jaw, once, twice, both times with a hint of wonder as if he couldn't quite believe how soft my skin was.

Kiss me, Trowbridge.

But he didn't, not right away.

The Alpha of Creemore's gaze held mine, perhaps for a second, perhaps for five. Who knows? Who cares? I was far beyond counting. All I knew was that he held it long enough to show me the naked longing in his soul—and the sweet soul of Robbie Trowbridge still alive within the shell of this battle-hard, beautiful stranger. His attention returned to my mouth. He took in the slightest, shallowest breath.

My lips parted.

I am beautiful. I am loved.

Then his mouth—wider than mine, harder than mine—lowered to gift me with a kiss that narrowed the whole, damn confusing world down to one perfect set of lips pressed to mine. Slightly open. Warm. The right pressure. The right angle.

The right everything.

The taste of him. The brush of his tongue. The smooth warm cavern of his mouth welcoming my exploration.

Every problem, every nuisance, every disaster looming— all that twisted ball of angst that made me feel like I was balanced on a tightwire holding a ticking time bomb— disappeared. It was just the two of us. And between us there was heat and confusion and want and desire and everything else all rolled into a thick, insulating cloud of lust and longing.

At last.

Oh Trowbridge, at last.

His tongue teased mine as his hands pulled me close. My belly met his hip. His erection was a long hot welcome ridge against my stomach. I was wet, and aching.

Fuck the spectators.

Carry me away, Trowbridge.

I lifted on my toes, straining—

You know, it doesn't take a whole lot to prick a girl's zeppelin of happiness.

Really, all you need is one high, anxious wolf whine and that airship is coming down.

Well, perhaps two.

Maybe three.

"Eeerrgh." The puplet from Merenwyn issued another mood-destroying canine protest and padded to where we stood entwined. And I mean, *right* to where we stood. Hot dog breath heated the back of my naked knee.

My man's mouth stilled on mine.

No, no, no.

I slit open my eyes. "Trowbridge, there's a bitch behind me."

He gazed down at my lips with something akin to acute regret. "You're going to hear some stuff you're not going to like."

My spine stiffened. "Explain to me why she carries your scent."

The Alpha of Creemore's face tightened. "There are things that will be difficult to understand. You need to listen carefully to what I have to say before you do anything—"

I backed up and almost tripped over the little brown wolf.

"Get out of my way!" I warned her in a lethal voice.

But no.

The bitch-from-Merenwyn stood her ground and dared to lift her lip toward me.

A show of teeth. *At me. In this room that stinks of blood—both his and mine—that was shed that night six months ago.* So, okay, maybe I lifted my magic spinning hand in a threatening manner, maybe I didn't.

But Trowbridge caught my arm and growled, "Don't use that Fae shit in this house."

And the world stopped.

Not for very long.

My heart slowed for two heavy thuds—as if someone had tossed first one bar of cold iron, and then another, inside my chest cavity.

Fae shit?

"I stuffed Trowbridge's finger back into his shorts before he went through the gates," offered Biggs from the hall, when the tense silence following that statement stretched out. "Thought it might be handy when he changed into his wolf."

"Shut up, you insensitive dimwit!" snapped Cordelia.

I found myself backing away from the guy with the dreads.

Merry swiftly ratcheted herself up her chain to the soft hollow of my throat. There she hunkered down, warming me, while from the inside of her amber belly, she issued her own commentary with a series of red blips of light that I'm pretty sure were actually Asrai code for "Shame on you!"

Yes. I nodded. *Shame on him.*

Which irritated my mate, judging from the way he flung

his dreads over his shoulder with a quick snap of his head. I watched the dust motes dance around him, thinking the whole damn universe was like a snow globe held in the paws of an unsupervised three-year-old, then numbly turned toward Lexi in query.

"He's not what you think he is." My twin's eyes were sad. "You don't understand what he's capable of. What he really is."

"No," said Trowbridge, speaking very, very slowly. "She doesn't know what her brother is. The Black Mage's Shadow. A traitor to his kind."

"I am not 'your' kind," said Lexi, through his teeth.

"You are an animal under your skin, just as I am." Trowbridge stepped between me and my brother. "Though maybe not a wolf. You're more like something that feeds on another's kill . . ." Trowbridge's eyes glittered. "A hyena—"

My brother sprang. Trowbridge swung out with his elbow in a blow that caught Lexi under the chin with enough force to snap his head back and send his body flying into the corner of the living room.

Before I could dart for my twin, Cordelia snatched me back, and folded her arms around me in a tight embrace.

"I can stop them!" I squirmed to free myself. "Let me go!"

She hissed as my foot caught her kneecap, then wrapped her fingers over mine, forcing them into impotent fists from which no magic could spring. "No. The Alpha must deal with this."

The Alpha did.

Lexi surged upward from the floor, hands clawed for battle.

Trowbridge transferred his weight to one foot, spread his arms high and wide, and met my brother's charge with a savage kick. His foot caught my brother mid-chest, and then my brother was falling again, his arms flailing in the air.

Thud. Lexi hit the oak flooring and slid across the living room, overturning a side table and its lamp, before his skid stopped. Eyes flashing, he grabbed something off the ground, flicked his wrist, and something—a box? a book?—hit Trowbridge on the cheek.

The projectile bounced off and broke open on the floor, the box's contents of silver chains spilling out. A gasp from the spectators crowding the hall went unheeded between the two combatants.

"Don't," I wailed.

But he did. Lexi made a fist. A quarter second later—as my brother's punch continued its harmless arc through the air where my mate had stood a second before—Trowbridge delivered a left-handed, lights-out blow straight to Lexi's jaw.

Chapter Sixteen

My twin's heels dug into the ground as he clawed at Trowbridge's foot. An understandable reaction, considering the foot was pinned across his neck, slowly choking him.

"Let him go," I sobbed, tearing at Cordelia's grip.

"Steady," she cautioned in my ear. "Have a bit of sense."

If I had a shred of that, I'd never have fallen in love with a Were in the first place.

My True Love stared down at my writhing brother, his expression merciless and savage as he observed my twin's color mottle into an ugly puce. "How does it feel to wear a collar?"

"You're suffocating him!" I cried. "He can't breathe!"

"He stinks of sun potion. Do you know why he swallows that shit? It's to keep his wolf from coming out. He likes to keep that hidden under his hat. Don't you, you bastard?" Trowbridge let Lexi writhe for another four seconds before he eased off. "Just like you enjoy hunting your own kind."

"No." My nails cut into Cordelia's wrist. "I know my brother. He wouldn't—"

"You know him, do you? Do you know anything about his life in Merenwyn? Or mine?" Hot rage blistered his tone. "Do you know that the Weres of that realm hold the Pool of Life as sacred as the Fae? Do you know your brother gets his hunters to set wolf traps around the pool and every spring that empties into it?"

No. That I didn't know.

Trowbridge's eyes examined me—for what? An answer? An apology? How could I frame an adequate response for either? *"Go to the Pool of Life,"* that's what I'd told his wolf. And now my mate waited, head tilted, for an explanation. *They trap Weres in Merenwyn.* Mute with horror, I covered my mouth with my hands and something died in his eyes.

"Jesus," Biggs muttered.

Trowbridge nodded, perhaps to himself, and then spat—whether or not he missed Lexi on purpose was debatable—before lifting his foot from my brother's neck.

My twin rolled to his knees, coughing.

Cordelia sighed, gave me a squeeze meant to comfort, and let me go. I wish she hadn't. My legs felt weak. I walked as steadily as I could to the wingback chair, and leaned on it.

Trowbridge said, "The Raha'ells are driven by instinct to drink from the Pool of Life. Come moontime, some of the younger wolves aren't strong enough to resist their need for the water. It takes the Fae three days to check the trap lines they've set up. If the wolf can't free himself before they find him, they shoot him for his pelt." He bit the inside of his cheek then said in a dead voice, "The real hunt begins when the Shadow finds a sprung trap and a blood trail. Your brother's got the tracking skills of a wolf and he likes to hunt. He chased me for four days."

Breathe . . .

My brother gazed at me for a moment, then planted a hand on one knee and heaved himself upward. There was no obvious mutiny in the way he stood there, weaving slightly. But Lexi was fighting for stillness—always a bad sign. It meant he was thinking—which was a worse omen, because you don't need to think to tell the truth.

"You'll lead me to the Safe Passage portal," Trowbridge told him. "Then you'll open it, and hold it open while I lead my people through."

My twin massaged his throat for a moment, considering his reply. When he lifted his gaze, there was no worry crease between his brows, and his eyes were steady and calm. "It's too late for that."

"Bullshit," said Trowbridge. "They won't expect us until nightfall."

Lexi's smile was exquisitely bitter. "You haven't figured it out yet, have you? It's been fourteen hours *here,* but it's been days, if not weeks, in Merenwyn." He gestured to me. "We were born within twelve minutes of each other, but she'll have to live into her nineties to be as old as me."

As long as that? I thought numbly.

Trowbridge swung to me. "How long have I been gone?"

"One hundred ninety-six days," I whispered. My restless hand found the piping on the seat cushion and my nail ran up and down its seam, over and over again, as I watched the slow crawl of disbelief cross my mate's face. "Trowbridge, I . . ."

"What?" Two red flags flamed on his cheeks.

My mouth worked, but nothing came out.

A tendon in his cheek flexed once, and then again, before he said quietly, "I've seen nine winters in the Fae realm."

Biggs gasped. "No wonder he looks so old!"

I heard Cordelia hiss, "Biggs, I swear to God, I'll rip your tongue out of your mouth myself if you don't shut it!"

"Shhh, don't fight." That's what I should have said, but words and pleas—and all the sorrys in my breaking heart—were trapped at the base of my throat.

"Get out of here before I do something I'll regret." Cordelia told Biggs.

"Should I leave the ferret here?" he asked her. When no one answered, he asked again. "Well, should I?" My gaze drifted slowly over to where Biggs stood, a question mark on his face, holding the Black Mage's bag from its strap. Its leather flexed. *It's the animal,* I thought. *Trying to fight for its balance.* "Jesus, it's not my fault," muttered Biggs. He stalked to the old coatrack and hung the satchel from a hook. Then he shut the door behind him, very quietly, as if it were a house of mourning.

"Time passes differently in Merenwyn," I heard Lexi goad. "Your Raha'ells died waiting for the Son of Lukynae to lead them to their promised land."

His Raha'ells?

The fetid stench in the room made me want to heave. I watched the bag swing from the hook, back and forth, and listened with half an ear to the faint scratch of tiny nails on leather, the tick of the clock in the kitchen, the start of the furnace. The heartbeats. The inhales and exhales. All the time thinking, *I sent him to hell. I told him to find his way to the Pool of Life, no matter how hard it was.*

The little brown wolf nosed Trowbridge's thigh. If she so much as turned her head and looked upward, his dick would be the last thing she saw in this realm. He looked down at her and then he said in a voice I found terrible, "The Raha'ells had enough water and game for the winter. We'll leave right away."

"Do you think the Black Mage's wolves haven't backtracked your trail?" Lexi asked, dripping scorn, and corrosion, and hurt—a splatterwork of destruction over all my hopes. "It's over!"

"What I think is that you made a bargain, and you're looking for a way out of it." Trowbridge's eyes were too bright, his face too still. "You listen to me, you Fae bastard. I did my part. You wanted to come home and now you're home. You're going to deliver your end or I swear to God I'll kill her myself—with my bare hands—right here in front of you."

"Stop," I said in a small voice.

Anu leaned against Trowbridge's naked leg, panting lightly.

"Kill her, then," spat my brother. "Her death means little to me."

The air grew heavier, almost a pressing foul weight on me. Lexi rolled his head on his neck then tucked his chin in. Morning light played over his tattoo. The wolf's eyes gleamed, yellow and feral.

No, no, no.

"Stop it!" I shouted.

And for once, everyone heard me. They stilled—even the ferret quieted. I rocked for a bit on my heels, a hand pressed to the base of my throat, then I whispered, "I don't understand what's happening, okay? None of this is making sense to me, so you guys have to stop now. Everyone just needs to . . . stop yelling and arguing and . . ." My voice broke. "Who does Trowbridge want to kill?" I turned to my mate. "Trowbridge? Who do—"

"It's Anu," broke in Lexi. "He wants to kill one of his own with his bare hands. The savior of the Raha'ells—what a load of shit that is. She's just leverage, isn't she, Son of Lukynae? Disposable—even though she has some of your pack's blood." His mouth twisted in a sneer. "You Raha'ells are as racist as the Fae."

"I don't use bear traps," growled Trowbridge. "I don't follow a bleeding animal for threescore miles, stretching it out. I don't sound a horn to let the wolf know it's being followed. I don't make it run until it can't anymore. I don't close in for the kill when my prey is close enough to see home. When I do it, it's quick."

"Lexi?" And I heard myself speak in a voice that sounded dead. "Tell me that's not true. Tell me you didn't hunt him."

"He's Raha'ell," said Lexi.

"No," I said slowly. "He's not. He's Robson Trowbridge, and he's my—"

Lexi's chin was out, begging to be hit. "If I hadn't hunted him down, someone else would have trapped him. The price on his head was too high. Every bounty hunter, every Fae who was looking for a brass ring was searching for him. He was *lucky* that I was the one who caught him."

Oh Goddess, I'm going to throw up.

"Don't you look at me like that," my twin spat. "You don't understand anything—"

"Then explain it to me!" I cried.

"Can't you see?" he shouted back. "He's not one of these watered-down wolves anymore! This wolf—this animal you bonded yourself to—is responsible for more turmoil and misery in my realm than you can imagine!" His chest heaved. "In the nine winters he's been leader of the Raha'ells, they've gone from a nuisance to a constant threat. A Fae can't travel from one city to another without an armed squad. You can't leave a gate open or even take a piss too far away from the campfire." A look of frustration. "Your Trowbridge is *more* than just their Alpha. They believe him to be the Son of Lukynae—sent by the Gods to deliver them from the Fae." Lexi gave me a bitter smile. "If you don't believe me, ask your 'mate' why he turned down my first offer."

First offer? I turned to Trowbridge. He closed his eyes briefly, then gave me a little shake of his head—his expression sad.

"I offered him freedom," Lexi said, when Trowbridge wouldn't—*couldn't?*—answer the question in my gaze. "His life in return for guiding us through the portal. Do you know what he said?" My brother's wolf crouched, ready to spring. "Your mate said, 'You need to sweeten the pot before I'll ever go through those gates again.'"

A heavy thing—ugly and dense—expanded inside my chest.

It fed on those words. It drank from the hurt.

If I let it, that heavy pain would grow so huge my knees would fold. I knew this. Just like I understood my twin wasn't quite finished. The prospect of victory—not yet his, but soon and certain—glittered on his face. It was there, plain as day, obvious in the anticipation widening his eyes, recognizable in the twisted smile he wore—the same gloating smirk that had always made me want to punch him when he slapped the final heart down on the top of the deck when we were kids. We deliberately edit our memories, don't we? Wanting to remember only the good? And so, I'd forgotten. How my brother liked to surge ahead of me, heedless of everything—caution, care, compassion—blind to it all, nothing ahead in sight except the sweet rush past the winner's tape.

He opened his mouth. *Here it comes—*

"He didn't want to come back," he said. "Not to Creemore, not to you—not unless he could bring his entire pack with him. He'd rather face the interrogation and the Spectacle again than leave his precious Raha'ells in Merenwyn."

But his eyes still glittered, and so I asked, "Then why is he here?"

"The only amulet that will open the Safe Passage is here." He gestured to Anu. "She wears it about her neck."

Ah, and there it was. The queen of hearts slammed faceup on top of the pile.

My gaze fell. Someone needed to wipe down the side table. It was gritty with accumulated dust.

"Hedi." Trowbridge's voice was a low, rough rumble. "I *told* you he'd do this. That he'd—"

"Lie. That's what you said before you turned into your wolf and went for your moon-run with the pack. You said, 'He'll lie and charm and steal to get what he wants.'" There was a palm print on the thick dust coating the table. Large. Probably a man's. If we were playing Clue instead of Truth or Consequences that print might have meant something. But now, it was just another element of grunge in a room swollen with all kinds of squalor. "Here's a truth," I said slowly. "When I look at Lexi, I don't see the Shadow. I see my brother and I *know* his lying face." I chewed my lip and thought back—double-checking my instincts. "No. Lexi wasn't wearing it." My gaze turned toward the man I'd loved since I was twelve. "Trowbridge, are you telling me that you didn't ask him to 'sweeten the pot'?"

The skin tightened around the Alpha of Creemore's eyes. "Hedi—"

Oh Goddess, why does this hurt so much? Why can't this heavy thing inside me smother all the sharp pointy parts of this terrible pain? "Just give me a one-word answer. Yes or no."

"There were reasons. You need to understand—"

"No I don't," I said quietly. "I already understand the most important point."

I'm a heart-blind fool.

Trowbridge's scent reached out for me, but I shook my head and took a step away from the chair, away from him, away from anything he'd ever touched. I stood, an island, in the center of the old Alpha's living room, thinking truths have sharp teeth and an endless appetite. They take a bite of you—one big sharp snap of their jaws—then, having found entry into your soft parts, they keeping nibbling, eating inward, until you're hollowed out.

Belatedly, my twin's expression softened into shame.

"I'm sorry, runt," he said huskily.

"I need to go," I said in a little voice.

"Where will you go?" asked Cordelia softly.

I shrank away from her touch. "I don't know. I just need to get—"

"You son of bitch," growled Trowbridge. "You filthy son of a whore."

Did he forget we were twins? That's my mother—

"I'm not the one who broke her heart!" Lexi grabbed the brass lamp from the table and tore the electric cord from the wall. "Come on," he taunted, waving the heavy end.

"I don't come at your bidding anymore." Trowbridge smiled. "My realm, my rules."

Stupid with pride, Lexi made a blind rush and a swing, which was countered by Trowbridge's quick side turn and crouch. If my brother had had a lick of sense, he would have stopped there—Trowbridge had always been graceful and quick with the fists, but now he had wicked timing and heavy muscle.

Lexi charged again.

Trowbridge delivered a gut-wrenching punch into my brother's stomach.

Lexi stumbled backward—almost tripping himself with the lamp cord—but recovered. He eyed Trowbridge with utter hatred, mixed with a whole bunch of busted manly vanity.

"Where are your hunters now?" asked Trowbridge softly, circling my brother.

Lexi threw the lamp at him and lunged, drawing his fist back for a blow. But he was too slow and clumsy compared to Trowbridge, who pivoted on one foot and spun. Before my brother even realized that his intended target had pulled another Houdini, Trowbridge had joined his fists and brought them down with bruising force, landing a blow to Lexi's back, right between the shoulder blades.

That was the end of it, really. The rest was blurred. Blows—some blocked, some not. But within a few seconds, Lexi's fine shirt was torn, and he was down for good. Trowbridge bent over and relieved my brother of his shiny flask.

He uncapped the bottle of sun potion, tipped it upside down, and watched my brother's face twist as the contents splattered to the floor. Expressionlessly, the Alpha of Creemore tossed the empty flask into the corner. "Come the next moonrise, your sister will finally see the animal in you, should you live that long." He tilted his head. "Let her judge whose wolf is worse."

And then . . . at last, I really was completely and absolutely numb. For 132 "Mississippis," I heard nothing. Saw nothing. Felt nothing except that heavy thing growing ever denser in my chest. In the background, I dimly understood that words were said, challenges exchanged, and threats and counterthreats issued, but all of it blurred into a meaningless hum, until—

"Cars!" Biggs exclaimed from the doorway. "Harry's truck's in front, but there's about nine more behind him—no, make that twelve. Oh man." He sighed. "The rest of them are behind that. The pack's coming."

"Wonderful," said Cordelia.

And so they came. In cars. In trucks. Hastily dressed. Eager to speak in words, not wolf thoughts. Questions—there'd be lots of those. But there were no clear answers, were there? Just half lies that would lead to more questions and more confusion. I stood, almost steady on my feet,

watching my twin, thinking that the blue shadows under
his eyes were the only thing left of color to his face.

Vehicle doors slammed—bang, bang, bang.

Gravel crunched beneath booted feet.

"All of you get back," said Harry. "You have no business on the Alpha's front porch."

"Is it true the Fae are coming?" some Were demanded.

"You guys are worse than a bunch of old women," Harry
bitched. "Now get back. You go wait over by the grass until
your Alpha's ready to speak to you." A squeak of the front
door, then my old second-in-command poked his head in
the room. "Cleanup's finished, boss. We've taken care of
the bodies and the scene, but I need a word with you."

"Biggs," Trowbridge said. "Go tell someone to jack up
the volume on their radio. Hey, Cordelia? Can you check
my old room and see if there's any jeans left?" The little
brown wolf made a noise somewhat like a car having problems starting. My mate murmured, "Easul." She settled, but
she used her back leg to satisfy an itch and demonstrate her
canine angst. She still wore the Royal Amulet, and Ralph
bounced—throwing out sparks of indignation—with each
thump, thump of her scratching.

"I'll get him back, Merry," I whispered.

Trowbridge swung around at the sound of my voice, and
for a moment—just for the briefest little nanosecond—I
thought I read something there. Hope? Entreaty? But whatever communiqué he sought to send me was lost in transit—
along with that solitary blue comet that had briefly
glimmered—when my brother said something low and
fierce in our mother's tongue.

"We're in my world now," said Trowbridge. "Your
threats aren't worth shit."

A bit of static, and then a station was chosen. "It's Intrepid Ian on the Edge. Next up, Temple of the Dog's 'Hunger
Strike.'"

"Seriously?" Biggs muttered from the door. "I'll tell
them to change it."

"Forget it." Robson Trowbridge moved to the bank of

windows. "Crank it up," he ordered. Faster than a minion could snap his fingers and say, "Sure, boss," I heard the opening lines. One guitar? Then Cornell's voice, low and plaintive. The Alpha of Creemore listened for a bit—his arm braced on the sash, his belly lean, his shoulders taut—then he heaved a heavy sigh and closed the windows, one by one.

"What's the problem?" he asked Harry.

Harry dug a cell phone out of his pocket. "I found this in Knox's jeans." He offered it to his Alpha, then he busied himself divesting his other pockets of the rest of Knox's stuff: a brown wallet, an ugly ring, a silver-toned necklace, and a small glass bottle half filled with colorless liquid. "You're going to want to watch the video," he told Trowbridge.

Forehead pleated, Trowbridge stared at the device.

Harry stepped closer. "Here, I'll show—"

The Alpha jerked his hand away. "I remember how to use a cell phone."

"That green ball of light came before the voice," said Harry, peering over Trowbridge's shoulder. "Okay, this next part's blurry. Knox was walking over to the edge to get a better picture." I heard Casperella hit the high note on the portal song. "And there's the money shot—he's got you coming through the gates with the Fae."

Cordelia swayed into the room, carrying a pair of jeans. "God, it stinks in here." Trowbridge accepted the Lees and dropped the cell on the couch.

Biggs asked, "Did he have time to send it before—"

"Yes," drawled Harry. "To some girl by the name of Brenda Pritty."

"Who is she?" Trowbridge asked, putting a foot into a pants leg.

His new second shook his head. "I don't know, but I'll find out."

The Alpha of Creemore flung his dreads over his shoulder again—*oh, for a pair of scissors*—and pulled the Lees up over his naked ass, then fiddled with the buttons on the fly. "Where are we on the moon cycle?"

Trowbridge hadn't looked in my direction once since he'd shut the windows. Which, come to think of it, must have required some mental discipline since the room wasn't that large. Why was that? Was he worried that one glance from him was going to send me sniveling into a handkerchief?

Look at me, Mr. Sweeten-the-pot. See my eyes? They're bone-dry.

Harry lifted a shoulder. "We have one more night."

"We should try to sneak out of town," mumbled Biggs. "Before the NAW sends people."

Lexi's gaze was riveted on the puddle of sun potion by Trowbridge's foot.

"Yes," I said, with thick sarcasm. "Let's do that. We'll fire up the GPS, load the car full of hamburgers and dog treats, and take a family road trip."

At that, Trowbridge gave me a quick searching look, then firmed his mouth. "No one will want to shelter us." He tucked the phone into his front right pocket. "In the meantime—Harry, find out everything you can about Brenda Pritty."

Biggs heaved a sigh and sank onto the stair's bottom step. "Why did this have to happen? We were going along pretty good until the NAW got interested in us. Who rattled their cage?"

One of the Hedi-haters. Probably a Scawens or a Danvers.

"I didn't get any sense of an Alpha power from Knox." Harry scowled. "Though there was something about his scent . . . Cordelia, did you catch it?" When she shook her head, Trowbridge went over to Knox's effects and uncapped the bottle of liquid. He took a sniff and then swore—rather fluently, in Merenwynian.

Lexi's nostrils flared and then his shoulders shook in silent mirth. "Looks like I'm not the only Fae in this realm."

"What is it?" asked Harry.

"Sun potion," Trowbridge answered. "How did this stuff fall into the NAW's hands?"

He looked at me. As if I'd been going back and forth between Merenwyn and Creemore with a tote bag and a guilty look. A sour taste filled my mouth.

I crouched beside my twin. "You okay?"

He nodded. "For now."

"We're so screwed," repeated Biggs.

Oh so predictable. Biggs moaning doom and gloom. Harry's jaw set, ready for action. Cordelia's gaze shuttered, her thoughts her own. The pack outside, hungry wolves hidden inside human skin. *Learn the way of the Were,* I thought.

"No, we're not screwed. There's a way out of this," said Trowbridge. "I have a mate, don't I?" Then instead of turning toward me, his head swung in Cordelia's direction. "Didn't *you* help me say the vows?"

She flinched.

Enough. Too much collateral hurt. "You were dying in my arms," I said, grateful for my sudden icy detachment. "So she did what she had to. Without my Fae blood in your veins, the portal's doors would have closed on you and you would have died, just like Mannus."

Pity about that, my gaze said.

"So," he said, his eyebrows lifting. "Instead you sent me into the Fae realm for eternity."

"Back then I wanted you to live."

A flush crawled over his cheeks.

"Biggs," he said. "Take the shotgun and the Fae to the kitchen. Shoot him if he moves." Then he walked to the doorway. "The rest of us are going out there as a solid unit. Whatever we're thinking in our heads doesn't show out there, got it? There's only way out of this, and everything depends on our solidarity." The Alpha of Creemore favored me with a long look of anger tinged with male frustration.

I took his evil stare, wrapped it with silver paper, put a bow on it, and sent it back to him.

Take that.

"Come with me," he said, too softly.

Chapter Seventeen

We filed onto the front porch, a Royal Family without the coronets, medals, and swords. Trowbridge in the front, me on his right, Cordelia and the others filling in the background. The crowd fell silent, except for two teenagers in the back. One of the Weres turned to shush them.

So there they are. My would-be murderers. A collection of plaid shirts, Lululemon yoga pants, and white T-shirts. The guy who'd wrapped the chain around me slunk back to the rear of the pack. A couple of the Danvers females returned my cool gaze with a belligerence that seemed crazy-ass stupid, considering their Alpha's paw rested on the small of my back.

I allowed my gaze to roam over the rest of the motley crew, letting my eyes do the talking.

I hate you, each and every one of you.

It had been an exercise in futility—trying to learn the way of the Were. Every time I'd tried to mimic their wolf-ish ways, I'd felt foreign and forced. A lousy imitation hoping to pass. All thumbs and dumb confusion, trying to slide a poorly fitted wolf pelt over my own too tight skin. Fae Stars, I have a Were in my belly, and a Fae in my gut. On the best possible day, when everyone is getting along, my skin feels stretched to the point of ripping.

I don't belong here. I never did, I never will. I dragged

my tongue over the top of my lower teeth and it gave a nudge to my salivary glands—my throat still painful from the tears I refused to shed. Water flooded my mouth, and the ache eased a fraction.

"I am Robson Trowbridge, son of Jacob Trowbridge, grandson of Stephen Trowbridge, great-grandson of William Trowbridge." The Alpha of Creemore snared my hand in his. "Who wishes to challenge my claim?"

His palm was calloused and warm.

Nobody stepped forward—evidence that none among the pack had the balls or the wish to lose them. Though there were a few sidelong glances followed by lowered eyes. *It's all stealth attacks on the weak and wounded with Weres, isn't it?*

Rachel Scawens stepped out of the throng. "Welcome back, baby brother."

He nodded. "Rach."

"I want it to be understood that I am not contesting my brother's claim to the title," she said, more for the pack than for her sibling. "There is no one among us—man or *woman*—who is ready to challenge him. And as of yet, there is no Were among us who can fully demonstrate the authentic blue light of an Alpha, *other* than my brother." Rachel eyed me for a second—all squinty-eyed and accusing—before she lifted her shoulders. "I acknowledge that. I just wonder if it's time for the Weres of Creemore to stop thinking like wolves and start thinking like people."

Good luck with that. Merry stirred inside my shirt.

No one hissed "Rebellion!" but the scent of the crowd sharpened. It frightened my inner-bitch—the last time we'd smelled this mixture of anger and anticipation we'd found ourselves tied to the old oak—and she sent me a silent plea to submit. *Like hell.* I locked my knees and stiffened my spine.

At which Trowbridge gave my hand a soft squeeze.

Screw you, Son of Lukynae.

Emboldened, Rachel continued, "Last night our new Alpha killed the NAW's envoy, and then he led our wolves

on the hunt for Knox's men." She shook her head. "I didn't
know their names, or what town they came from. For all I
know, they could have family waiting for them. I followed
the hunt because I was wolf, and my wolf wanted to please
her Alpha. To her, those men were just . . ." A sick expression flitted across her face. "Prey. I've never hunted one of
our kind before, have any of you?" The guy who called himself Tank scratched the side of his cheek and tried to look
invisible. "This morning I woke up as me." She thumped
her chest twice. "Me, Rachel Scawens. And it's me who
has to live with the consequences of my wolf's actions."

Bring me a hankie.

"What we did last night—what we participated in—
will certainly bring the NAW to Creemore. And mark my
words, they *will* extract justice for their losses. You don't
need to be psychic to predict that the next person to die in
this town will be one of ours." Trowbridge's sister looked
blindly at the ground. "When the bloodletting is over and
you are mourning one of your children, the NAW will still
be here. Trust me. They'll use this opportunity to absorb
the Weres of Ontario into Quebec."

Anu yawned.

Trowbridge held up his hand. The left one—all perfect
fingers splayed open. "My sister is assuming that our actions were illegal, and that we will lose in any contest
against the NAW."

"Of course we'll lose," she scoffed. "Look at us. We're
shopkeepers and accountants. Salesmen and factory work-
ers. Our game is deer and rabbits, not other Weres. We
don't know how to fight against the NAW's enforcers."

"It's never going to come down to a fight." Trowbridge's
tone was unruffled and totally at odds with the beard, the
dreads, and the scent of dominance wafting from him.
"Everything my pack did last night will hold up when the
Council reviews our case." He raised his right hand—and
therefore mine—high enough to lift me to my toes. Teetering slightly, I gazed resentfully up toward the symbol of
our love and unity. Talk about imbalance, his paw nearly

swallowed mine. "Hedi is my mate. We have said the words. For the rest of our lives, we are bonded."

You could almost see the "uh-oh" thought bubble over the rest of the pack. "*Shit. Time to backpedal. The bitch is back.*"

Trowbridge lowered our hands. But he didn't release mine and kept it trapped, close to his hard thigh, forcing me to either shuffle closer or lean into him. I did a reluctant hokey-pokey to the left. "The NAW asked for everything they got. They sent a hit squad to my territory, and their representative tried to kill Hedi. That amounts to a direct attack on me. As a mate, and an Alpha, I met their challenge with equal force."

I smiled faintly at the woman who'd elbowed my head.

"It's a clear case of self-defense," their Alpha emphasized for those too dim to grasp the miraculous loophole being presented to them. Babble erupted until the guy from the insurance office pursed his lips and let out sharp whistle. He held up his hand.

Trowbridge nodded toward him.

"No disrespect, Alpha," the claims adjuster began. "But that little wolf at your heels carries more of your scent than she does."

I felt a sudden and deep kinship with every one of those political wives that found the inner resources to smile at the public as they listened to their dickhead husband explain how one call girl does not equal a marital indiscretion. It hurt to smile, but smile I did. Wider than before. Showing teeth and maybe a little gum. *Yeah, Trowbridge, answer that—tell them about that little bitch who carries your scent and basically does everything but wear a sign saying,* I'VE SLEPT WITH ROBSON TROWBRIDGE.

Trowbridge pinned the whistle-blower with a cold glare. "If I ever hear you call my mate 'she' like that again, I'll take you out." When the claims adjuster's shoulders were sufficiently hunched and humbled, he continued. "The wolf's name is Anu. She is a half-bred Were and does not have a scent of her own."

Rachel smirked at me. "And why hasn't she changed?"

Trowbridge shrugged. "Traveling through the gates has messed up our clocks."

"But why'd you bring the Fae?" a woman cried out.

"He is not a Fae. His name is Lexi Stronghold and he is the brother of my mate. He was born here in Creemore, sired by Benjamin Stronghold. Ten years ago, he was stolen from the pack by the Fae, but now he is home, returned as part of our pack."

Another round of murmurs. Then, because I'm part Were, I heard (probably as she'd hoped I would) one woman's aside to Rachel. "I still don't get it. Who is Anu to us? Is she another mate?"

"If you have a question about the pack, you address me. Not my sister, not anyone else." Trowbridge's thumb stroked my knuckle.

Seriously? I dug my nail into his palm.

Then the Alpha of Creemore said something that made everything in my world tilt sixty degrees toward WTF. "Anu is Lexi Stronghold's daughter."

I didn't see that thunderbolt coming. *Anu is my niece.*

Rachel threw up her hands. "The NAW didn't just come here because sh—" She stumbled on her words. "They didn't show up here because my brother's mate doesn't carry his scent. They came here because the treaty has been broken. His consort summoned the fairy portal twice. Just how many times do you think we can get away with that?"

Anu is my niece, and she smells like Trowbridge.

"We keep propping open that door, and the Fae will walk through it. They'll follow him back here, and then—"

"The Fae will come!" Trowbridge mocked softly. "The bad guys are coming. Be afraid. Did we ever worry about the Fae coming through our portals back when we were kids?"

Anu is my niece, she hates my brother, and she smells like Trowbridge.

The Alpha of Creemore looked around the group, eyes faintly narrowed, until his gaze lit on the large Were at the edge of the crowd. "Hey, Tank, how've you been? Do you want to tell me where the bad guys are?"

The Were in question chewed his lip, considering how best to answer the $64,000 question.

"The Fae closed the portal, not us." Trowbridge's voice rang with authority. "They don't want any part of our world. The day humans learned to melt iron was the beginning of their exodus from our realm."

"Yeah!" cried a male voice.

"Damn right!" called another.

"Well, I've seen them around metal and steel," said the woman from the real estate office. "Your mate's proof of that. Hedi's been living in a trailer for half a year, and she—your mate—looks pretty healthy."

"My mate is half Were and we've exchanged blood," said Trowbridge without looking at me. "It has raised her tolerance level for such things."

Not true. It hadn't raised my tolerance level for Weres. The gauge on that particular measure was sinking closer to empty with every little hoo-yah from the boys at the back of the pack. *Anu is my niece, she hates my brother, she smells like Trowbridge, and she can change into her wolf.*

"You will not see another Fae walk through that portal." Trowbridge's voice rang with authority. "They're demigods in their realm, not ours. There is nothing in our world that they want enough to stand the discomfort of coming here. This is our territory and shall always be *our* territory."

All he needs is a horse and some blue face paint and he'd be good to go.

"Some of you have the ability to scent a lie. Test the wind for the truth. Do I lie?" The Alpha waited, posture easy, as the nose police did their job. One guy made a production of it, taking in a huge lungful of air that swelled his chest.

"He tells the truth," nose police announced.

Approval rippled through the crowd.

"Your concerns about a Fae invasion are based on fear, not reality. We will be as we have always been. United!" Trowbridge's mighty chest rose. "Wolves of Creemore! Kneel!"

And bam, they did.

Then the guy I'd bound my life to lifted our conjoined hands skyward one more time.

"I am your Alpha by birth and by right," he said to his Weres.

They roared. A collective sound—very mortal.

"I vow to protect you and lead you."

Some starstruck girl opened her mouth and let out a high, keening, plaintive howl. And that's all it took. Their voices swelled, wolf songs from human throats. Silently, Anu padded over to where we stood, dead under the porch light, and sat down, her flank brushing my mate's knee. Her tail gave a thump.

Anu is my niece, she hates my brother, she smells like Trowbridge, she can change into her wolf, and she knows no fear.

I gritted my teeth, trying to maintain my balance on my toes.

"My mate and I will never leave you again!" their Alpha cried.

Then to me in a soft aside, "Will we?"

I jerked my hand free, and pushed my way through Harry and company.

And the pack roared.

The house still reeked of dead stuff.

I stood in the hallway, fighting the urge to run. It would be so much easier to scurry away than to stay. *Oh Goddess, I need to run.* From the pack, from a man who may or may not want me, from all the failures and miscues following me like a shaming trail of bathroom tissue stuck to my shoe.

Run.

In the past, it had been the answer to all that sickened

and infuriated me—run. A sprint down the hall, fast as hunt-terrorized deer. A right at the end of the passage, a quick jaunt through the kitchen, and then straight out through the back door. I'd be halfway across the back lawn before the screen door slammed behind me.

But I couldn't.

Not now, anyhow. Not while my drug-addled brother waited in the kitchen with a laundry list of problems too long to solve in a few hours. Even I, the girl who preferred to ignore the obvious, and run hell-bent from the painful, could understand that.

There were twenty-nine days before the next full moon when, supposedly, Lexi would turn glassy-eyed with moon-lust. Plenty of time to make plans, to pack a bag, to pur-chase a road map . . . to leave if that's what I really wanted to do.

How could everything have changed so fast? Yesterday I knew without question what I wanted: My One True Thing returned to me . . . *And now?*

My fury was a spoon stirring the stew of me—mortal-me, wolf-me, Fae-me. I needed to lift the lid and allow the steam to curl. Too many months had been squandered on keeping my dark urges—don't lie, don't steal, don't rage—from escaping in a black, bubbling boil.

For what? my Fae whispered. *For whom? Can I please come out now, too?*

Damn right she could. I gave her a hard nudge, and she swelled upward, brushing past my inner-Were with a sly grin. Magic, fat with temper, fed itself into the tips of my fingers. No more compartments, no more rationing of base desires, no more stomach squeezing, stomping down on nat-ural instinct. *I am Fae.* I flicked my wrist and felt my mouth shape into a snarl as my otherworld talent spun from my fingers in a long, supple line of green. Fast as a whip, it trav-eled to the end of its reach, strained for another greedy inch, then—blind as a cave-dwelling snake—turned back toward me. It curled itself over my head, bobbing faintly on a current of air, shimmering with impatience under this world's sun.

"Where? What?" it hissed.

"Window."

It flew across the room to the bay and attached itself to a sash. "Open," I said. Bang! Up went the double-hung—glass panes shuddering—an ample demonstration of my Fae's willingness to work with me. Forget words. It read my mind, and magic flew to the next sash. Bang! Onto the next—bang! Up all four of them went, one after another, jerked hard right to the top of their frames, in pretty much the same order as they'd been sealed by the Alpha of Creemore, except a hell of lot less pretty and a whole lot faster.

"Isn't this better?" my Fae purred.

Clean air drifted through the gaping windows, trying to cool my heated throat.

I need to destroy something. I surveyed the place where everything had turned to crap. *That's where it happened—over there in the living room, in that dark corner. That's where they'd tortured Trowbridge. Everything went to hell after that.*

My inner-Were was restless inside me, distressed and fretting to be let out, too. *Yes, there,* she whined—in rare, but perfect, agreement with my Fae. *Hurt that place.*

Remember that slash on his belly, those wounds on his thighs.

I stepped into the room and considered my targets. The chair they'd bound him to? The table to which they'd pinned his hand? The floorboards with their dried gore? Or how about the ladder-back chair on which they'd propped me up so that I had a front-row seat to his mutilation? Remnants of my duct-tape manacles still clung to its battered front legs.

Something needed to be turned into kindling in the next minute or I was going to explode. Just as I lifted my hand, target chosen—*the table, of course*—the front door opened with a protest of its hinges, and the scent of Chanel entered the house, followed by a click of claws on oak floor.

"Leave me alone, Cordelia." My cable of fluorescent-green magic slithered over the furniture, nose forward, testing the density of the easy chair, slipping over its rounded back to shoot across the open space toward the bookcase.

"I'd love to," she replied blandly. "But your niece looks ready to shed her wolf, and Bridge sent me in to babysit."

I slowly pivoted to face my old roommate and my magic curled around me, a sinuous shimmering snake.

Heels, a nice skirt, a twin set. When had she found time to change? All that was missing was the heavy makeup—and she needed a shave. My roommate's eyes narrowed into slits when my hot gaze rested too long on her jaw.

"Did he ask you to watch his baby or babysit?"

"Let me think," she drawled. "I believe his exact words were: 'Take the wolf into the house and find Hedi something sweet to eat. We'll get this shit-fest straightened out as soon as I'm finished accepting their oaths.'"

Behind her, my niece paced in the small hall, anxious as a dog in need of a pee.

"Trowbridge's full of orders now, isn't he?"

"It's part of the job title, as you'd have known if you ever bothered to listen to me." Turning to face the hall mirror, Cordelia frowned and rubbed a spot by the corner of her mouth. Long fingers, big knuckles. A square, solid thumb. "So, darling, what sweet thing do you wish? Choose something that takes a long time to assemble—I don't particularly enjoy the pageantry of the 'bear my mark' ritual. As far as I can see, it's a needless pain for something that amounts to little more than a temporary blood tattoo. Besides, it's not *my* duty to stand beside him while he does so."

She added a long sniff to that last statement—just so I would understand that she considered it my responsibility to stand smiling inanely at the people who'd tried to skewer me to a tree not fourteen hours earlier.

Another small ladle of acid added to my roiling stomach. Instinctively, my free hand went to my amulet friend, hoping for a measure of calm. But Merry was not in a

comforting frame of mind. She flashed a light—deep red—
from within her stone and then, faster than an old station
wagon caught in rush-hour traffic, her temperature rose.

"What?" I hissed, hunching my shoulders against her
stone's sudden scorching heat.

In answer, a strand of ivy pointed an accusatory finger
at Cordelia.

And then, I realized, belatedly, what I'd missed.

"You're wearing Ralph?"

Cordelia examined my serpent of magic coiling in the
space between us for the count of three—she was the only
Were with eyes clever enough to actually *see* my magic—
then calmly shut the door behind her. Indifferent to the
danger. Dismissive of our rage. "Yes. I am the temporary
guardian of this amulet. Mine to serve and protect, at least
until Trowbridge finishes outside."

"Temporary guardian?" I repeated.

At that, my amulet friend gave herself a vigorous shake,
and presto! She'd morphed from pretty pendant to Merry-
the-stick-figure—four strands of ivy called into duty as
appendages. My incensed Asrai pal stalked up the Valley
of the Boobs, her golden chain looping behind her, and
found a place about two inches below my right collarbone.
From there, she glowered at me; the pulsing red light deep
in the heart of her amber now distinctly tinged amethyst.

"I *did* protect him, Merry—"

One ivy arm took a tighter grip of my T-shirt, the other
undulated in the air; a cat's tail, twitching with irritation.
She canted her body back, ready to deliver a slap-down.

"Really?" I asked through my teeth. "I did two A.M.
feedings. For *five* weeks. I found him the best shrubs, the
sweetest trees. And, I did *not* give him up to the pack. He
made the choice himself last night when he opted for a
wolf's protection over mine. If you don't like seeing him
hung around a Were's neck, then you should talk to him,
not me."

Cordelia said, "Now there's a conversation I'd like to
listen in on."

"And you!" I growled. "Have you forgotten how Ralph likes to strangle people? With no warning? Usually when you're not expecting it?"

She peered down her nose to study the amulet in question with about as much enthusiasm as one would a third nipple. "If it snags even one thread on this silk shell, I'll turn it into a coat hanger."

The Royal Amulet, clearly offended by her lack of deference, flushed red from deep within his blue jewel, suffusing his stone with a hint of purple far pissier than Merry's most outraged hue.

There's a match made in heaven—Merry and Ralph's fights would be more awesome than Canada Day fireworks.

My amulet fought for balance as I ran a distracted hand through my hair. "I need everything just to stop for a second. I can hardly think anymore."

Karma gave a toothy grin to her friend Chaos.

And suddenly Anu cried out and did a drunken sprint toward the back door. She got about three feet before her paws went out from under her, and she slid, belly-first, down to the floor.

"Damn," said Cordelia, moving the hall table out of the way. "I'd hoped to get her to the mudroom before she fell into her change."

Un-freakin'-believable. I had to witness my replacement's transformation?

"That's it." I turned my back on Cordelia and the she-wolf from Merenwyn. "I've had it. You need to shovel Anu-the-new-dog-treat from the floor, and take her elsewhere. I don't care where, just get her out of my sight." Fingers hooked, I sketched an angular figure eight in the air with the marker, watching with grim fascination as my magic rolled through the loops with exquisite precision.

Silence from my ex-roomie, a guttural groan from my new niece.

I shot a glare over my shoulder. Cordelia studied me with pursed lips. "I perceive your feelings have been hurt."

"Ya think? The Alpha of Creemore raised my hand and said, 'We'll stay forever.'"

"And you take issue with that."

I shook my head in disbelief. "Have you forgotten that the pack tried to *kill* us last night?"

"They won't try it again."

"Everybody keeps on saying that." My Fae floated over toward the bad corner, touching first this and then that bad stain. Tasting them with a shiver. She turned her blind head back toward me, as if to say, "Mmm, wolf blood. May I have more?"

No. You can't. I jerked her away from it.

"You know," Cordelia drawled. "Bridge didn't have any other choice than to do what he did. The man returned home last night, and found what? A welcome banner? No, he found you—presented in a wonderful homage to *The Perils of Pauline*—and a leaderless pack in a positive agony to tear something apart. And from that moment onward, his choices were whittled down to kill or be killed. Dominance or death."

The end of my fingers ached from the strain of my curious Fae. "Stop it," I told my magic savagely, fighting to bring her back to heel. She resisted briefly then acquiesced, returning to undulate above my head.

I twisted around to frown at Cordelia. "Who the hell is Pauline?"

"The quintessential damsel in distress." She pressed the back of her hand against her forehead to whine. "Oh! Oh! Save me. Oh please. Someone save me."

"You take that back," I hissed. "I am not a damsel in distress. I've never been a—"

"Have you once stopped to think about the fact that Bridge has been on Hedi's Train to Hell from the moment you found him in that motel room?" She jabbed a finger at me. "And *you* don't know what choices were offered to him in Merenwyn."

"I know what he passed on!" My magic whiplashed over her head as I whirled to face her.

Cordelia flicked her head upward and gazed at its coiled menace for a long, steady moment, then slowly lowered her chin. She gave me a poisonous smile. "Go ahead. Try it again."

Oh, I wanted to. I did indeed.

Six months she'd been riding me. Pick up your clothing. Eat some protein. Do something about that amulet, he's looking sulky. She'd taken the better bed because "I'm bigger than you." She'd hissed, and hummed, and driven me three-quarters batty. Even now, when any other idiot would have walked away, she stood there, daring me.

She knew no fear, my six-foot mother hen.

For a beat, we had a stare-down. I shook my head. "Maybe Trowbridge did what he had to do. But you heard what he said before the pack arrived. He hates my brother, grieves for his Raha'ells—he's willing to travel back to a realm where they hunt wolves with bear traps just to bring those wolves to freedom—and it seems he'd rather have faced more torture than come home to me."

I gestured with my chin to where my blood relative writhed on the floor, one quarter human, three quarters wolf. "To top it all off, I'm pretty sure he's slept with my niece, who has absolutely no problem turning into her wolf."

"If she's a threat, then kill her," she said softly.

"I can't," I replied automatically. "She's my brother's daughter."

Another fact that Lexi hadn't shared with me last night.

Cordelia's gaze was scathing—a bristling hedge of fake black lashes around an angry shimmer of icy-blue. "You're giving her more importance than her presence warrants. *She* is a nobody. He didn't even properly introduce her to the pack. *You* are the mate of the Alpha of Creemore. It's simple. If you can't bloody your hands then just kick her ass out of your bedroom."

"You don't get it," I said in frustration.

"What don't I get?"

"It's all messed up!"

"Of course it is," she replied. "It's life. And life is inevitably messy." She tilted her head to study me. "Darling, what did you think was going to happen if he came home?"

Bored of the conversation, my serpent of doom drifted to the fireplace's mantel. There, it slid along the smooth pine until it met the obstacle of a family photo. This object was briefly investigated, a curious tongue testing the rounded contours of its brass frame. Evidently, not tasty. It brusquely knocked the picture off its perch. Glass shattered on its impact with the slate hearth.

I gave it a hard leash correction and pointed to a spot near my feet. "Stay there."

"That's a good idea," Cordelia said, brushing past me. "Your feet are bare and your temper's up."

Got that right. My Fae wrapped itself around my ankle—feigning remorse—as Cordelia bent to pick up the broken frame. She tapped it on the floor to rid it of clinging glass slivers, then replaced it on the mantel.

We both stared at the family group shot—Trowbridge in the center, wearing a rented tuxedo and an uneasy smile, standing beside his new bride, Candy. Two teenagers married too young with no idea what was coming their way.

Without comment, she flipped it facedown.

Fatigue. It had been hovering in the distance, a dark threatening thundercloud, and now it hung over me. Pressing down on me. *I need to sit.* The couch was behind me but with it came the memory of Dawn Danvers's sly smile as Stuart Scawens nuzzled her shoulder. Were they the last to sit on those cushions?

I chose the floor instead, and rested my back against the side of the sofa, watching my Fae nose dust balls while thinking about would-haves and could-haves.

Those "could-have" thoughts are dangerous things. They can live forever in your daydreams, untested and lovely, unless you pull them outside of your head and give them a good shake in the light of the real world. I should know. I'm a real champ with dreams.

Tell her.

"We were going to fill up the gas tank in the old red van that Harry's got in his garage, and head west for British Columbia," I said quietly. "You and Biggs were going to argue all the way across Manitoba and Saskatchewan. Once we got there, Trowbridge and I were going to find us a farm or a house—someplace we could all live together in peace. Then, you were going to coach pageant brats and Biggs was going to get a girlfriend who was shorter than him. Harry was going to keep us neck-high in kindling. And I was going to get a job—one I wouldn't have gotten fired from . . ."

My voice trailed away. "None of it's going to happen, is it?"

"No." Cordelia's eyes were sad and knowing.

"How did it get to be such a mess?" I whispered. "I can't abandon Lexi. He's my brother. I won't—I can't—leave him to fend for himself while he tries to get over his sun-potion addiction."

"Some would think your mate should come first."

My wrist ached, my fingers were swelling. "Let's stop pretending, okay? I tricked Trowbridge into saying the words. I took what wasn't mine and now I'm paying for it."

"Exactly how are you paying for it?"

"Because I got what I wanted—I got *exactly* what I wanted. I sat on that damn pirate rock and I stared up at that bright star in the sky and made a wish. 'Please, Goddess, send them back to me. Bring me back my mate and brother.'" My voice rose in hurt and frustration. "Well, she did. And now I wish . . . Oh hell . . . I don't know what I wish—all I know is that nothing's going to work."

My cable of magic slithered up to my lap. I gazed at it, feeling older than Cordelia, Trowbridge, and Lexi all put together. "I can't be what Trowbridge wants me to be. I can't leave my 'Fae shit' outside of this house. It's part of me. It goes with me where I go. And I'm tired of trying to keep everything nice in little separate boxes. It's just . . ."

"Exhausting," she said softly. "Almost impossible to carry on, pretending to be something you're not."

I nodded in quiet misery.

"Stop worrying about what you *think* other people expect of you. And stop worrying about being anything other than what you are. It's a mistake we all make when we're young—fooling ourselves into believing that we've hidden from the world what we truly are. Most of the time, we haven't. People understand far more about us than we imagine."

She lifted her penciled brows.

"As for the 'Fae shit' issue—Bridge made an unfortunate comment in the heat of the moment. Wrestle an apology from him and move on." She fussed with her sweater. "You two definitely need some alone time."

"I'm afraid of what he's going to say when we are alone."

Cordelia heaved a sigh. "God, how I loathe living in high drama."

"Says the ex–drag queen."

Her features twisted into an impressive scowl. "Brat." Then she sat down on the floral-covered settee, and for a minute or so, neither of us said anything. Not even my Fae—who drifted off my lap, and headed back toward the edge of the hearth, seemingly intrigued by the dark hole of the firebox.

Moodily, Cordelia said, "I loved someone once."

I risked a sidelong glance. "How'd that work out?"

"Not very well." Her five o'clock shadow rasped as she scratched the side of her neck. "Possibly because I decided—based on one off-the-cuff comment—that he wasn't going to go the distance with me. And then I left Creemore before he had the opportunity to prove me wrong."

"Another pack member?" At her brief nod, I asked, "He's still here?"

"He'll never leave Creemore."

"That must be hard."

"Harder to face the fact that I was never going to replace him—that not one of those sweet young things who drifted into my life to bleed me dry has ever filled that hole inside me." She stared blankly ahead. "I want you to be smarter than I was."

My shoulders slumped. "I don't know what to do."

A size eleven Stuart Weitzman gave my hip a gentle nudge. "Why don't you start with doing something about that little snake? You've been mislaying your magic—little pieces of it—everywhere. It is a gift, is it not? Isn't that how your people refer to it? A talent or a gift? And look. You're letting it nose around in the ashes."

Surreptitiously, I swiped at my damp eyes. "You and Lexi are the only two people who see my magic."

"Really?" She busied herself with a thread on her skirt. "How odd."

"Return to me," I said. A moment later, my Fae sat sullenly in my gut, nestled close to my inner-Were. I felt marginally better. Spine stronger, belly full again. Merry slid down her chain and settled herself dead center over my heart.

Enough. I stood.

Cordelia observed, "Your niece is almost finished."

I turned my head toward the female huddled on the floor in the final throes of her change. *Hooray.* Anu's human form was going to be depressingly fit. Her shoulders were on the wide side, but since she was about as thin as a catwalk model, their width only served to make her waist look even smaller.

"She'll need a blanket." Cordelia headed for the stairs. "Stay with her?"

"Yup," I said without much enthusiasm. "You got to admit, this is the perfect end to a perfect day."

"Don't get cocky." Cordelia's voice floated down the stairwell. "It's only the morning."

"Even Karma has got to know when to call it a day," I called back.

Sucking in my lower lip, I leaned against the door frame and settled in for the rest of the show. Another forty seconds

of moaning and leg jerking before Anu was finished. My
brother's daughter lay on the dusty floor, naked—a long-
running Were theme I was getting more than a little tired
of—and protectively curled into a ball. She gave a watery
sniff. Then she pushed a heavy swath of hair from her
cheek, knuckled away some eye goop, and lifted her gaze.

Oh Fae Stars. Green eyes, so pale they were almost
translucent, widened and filled with tears. *They're the
exact shade of mine.* A minute comet of green fire spat at
me—like a cat's hiss—before it circled her dark pupil and
faded.

"You're nothing more than a kid," I said in shock.

Lexi's brat looked down on herself and uttered a bleat
of dismay.

Yup, you're naked. But it appeared my niece was definitely not comfortable with that concept because she executed a frantic scramble for a place to hide or something to
cover her nudity. Which was too bad because there was
nothing except a wall, a staircase, and a carpet runner
nailed down to the floor.

"Hurry up with the blankie," I hollered.

Cordelia leaned over the railing to toss me a wedding
quilt. "Here."

I caught it. "You couldn't have found something that
didn't smell like Trowbridge?"

"I have an aversion to Mannus's scent," she answered.

"Good God. Has she been weaned yet?"

At the sound of Cordelia's drawling voice, Miss Woebegone uttered another wrenching cry then buried her wet
head into her knees. Her shoulders shook and she began to
cry, but quietly.

I grimaced and edged toward her. "What is she, twelve?"
It was tempting to toss the thing over her like a dust sheet.

Cordelia frowned. "I'd say more like—"

"Fifteen," piped up Biggs from the end of the hall.

"Shut up!" Our voices rang in perfect unison. Biggs
pulled a face and melted back into the kitchen.

"Don't bite," I warned, crouching to drape it over her

shoulders. My knuckles grazed baby-soft skin, and with that came a flea of a thought: *Trowbridge would never touch a child.* I verified that certainty with my nose. "Her skin doesn't carry his scent."

Cordelia huffed as she descended the stairs. "I can't believe how long it took you to figure that out. Of course she wouldn't have a scent. She has Fae blood in her, just like you do—which means—"

"She'd pick up whatever scent she's been around. And since Lexi doesn't have one, she'd smell like Trowbridge." I sat back on my heels, thinking that life was a freakin' scale in front of me. One side was already heavily weighted, and Cordelia kept tossing handfuls of pebbles onto the other. "You know you're biased?" I said. "You're definitely Team Trowbridge."

"Of course I am," she said simply, her tone gentle. "He's beautiful, and I've always had a weakness for lovely things." Her gaze grew penetrating. "But I gave you a promise six months ago that I'll never take back. Come what may, I will always be your friend."

You're more than that, I thought. *And Trowbridge isn't pretty anymore, not the way he once was.* Hard, yes. Honed, definitely. And maybe—my heart twisted at the thought—more than a little tortured. "Do you think everyone has One True Thing?"

"Yes." Her mouth twisted into a sad smile. "And no."

"What do you mean?"

"I think it's time for tea." She pushed me toward the kitchen. "Come along. My tolerance for babysitting is limited to one hour. Let's see if I can rustle up anything sweet before the meter runs out."

"I'd kill for a piece of chocolate."

"Wouldn't we all, darling. Wouldn't we all."

Chapter Eighteen

Cordelia poured boiling water into the old china teapot.

Biggs was on the job. Cheeks sucked in, he attempted to level Lexi with a De Niro. I was hoping it would be sooner rather than later before he gave up on his glower. His "You looking at me?" only added more tension to a room already swollen full with it.

I was hungry and there was nothing sweet in the cupboards except sugar for the tea. We were making do with hot English Breakfast mixed with as many spoonfuls of the sweet stuff as we could tolerate.

Yay.

Lexi's head had lifted when I entered the room, but since then he'd retreated inside himself. Yes, on the surface, he appeared to be relatively content to sit at the table, his hand slowly stroking the ferret he'd freed from the Black Mage's bag. But inwardly? Another story. His booted foot kept rocking against the chair rung.

Annoying.

The only living creature in the room who wasn't irritated, depressed, stressed, or pissed off was the ferret. Biggs hadn't wanted it to be released from its captivity— which Cordelia had ridiculed. "Oh, shove off. What's he going to do with the animal? Throw it at you? Besides, the Fae won't do anything that could cause his sister harm."

Then she'd given Lexi her patented sneer. "Now, will you, darling?"

There it was again—no one wanted to hurt me. But my throat was still so tight it felt like an aching sore. Things had been said. Promises and threats had been made. Family lost and found. Cordelia placed a mug in front of me, then filled it with tea. "Chin up," she said severely.

"You betcha," I muttered, reaching for it with my left hand—my right being temporarily out of action, thanks to the blister forming on the web between my thumb and my pointing finger.

She gave my twin the same then pushed the sugar bowl closer to me.

"Don't you have anything stronger?" Lexi examined the contents of the mug with disgust. "Something with a kick in it?"

"No," Cordelia said flatly.

A lie. Two minutes ago, she'd opened a cupboard and closed it fast, but not quickly enough to keep me from catching a glimpse of a liquor bottle. I killed the sigh birthing in my chest and added five teaspoons of sugar to my tea. Merry rested on my shoulder. Her movements were slight—I doubt if either Biggs or Cordelia had noticed it—but I was conscious of how she kept herself oriented in Cordelia's direction. Wherever Ralph traveled, so did her interest. *How am I going to reunite them?*

I swiveled in my chair to check on my niece—not because I felt responsible for Miss Woebegone, but because the wholesome Norman Rockwell kitchen with its old stove, pine cupboards, and blue and white curtains was making me uncomfortable. Anu had edged herself to the doorway. Another foot and she'd actually be in the same room with us.

"Does she know who you are?" I asked.

"Of course, I am the Black Mage's Shadow." His voice was bland, but there was a line of sweat on his upper lip. "The Fae who creeps into his mistress's boudoir each night and leaves before daylight."

"She's got green eyes." I herded a few granules of spilled sugar into a miniature molehill. "They're almost as pale as mine."

"They're *exactly* the same shade."

"That eye color standard issue in Merenwyn?"

"No." He'd said it in a clipped fashion as if the subject bored him, but my twin radar lit up. *Something more there,* I thought. Twelve years of sharing meals and fighting for homework space at the Strongholds' cramped kitchen table had cued me to detect the slightest weak spot. I waited until he'd torn his gaze from the 2002 calendar tacked to the bulletin board, before asking in a casual voice, "Who's her mother?"

He inspected the metal teaspoon as if it might bite him before adding three measures of sugar to his tea. "A Raha'ell bitch."

I winced at the coldness in his voice. "She couldn't come with you?"

"She's dead." He took a cautious sip and grimaced.

"Oh, Lexi, I'm sor—"

"I fucked her, not loved her," he said with a faint lift of his shoulder. Cordelia made a noise at the back of her throat that could have been classified as a refined growl. Seemingly oblivious, my brother reached for the sugar bowl again. He tipped a thin stream of the sweetener into his cup. "You were always such a romantic, runt."

"Says the guy who used to stand on top of our pirate rock and holler, 'I'll save you, my lady.'" I stroked the peak of my pointed ear for a moment or two, watching my brother play catch-the-paper-towel-ball with the ferret. "How old is Anu?"

"She's seen thirteen winters."

One year older than he'd been when the Black Mage had taken him away. "Her eyes do that thing mine used to do. You know . . ." I slid a shy glance toward Lexi. "The spitting light, the miniflares. Has she produced a full flare yet?"

"No."

"So she hasn't found her One True Thing," I murmured.

Lexi rolled his eyes. "Do you still believe everything that Mum told us? A full flare isn't as common as she said it was. Believe it or not, it's considered a mark of high nobility among the Fae. I didn't even know I could do it until I was well into my manhood, and even then what I have is more of a flash than a full flare."

Aha, that's another thing I do better than Lexi.

Cordelia filled a mug with tea and lots of sugar and placed it on the floor a few feet inside the kitchen door. My niece gazed at it with a longing that spoke of a dry mouth and hunger. "She hasn't had anything to eat or drink since she got here," I said, feeling an unpleasant twist of guilt.

"She wouldn't have accepted anything from either one of us." He turned a spoonful of sugar into a serving of sugary tea paste then offered it to his pet. Not something you see every day. A ferret eating from a spoon.

"I thought they were carnivores," I said.

"Ferrets like sweet stuff like any other Fae. Don't you, Steellya?" Yellow wolf eyes seemed to blink at me as he absently rubbed his tattoo. "You know what I was thinking about?"

"What?"

"How we used to cheat in school."

I smiled.

"Permission?" his hooded gaze inquired.

A thought picture? Here? I let my gaze innocently roam. My niece's attention seemed focused on the pink coffee mug, Cordelia's on the sink, and Biggs's on Anu (I knew he'd waver from the job). I bit my lip and nodded. A slip, and a slide, and then the real world—the back door with its four-paned glass window and old-fashioned door handle—disappeared. A moment of haze, then ta-da! I received Lexi's thought picture in vivid, full color.

Huh. I'd expected something that would stir my heartstrings, maybe a picture of the four Strongholds, prefire, prekidnap, preheartbreak. Sitting at our own table—Dad, Mum, Lexi, and me—happy. Instead I got this: Knox's minibottle of sun potion. *Not going to happen.* The skin around his eyes tightened when I mouthed my reply.

He let Steellya have the spoon. A small smile then another image. But this time, transmission was faster and harder—more of a mental shove. I pressed my hand to my forehead, and waited for the picture to settle. Lexi and me, sitting in the front seat of a car—me at the wheel with him holding a map.

I blinked to erase it then glanced at the clock. *Less than an hour left till noon.* Did Lexi really think that it was as simple as stealing a car and hitting the road? Fae Stars— what about his daughter? How about Ralph and Merry? And here's one that was at the top of my list: what about me? And the long-held fantasy of mates-forever that was poised on a knife's edge?

"Promise me you won't leave with him," Trowbridge had asked. *"Let me explain."*

Could anything get us past this? Brother gone bad? Mate bond fractured? Trowbridge coming back so foreign he barely matched the man of my memory?

And really, could he—the man of few words—find the right ones to "explain" all this?

I thought back to that slow stroke of his thumb on my knuckle as we stood in front of the assembled pack/ would-be Hedi murderers and wondered if he'd been dumb enough to think a touch, a feel, a press of skin was the equivalent of a talk. I had a growing sense that he'd been trying to bypass the awkward necessity of speech, cagily trying to speak to me with his skin and his heat.

Cheater. Some words are important. Strung together, they can save people a world of hurt. For instance, "No, Hedi, I never told your brother to sweeten the pot."

My twin drummed his fingers on the table, impatient for my response.

I answered with a vehement headshake.

"Why not?" he said out loud.

Cordelia turned, sponge in hand. Biggs straightened from his slouch against the door.

"Because I'm not ready to," I snapped.

Without permission or delicacy, my brother shot one final image through the open channel between us. It surged into me like a tidal bore, too fast to repel, too powerful to outrun. A small pack of wolves—maybe seven or eight of them. Viewed from some vantage spot above them. Freeze-framed in the moment of their bloody victory. Prey had been felled—a man, legs akimbo, arms flung out, mouth open in a soundless scream—and the wolves were clustered, shoulder to shoulder, around his body. Slick smears of red on the grass. One large, gray wolf tearing a sinew from the man's neck. The others' lips curled into snarls, poised at the point of a rumble for the choicest meats.

I gasped and tried to rinse the image out of my head, but the vision was so ugly, so sickening. "Don't ever do that again," I said in a shaky voice.

His face was sweaty and pale, his eyes bruised. "That's who they are."

Cordelia moved to stand between us. "What's going on?"

I focused on slowing my breathing, clearing my mind.

"You're a fool if you ignore that." His Merenwynian accent was back. "Can't you see them for what they are?" Then he dared to send another mental nudge.

I stood up so fast, my chair overturned, and Merry tumbled off my shoulder. She swung from my chain, flashing yellow-orange in alarm. "I've had enough of being pushed around today," I said in a raw voice. "If you ever try what you just did again—I swear I'll level you."

Lexi lifted his lip in a superior sneer that pushed buttons I'd thought long buried, then said, "You needed a few home truths delivered."

I did, did I?

"I've had enough truths to last a lifetime." I flattened my palms on the pine table and leaned into his space. "Why don't you take a turn? Here's a home truth for you. Our father would be ashamed of you. He would have been horrified by what you've done."

"Move away from him," Cordelia murmured to me.

But I couldn't. Lexi's eyes had widened with a hurt that somehow had turned around and bit me. *Oh Goddess. What had I done?* "Lexi. I didn't mean it. I'm so sorry. I'm just tired and—"

"You think you're fit to judge me? You?" Lexi rose slowly, cradling the ferret. Sweat dotted the shorn side of his scalp. "You have no fucking idea what it's like to find yourself in another realm, cut off from everybody. Look at you." He flicked a dismissive hand. "You've never gone hungry. You've never been too afraid to shut your eyes. You haven't got a clue."

No. I didn't know what life in Merenwyn was like, and for that, I owed him. Ten years ago, when the Fae had carried him through our kitchen, Lexi's gaze had swung to me. He'd seen me, sitting hunched in my hidey-hole, and then, he'd deliberately looked away. He'd done it to protect me. And because of his sacrifice, I'd had a life of sorts. Boring and quiet, and yes, equipped with my own set of nightmares. But nothing like the horror his life had been.

His ferret looked at me with accusing eyes.

"I'm sorry," I said, shamed. "I'm so—"

"Save it." Lexi cocked his head to the side. "You know what I see when I look at you? Just another one of the Son of Lukynae's well-trained bitches. Sit," he said, his tone set on hurt. "Come on, 'sit.' Or do you only answer to your master?"

And bam. Just like that my emotions heated right back to simmering rage.

"You have *magic*," he taunted. "Do you know what I could have done with that back home? Even gifted with a minor talent like yours, I could have made something of myself with it. I would have taken it, shaped it into something useful, honed its edge every night until it was sharp as a blade, and it would have protected me!"

"You *were* given a magical gift," I said through my teeth.

"Being able to see magic isn't a *gift*. It's a fucking curse!" he shouted. "Sure, I can see it—even steal it and use it for an hour or two—but it won't stay with me. It's not *mine*. I have nothing of my own except my wits and my balls. The rest of it—my clothing, my food, my bed—it's all a short-term loan. One misstep, one stupid gesture—it's gone and so am I. No one except the Black Mage knows that I have a talent. The men of the Court give me a nod, but I know what they're really thinking behind their masks—that I'm just another of the Black Mage's pets and it's only a question of time before he loses interest. As far as they can tell, I butt-fucked my way out of the kitchen, and sooner or later, my protector's going to tire of me, and then all his little bonus gifts—like the temporary magic I sometimes demonstrate, or the right to eat at table—will be taken away. The bets are already being laid about his newest acquisition." His mouth curled into a smile of self-derision. "You know what the worst part of it is? I'm the dickhead who brought that little mystwalking freak into the castle—"

"Mystwalkers aren't freaks."

"They should have let the trait die out." He swiped his hair over his shoulder. "Drowned each and every one of those abominations at birth."

My mouth fell open, so deep was my shock. *Abominations?* I'd pried open a can of sardines with my teeth to discover it packed instead with scorpions, stingers raised. Now all I wanted to do was reseal the lid. Painfully, with a sledgehammer of harsh words, but dismay and rage had temporarily choked me of a vocabulary suitable to the task.

"Instead the Black Mage sends me searching for them." He shook his head, his gaze unseeing. "I brought that little shit in—had to fight off half his family first—thinking he would keep my master occupied for a week or two. Instead, the mystwalker turned out to have true talent. He'll travel to Threall soon, if he hasn't already."

I think he already has. You wouldn't believe the mess he's made of Threall.

"I'll be as worthless as two teats on a boar hog if the little prick succeeds." True worry creased Lexi's brows,

and the ferret placed a soft paw to his tense jaw. "The
Black Mage trains his pets in secrecy, but I know what he
means to do. He wants to steal the Old One's soul, and
with it, all his knowledge."

"You can't steal a soul," I said flatly.

"He'll send me to the Spectacle again." The hand that
petted the ferret faintly trembled. "But this time he'll have
them blind me first, so I can't use my flare to save myself."

I don't ever want to see inside my brother's soul, I
thought bleakly. *It would be fear plus bitterness plus fear
plus crazy . . .* I softened my voice. "It doesn't matter what
the Black Mage does or thinks. What happens in Merenwyn no longer matters. You're home. You never have to go
back to that nightmare."

"Of course I'm going back," he said scathingly. "Earth
has no sun potion."

"Well, get over it," I replied. "You don't need it."

His face grew as mean as the day I'd won his stack of
Pokémon cards. "You know, when I crossed that portal, I
thought there was a good chance that you'd died of old age.
It grieved me. Well, look what I found. My twin's only
twenty-two. She's still got her whole life in front of her.
Not a cloud in her sky, or a useful thought in her head.
She's mated herself to the Alpha of Creemore, and she's
going to live in this nice home, and everything's going to
be roses and sunshine."

Enough. Nasty did a push-up inside me and said, "Let
me at him."

"Roses and sunshine?" I said acidly. "You think I don't
live with a knife over my head? Well, try this on for size—
I'm an 'abomination,' too." I read confusion on his face,
and the ugly side of me preened. "My true talent isn't
minor—it's unique. I'm a mystwalker. I started walking
through your dreams back when you were still playing
with your G.I. Joes. And you know what? I must be a
damn good one, because I don't need some mage to train
me to travel to Threall."

Disgust rippled across his face.

I gave him a twisted smile. "I could go to Threall and thumb through your memories like they were the yellow pages." My Fae stirred inside me, dragon eyes slitting open. "You want to know what souls look like? They're round as a ball, and as bright as stars in the sky. They have absolutely no defense against a mystwalker—they hang like fruit waiting to be plucked from ancient trees. All I'd have to do is touch your tree, and I'd be in your mind. I could see past every lie. I could mine every black deed you ever did or even thought of doing. I could examine your life as ruthlessly as you've dismissed mine."

What caused what happened next? The raw exchange of truths? The reality of my true talent? Or the sudden ugliness that spewed from me?

Whatever it was, it only took Lexi a split second to act.

He whipped the sugar bowl at Biggs.

Fast as a pit fighter, Lexi pivoted—chair in hand—and brought it crashing down on Cordelia. She fell with an operatic moan. Two steps and he was by her side, yanking Ralph up and over her head. Her wig came off with it, and when she made a quick instinctive snatch for it, he lashed out with his foot. She rolled away, her hand covering her balding head. But she didn't rise—vindictive and snarling—and bitch-slap him right back to Merenwyn.

My fleeting thought—*this from the woman who threatened to hurl me into the pond for forgetting to put the cap back on the milk bottle?*—was interrupted by Anu's scream.

As shrieks go, it was as piercing as a banshee on moonshine. She charged, mouth in a fearsome grimace, wedding quilt a flying cape behind her. Her father half turned, caught her in full momentum. For a split second he held on to her, their bodies twisting, and then he let go, and she stumbled backward.

That's your daughter.

My niece's hip caught the Welsh dresser, toppling some china off its pine shelf. The old earthenware platter—pink spring blossoms on a cream background—fell and cracked into two jagged pieces. Lexi spun for Biggs, but the younger Were appeared to be dazed. A trickle of blood streamed from a cut on his cheek. *Seriously? He got nailed with a sugar bowl, and he's near out for the count? I've seen Biggs face far worse.* My brother snorted, snatched up the knapsack, and pulled open the back door. He glanced outside, then flashed me one last penetrating glance over his shoulder. One I had no frame of reference for, nor any inclination to untangle its meaning.

He ran.

And for a second I just stood there, stunned, my anger doused by a disappointment so wretched all I wanted to do was sink down to the floor. Was there anything salvageable in my brother? *Anything?*

Damn right there was something salvageable. He was my *brother*.

I started for the door, crying, "Lexi, come back!"

Biggs stepped in front of me. "No," he said, blocking the doorway.

"Get out of my way!" I slapped at the arm stretched across the threshold. When a hard-eyed Biggs didn't budge, I ducked and tried to slip under his armpit, but Cordelia hooked the back of my T-shirt, and when I tried to slither out of *that,* she grabbed my hair. My eyes slit as I strained against the tug on my scalp.

I spat through my teeth, "I order you to—"

Cordelia's voice was firm. "You don't give the orders now, darling."

Yeah. That sent me straight into orbit.

What followed was a three-second, undignified scuffle of slapping hands, pulling hair, and blinding fury that ended with my own horrible shriek—not a Xena banshee yell— just a woman's howl of absolute frustration and impotent rage. They were bigger than me—physically subduing me was a given. Biggs wrapped me in a bear hug, trapping my hands so that no magic could fly, and as he did, the ferret slipped through the maze of our feet.

It raced across the grass, seemingly intent on catching up to my twin.

"Lexi! Come back," I choked out once more as Biggs lifted me off my feet.

My brother was past the clothesline by the time Trowbridge slid into the room. He'd cleared the hydrangeas when Biggs hauled me away to the back corner and was beyond the old sugar maple when Cordelia passed her Alpha the loaded shotgun.

Oh Goddess, no. "Don't hurt my brother," I said in an awful voice.

"One of you take Hedi out of the room," growled Trowbridge, raising the gun to his naked shoulder. Biggs gave me an apologetic squeeze and started to back us toward the other door—the one that led to that dimly lit hallway and a room with dark memories.

"Don't shoot him! I'll make him show you the Safe Passage. I will—"

"Biggs, now!" snarled Trowbridge.

It was an instant, visceral reaction—hands caught, escape impossible—I called up my flare. It came on powerfully hard, its progress from sleep to full light fast as flipping a switch. With it came heat. I felt incandescent, a Fae blowtorch primed for some destruction.

My Fae brushed past my quivering Were—a thinking, clever entity no longer a serpent of doom—and she told me, "Use our wiles."

"Biggs," I said in a pathetic whimper. Fool that he was, he looked down to my upturned face and I nailed him. Up close and personal—a sucker punch of a flare. Undiluted by reason or caution. Green fire, made of pure vexed will and Fae spite. At that moment I didn't give a shit who he was or what he'd done for me.

Biggs made a noise awfully like a baby's mewl and dropped me.

And I didn't care.

I was Hedi the Destroyer, and my flare was me laying

down the law. Touch my brother and I'll never forgive you.
Stop me from coming to his aid, and I'll kneecap you. A
nicer, kinder person would have let Biggs back away. Part
of me recognized that, but it amounted to a white-hankie
wave from a limp-wristed sissy. I wasn't in the mood for
taking prisoners or sitting in a sharing circle. My Fae
swelled inside me—*we are Fae*—and my light grew mercilessly fierce. Biggs made another noise—one of utter
shame and dismay—and shuffled backward, shoulders
hunched, eyes downcast. Then I swung my gaze toward the
door, where the man with the dreads stood. *You will stop.
I will make you stop.*

For the record, I used everything I had on him. Theoretically, he should have felt at least a little singed. But
Trowbridge is, was, and will always be incombustible. He
grimly lowered his eye to the gun sight.

I darted forward—I don't know what I meant to do,
pull his dreads? I was beyond thought, beyond plan, beyond reason. Half of me was protective twin, half of me
was pissed-off Fae. So, I never saw it coming when Cordelia intercepted me, her square hand already primed.

She slapped my face so hard I saw stars.

I tottered for a second, holding my cheek. My BFF took
quick advantage of my shock—one light kick behind my
knees, and I crumpled. No sooner had I hit the floor, than
she'd clamped my head between her big hands. Slowly, she
forced it downward. Nails, blunt and wide, dug into my
scalp. My neck was strong, but her hands were stronger,
and soon green light bathed the Trowbridges' golden oak
floors. "Put it out," she hissed. "Right now."

My Fae recognized the odds, even if mortal-me was
beyond calculating them. She gave up before I did, sinking
back to my gut, where no one could hurt her. Without her
presence to bolster my all-too-mortal fury? My rebellion
was pitifully short. My light sputtered, and then—as despair filled me—it flickered out.

Only then did Cordelia ease her pressure. "That was
unforgivably stupid," she growled.

I stubbornly lifted my chin, and stared with watering eyes past her.

My twin's flight had brought him to the line that divided civilized from quasi-tamed, where overgrown grass gave way to a beaten track leading to the pond. His long blond hair streamed behind him, his feet were light and fast.

Run.

And he did. Fae Stars, he did.

Trowbridge's muscles tensed, and I thought I saw his finger tighten on the trigger.

"Don't do it," I said, my voice thin and small. But I knew, even as I tightened my blistered hand into a useless fist, that what followed would be ruin and despair, and the heavy thing inside my chest would grow, and grow, until I couldn't take another breath.

"He can't leave this realm with an amulet," said Trowbridge, his voice warrior hard. "He's chosen his end."

"Then let me take him back to Merenwyn."

He stilled then said, "I can't risk you or Merry falling into the Black Mage's hands."

I figured that was his final statement—Trowbridge's justification if there was ever to be one declared. And I prepared myself. Holding my breath, tensing my muscles, knowing—*it's going to happen any moment now.* This time I couldn't stop death.

Then Harry stepped out of the bushes at the edge of the cliff. Old man, my ass. He swung a bat at my brother's knees with the strength and accuracy of a ballplayer in his prime, and Lexi dropped to the turf. My twin rolled, once or maybe twice—I was losing detail because my vision was so blurred—trying to dodge another blow. The two Weres who'd lain in wait with Harry slunk out of their hiding spots. All three fell on him, with fists and rope. He fought and cursed in my mother's tongue.

Wolves in human skin, I thought.

My gaze fell to the floor as he was trussed, and I stared at the dark seam between one aged plank of oak and another, telling myself, *I'll think later. I'll feel later.*

"Biggs." Trowbridge's tone was as empty of inflection as an old gunfighter's. "Put the shotgun back where it belongs."

Red sneakers shuffled past me. "He was after the amulet, just like you said he was," I heard Biggs mutter to his Alpha. I must have flinched, because Cordelia patted my shoulder—gently, the way you do when very bad news is given.

"Cordelia, step back," the Alpha of Creemore said sternly.

"She didn't know what she was doing," Cordelia said in an undertone, but she did what she was told. Knowing that it was time for my ass-whipping, I lifted my eyes to stare into my mate's harsh face.

Blue comets spun around his dilated pupils.

Don't use your flare on a Were. Don't use that Fae shit in this house. Well, hadn't I just done that. I'd aimed my flare at a pack member. More significantly, I'd tried to make *him* submit to it. In front of his people, who used to be my people, but evidently lines had been blurred, and polarities had been exchanged.

And now? I had no people.

Except a brother, who'd hauled ass as quickly as he could from his mystwalking sister, and an amulet whose affection for me was momentarily questionable. I glanced down at her. No, not questionable. My pal Merry had gone chilly; her stone muddy brown. Usually, those were her indicators for being sick, or sickened. I was thinking it was a double dose of the latter when Trowbridge hit me with the true flare of an Alpha.

I thank the Goddess and all her little brats that I was already kneeling.

Oh Fae Stars.

For all my inner resentment toward the pack, overall I'd been a pretty good kid in Creemore. The old Alpha had never had reason to look at me, much less gently chastise me with a spark of his signature flare. And I'd already gone through a spin under Lexi's light show, which had felt stomach-heaving, but three quarters of that had been shock and surprise.

But this? It was so much worse.

Trowbridge's flare was totally impartial—and perhaps that was the cruelest thing about it. There was no recognition in it that I was his mate, his One True Thing. I was the creature who'd dared to threaten a natural-born Alpha. It was a full-out reprimand. Solid and heavy—an anvil on my soul, draining me of my pride and self-will.

Crushing.

Hurting.

The urge to prostrate myself under its heat was so crushing that I almost forgot how to breathe. I wanted to fall to my knees under its weight, to stretch out a pleading hand.

"*Submit*," his flare demanded.

No.

So I held my breath—who needed it?—and I bade my spine not to fail me. Even if my inner-bitch howled at me to go on my belly, to beg forgiveness. Even if we both wanted his eyes to soften into approval and his scent to wrap us in its fragrant, loving embrace.

Fold once, and it will be a lifetime of coming to heel.

I ignored her instincts to heel. Shut her down, and listened to one voice, deep inside me.

The me-of-me.

And she said, "Don't you dare fold. Strongholds hold."

So I did just that, even if I trembled like a pooch at its first visit with the vet.

Anu uttered a whine as the kitchen turned electric blue. What would have happened if Biggs had taken longer to put the shotgun back in its place over the mantel? Or if the three-man crew who carried my brother back to the Trowbridge manse had stumbled on one of those prairie-dog holes? Or if Cordelia hadn't made a humming noise that sounded almost like an involuntary protest?

Would I have held tough? Who knows.

I swayed, but I stayed. Upright. Dry-pantied. Stiff-spined.

And yet . . . Before Biggs had rejoined us, before Harry had laid my brother at his Alpha's feet, before I'd swooned and plunged into a pool too frigid to swim out of . . . Before all of those humbling and hurtful things, Trowbridge's light eased. From harsh blue, to bright blue, to finally, a pair of tired eyes doused of all fire.

We studied each other.

"Why did you make me do it?" his gaze asked.

"Because you wanted to hurt my brother," I tried to tell him with mine. "Because I'm never going to roll over for you like a well-trained bitch. Because I was angry and part of me wanted to challenge you. Because I forgot where we were. Who was watching . . ."

Yeah. I know. Too many sentences.

He brought down a shield between us.

And I was glad.

Because the last thing I read in his eyes was pain and a bitter, aching loneliness.

Chapter Nineteen

Situation normal, all fucked up.

The Weres held court, and the Fae waited.

I was good at that, though—waiting. I'd earned a PhD for it, with minors in Lingering Hopefully, Abiding Patiently, and Marking Time Before Being Royally Screwed Over.

An unasked question hung heavy in the Were-scented air. What should be done with the Fae? With no immediate answer forthcoming, Cordelia had righted my chair and eased me into it. Harry had returned—he of the wicked swings—and had laid a sullen and bound Lexi at Trowbridge's feet. The grim-faced Alpha of Creemore had rolled my brother over, and pried the Royal Amulet from his bloody hand. Ralph now hung from Trowbridge's neck. Biggs had found a new place for himself, a little to the left of his Alpha's shadow. And Merry had slowly—almost thoughtfully—ratcheted up her chain, until she hung like a loose choker, her pendant a warm comfort against the hollow of my throat.

I hadn't figured out why she'd done that—at that precise moment *I* didn't even like me.

True, my brain wasn't working very well. It kept picking up stupid stuff such as that the seat cushions on the old

Windsor chairs were mismatched, and that no one had ever thrown out the dead houseplant on the kitchen windowsill. The cap on the saltshaker was unscrewed, and half of the salt lay on the table. I wondered who'd done that. Mannus, always so hasty and greedy? Or maybe one of his crew? Out of the corner of my eye I saw Cordelia reach for her wig, then slap it against her knee to shake free the dust. "Biggs, sweep up the crockery," she ordered, breaking the tense silence.

"That's not my job," he started to whine. But then Harry made a discreet rumble-growl low in the back of his throat, so Biggs stomped over to the broom leaning in the corner, anyhow.

The Alpha of Creemore's back was to us—and had been for 216 "Mississippis." Arms folded, he stood square in the back door's threshold, silent and broody, seemingly engrossed by the awesome weed display growing on his father's back lawn. That was another thing different about him. Before, he always leaned against something—be it a car, a door frame, or a piece of furniture. Now he was given to standing alone, legs spread and planted. Spartacus without the skirt.

Then Lexi whispered, "Ask him to let me go."

I'd been doing a pretty good job of avoiding my twin's gaze—I was too bruised by his sledgehammer of home truths, and too conflicted by the emotions stirred at the sight of him trussed like some turkey ready to be fed to the oven, to have the stomach to look at him.

"Be quiet," I murmured, glancing toward the floor. Oh, what a lovely picture he was. A rope had been twisted around his torso, binding his arms behind him, and another shorter length had taken care of his legs. He lay on his side on the kitchen floor, his head lifted, anxiety and anger twisting his features. A streak of sweet-pea-scented blood oozed from the cut on his lower lip, and his usually sleepy green eyes were wilder than an infuriated tiger's.

"He'll do it for you," my twin coaxed in another stage whisper.

Trowbridge stiffened, just slightly—enough to let me know that he'd heard, and processed, and already decided that the answer to that was, "Hell, no."

"You're only making it worse," I muttered.

Sun potion leaked from my brother's pores, a thin layer of too-sweet squeezed in between all those other more dominant strata of scents. He clumsily changed tack. "Hell, it's not what it looked like. I can explain—"

"It's not?" My frustrated instincts to right something bit at me. I replaced the cap on the saltshaker and twisted it until it was tight. "So, you didn't steal Ralph and run hell-bent for the portal?"

He rested his head on the floor, and said hollowly, "I had a reason."

"If you wanted to go back so badly," I said quietly, lining the saltshaker against the pepper so they stood side by side, "you could have asked me. I would have asked Merry to take both of us through the portal."

I brushed some of the salt into a pile, then glanced at my brother.

His expression was mutinous. Little spits of green fire circled his dilated pupils. "I didn't steal anything. The Royal Amulet belongs to the King of the Court. I was going to return it to its rightful owners."

Merry's chain tightened. Just one notch.

"There's a huge reward for the Royal Amulet," he continued. "If I was the one to bring it back, I could write my own ticket. It could change my life for me back—"

"Home," I said dully, feeling my cheeks flush.

My answer only served to infuriate him. He struggled against the bonds, and when I didn't fall to my knees beside him and plead, "Please, sir, I beg of you. Untie my wretch of a brother!," he reacted poorly.

"I can't talk to you like this!" Lexi shouted. "Tell him to unbind me!"

I wanted to say a lot of things. Like "Don't ask me for something I cannot give you, brother-mine." Or how about this? "Don't make me want to slap you and hold you and yell at you all at the same time, you broken and fouled shadow of my twin."

But I didn't.

"Taking the amulet was the only way I *can* go back," he pleaded, his voice too loud in that pin-drop silence. "Don't you understand? I can't return without it."

For a muzzy second or two, I considered the question seriously. Did I understand anything of this day? Of last night? My aching fingers crept to the peak of my ear. That's a big fat no. "I have been near drowned in lies and truths ever since you landed here, and I don't know what I believe or understand anymore." I closed my eyes briefly, but even that didn't magically reshuffle all the puzzle pieces, any more than stroking my ear soothed all the conflict inside me. How could it? My brother lay bound near my feet, and my mate stood brooding in the doorway. And I was in the middle of them. I'd always be in the middle of them.

I shook my head. "I'm so damn confused. I don't know what to believe."

Trowbridge slowly turned around, arms still folded over his chest. "He can't return without the Royal Amulet, because the Black Mage sent him to steal it."

Blue eyes watched me. For what? For me to stand up and say, "Well, that made it all clear!" I went back to herding my salt pile into a tidier mountain, thinking Trowbridge was going to have to dumb it down for me, and feed it to me in tiny morsels, because I still wasn't connecting all the dots.

"Hell, I think one of my legs is broken," Lexi pleaded. "It's hurting me to be tied up like this."

He's hurt.

I chewed the inside of my cheek. "Does he have to be tied up?"

"Go ahead, Harry," Trowbridge said, his face shuttered. "Untie him."

Harry shook his head, but Biggs and he untied Lexi and propped him on the chair. My twin's gaze darted around the room. From the window, to the door, to the knife stand, to the sharp broken shard of crockery by the Welsh dresser that Biggs had missed.

My brother was evaluating everything as a potential weapon. Just like Trowbridge did. Except his jittery nerves made his thoughts transparent whereas Trowbridge's inner mind-spin was becoming more obscure to me by the minute.

Lexi stretched his mouth, as if his lips were too dry. "You saw us come through the portal. We were *running* from the Black Mage. He and his men were on our heels."

Trowbridge's voice was completely flat, not one iota of wheedle in it. "They had horses. We had feet. They could have caught up with us at any time. The only reason we reached the portal was because the Black Mage wished us to. He needs something from this world, and he sent his Shadow to get it. I've been waiting to find out what exactly it was."

Ah. That explained the little kitchen opera I'd just witnessed. All those peculiarities of logic and reaction—my former inner circle had been given a new playbook. Trowbridge had told them to let Lexi make a break for it. It was the reason why my brother had been so laxly guarded, and why Cordelia hadn't knocked Lexi right off his feet when he stepped on her wig.

Though . . . Was that the reason Trowbridge hadn't pulled the trigger right away? He could have shot Lexi. He had a clear view, a gutload of hatred, and a valid reason. It would have been one sure way of making sure my brother never crossed another portal.

I traced a circle around my salt pile, and then asked Trowbridge, "You never thought that my brother just wanted to come back home?"

To me, I didn't add.

"No." Trowbridge lifted his shoulders. "Your brother's addicted to sun potion, and as he said, there is no juice in Creemore. It was a given that he was planning a smash and grab. I just wasn't sure if there was anything else he wanted."

Ow.

Stubbornly, I said, "Still, he could have just come to see what—"

"No one with any Were in them would take traveling through those gates casually," Trowbridge said harshly. "It's like a whacked-out ride at Wild Water Kingdom. Except the walls are made of water not fiberglass. And instead of sliding down, you're being pushed upward by a wind. Everything's blurry, but . . . there are people on the other side of the wall. You can see them. All tight together, twisted, pressing against the surface on the other side. I'm not sure if they're dead or alive. Their eyes . . ."

He shook his head. "In some places the passage gets real tight, and then it seems to split into two, sometimes three channels. If Merry hadn't led me, I'd have . . ." His lips tightened, then he dismissively lifted his shoulder. "It's a fucking nightmare in there. Your sense of time is shot. Your wolf wants you to change, and you're worrying how it will react to all the things it hears and sees. Last thing you want to do is go down one of those blind alleys."

I gazed at him, remembering how I had sent a half-conscious man through the gates and seen a wolf leap through the other end. *Another sorry to add to the list. Another thing to thank Merry for.*

"Don't listen to him," Lexi said in a soft hiss.

"Just for once, shut up," I said.

"You don't forget what it felt like," said Trowbridge. "And you don't look forward to doing it again. Your brother had already traveled through once. He knew what to expect. Add that to the fact he's half juiced on sun potion ninety-nine percent of the day . . . The trip here was hard." He lifted his gaze to mine and held it so I could read the truth. "Your brother was sent on a mission. I could only think of two things that the mage would consider valuable. One of them was the Royal Amulet."

"What was the other one?" asked Biggs.

"Hedi." A muscle moved in Trowbridge's cheek. "That was one thing your brother didn't lie about—there aren't a lot of mystwalkers in Merenwyn. They're right up there with the Sasquatch. I didn't know if he knew that Hedi was a mystwalker right up to ten minutes ago."

Just what every girl wants to hear—being compared to Bigfoot. I drew a moat around my small salt mountain. "Why's Ralph so important?"

He walked over to the fridge and leaned against it. "It has another name—the Opener of Doors. Doesn't mean shit to me. All I know is that the Black Mage wants it, and as long as I'm Alpha in this world, he's not going to get it."

Lexi saw the last boat sailing away without him. "He's trying to poison your mind, and you're letting him. Don't you see? He hates me because back in Merenwyn, I'm a somebody, and he's worth less than a farm animal!" Lexi groped for my hand, and when I pulled it away and tucked it in my lap, he exploded into full rage. "He didn't even want to come back to you! Remember, I had to 'sweeten the pot' before he'd agree to a deal!"

Trowbridge pushed away from the refrigerator. Standing alone and tall again. "I am—was—the leader of the Raha'ells. I owe them. If there was any way I could get them through the Safe Passage, I had to try."

"I can't deal with this," I said numbly, covering my face. "I can't think anymore."

"Hell, don't let them do this to me," my twin threatened. "I've got to go back. You don't understand—I'll die without the juice."

My twin, the drug addict.

"Here's the sum of what I understand," I said, my voice cracked and low. "You're wearing your lying face."

"You whoring bitch," my twin hissed.

"That's it." Two red spots on Trowbridge's cheeks. "Lock him in the room downstairs. We'll figure out what to do with him tomorrow."

Suddenly, Lexi sprang up—like hell he had a broken leg—and overturned the table in my direction. I dove for the floor and cried out when I landed on my burned hand. Trowbridge let out an ungodly roar and threw a roundhouse punch into my brother's face. Lexi went stumbling backward, tripped over my overturned chair, and fell on his hip. The Alpha of Creemore was on top of him before he'd even had a chance to roll. Trowbridge caught Lexi's collar in his bad hand, and he went to town on Lexi's face with his left.

Blood flew, and the scent of pink sweet peas blossomed again.

When a splatter of the red stuff hit the cabinet, something broke inside me. I screamed. Sharp and shrill. I kept it up until Cordelia had pulled my face into her lumpy breast. "Hush, hush," she murmured, rocking me.

"Don't let them do this," I heard my brother call to me. "You don't know——" Another smack of fist on flesh made me tremble and cringe. I turned my head to watch as they carried Lexi past me——the Alpha of Creemore and his trusted second, Harry. And it was hard not to remember another kitchen——this one in flames——and another time when my twin was carried away from me. But this time, in this homey kitchen, when everything had given over to ruin——through the destructive flames of home truths and broken loyalties——our gazes held.

Betrayer, his said.

A little part of me turned to stone. I crawled away from Cordelia's embrace and kept going until I hit the corner. There I crouched, a hand pressed against Merry. She wrapped a tendril of ivy around my thumb as doors were shut, locks were turned, and my brother's cries were finally silenced.

By the time Alpha and crew came upstairs, I felt leaden. I rocked on my heels, staring at the blister, now fat and yellow, on the web between my finger and my thumb.

Ugly.

Trowbridge came to me directly. No detours, no pausing to judge the relative dangers of the kill zone. The Alpha of Creemore sank onto his heels, his knees bracketing mine. We were so close I could have counted the lines radiating from his solemn eyes, if I'd had the time or a piece of paper to tally up the numbers.

He'd buried the loneliness. There wasn't any whiff of it in his gaze.

But he hadn't figured out how to hide his bone-deep fatigue.

It aged him.

I'll never catch up to him. I don't even want to anymore.

"Are you all right?" His scent spoke to my Were. Told her that his protective urges were hanging on to control by a very thin thread.

A regretful thump of a tail, low by my spine.

"I hate this kitchen," I muttered. "It smells of death like the rest of the house."

"This is your home." His voice was a low rumble. Lids lowered, gaze fixed on my twisting hands. "I'll have them scour it from top to bottom and put flowers in every room. It will be cleaned before the sun goes down."

"I don't think Lexi knows where the Safe Passage is." Trowbridge visibly tensed as I tested the edges of my blister with my nail. "If that's why you didn't shoot him."

So fragile, I felt. Poised on the edge of either violence or another meltdown.

Let it be violence. Don't let me cry in front of them again.

"Can I see your hand?" he asked, choosing to ignore the Lexi reference.

"No," I said flatly. He had a little piece of something green caught in his beard. Was it a bit of Merenwynian fern? I focused on it—not on the slope of his hard shoulder peeking through the dreads or the way the denim stretched over his thighs or the fact that a tiny smear of my brother's blood was glistening on top of his arm hairs, right by his elbow.

Cordelia cleared her throat in a meaningful way. Then I heard Harry say, "We've got some cleanup to organize. Biggs, bring the girl."

"Are you serious?" he whined.

"I could neuter you with one twist of my wrist, you featherbrained Chihuahua," said Cordelia.

I heard Biggs sigh and then we were alone.

Trowbridge hadn't moved a muscle during all this and I found myself thinking that he must be a good hunter. Able to pick his prey and wait for the right moment to pounce.

Don't pounce. I'm not prey.

He waited for a beat and then said tersely, "You've got to stop messing with that blister. It's driving me crazy to watch you hurt yourself."

Don't do that, Trowbridge—don't get all tender with me—I'm not ready.

I folded my arms—awkwardly, since a blistered mitt is resistant to being tucked under an elbow. It sent prickles of pain messages.

He stared at my pose for a moment or two, decided not to go for the challenge, then let out some anxiety by blowing a stream of air through his teeth. "I knew Lexi didn't know the location of the Safe Passage," he said heavily. "If Lexi had known its location, he would have used it himself so that he could have avoided the Black Mage and collected the bounty for the Royal Amulet. I knew that, Hedi." The general shape of his mouth got lost in his thick beard as he scowled.

Not a good look for you, Trowbridge.

"There really is a mother of a reward for the person who returns that pendant to the King of the Court," he said. "But your brother ran for the fairy pond, which meant he had to be bringing it back to the Black Mage."

"Ralph's a person, not a pendant or an 'it,'" I corrected darkly. Though His Nastiness sure looked like some sort of quasi-Celtic piece of flummery, resting placidly on Trowbridge's manly chest, his stone not sending up one tiny spit of light. Why was that? I needed tongs to handle Ralph in a pissy mood and now he was all cheery blue stone, content and smug. "I don't know why he's not throttling you."

Trowbridge lifted his eyebrows. Tested the emotional climate with an experimental waggle of them. "The enemy of my enemy is my friend?"

Probably more a case of like recognizes like. I mentally shrugged, dismissing the Ralph puzzle. There were more pressing questions to pose than the motivations of an Asrai amulet, and answers that might prove as painful as the blister I couldn't leave alone. "Once you figured that out, why didn't you just pull the trigger?"

He stared at my mouth for a moment, either gobsmacked by its lushness, or killing time as he tried to figure out what he should and shouldn't tell me.

Just say the right thing, Trowbridge. It's not difficult. All you have to do is tell me that you don't mean to kill my brother.

But he surprised me. He gazed at me for a second in consideration, then firmed his shoulders and told me the truth, flat and unvarnished. "You needed to hear him lie. You needed to see him as he was."

Did I? Everyone was telling me what I should be hearing, what I should be thinking, what I shouldn't dare do. It didn't change the inside of me. It didn't stop me from wanting to fix things, or change things, or do something, *anything*, to stop things from going to hell.

"But now what?" I probed. "Lexi can't return home—you won't let him cross the gates with an amulet. Unless you'd let me . . ." My voice trailed off, because Trowbridge had lowered his head. "You can't," I said to the top of his dreads. "The pack has seen him steal from you. You can't let that go without doing something. What are you going to do? If you hurt him, Trowbridge. If you kill him anyway—"

"Hasn't he hurt you enough?" His chin lifted. "Can't you see he's no good?" That's what his expression asked.

I chewed the skin on the inside of my mouth rather than answer either question.

Trowbridge shook his head in silent frustration—man-style—ear cocked toward the ceiling, eyes downcast and hooded, mouth thinned. "You can drive me right up the wall and back again." He exhaled, long, slow, measured. Then he cautiously reached to touch my hair—just lightly, not quite a stroke, or a pat—as if he just wanted to make sure this time he could without me biting.

His voice was regret-heavy and sincere. "I promise you that I won't kill him."

There must be a special on promises today.

It should have been enough. I should have thrown myself into his arms right then, smothering his hairy cheeks with thank-you kisses. But there was something about the way his expression momentarily darkened after he'd made that vow, as if my happiness were something sharp sticking him in the ribs.

"Tink," he said softly.

Damn you. Don't you dare look like the weight of the world is on your shoulders.

"I haven't slept for days. Or bathed for a week. Let me get some rest, and then I'll think up something."

There were blue shadows under his eyes to rival Lexi's. "Will my brother be all right?"

"He's locked in a room. No one will enter without my consent."

Is there a loophole in that?

"Come upstairs with me. Keep me company," he coaxed, his faint, hopeful smile half hidden by his heavy beard. "Promise me that for the next ten minutes you won't worry and you won't think. At least give me that."

I let him pull me to my feet and gently tug me down the hall. At the living room's threshold he paused. He lifted his chin in the direction of Harry, who stood by the open bay windows. "Do you still have contacts with people inside the NAW?"

Harry pruned his mouth. "I know one that could be bought."

"Tell him there's ten thousand dollars in it if he gives you a heads-up about any movement from the NAW."

"He'll want more," warned Harry.

A sour look fouled Trowbridge's face. "Of course he will."

Anu shot out of her chair as he pulled me toward the stairs. Biggs had given her the shirt right off his back and her legs looked dainty and trim beneath its hem.

"Verstaler," the Alpha of Creemore murmured. Lexi's daughter broke into a brilliant smile and fell in behind us.

I balked. "Sharing a bedroom with her falls into the 'In Your Dreams' category."

"Kid, I'm too tired to dream." His fingers bit into my wrist as I stumbled on the first stair and again on the third. On the fourth step, he slid me a glance—a slant of Trowbridge blue through sooty lashes.

Your eyes are the only thing I still recognize of you, wild man.

His grip gentled. I knew that if I truly wanted, all I needed to do was slip my hand free of the manacle of his fingers. When I didn't, his expression lightened—I hadn't even realized he'd been worried—then he gave me an almost imperceptible nod and put his foot on the fifth riser. That's how I followed him up the staircase, always lagging a step behind, my legs of jelly trying to keep up with his long muscular ones, a little Raha'ell breathing down my neck. *Is this going to be my place now? One step behind the Alpha with another bitch at my heels?*

Daylight streaked through the dirty window on the landing.

One step behind inevitably led to two steps behind.

I can't do that.

"You're thinking again," he muttered as if he read my mind.

Yes. I was. Fate had propelled us willy-nilly to this point. And that was a problem. Because I suddenly didn't know if I wanted to go or I wanted to stay. Whether I needed to be with him or needed to leave him. He came with so many problems. A pack. A hatred for my brother . . . Let's not forget that "Fae shit" attitude.

We crested to the second floor. A layer of grit marred

the soft golden gleam of the old oak floors. And the air—it smelled dead up here, too. Under Mannus's squalid scent layer, there were faint signatures of lives lived before his tenure. The Trowbridge family had once slept here. Lived. Fought. Loved. And died.

Yes, I could smell their stale blood, too.

Despite that, my Were's tail started to thump. She recognized a familiar scent, faded now, and mixed with other, less wonderful things. But she'd been searching for something to ease the growing anxiety inside her, and now, here in this dark passageway, she'd finally found it. There—coming from the bedroom to our right—Trowbridge's old scent, so faint it was hard to catch, mixed with the scent of his dead wife, Candy. Mortal-me faltered. He'd called me by her name once. Did he still love her? A muscle moved in his cheek as he towed me past that door, but he kept his eyelids lowered, shielding me from whatever grief his gaze might reveal.

At the third bedroom, he said something in Merenwynian to my niece. She gave him melting eyes, a hard thing to accomplish when your irises are such a pallid green, but heaved a heavy sigh, and walked over to the bed. "Good night," he said in English. She sank down on the mattress, all woebegone, as he firmly shut the door.

My Were's tail thumped against my tailbone: happy, happy, happy. He's all ours.

But mortal-me? Not so happy. I was one of the following: angry, heart-bruised, or confused.

When in doubt, opt for anger.

Chapter Twenty

The master bedroom was a corner room, one door down the hall, dominated by a king-sized bed. The room had been frozen in time, its hour hand unmoving beyond the night Mannus lost both his empire and his head. The pale green sheets were still twisted from the activities of its last occupants; a dark sage comforter was kicked to the floor. Mannus's scent lingered—a corrosive layer over older, half-buried ones.

Trowbridge's hold slackened on my wrist, and I pulled free, pivoting in place, sniffing delicately. *Ah—there.* It was little more than a thin thread of woodland wafting from the easy chair in the corner—but it was there, part of the olfactory composition of the room. This cozy room with its fussy wallpaper also smelled faintly of Trowbridge's father and his mother.

A muscle tensed in the current Alpha's jaw as he stared down his nose at a pair of jeans lying in a discarded puddle on the floor between the massive bed and the doorway. At the sight of those abandoned Lees, my stomach roiled. Was it always going to be like this? I wondered, curving my arm around my belly. I'd run into a Mannus memento and find myself wanting to hurl as I remembered the night when my aunt's mate turned me into a whimpering pile of woe?

I'd rather stay mad than feel small and lost.

Trowbridge hissed through his teeth and strode over to open the windows. The first double-hung resisted, and he said something harsh and sharp under his breath in my mother's tongue as he tried to force it up without breaking it. "Shit!" he cursed, slamming the heel of his palm on the sash. Success. The window screeched upward, and cold fresh air poured through the opening.

He braced his arms on the windowsill and bent to stick his head outside. *The man's too thin.* The skin over his taut belly pleated as he sucked in a deep breath. "Your brother said a lot of stuff downstairs," he said gruffly. "Meant to destroy whatever we have going between us. Don't let him."

I hooded my eyes. *Another don't.*

He half turned and froze—just like that—twisted at the hips, his mouth a little open, ugly hair brushing his sharp cheekbones. "I used to dream of you. Looking like you do right now."

My heart stopped for a beat, then picked up.

He said slowly, "For nine years, I had the same dream. I stood buck naked in the Pool of Life. You stood under the apple tree."

My breath caught. "It was a cherry tree."

You died. Every night you dived under the water and never came back up.

"The nightmares started petering out this year," he said tautly. "I haven't had one in a month."

But I dreamt of you the other night, I almost protested. Then I thought of how a single day in this realm equaled many in Merenwyn, and remembered how the dreams always ended—with arrows raining down on the pond.

Yes. For both of us they were nightmares.

A light flickered in his eyes. "We always—"

"Argued."

I looked down at my blistered sooty fingers. Silence stretched. When I glanced up, I caught him staring at me moodily. The front of his pants was tented. He blinked then his features rearranged themselves back into his new default expression. Broody Alpha with a touch of Neanderthal.

"Yes," he said, adjusting his jeans. "We always fought."

"But the dreams stopped. Maybe that's the problem with fairy tales in the real world," I said quietly. "Sometimes the princess doesn't get the right frog, and sometimes the prince is having too much fun slaying dragons to come back home."

Irritation thinned his mouth. "You *know* why I didn't accept your brother's first offer."

"Right. Obligations to your Raha'ell and all that." Then I cocked my head. "You just vowed to *this* pack that I would stay here forever. Knowing that they tried to kill me."

"Yes, I did," he said flatly.

"What if I don't want to play housemother to a bunch of murderous wolves?"

"Well, that's the thing about vows," he said, his tone hardening. "Sometimes other people can make them for you."

To bring up the mate issue so casually. My cheeks heated as I searched for a good comeback. There wasn't one. Instead, I studied his body and face, searching for ammunition. Some men were meant to walk around barefooted and shirtless. He was one of them.

So I said, "I hate your hair."

"I'll add that to my list," he drawled.

Fraud, I thought. He was shooting for cool and detached but his frustration was evident in the glitter of his eyes and the flush across his upper chest. It had sharpened his scent, too—if his had shape and form, it would be curling into a fly swatter.

He blew air through his teeth and muttered, "No one can push my buttons like you." Then he jerked his chin at my swollen hand. "Can't Merry fix that?"

That would be a "yes," except Merry hadn't offered.

"I'll heal on my own," I told My One True Thing.

"Hmph," he replied.

But I heard him mutter, "Stubborn as a mule," before he set to a bit of energetic housecleaning. He tore the sheets off the bed, wadded them into a ball, and tossed them through the window without so much as a heads-up. A second later, the jeans went sailing after them. From the side table, he grabbed a book, a mug, and a yellowed newspaper. Those were pitched, too, with more force than required—the I ♥ CREEMORE mug bounced along the roof of the portico before it fell to hit the walkway with a sharp crack.

I stalked over to the bedroom chair and picked up the woman's blouse that had been left draped over its arm. My aunt Lou had worn one like it—I frowned. Was it *this* shirt? If so, remnants of my lying aunt could go with the detritus of his land-obsessed uncle. "Here, chuck this, too," I told Mr. Clean, tossing it to him.

He caught the shirt, balled it, and made a free throw. "So, this place Threall, it exists? The fog, the big motherfucking trees, and all the lights in the sky?"

"Not lights, soul balls." I ruthlessly banged the seat cushion free of dust and then collapsed into the chair, curling my legs under my ass. "Yes, Threall definitely exists."

Evidently, the correct answer for that would have been "no."

Grim-faced, he strode to the bathroom, where he continued his ruthless eradication of all things Mannus. Cabinets were emptied, shelves ransacked. When he was finished, he'd filled an entire drawer with rejected personal-care items. He exited with it balanced on his hip. For a second he stood there—Suzie Homemaker in blue jeans and a beard—eyes choosing his next target. *Aha.* The cherrywood dresser. One quick swipe of his forearm swept all the surface litter—a beer bottle, a stack of road maps, another mug, and probably an inch of dust—on top of the now brimming drawer, before he padded barefoot over to the windows for another purge.

Good-bye, Mannus. The new Alpha shook the contents of the drawer outside.

Outside someone said, "What the hell—"

"It's the *Alpha*," answered another.

Trowbridge stuck his head out the window. "Hey, you. What's your name?"

"Jeff," came the answer.

"Tell Harry I want all this shit out of here in the next ten minutes. And Jeff? I want the downstairs scrubbed down right away. Also get him to send someone for a few of those candles that smell good, too. Something with sweetness to it like those flowers in the—"

He scowled and said, "Forget it. Get something spicy."

"On it," I heard Jeff reply.

Trowbridge moved to the closet. "The Raha'ells say that a trained mystwalker is the ultimate weapon. They can destroy people just by tapping into their dreams." Hangers screeched then he stalked past me, his arms full of clothing.

"You think I'm a loaded weapon?"

"To the right guy, you're kryptonite," he muttered, dropping his armload outside. Someone said, "Ow!", but Trowbridge was obviously feeling all kinds of honey badger—without any apology he returned to the closet and crouched to investigate the bottom of it. "So you've gone to Threall, where you've 'thumbed through people's memories like they were the yellow pages,'" he said. Viewed from the back, his dreads were an awesome mess—dusty and grizzled, sun damaged and discolored. Quite a bit of gray in them, too.

What would I do with such an old man as you?

"I've visited it twice." I blew on my tender palm, hoping to cool some of its burning heat. The whole damn room felt hot, the air heavy and potent. "The first time right before I pulled you out of that strip bar."

He twisted on his heels, a loafer in his hand. "You shot me in that strip bar, and I pulled *you* out of it before we both got thrown in jail." A missile of brown leather went whistling past me and disappeared through the open window, without even grazing the sash. "And the second time?"

"After Knox used his blade."

His mouth turned into a forbidding slash. "Why did you go there?"

"I don't know. I just landed there."

"You used to think about Threall sometimes—in those dreams we shared. I'd get flashes of a field. Big trees and lots of fog." He sent a quick sideways glance in my direction. "You worried about the place. That it would get its hooks into you and you'd never return home."

"Yes." He remembered that, at least.

"But this time, you came back."

"I did." Emotions that I thought I'd quelled started to bubble inside me. For instance, I couldn't seem to keep my attention from flitting to his body. No man should look that good balanced on the back of his heels. In Trowbridge's case, the position only served to emphasize the swell of his shoulder, the tautness of his belly, the solid strength of his thighs. My gaze bounced from all those landscape delights and then settled on the curve of his ass.

Goddess, buns of steel.

I looked up and found him watching me, a corner of his mouth quirked.

Annoying. I feigned a deep interest in his mother's decorative touches. There was ample evidence of her love of needlecrafts—a cross-stitched sampler on the wall (FAMILIES ARE FOREVER), a Log Cabin quilt folded over the quilt rack, a scattering of crocheted pillows. I rescued one that someone had dumped on the floor by my chair and gave it a good shake to rid it of dust mites before I hugged it to my chest, hoping it would hide the fact that my nipples were poking through my T-shirt.

He growled something unintelligible—I swear I don't know if it was jumbled English or mumbled Merenwynian—before he headed for the bathroom. There he studied his reflection for a long, long time (eight to twelve seconds—depending on whether I started counting the moment his brows drew together in a WTF or after he'd placed both palms on the counter and leaned into the mirror for a closer inspection).

Don't they have mirrors in Merenwyn?

"Jeezus," he finally muttered, raking his fingers through his graying beard. Grimacing, he bent to open the cabinet's bottom drawer. "So did you rummage through *my* memories? Plant anything in my head you need to tell me about?"

"No," I said, truly affronted. "I'd never do that."

He pawed through the hair rollers and brushes, until he found a pair of scissors and a set of hair clippers. "But you used your mystwalking talent to summon me at night to that damn Pool of Life—"

"I didn't summon you," I snapped. "We were both taken there every night. Blame Karma—"

"That bloody place was so damn—"

"Cold," I said, thinking of the chill in the air.

"I was thinking wet, but you're right; it was cold." He plugged the clippers into the wall, and tested them. "You always stood under a tree, talking to me about books and stuff. Arguing with me. Both of us knowing what was going to happen." Flicking off the electric shears, he asked, "Why'd you keep doing that to us?"

"Do you honestly think I had any control over those dreams? That I liked standing there, watching you—"

"Learn how to swim the hard way," he said grimly, picking up the scissors. "Remind me never to really piss you off." He chose a dreadlock, hesitated long enough for me to worry that he might actually think he looked good with all that Rastafarian nonsense, then set the blades to it. Snip. One fourteen-inch length of twisted hair fell to the floor.

Downstairs in the kitchen, the League of Extraordinary Bitches were filling their pails with hot water in the kitchen while discussing us in voices pitched low. "How much do you really remember of the dreams?"

He scowled at me in the mirror, scissors poised. "Well,

the diving into the freezing pond was hard to forget. The rest is just bits and pieces." Snip. "Most of it was gone by daylight."

So it was forgotten. The minutes—sometimes a full hour—before the arrows flew. The intimacy of just him and me, talking and arguing. Along with the tenderness sandwiched in between the fear, and the tears.

Then we were to start as strangers again.

An Alpha and a half-breed Fae.

Impossible.

He lifted a dread from the back of his head. Pulled it tight then went for the chop. And so it went. Thirty-two more snips and he was near shorn, heaps of hair littering the floor by his callused heels like small dead rodents. "But I do remember a few things," he murmured as he considered his Grizzly Adams beard.

"What?" I flexed my fingers, wondering how long it would be before I could actually fold them into a clumsy fist.

"You spend too much time overthinking the little stuff. And when the chips are down, you run on courage and instinct."

Startled, I looked up and found his reflected gaze fixed on me.

"I missed your dreams last month," he said softly.

"How could you? You kept dying at the end of them."

"Did you ever see me really die? Did you ever see an arrow get me?"

I thought back. "No."

"All I had to do to end the dream was dive into the water. I knew that. I was never in true mortal danger." His gaze was bleak. "Please don't go to Threall again."

My eyes burned. *I'm not going to cry.* I heard a lawn mower start up and turned my head toward the sound and found peace outside the window in the hypnotic movement of the swaying trees. After a bit, I whispered, "I'll try."

"Shit," Trowbridge cursed. "Got myself."

I closed my eyes and leaned my head back on the chair.

A couple minutes later, I heard the bath curtains being pulled, the taps turned, the beat of water pattering on an acrylic tub.

I imagined him slipping off the jeans. Standing under the spray.

Soaping his chest.

Don't think. Don't feel.

Back in May, he'd asked, "Promise me that I'll never come out of a shower and discover you gone again." I told him that I wouldn't, and I'd made him make the same pledge. Because we were equals. That's what I thought back then, when I'd believed that taking a blind leap into love required nothing more than sucking up your courage and following your instincts.

I hadn't tallied up the negatives. The possibilities. The sheer cruelty of Karma.

There wasn't six years between us anymore. There was a daunting fifteen. No matter how fast I tried to speed-mature, I'd never match him in experience. I'd always be too young, too soft, too fluffy. The girl with the traitor brother. The Were with the Fae inside her.

Not a battle-hard Raha'ell.

But still, I had given my word, hadn't I? That afternoon in the courtyard?

I opened my eyes and listlessly watched the young Were mowing the grass come to the end of the lawn and turn. He had light brown hair. Maybe he'd gone to school with me. He looked about the right age.

I still couldn't remember his name.

Likely, I should never have given in to the urge to rest my eyes when I felt worn down to gristle and bone. Nor should I have dug myself deeper into the comfort of the chair. But I forgot, didn't I? There were two other Fae in the house. Both as tired as me.

I opened my eyes in Anu's dream and discovered that fear is a thing with a threshold that moves ever higher. We were back inside the pen within the pen. The moon was heavy and full in the night sky. Wolves slunk along the dark shadows near the forest's edge.

Anu looked through the bars to the grandstands. Lexi was there, standing on the platform to the right of the seating, his bowler worn at a jaunty angle, his body canted toward the row of spectators.

Her terror flooded into me, drying my mouth.

Beside Lexi's elbow was a lever that was attached to a hook and a rope strung between the stands and the ceiling of her cage. She understood that when the Shadow pulled on that lever, the hook would open, the rope would fall lax, and the walls of her pen would collapse.

No longer would she be the prey safely caged.

Lexi barely glanced at her. His attention was fixed on the tall man with the long face who sat in the choicest seat. The Black Mage's vanity extended to his clothing. It was all funeral black, embellished with silver buttons, and lacing at his throat. And when he smiled—both ends of his long mouth turned up, his teeth bright white, his eyes wicked and sly—Anu's grip on the bars tightened.

"Dearest Mother of the Goddesses, hear my final prayer," she whispered.

The ladies in the stand tittered when the mage lifted his hand and held it in the air.

"Forgive me for—"

A noise behind us. Another surge of acid-mouthed terror.

I heard her thoughts, as clearly as my own. Should she close her eyes, and let the end come? No. Not she. Anu turned her head, but slowly, so as not to frighten the beast.

She expelled her breath. He was not in the throes of his moon-change.

He was in man form, with no distortion of limb or jaw. A dark beard covered his lower jaw, ropes of his black hair hung down to his waist. He stood swaying, and then he cocked his head, eyes narrowed on hers. "How fast can you run?"

"Like a deer," she whispered.

"Then stay close behind me," said the man. "There will be an opportunity."

The Black Mage waggled his hand at my brother, coyly, extending the moment of truth.

"We will live through today and tomorrow," said the beast.

"How do you know?" she dared to ask.

My Trowbridge gave her a feral grin. "Because I'm the Son of Lukynae."

Chapter Twenty-one

I woke up with a gasp.

It was quiet in the Alpha of Creemore's bedroom. Too quiet. Technically, if you've got any Were in you at all there is no such thing as near silence. You register the hum of the appliances over the sound of the lawn mower chewing up the grass, the discreet vibration of the heater under the chatter of the women working in the kitchen below. But if you stay motionless and let the outside world fall away, so it's just you, and this room, and this man whom you thought you knew but didn't . . . You might perceive the absence of breath. You might notice, as you stand there, feeling somehow naked again, that the person with whom you shared the bedroom has stopped breathing. That he is holding his breath, so that he can measure the hard hammer of your heart in your chest.

Without lifting my gaze, I knew he stood at the door's threshold, watching me.

I can't look at him. I really can't.

"What is it, Tink?"

I wanted to howl. I wanted to pound my fists.

Feathers protested as I hugged the pillow to my chest. "I was in Anu's nightmare . . . She was in a cage set inside a field. There were grandstands and wolves watching from under the trees."

"You always going to walk through people's dreams? If I go to sleep right now, are you going to do a drive-by?"

"I don't know," I said bleakly, staring at the floor. "She was so terrified of those wolves . . ."

A moment of silence, then he said, "Of course she was—she was scheduled as prey for the night's entertainment. The kid wouldn't have stood a chance against a pack of half-starved wolves."

"Why didn't she change into her wolf? Why didn't you?"

He drew in a long breath and released it. "I could hold my transformation off. Not forever—no wolf can do that—but long enough for me to figure out the lay of the land. They'd given Anu a double dose of sun potion to make sure her wolf couldn't break through." His tone was flat. "The kid was defenseless. She'd been raised as a Kuskador—that pack chose to submit to the Fae following the Treaty of Brelland. Most of them have been on sun potion from puberty. They've never met their own wolf."

"But Anu was wolf when she came through the portal." The horror was spreading, spreading. Like water coming through the dam. Finding crevices to widen, cracks to pry open.

"I wouldn't let your brother give her another dose while we were on the run—I didn't want her going through the gates with that shit in her veins. The kid went through her first transformation two hours before we made it to the portal."

"You were there in her dream." I'll never be able to rid my memory of the whip marks marring his flesh. Ugly red hatch marks. Rivulets of his blood staining the backs of his naked thighs. An ache in my throat, tearing, hurting pain. "Oh Goddess." The pillow fell as I stood. "What did I send you to? Your back was so torn up . . ."

"Forget it," he said harshly. "It was just a dream."

"No it wasn't!" I hissed, my gaze jerking to him.

Fae Stars, look at him.

The elements that had so distracted me—the dreads,

the beard, the foreign quality to him—had been mowed away by a pair of clippers, and now it was easy to appreci-ate again the cut of his cheekbones, the length of his long nose. He'd wrapped a towel around his hips, which made him look like one of those male models who, between stints of hawking man-perfume, filled in time alternately starving or bench-pressing fat people. Now his eyes domi-nated, and they glowed with a fire that wasn't bred of an Alpha's dominance but of a fine-edged human hatred. Deep inside them, I read a deadly, relentless loathing.

My heart sank to my belly.

"It was real," I said, my voice hollow. "I've learned the difference between a dream made of fiction and one made of memories . . . They whipped you."

"Not 'they,'" he said harshly. "Say it. The Fae."

I wanted to rock myself, I wanted to wail. "What *was* that place?"

"It's called the Spectacle." A muscle tightened in Trow-bridge's jaw. "Not every Raha'ell is shot for their pelt—the ones worth sport are brought to a field surrounded by twelve-foot walls. Less than half an acre for more than thirty wolves. Never enough food or water. When the moon is full, the Fae come to watch us tearing at each other for a share of food. To those bastards the Spectacle's a morality play about the beast hidden within. But for us . . . it's a choice of death or hunger."

"My brother was there," I said thinly. "And the Black Mage." Shutting my eyes didn't help. I kept seeing the field, those shadows slinking along the edge of the woods. "Those wolves—were they part of your pack?"

"Some of them." Trowbridge turned, yanked an appli-quéd coverlet from the quilt rack, and gave it the sniff test before he tossed it on the bed.

I shook my head. "How did you escape from that?"

He threw a pillow on the bed then bent for another. "Your brother set up an explosion that destroyed a section of the outer fence. My wolves saw freedom and went right for it, just like he intended them to. It was a bloodbath. Half of them never made it through the gap in the wall."

"You could have been killed," I said in horror.

And I wouldn't have known.

"The Shadow used the diversion to lead us to another exit. When I saw what was happening, I tried to go back to lead my brothers to safety, but he pointed his hand at me, like you did downstairs at Anu, and I felt this thing, like a band of something invisible . . ." A look of disgust. "It felt alive. And when I tried to claw it off me, I could feel the burn of magic. It wrapped itself around my chest, binding my arms."

Goddess, like Dawn Danvers. That's what he meant by "Fae shit."

"I couldn't pull myself out of it. It was like being caught in the jaws of the wolf trap all over again." He swallowed. "One of my pack got hit in the flank, he was dragging himself toward me . . . and I couldn't go to him. I wanted to. I tried. But I couldn't. I followed your brother out of the field like a whipped puppy on the end of a leash." Mouth sealed, he ran his tongue over his top teeth, then gave a shrug that strove for indifference, but failed. "When the magic wore off, I almost killed him. But he kept saying, 'You can make it up to them. I know the location of the Safe Passage. I'll take you to it, once we get back home.'"

"I thought I was sending you to paradise. I just wanted you to live. To heal." My voice cracked. "Not to spend nine years—"

"I did heal. I did live." Comet trails spun around his pupils.

What was it? The faint eau de Mannus? The knowledge that I'd done to Dawn Danvers exactly what Lexi had done to him? Whatever the impetus, all I knew was that I needed to be out of that room as fast as possible. To find a place to hide, to think, to rock myself as I mourned for all those stupid happily-ever-afters that had kept me afloat for the last six months.

I spun for the door—

"Don't." That's all he said. "Don't." Spoken so softly—
not an order, but a request, maybe even a plea. And it
stopped me—that faint underlying thread of "please"—
right in my tracks.

The door's glass knob cut into my palm. "I wasn't running."

"You sure?"

Forehead against the door, I nodded miserably. "I just
need some space for a bit."

"I'm done with that," he growled. "No more space
between you and me."

The air stirred between us. "If you touch me," I quavered. "I'm going to break down."

A man-sigh. Then, softly, "I hate it when you cry."

"I'm not crying," I said through my teeth. Not yet, anyhow. Even if it meant locking my knees and blinking like
a caution light that never was going to turn green. *Don't
fold,* I told myself. *Hang on. Count to seventy, then turn
around and face him.*

Because sooner or later, I knew I had to do that.

And I would. In a minute or two.

"Forget that," grumbled his scent. Just when dry land
was virtually in sight, an invisible stream of Trowbridge
yum stretched out and touched me. With delicacy, at first—a
deft brush over my white knuckles, followed by a sweet
"steady, girl" caress along the back of my hand. Then, ever
possessive, it wound itself around my wrist, pausing to give
a soothing and apologetic stroke to the bruise beginning to
form on my skin. Onward it spread over my skin—fondling
and touching the things it considered its possessions.
"This is mine," it said, licking the inside of my elbow.
"And these are two of my most favorite things," it crowed,
as it made a quick and impertinent detour to graze my
breasts.

It slid up my neck. "Remember me?" it asked.

My chin crumpled when his scent touched my cheek—
tender-sweet.

"I'm walking now," Trowbridge told me. "You don't have to move. I'll come to you." And he did, crossing the distance between us faster than I could think. "All the honeyed words in the dictionary aren't going to get us out of this mess."

Because that's what "this" was. A huge hodgepodge of daydreams and nightmares; sun-spun myths and gritty facts; bleeding wounds and toughened scars.

And now—thanks to the consequences of my desperate decision revealed to me in a Goddess-cursed dream—it felt like our fate was written four ways, the answers hidden within the folds of a paper fortune-teller. There were no easy choices written on those wings of paper; instead there were symbols—a Fae, a wolf, a black walnut tree, and a twin.

I still wanted him. I couldn't be in the same room with him without my body reacting to his. But how could he get past this? How could I?

Guilt.

It swarmed over me, biting like fire ants.

His heat warmed my back. I knew all I had to do was lean back a little, and I'd fall into his arms. But unspoken words were the Hoover Dam between us.

My One True Thing leaned into my ear and whispered, "Listen, I got over hating you."

And with that—bang! The Hedi floodgates flew open.

"Aw shit!" He cursed as a sob broke through my control. "Don't cry, sweetheart."

There went my chin; there went my knees.

Trowbridge said, "Aw shit," again, then suddenly, I was being swept into his arms and carried—a rigid, half-curled ball of sobbing woe—five paces across the floor. He paused, possibly to consider—chair or bed?—and went for the safest choice.

I cried into my hands as he sank into the easy chair and tucked me into his lap. I shuddered as he coaxed my head toward the convenient hollow below his collarbone. I sobbed into his neck when he wrapped a comforting arm around me.

The man, not the Alpha, rubbed my back. "You cry it out, okay?"

And I did, long and hard.

"I like your hair when it's loose," he observed, after the storm had passed. A tug from him, a wince from me, and then my hair was free of the elastic's hold. He threaded his fingers through the uncombed mess and fanned it down on my shoulder. "I like it just like this."

Thousands wouldn't.

"You going to listen to me now?" When I gave a silent nod, he pressed his chin on the top of my head. "That first month in Merenwyn was so fucking hard, it would have been easier to die. I thought if I ever got my hands on you . . ." He stretched to reach for his mother's crocheted pillow, then passed it to me. "Here, wipe your nose with this."

"I can't," I quavered. "It's too nice."

"Okay, hang on." He did a thigh press, reached under himself, and pulled off his towel. Back down we went. "Here, take this." A vague wave toward my nose. "Blow, and then I'll tell you the rest."

I did.

"I was thinking about you one night before I fell asleep." His fingers combed my hair away from my ear. "And then . . . There you were. Real as life. If I could have waded out of that damn water, I would have wrung your little neck."

I dabbed at my leaking nose.

"Then this . . . thing happened." His tone turned bewildered. "I remember thinking, 'I'm going to kill her,' and then . . . I don't know how to describe it. You just . . . flowed into me. Like I'd opened a book, and I could read you. All of a sudden, I heard your thoughts like they were mine. Not only that, I could see some of your memories. I know it sounds whacked, but it was like I stood inside you, and if I turned around, I'd see every part of you."

"You told me you don't remember the dreams," I whispered.

His thumb stroked the curve of my peaked ear. "What I said was I forgot the details. I'm a guy, okay? Some things aren't worth remembering. But I think I remember the important stuff."

"Like?"

His arm tightened. "You were so sad," he said. "So young. All filled up with grief and guilt. And . . ." A lift of his shoulder. "All I wanted to do was to hold you. Protect you. But you wouldn't let me—night after night you stood underneath that tree beating yourself up and making me stay in the damn pool. Every night, you fought with me. Every fucking night. You are *so* stubborn."

Up to that moment his penis had been forget-about-it soft. But now, I could feel it, hardening underneath me. "You know I hate water now, right? Can't stand ponds or lakes . . . I'll even go out of my way not to walk through a puddle." A soft huff—hot and Trowbridge scented—into my ear. "I don't hate you, sweetheart. If anything, you're my personal addiction. I'd wake up every morning wanting you so bad my balls ached."

My Were did a somersault as his scent grew spicy with musk.

"I learned something in Merenwyn," he said pensively. "All my life I wanted to avoid the future I saw ahead of me—I didn't want to run a pack. I hated being led, and figured that meant I'd be happier as a rogue. But life with the Raha'ells—it made choices real simple. It was either step up or die."

All I could feel was his heat and his arousal hard against my hip.

"I was forced to become an Alpha in Merenwyn," he said in that crystal-fragile silence. "And I found out that I really was born to be one. I'm a natural leader." He gave up on my ear and used his hand to tip up my chin. "I've had enough of you standing under some damn cherry tree." Blue eyes gleamed. Then he gave me a sweet smile and nuzzled the corner of my mouth with his warm lips. "Stay with me. Be with me. All that other shit, we'll figure it out."

"Promise me you won't kill him."

"I promise."

Love's a sneaky fighter. She whispers to your greatest need. She wins her battle not through sweat and logic, but with a look, a gesture, a feral recognition of weakness. And the other part of you thinks, I can do this. I can take a thin thread of bliss and spin it into a length of silk that will stretch a lifetime.

I gently touched his cheek and felt the smooth spots he'd shaved clean, and the bristly parts he'd missed. "There's so much—"

"Just for once, stop thinking." He ran a thumb over my bottom lip. "I love your mouth," he said, his voice raw in a way that sent a shiver up my spine.

Kiss me, kiss me, kiss me.

His hands went under my butt, and he lifted me as he stood. Desire swamped me as I wrapped my legs around his waist.

Four strides took us to the mattress.

Trowbridge turned at the foot of it. Lifted me a little higher. I tightened my hold, preparing for the long sweet slide to the bed, but instead of falling backward, he sat us on the edge of the mattress. His strong hands cupped my waist. My knees bracketed his long thighs.

Goddess, he was aroused.

His erection was hard as a staff—a long, hot ridge against my belly. Delicious and sinful was the smell of his desire—heady, too, the combined scent of us.

Finally.

Eyes hooded, Trowbridge eased Merry off my neck. I took her from him and twisted to place her on the bedside table, but the surface was coated with grime, and befouled by a dusty coffee mug ring. With a murmur of apology, I hooked her chain on the bedside lamp's finial instead. As I did, my lover pulled the Royal Amulet up over his head with a great deal less ceremony and delicacy than he'd accorded Merry. He passed him to me.

Ralph spat a flash of reproof as I stretched to hook him on the lampshade. The moment the two Fae gold lengths touched—Ralph's heavier, serpentine chain covering Merry's fine delicate filigree—the air sparked, brilliant blue-white.

My best friend's amber stone flushed a brilliant red-orange.

"They've got some electricity going on between them," I said, watching Merry hurriedly put some distance between her and Ralph. Trowbridge nodded—a quick, harsh bob—then stretched to rotate the shade. Three quick turns and our amulets were facing the quilt rack.

Alone at last.

With exquisite tenderness, Trowbridge used the pad of his index finger to blot away a tear lingering on my lower lash. "I really do hate it when you cry," he said quietly.

"I don't do it often."

"I know." Thoughtfully, he used the back of a knuckle to gently trace the slope of my cheek all the way to the edge of my jaw. There he paused for another swipe to dry my damp skin once more before his finger followed the line of my pounding pulse from my ear to the base of my throat.

"Your heart is beating so fast," he murmured with a faint smile.

I flattened my hand on the mat of soft hair nested between his small nipples. Under my palm, I felt the surge of his blood. "Yours, too."

My mate cupped my face. Eyes serious, face taut. He examined me—my nose, my hair, my lips, the curve of my jaw. Then he angled his head and touched his lips to mine. Softly. His mouth was slightly open, his breath mingled with mine.

It was a different type of kiss than what he'd given me downstairs when his wolf was still upon him, and his restraint was thread-thin. Gentler. A tad strained, as if he knew me to be someone very soft, and very round, and prone to injury.

But desire streaked through me—that fast. One touch, one intimate exchange of spit and breath, and my core dampened, my breasts swelled. I needed to be closer. Instinct told me to hug his thighs tighter, to curl an arm possessively around his neck, to press myself against him until my breasts were flattened against his chest.

Trowbridge, Trowbridge.

This was what my body had been made for—his touch, his scent, his hands.

Heat built inside me as my guy's firm lips moved over mine, skillfully stoking the fire within me. His clever tongue lightly traced my full upper lip, teasing for a response. I opened my mouth, and touched the tip of his tongue with mine. With that, his hand slid up the nape of my neck and our kiss deepened.

The soft rasp of his tongue against mine, warm and wet. *Oh sweet heavens.*

My heart hammered as I slid my fingers to the nape of his neck. Short bristles instead of long locks. I tested the steely sinew of his neck, the rounded bulk of his shoulder, the little knob of his spine, the hollow behind his ear—*oh, he liked that.* This I stroked again, emboldened by the sudden tension in his body.

Goose bumps as he turned my head to nuzzle my ear.

Eyes hot, he slid his hand under the gaping neck of my T-shirt. This, he pushed aside, so that it sat low on my shoulder, baring the skin above the shadow of my collarbone. Head tilted, he ran his palm over the place where his teeth had torn my flesh the night we'd exchanged the mate vows.

"There's no scar," he said, his brows drawing together.

No. The bite mark had healed. Slower than usual, considering I was half Fae and half Were, but like most wounds, it had healed. I'd worried about that—in the back of my mind echoed a fragment of conversation overheard in St. Hubert's cloakroom about mate bonds and teeth marks.

"Do you have one?" I asked, feeling a tightness in my chest.

My One True Thing arched his neck to the side so I could examine the place where I'd bitten him. His trapezoid muscle was as unmarred as mine. My gaze flicked downward to his hard abdomen, which bore a jagged silver line—a permanent memento from the wound he'd received on the dark night when the scent of sweet peas had mixed with the raw perfume of the wild and the woods.

"*Should* there be a scar?"

"Sometimes the act leaves one on the woman." Pensively, he touched the place that had no spot to mark something so precious and wonderful. "But it's good. It would be a crime to ruin your skin."

He stroked my shoulder softly, his downcast gaze shielding his thoughts. My skin looked very white, and very smooth, in contrast to his tanned, scarred hand.

"It's soft as a baby's," he said. "I'll need to be careful or I'll bruise you."

I don't want careful. I want God-I'm-dying-for-you passion.

That's when it occurred to me—right at that moment when I was astride his lap wearing nothing but a pair of damp cotton panties and his well-worn T-shirt—that the gap between our ages and experiences was in danger of becoming a freakin' fjord. And if I didn't find a way to span it—if I let him point to someplace up ahead where presumably a rope bridge swung—all would be lost.

Soft as a baby? Tender as a chick? Is that how he saw me now?

Probably. He'd carried me to this bed, and wiped my eyes dry of tears. To him, I was still Hedi, not much changed. Impossibly young. While he'd evolved into the savior of the Raha'ells and the Creemore pack's returned hero.

Talk about a disparity.

Suddenly his gentleness felt less worshipful than cautious. His kisses practiced and controlled.

He was holding himself back.

No. No. No.

The guy I'd shoved through the gates had been an eager,

impetuous lover. That is where we'd communicated. That is when I'd known that his passion matched mine.

I'd felt his equal when we lay skin to skin.

I'm not giving that up.

With a sigh, I cradled my mate's face between my hands.

"What?" he said, his eyes narrowing.

So this was my new lover?

This complicated man with all his new complex angles, and unexpected hollows, and thin, tight skin? Given to command. Tempered to the role of leader?

Yes, mine.

If I was willing to dig for the Robbie Trowbridge buried deep. If I didn't let him relegate me to the fragile and breakable category. If I believed that he meant what he said before he'd carried me to this ancestral bed. That it didn't matter that he was one thing, and I was another. That all the other stuff really amounted to shit that we'd figure out later.

Well, here was Part I of the later shit.

His face had grown shuttered under my silent inspection.

I brooded over his mouth. Upper lip sharply defined, lower lip wide and firm. It used to be mobile and prone to ironic grins but now, more often than not, it was taut and tense. No longer the mouth of a man rebelliously clinging to his rogue status. This mouth belonged to a man who'd seen too much. Lost more than he'd owned. Thinned his lips and clamped down on private suffering too many times.

I can't make love to the Son of Lukynae.

Not with this reservoir of guilt ceaselessly circling inside me like a dirty whirlpool.

Within days of pushing him through the gates, self-loathing and reproach had started twining itself around my battered self-esteem. How could I not remember the words to bring the portal back? I couldn't reconcile myself to the enormity of that stupidity, any more than I could dismiss the fact that the mantle of leadership did not fit me.

And now, I'd seen the whole measure of my crime.

Remorse could drown me if I let it.

Yes, I could tell him "I'm sorry" again—hoping he'd give me some get-out-of-jail pass that would make me feel better—but even if I did, and cried another monsoon of tears, it still wouldn't change one damn thing. Because my "sorry" was both a truth and a lie, all at the same time.

I'd known that, too. Whenever the whirlpool had dragged me down to the choking mire of self-hatred, I kept on finding the skeleton of the truth lying at the bottom.

Because I was sorry, and yet I was not.

I opened my mouth and out popped the truth. "You should know that this 'kid' would do it again."

He tilted his head, his brows drawn together.

I hardened my voice. "Even knowing what world I was sending you to. As long as there was a chance that we could be here together—that I could see your face, smell your scent wrapping around me—I would do it again. I'd shove you through a thousand portals, over and over again, if I could save your life. I'd close my ears to the sound of the whiplash just so that I could bargain for another hour with you."

In this bed, let there be no lies.

"I'm not a noble person. I'll never be one. I don't want to be. Not if it means I have to lose what I have. I have too little left, and what I have, I value too much."

A flush tinted his high cheekbones as I cocked my hip, so that the soft folds of my sex eased to fit against his erection.

Yes. This is the way to find him again. Through words and action.

Blue eyes fixed on me.

And me alone.

I pulled his chin down—so slowly, so deliberately—and placed a hard kiss on the corner of his tense mouth. "I value *you* too much." Then I forced his head back so that our mouths were aligned to my satisfaction and comfort and kissed him over and over again, with tongue and little tugs on his lower lip, and sneaky little rocking motions of my hip, until his arms were hard urgent bands around me, and I felt a deep tremor rack through him.

That's when I flattened my hands on his hard chest.

He lifted a brow—his only outward comment on the ludicrous notion that I could overpower him—but he let me slowly push him flat.

There he lay, all parts of him rigid with desire, his body laid out for me to feast on. Face of a warrior. Hard belly, so much definition in his muscles that they looked like they'd been carved from a piece of marble. Light scattering of dark hair between those two slabs of pectoral muscles. A thinner trail leading south from his tight navel to his heavy cock.

"This is new," he said huskily, his lids at half-mast, his head tilted back.

"I want to make love to the guy who stalked across the living room," I informed him as I crossed my arms and took hold of my T-shirt's hem. And then very slowly, I lifted my arms and the shirt rose, exposing for both our pleasure the rounded curve of my hip, the white skin of my soft belly, the rib cage within which my heart pounded, the undercurve of my heavy breast, and finally, the hollow of my tender throat.

The woman in me preened as his lips parted.

For another taunting second, I held my arms above my head, slightly canted back, knowing that it lifted my breasts up in a seize-me salute, before letting the T-shirt fall to the bed.

I gazed down at my lover.

A blue comet spun in a lazy circuit around a dark dilated pupil.

My eyes began to burn, a prelude to my own flare. I removed the hand that seemed intent on working its way to my pussy, and splayed open his fingers. A hard callus sat at the base of what was left of each digit, testament to the harshness that he'd endured.

"I'm so sorry you suffered." His brows slanted downward in an expression almost akin to pain as I brought his palm to my mouth and pressed a kiss to that callus, then did it again, and once more, following the rough line of them all the way to that rounded nub of that pinkie—all the time watching the skin sink in the hollows of his cheeks as he fought to hold on to his emotions.

"But you have to understand, Trowbridge. I'm no kid."

He sucked in a sharp, quick breath through his teeth as I moved his hand to my breast. The women of the Creemore pack had small, high apples. I'm shapely and bountiful—a veritable harvest of flesh. And my Trowbridge was definitely a boob man. Without any urging his other paw reached for my breast's twin. He lifted them so that they plumped, creamy and full, in his palms.

I raised my voice to get his attention. "I am the girl who crept into your motel room. Who tried to steal your amulet. Who killed Dawn Danvers. Who pushed you through the gates to hell."

His thumb brushed my beaded nipple and I felt the tug of desire all the way to my lady parts.

"And I am no innocent."

I coaxed his hand to trail down my ribs, to follow the sharp dip of my waist, to slow on the curve of my hip. Cheeks flushed, he rolled his head to the side and gazed down to where my legs were spread and his cock lay curved. Eyes hooded, his palms began to slide toward the temptation of the soft inside crease of my inner thigh.

"Uh-uh. You can explore that later."

I caught his cock and held him, pulsing, in my tight grip. Silken skin over a hard, hard shaft. Scented of his lust. His knees drew up as I moved my hand along his length. My thumb found that pearl of desire leaking from the slit, and rubbed it in a circle.

"Right now, I'm going to take what I want."

Swiftly, I rose on my knees, eased aside the leg of my panties, and brought the heat of him to tease the aching, damp core of me. Back and forth I dragged him along the folds of my pussy, wetting his cock with my own moisture.

Then with a smile that promised him hell and heaven and everything in between, I guided his length to my entrance. Eyes closed in pleasure, I sank down, slowly, inch by inch, feeling the stretch, the slow hard slide, the wondrous sensation of being filled once more.

He flexed his hips so that I felt him right up to my womb.

"I don't want to make love to the Alpha of Creemore," I said shakily. "Any more than I want to sleep with the Son of Lukynae."

Our gazes locked as I rose slightly, just enough to let him come close to slipping out from me, then sank again, parting my legs wide, and leaning forward so that the bud of me rubbed against him. His breath was shallow, quick and sharp, through parted lips.

"In this bed, it is just you and me. You are my Robbie Trowbridge." I flattened my hands beside his head and bent until our mouths were inches apart. His breath and mine mingling. "And I am reclaiming you."

Then, the terrible stillness that had held him splintered into lustful shards of lost self-control and then . . . there were no words.

I was being caught in a grip that forgot to be gentle and tender. He rolled me, tearing away my panties as he did, and then I was flat, one arm pinned over my head. And he was leaning over me, plundering my mouth. His knees pushing my thighs wide apart. Reaching between us again. Pressing himself into my soft wetness. Entering me again, with one sweet sharp thrust of his hips.

Yes. His hips heavy on me, his weight balanced on arms bulging with muscles. Comets swirling in his beautiful, beautiful eyes. I hooked a leg over his back and pulled him close.

And then it was a blur of sensation.

And there was no awkwardness. There were no more counterfeit grins. Or a self-conscious girl, thinking herself too young, too round, too short, too small.

No strangers in this unmade bed.

There was this: the lush softness of a woman's breast

and the hard button of a man's nipple. Sucked-in guts—
from touch-me, touch-it, touch-us need. A woman's heated
core, a man's swollen cock. Hard mouths and tender mouths.
Trembling hands and sure hands.

And limbs twisting and friction mounting.

Hearts thudding. Slick skin sliding. Sweat building.

The right angle—there. The right rhythm—yes, there.

High choked baby cries and deep groans.

And finally—oh sweet Goddess, thank you—

Two hearts, beating as one.

Chapter Twenty-two

It's all kinds of wonderful to wake up draped over my Trowbridge. My head tucked under his firm chin, my arm over his taut belly, my short leg swung over his long one. A thump from below made me stir, yawn, and snuggle in a little closer. Drowsily, I slid my fingers under the thatch of hair growing on his chest.

Mine.

I hadn't dreamt at all during my short nap. No ponds, no pools, no pens within a pen.

Safe.

Kind of amazing I'd dropped off at all, considering how the cleanup effort going on downstairs had swollen the house with sound. Unseen brooms swept the porch. Taps groaned, sinks gurgled. Scouring brushes swept back and forth. If I just listened to the noise and subtracted the people, I could almost imagine myself as Belle waking up in the Beast's castle. Mrs. Potts puttering in the kitchen, the little hassock dog doing circles around Cogsworth. Except of course, I'd knitted the middle of the movie to the ending—my beast had already transformed into the very beddable prince.

But the house? It was waking up under their ministrations, as if it, too, had a life.

Yet another example of how I'd gone wrong with the

pack. I should have given them some jobs. Kept them occupied. Clean that hearth, scour that sink.

Wait till they see all the hair Trowbridge left on the bathroom floor.

Another thump.

I glanced at the bedside clock then at the amulets dangling from the lampshade. We'd been snoozing for over an hour, during which time neither Ralph nor Merry had snuggled up. So clearly it wasn't bashfulness keeping the lovers apart. Something was wrong there, but what?

I'll get to you soon, Merry-mine. Promise.

Then I put my best friend's problems in a box, labeled it LATER, and shelved it.

My life had a huge knot that needed untangling, and I wasn't sure which end to tease loose first. On one end was Lexi—so fouled and broken I wasn't sure how I was going to fix him—and on the other, My One True Thing, who came with his own list of problems. Packs and fur loyalties. Moon-runs and fleas. And in the middle of the larger knot was the small tight one of me—a girl who'd found herself tied to the old oak tree.

A life among the wolves without being a wolf.

That made my head pound, so I went back to the problem of Lexi and Trowbridge.

Somehow, without undermining the Alpha of Creemore's top-dog status, I had to get my brother out of that locked room downstairs and into some place of safety while he wrestled with his withdrawal symptoms.

"Mrrph," Trowbridge sleepily sighed as I traced a circle around his nipple.

How deeply buried was my twin under the weight of his addiction? Would I ever find the boy who cried, "I'll save you, my lady," underneath the man who'd flung his daughter across the room like she was a used sock?

Thump. Pause. Thump.

"What is that?" I heard one of the league's bitches ask.

"It's the Fae," a man replied. "He keeps throwing himself at the door."

Lexi. Before Trowbridge had blearily lifted his head, I'd rolled off him, swept up Merry, and bent to retrieve his crumpled T-shirt from the floor.

Covers rustled. "What's going on?"

I hurriedly tugged his T-shirt over my head. "Have you seen my panties?"

"You don't need them," he murmured, sitting up and stuffing a pillow behind his back.

"Yes I do," I replied, centering Merry on my chest. "I'm going downstairs. Lexi's hurling himself against the door. He's going to hurt himself."

"You can't help him," he said flatly.

There was a quality to his voice that should have stirred my instincts, but I wasn't listening to my inner voice. I was Hedi the mate-claimer, and she was lifting the quilt intent on panty retrieval, her Nightingale instincts on full alert. "Is there anything I could give him that would make his withdrawal easier?" I asked, sweeping the mattress with my hand.

No answer. No panties, either. Frowning, I flicked a glance upward.

My Trowbridge studied me, then chewed the corner of his lip, and then drew his leg up so that he could rest his wrist on his knee, and then—finally, after all those thens—he said quietly, "Don't go down there. That's not the way you're going to want to remember him."

And bang. The wheels on the bus stopped turning.

Remember him? "You promised me that you wouldn't hurt him," I whispered, fear starting to crawl up my spine. "You said flat out, 'I won't kill him.' "

A flush tinted his cheeks. "I won't have to. Your brother's been on the juice for decades . . . He can't go without it." Pity on his face. Regret in his tone. "In a day, maybe less, he's going to go into convulsions, and then he's going to die." Blue eyes steady on me, he delivered the final slap. "There's nothing you can do to stop it."

No. There's always something I can do. My fingers

curled around Merry. "Then I have to take him back to Merenwyn."

He shook his head. "I won't let you cross that portal."

Merry scratched against my palm as if to say, "Let's have another think on this." But *this* was not the time for deep thought—not now with the hours melting away. *This* was the time for action. "We can slip in and out before the Black Mage even knows we're there," I said, as much for her as for Trowbridge.

The man who'd trailed a line of kisses along my spine only an hour ago now swung his legs out of his bed and stood. Legs spread and planted. "No. You can't."

And then I understood.

Everything. Welcome to Part II of the "later shit."

"You knew," I said, backing away. "You knew even as you promised me that you wouldn't hurt him, that the worst had already been done. You've known since this morning." Disbelief and disgust churned my gut. "All the time we spent making love . . . Oh, you ripe bastard, you knew."

"You said that in this bed it was just you and me!"

"You could have—"

"I didn't cause this," he said harshly. "He's been a dead man walking for a long, long time."

No, no, no.

An expression of such sadness swept over his face, as if he could see the hurt ahead, could already measure the size of the resulting scar. "Don't, sweetheart," he said.

I spun for the door—just as he knew I would.

Weres.

They're so fast when they want to be. Before I could turn the handle, Trowbridge had caught me by the hips. Then I was being turned, and his body slid between me and escape as he repeated, in a voice laced with sadness and awful knowledge, the same utterly useless request. "Don't, sweetheart."

Don't what? Don't fight?

Let death win?

Never.

I launched myself at him, striking out blindly with my nails, my fists, my feet. Ever stoic, he weathered my abuse silently. Never striking back. Never flinching. His gaze filled with so much pain for me that I wanted to scratch out his eyes.

Unmovable. The ultimate doorstop.

When most of the fight went out of me, and I slid to the old wool carpet, he followed, wrapping his arms around me, absorbing my weight and my misery as my knees collapsed.

We knelt together. His body curved around mine.

And I hated him.

Dust bunnies quivered against the baseboards as I panted and seethed.

"I don't care if you hate me," he said in a fierce whisper. "I won't let him hurt you again. I won't let him take you down with him."

It was there, inside me—black and bitter—my Fae's dark and wicked wish to render him as helpless as me. She lifted her dragon snout to murmur, "Teach this wolf our strength."

It would be so easy. He'd forgotten the danger of our hands, hadn't he? Past his shoulder we could see a variety of things we could use to stun him. The old bulky television, the lamp with its fussy shade. We could turn this room into a maelstrom of Fae might.

My Fae smiled, the tip of her forked tail flicking.

We could destroy this room, this man, this unsettling love.

I came close. Right there, in that room of ugly wallpaper and easy chairs with broken springs, I could have splintered into three separate pieces, because all the straws had been piled, one after the other, on this camel's back.

Was it always going to be like this?

Always caught in the middle between two loyalties?

Never Fae enough for the Fae. Never Were enough for the wolves.

Never knowing which side to pick.
Oh Goddess, I can't, I can't.
Trowbridge pressed his chin to our sweating brow.
And finally, found the perfect words.
"I love you, Hedi Peacock."

Okay, if there really was a fairy godmother, and sweet
wishes turned plain cupcakes into red velvet cake batter, I
would have told him that I loved him right back. Right
then, right there. Cue round three of hot sex. But I knew
suddenly, just by the hurting squeeze on my heart, that life
isn't baby-fat cupids, and valentines with two lines of *x*s
and *o*s. My One True Love could live with a little temporary insecurity while I figured this out.
I am loved.
It should have filled me with unholy delight. Hadn't I
longed for those words? Then why did I feel like I was
wearing hip boots and a rain slicker while fireworks burst
over my head?
*Because I am loved, but the price of that love is so
fucking awful.*
I took a time-out, and once more let him gather me up
like I was a witless rag doll. I said not a word as he deliber-
ated between bed or easy chair once again, nor commented
"smart" when he opted once again for upright over horizontal. I lay unprotesting in his arms as he dragged his
blunt fingernails lightly up my backbone. Remained unmoved as he parted the hair at my nape to press a melting
kiss on the knob of my spine.
It's not going to be that easy, Trowbridge.
Not for us.
"Love doesn't triumph over all," I said, resting my ear
on his warm chest. *My brother the Fae. My brother the
wolfhunter.*
"I'm tired, Trowbridge," I said slowly. "I've been trying
to make parts of me invisible, and I'm pretty sure I can't
do it anymore. I am all three things—the Were, the Fae,
and the girl. Which means that I'm never going to be the

easy—or even the right—fit for you. My inner-Were isn't a dominant wolf, and my Fae comes out at the worst times. I'm never going to run with you under the moon with your pack. And I'm always going to be fifteen years younger than you."

"I know," he murmured, combing my hair with his fingers.

"I'll never forgive your pack," I told him. "They tried to kill me. And you'll never forget who my brother is. Or what he has done to you." I knew the answer—in my heart I *knew* it—but I asked anyhow. "Who ordered you whipped?"

A pause, soaked with bitter memories.

"Your brother did."

I bit down on my back molars, clenching my jaw against the need to release a ragged sob.

"You are not your brother. And I promise that I'll never let any of the pack hurt you again. No one will lift a hand toward you, no one will ever treat you with disrespect." His voice was firm, his intention absolute, but how could he say that? Not even the Alpha of Creemore could hold back the shit-storm that was coming our way. His hand stilled on the spot right between my shoulder blades, and flattened there, as if he wanted to feel my heart through his palm.

"I'm twenty-two years old, and I can count the things I love on one hand," I said, slowly running my finger along the contours of three fingers on his bad hand. "I love Merry, and Cordelia, and Cherry Blossoms. I'm fond of Harry, and I'm softening on Biggs, though that could still go either way." I gave up on his hand, and moved to his arm, stroking it, trying to flatten hair that seemed to bristle.

Then I lifted my head and looked into his eyes.

"You'd need to be blind, deaf, and dumb not to know this already, but I love you, Robson Trowbridge." His mouth broke in a wide smile, and suddenly I wanted to cry so badly that I had to clench my teeth and draw in a shallow breath before I could continue. "That's the truth," I said shakily. "There's no getting around it. I love you more than the sum of all the people I've ever loved in my life."

Blue comets in his eyes, deep happiness in his scent.

I covered his mouth with two shaking fingers when he opened his lips to speak.

"I'm not done yet, okay?" I whispered.

His expression grew serious, and he gave me a grave nod.

"If love was all it took, then whether you're the Alpha of Creemore or the Rogue from British Columbia wouldn't have made much difference. I could have got past all that."

His body tensed on the last sentence.

"I've got to get up," I said, fighting the urge to smooth his brows. "I can't think when you're touching me."

"Don't," he said, his voice low.

"Gotta," said I, slipping off his lap.

Folding my arms over my chest, I walked over to the window and stood there with Merry on my shoulder, looking at all the Trowbridge land. His empire. Once, for a brief and dreary moment, mine. "Being with you is what I always wanted. This should be the happiest day of my life, but now you're telling me that there is no way to save my brother, and it feels like the saddest."

The seat cushion crackled as he stood. "Hedi—"

"Shh!" I said, not turning. "I'm going to have to watch him die, here. In this house. While he's under guard. And you're going to ask me to do nothing about it. And that's the thing I'm not sure I can get over." The old glass shivered in its loose moorings as I rested my heavy head against it. "I know what my brother's become. He's everything you say—a lying, drug-addicted wolfhunter. I know that's the truth, just like I know that I owe the boy he once was a debt that can't ever be repaid."

Truth is born when you say it out loud. Until then it's thinking, and somehow, thinking isn't as painful. But now, as I absorbed all that had been said, guilt swept over me, its weight so choking, it almost smothered the pain.

Breathe. There is a world beyond this minute.

Outside, two Weres inspected a sugar-maple sapling that had seeded itself near the edge of the property. It didn't belong there—clearly the five-foot specimen had encroached on what had been once designated for lawn, but it was beautiful within its vibrant show of fall color. Ivy had discovered it and had wound itself up the tree's thin trunk and threaded itself through the lower branches. That, too, was picture-book lovely, its greenery having turned a brilliant red. As I watched, one of the men reached for a vermilion loop.

The sapling bent as he started to strip the ivy from its branches.

I thought about what had to be said next and fought to force the words out of my throat. "The night the Fae came, Mum told me to go wake Lexi up. But I didn't, which meant that Lexi was sound asleep when the Fae came into the house." I swallowed. "He was a kid, Trowbridge. Just a little boy, who woke up to find the boogeyman in his bedroom and the house filling up with smoke."

So small. So feisty. "From the sound of it, he threw every book, video game, and G.I. Joe he had at them. But in the end, he was just a kid. When they carried him past me . . ." *His eyes were so wild.* "He saw me hiding in the cupboard, but he never let on to the Fae. So I got to live this life, and he got to live that one. All the things he endured? That could—should—have been me."

The maple was now rid of its pest, but it had suffered in the process. Branches had broken. Leaves were shed. Now the two men stared at the sapling, one with hands on his hips, the other idly scratching his shoulder.

Leave the tree alone.

"I'm sorry, sweetheart," Trowbridge said simply, and his scent stretched for me, landing softly on my shoulder, curling down my back and around my waist. It was sweet, and tentative—an extension of the man, not the Alpha. I twisted around to look at him. My mate's expression was hurting, his arms hanging by his sides.

He's hurting for me.

"Trowbridge, the truth," I said. "Is there any chance Lexi can get through the portal without the Black Mage knowing?"

A pause—and for that, I'll always love him—as he thought it over seriously.

"No," he said finally. "He'd have to have some pretty serious magic to get through what's waiting for him at the other end and he doesn't."

I nodded and turned back for the window.

"Coming here was the act of a desperate man, sweetheart," he said as he crossed the room. His tone was careful, just as his steps were slow and measured—a man gingerly navigating himself over a piece of thin ice.

Did he think I was on the verge of breaking?

Not me. I'm almost numb.

My mate touched my arm, and when I didn't jerk away, he carefully eased me back into his warm embrace and folded his arms around my crossed ones. "Your brother was being put out to pasture, and he knew it. Back in the day, his wolf blood had been overlooked, but tolerance isn't what it used to be at Court, especially not for a guy whose addiction had become a liability. He was on the way out. The Shadow had outlived his usefulness to the Black Mage and become an embarrassment."

"I can't think of a way out of this," I murmured, watching Merry slide down her chain. She met the obstacle of Trowbridge's arm, and settled into the vee between my breasts. "He can't go back; he can't stay."

His chin rested on my temple. All I'd have to do would be to lift my chin, and he'd kiss me, and somehow in the moment, I'd forget everything.

Right?

"If it's any help," he said. "I could tell you that life for someone with wolf blood is only going to get a whole lot worse in Merenwyn. Once the Old Mage dies, the Black Mage will have full access to the Book of Spells, and he'll be as powerful as his teacher once was, but he won't have the tolerance for wolves and other races like the old one.

The first thing he'll do is wipe out anything and anyone that has ever thwarted him."

"Your Raha'ells?"

His tone hardened. "The Raha'ells have made him look weak. He'll take care of them the moment the balance of power tips. Anyone with wolf blood in them will be at risk."

"I'm sorry," I said.

"I'll learn to get over it," he lied, tightening his embrace. "You know, it won't just be the wolves who will suffer when the Book of Spells's wards dissolve."

All this suffering attached to the actions of one mage.

The wish for revenge. It burned inside me, as fierce as it had the moment Rachel Scawens's son sawed through Trowbridge's finger.

Very lightly, Trowbridge brushed his thumb over Merry's warm amber belly. "I used to hate the sight of her on your chest," he mused. "But I wouldn't have made it without her in Merenwyn."

He opened his palm, and Merry crawled into it with practiced ease.

They've done that many times before, I thought, feeling a stab of jealousy.

"She doesn't belong in this piece of rock. She's got heart," he said somberly. Merry-mine wrapped a tendril of ivy around his thumb. "When the Black Mage knows the magic, there's nothing to stop him from making another Merry or Ralph."

A beat of red deep inside the heart of the amber. It hurt me to look at her, and so I stared outside to the scene on the front lawn. The men had finished raking up the debris from under the tree. One of them glanced at our window, and I reared back.

"They heard us, didn't they?" I asked.

"Yes."

My cheeks heated. *They probably heard us make love, too.* "Don't you worry that they'll speak to the wrong people?"

"Those two gave me their blood vow. Anyone who's on the property has, and their loyalty is absolute. Those who haven't, have twenty-four hours to do so."

Or what? I wanted to ask, but didn't. "Did your sister make the vow?"

His chest lifted and fell. "No."

"It's such a mess, Trowbridge," I said. "If the Black Mage has an amulet, will he come here?"

"If he believes the Royal Amulet is here, he'll come."

"You lied to the pack."

"It's a skill I picked up in Merenwyn."

"Is there any way we can stop it?"

"Not unless someone kills the Black Mage." Suddenly, Trowbridge swiveled around, his ear cocked toward the door. A moment later, I heard the sound of boots coming up the stairs. "It's Harry," he told me, as if I didn't recognize the sound of those cowboy heels. "He must have some news about Brenda Pritty."

I tried for a smile and failed. "Then you better go talk to him, hadn't you?"

"It can wait," he said.

"No, it can't, and you know it." I headed for the bathroom.

Harry knocked on the door. "Sorry, boss, I didn't want to disturb you, but I just got the information you needed."

I shut the door, then turned on the tap so that Harry wouldn't hear me pee. (Yeah, I know he could still hear me but it's a mental thing, okay?) Trowbridge's hair littered the floor. One long dread hung over the rim of the garbage can by the toilet. I picked it up. It felt soft in my hand.

Not dead to the touch at all.

I flushed and washed my hands. As I stared at my reflection in the mirror, I thought about how I hated death more than anything else in the world. I'd lost to it twice now, and I'm a really sore loser. Maybe that's what drove me to protect those I love even when common sense told me not to.

So fix this.

My brain spun around the problem. Lexi needed to return to Merenwyn, but if he did, he'd be facing one very angry mage. Everything always came back to the Black Mage. His soul ball must be as dark as—

Ohhhh.

Contrary to a popular misconception, and the vampires of *Buffy the Vampire Slayer,* you really can't survive without a soul . . . The Black Mage's dark heart was easy pickings in Threall.

All I needed to do to change everything from terrible to bearable was travel to the land of myst, dodge Mad-one, take a stick, and break his soul ball. And then . . . I could return home. Tell Lexi that his sister, the mystwalker abomination, had slain the monster. That it was safe to go back to Merenwyn and thumb his way through the Old Mage's spell book until he found the antidote to his addiction.

Murder of the most sinister kind.

But if I did it . . . If I killed the dark wizard's twisted soul, I could save Lexi, and Merry's people, and even Trowbridge's Raha'ells, so much hurt, so much pain. All I had to do was to be willing to extinguish one light in Threall.

And yet.

Murder.

I killed Dawn Danvers. I rubbed my mouth, thoughtful. Most of the time, I didn't think of her too much. She'd had to go; she'd hurt mine, and was planning to kill mine. But some nights—when the wind stirred the trees—I found myself thinking of her. I couldn't seem to erase the memory of her terrified expression when my Fae dragged her toward the pond. I couldn't seem to forget the way her nails had tried to gouge the cable of Fae magic wrapped around her waist. Sometimes I woke up, heart thudding in my chest, remembering her wild and terrified eyes staring at me from under the water.

If I could do that, I can do this.

Merry scratched my neck, as if to say, "What's up?"

I shook my head.

The end justifies the means, right?

I turned the idea over, inspecting it from all sides. One speed bump was Mad-one—she'd finally completely lost it. You had to be three-quarters cracker dog to believe I was "the chosen one." *Talk about wishful thinking.* She must be dying to find a replacement.

What would I do if she started hovercrafting after me, tossing fireballs?

I'd run damn fast, that's what I'd do.

Though, no matter how quickly I sprinted down the field, I'd always been a slow tree climber—partly due to my fear over the prospect of falling, partly because I'd never had Lexi's agility. And from what I could remember, the specimen I intended to scale was a monster. Heavily foliaged, its trunk twisted and fat, garnished with knobs of bulbous growths uglier than warts on a witch's chin. Even now, safe in the Alpha's bedroom, my skin crawled at the thought of touching that bark. What thoughts would I hear, when I touched his tree? Goddess, it would be like sticking your hand into a pile of offal.

Oh crap. What if he saw into me?

I held a glass under the faucet—*hey, look at that, the water pouring out of the tap looks a lot like the portal to Merenwyn when you see it from Threall*—and filled it up. Tossing my head back, I swallowed it right down, all the time thinking, *Protect, protect, protect.*

Okay. The simplest solution would be to put everything precious in a strongbox—Trowbridge, Lexi, Cordelia, Merry and Ralph, Harry, and even Biggs. Everything that was crucial to me sealed in a treasure chest. I wiped the corner of my mouth. I could do that. I was great at compartmentalizing.

Would that be enough?

"You think too much," Trowbridge had just told me.

Don't think. Do.

I turned off the tap, and eavesdropped for a second.

"They say she has a drug problem?" asked Trowbridge.

"Yup," said Harry. "A big one, from all accounts. Which means—"

"We've got to track her down," finished the Alpha of Creemore. "Find out who she's told."

Harry cleared his throat. "Before you arrived Knox said he'd contacted his superior at the NAW, which means Reeve Whitlock probably has at least a verbal report on what's been going down in Creemore."

"Doesn't matter. Without the video, there's no proof that the portal ever was opened. If it only went as far as Brenda Pritty, we're good."

Pack business.

Let Trowbridge take care of his people while I take care of mine.

I closed my eyes. Concentrated.

Pull away from here. Think of Threall.

I imagined myself as a bird, flying in from the south, my eyes opened wide instead of squeezed tight. Threall was an open field, roughly the size and shape of a hockey rink. Forests to the left and right of the clearing, each separate grove of trees hedged by overgrown hawthorns. Blue mysts weaving across the moss-covered ground. Tree stumps dotting the ground, their jagged edges worn smooth by Threall's ever-present, soft and fragrant wind.

Yes! I felt a lifting of my soul. A stretch of my skin.

I had feathers, I had wind.

Imagine every detail.

Three trees to avoid in the pasture. Two black walnuts, down at the far end. Skirt over them, be careful of—

I could hear the outside world again.

Detach from the world.

Another swoop and then another run. A close-up of the lone tree at the dead end of the clearing: one ancient beech tree, growing under the lee of the sheer wall of rock. Surrounding it, a hand-constructed fence, made from broken branches and sharp spars of wood, all of them jammed hard into the ground at a forty-five-degree angle so that each dead bough was fitted into the complex embrace of the one below it.

I circled Mad-one's lair, trying to see through the deep foliage. Past the knotted and gnarled boughs. Looking for a mystwalker, dressed in a long blue gown.

"Hedi?" I heard Trowbridge cry.

No, not back down to where there was nothing but a terrible future. Not there. Choices—the repercussions that would follow them—were being pursued, and things—precious and irreplaceable—were going to be destroyed, unless I did the thing that only I could do.

Fly.

I flapped my wings, hoping to soar.

One last, terrible pain.

I heard one last despairing, "Hedi!"

And then finally, I was free.

Chapter Twenty-three

This felt a tad repetitive.

Once again, I was flat on my stomach, eyes closed, skin registering the prickling resistance of the moss beneath me. For a bit I lay there, recovering, because, for the record, deliberately growing a body is just as horrendously painful as purposely cutting yourself off from your mortal shell. It's all about gravity, you know? Most of us don't realize the constant tug of it or even recognize the weight of our bodies.

Then again, most of us can't travel to Threall.

A faint breeze, sweet and floral, teased my hair. It picked up a paper fragment of a soul ball and played with it with sly cruelty, impaling it for a taunting second on the curved thorn of a hawthorn before sending it skipping across a brackish puddle. I tracked its progress with my eyes—this fluttering scrap, once the sheath of a soul, now a toy to a heartless wind—feeling strangely sad and old, as it was carried past the scaled trunk of the Old Mage's black walnut tree.

Each time, I land here. Not under the canopy of the Black Mage's specimen, but near this wind-battered relic. Why? Was I more like Lexi than I knew? Did my covetous soul recognize that magic lay beneath Threall's thin crust?

That beneath my belly were the wizard's roots, ebbing life—a fibrous pathway to a mind both agile and—

Goddess, stop. Get up. Roll away.

Rolling to my knees, I forced my attention from his dying tree and found things, if possible, had only gotten worse in Threall during my absence. Daylight was waning and with its creeping loss bomb craters had proliferated, trees had suffered limb amputations, and the once serene, mossy clearing had nearly finished its de-evolution into an unloved wetland.

So much water. So much mud and mangled moss.

A few feet to my left, just past her foxhole, the Mystwalker sat slumped on a tree stump, her feet resting on a broken tree branch. She half turned, her lip twisted in a predictable snarl. " 'Tis but you," she noted.

Evidently, I'd been recast from threat to irritation.

I rose to my feet to gaze better at the disordered forest beyond the straggling line of hawthorns. The woods were dark and quiet. *I'd like to wander through them one day. When I'm not running from something. Or for that matter, running to something.*

"It is the wildness in you," Mad-one said quietly.

When I turned, she nodded toward the sanctuary of the trees. "Your soul recognizes its loss and wants it to be reconciled. It is why that side of my Threall fascinates you." Then she studied me, her head tilted, her eyes weary and bleak. "You should find a place of concealment. It would be a pity to lose the chosen one before she is of practical use."

"And who or what am I hiding from?"

"The same vile beast as before—the devil's spawn."

He had to be one big-ass monster to have done this much damage. The cudgel lay where I'd dropped it. I bent to pick it up, and said, with as much casual indifference as I could muster, "I see no spawn."

"He will return."

"Where'd he go?"

Her mouth flattened.

Ah. So he'd returned to where she could not—home to Merenwyn.

The sudden leak of sympathy I felt for the Mystwalker of Threall turned me testy. "You want to tell me why you haven't blown the 'devil's spawn' off the edge of the world like you once tried to do to me?"

"He is fleet of foot," she said sourly.

Great. The Threall destroyer was a *fast-moving* guy with a pitchfork and horns.

I blew some air through my teeth. "If I could fly like you, I'd have nipped up to the top of the Black Mage's tree, and ripped his soul ball out of its boughs faster than you could say rock-a-bye baby."

Using the slow voice usually reserved for speaking to very young children, she said, "He has cast a ward of protection around the citadel of his cyreath—surely you can see that? And even if I wished to pass through its cloying barrier, my soul is bound. I cannot hurt a member of the Inner Court or its mage. If you were a *bound* mystwalker instead of an ignorant fool you would know that."

*Always with the cheap shot*s. "What is a citadel of your cyreath?"

A long finger, soot tipped, smeared with mud, pointed toward the nearest tree. "That is a citadel." Then she gestured toward the soul ball. "That is a cyreath." With a look of utter disgust, she wiped her hand clean with her skirt. "Also, that which you would know if you were a mystwalker with the most rudimentary education."

I had a comment for that—something along the lines of "Oh shut up, Miss Smarty-pants"—but refrained. Instead I asked, "How bad is his ward?"

"You could pass through it," she replied, her voice thoughtful.

Could I?

If there really is a ward then it's damn near invisible, I thought, gazing at the citadel of the Black Mage's twisted soul. I might have miscalculated how easy of a task a little soul destruction was going to be because I hadn't factored fear into my stunningly simple plan of scaling his walnut tree and beating the shit out of his "cyreath," and, oh sweet heavens, I should have. How could a thirty-foot tree seem to be so alive? So sentient? So malevolent?

Gray-green lichen crawled up its twisted trunk.

Climb that? How? That first fork was chin-high, if not higher. I'd need to perch my foot on top of one of those bulbous growths, and insert my hand into a dark knothole—*oh please, no spiders*—just to reach that first fork. After that I'd have to pick a path to where his mottled purple soul ball swayed from its perch over the abyss that had no bottom, trusting that my weight would be supported by branches that grew steadily thinner and weaker the higher I went.

All of it accomplished under the watchful eye of the Mystwalker of Threall.

She of the fireballs and bad temper.

I tapped my cudgel against my thigh, thinking how much I'd like to use it on Mad-one, while she busied herself by daintily rearranging the folds of her scorched skirt. After I'd counted all my toes and fingers, I slid a glance toward her in time to see her quickly avert her eyes.

This is ridiculous. I'm playing "who's the bigger bitch" with Mad-one while Lexi is throwing himself at the door of his prison. "So, am I right in thinking that you don't have any particular problem with me killing the Black Mage?"

Her answer was a slow, chilling smile.

I jammed the piece of oak down the back of my pants so that my hands were free. "Well, watch and learn, Mad-one. I'm going knock the Black Mage's twisted heart straight into the abyss of hell."

When, out of nowhere, I heard a voice. "This is ill-advised."

Who was that? I whipped around, searching for a face, a shadow, anything to explain that cool observation that seemed to come from either inside my head or right behind me. *Let it be someone behind me.* But there was no one. Just the wind, the moss, the myst. An errant breeze goosefleshed my skin as I turned back to Mad-one. Her head was tilted; her eyes narrowed in consideration.

"What did you say?" I asked Mad-one hopefully.

The Mystwalker lifted a single blond brow, very delicately. "I did not speak."

The wintry voice inside my head spoke again. "I shall not aid your travel to that one's embrace. The Old Mage calls us, can you not hear his summons? We were born to serve him, not the foul one."

Oh crap.

Up to now the few times my Fae had opted to comment on Hedi-land, she'd been basically all "Fee-fi-fo-fum. I'm going to fuck with this dumb-dumb." Sly quips. The Dorothy Parker of ride-alongs. And *usually,* she strung together two or three words at most.

Six tops.

Never had she spoken using a distinct sentence structure, with verbs and stuff. Never like a fully formed person inside my freaking head. Well, that wasn't quite true . . . there was that time the three of us had killed Dawn.

No. Not that again.

Not up here, when I was Were-less. When it was just mortal-me pitted against Fae-me.

"Do *not* talk to me," I said. "You're not becoming top dog in Hedi Incorporated, got it? Just because we're in Threall where you're feeling all . . ."

"Forsooth, she is witless, this one," the Mystwalker murmured.

My voice trailed away. I stared at Mad-one, wondering, was this how crazy had begun for her? She'd started out reasonably normal and then the voices started? Two or three Threall visits later, and she was the resident whack-job having long heart-to-hearts with herself?

Scary. *Get out of Threall before you turn into an inmate.*

Without another word, I launched myself out of the

foxhole, and sprinted across the field with the speed of an infantryman under sniper fire.

I'm coming for you, you black-hearted bastard.

Puddles sprayed as I dashed toward the dastardly and all was going swimmingly until twelve feet from the walnut when I hit an invisible and viscous pocket of something . . . terrible.

His ward was thick and oily.

Horrible. It swamped me with a near-overpowering urge to backtrack bowing and whimpering from that wall of the dreadful and the bad. Even breathing became a Herculean task because there was no air in that bubble. Just horrible, stinking pressure. It squeezed down on me . . . Fae Stars, I was the bruised raspberry suspended in a bowl of setting gelatin.

"Go back," said my Fae.

I couldn't do it. Retreat required a one-hundred-eighty-degree turn. Too much effort.

"Fool, push through it," she cried.

The command congealed before it ever reached my toes. How could I move my foot? It was a cinder block affixed to a concrete pad bolted to a unyielding slab of bedrock.

"We're going to perish!" She flooded me with bitter frustration.

No we won't. Not if I lift our foot. It isn't a cinder block. It's a foot. Toes and heel. A callus on the back of your heel. Always missing a shoe or two. I can do it. All I have to do is take another step. I don't need air.

Lungs screaming for air, I took a shambling step.

Followed by another.

"We're seeing dots," she hissed.

Stop whining. I'm concentrating.

One last push. Come on. You can do it. Use the momentum of your weight. Stick out your goddess-cursed chin and fall forward.

Sometimes I amaze myself with my brilliance. I thrust

out my jaw and willed myself to become the Leaning
Tower of Hedi. A sense of reluctant parting—choking
hands being forced to open—and then I was out of its sickening grip. Release. Oh, wonderful release. I fell onto my
hands and knees, and stayed like that, gratefully sucking
in air, the piñata stick digging into the upward swell of
my ass.

I'm going to have to go back the same way I came.

My mouth filled with bile as I twisted around. There
was nothing to mark the place where the invisible wall
began or where it ended beyond a long track of moss pleated
up during my zombie walk. Even as I watched, a stream of
blue myst slid right through the ward, did a lazy circuit
around me—*go ahead, rub it in*—then merrily flitted away.

"Kill him," said my Fae. "The ward will die with his
soul."

"Works for me." It took a brief second to puzzle out the
toeholds and stretches required, then I placed a foot neatly
on the big bulbous growth sprouting on the trunk and
sprang upward. My hand caught the edge of the knothole a
foot higher. One big heave, a bit of awkward scrambling,
and I was crouched in the fork of the black walnut tree.

Stupidly, I grinned—oh evil murderess me—at how
easy it was. Success was just a quick scramble up through
the foliage. And then, as I was reaching for my piñata
stick . . .

Oh sweet heavens.

The Black Mage's dark soul poured into me, as if someone had pulled the stopper on a bottle of something vile. I
didn't see pictures, I didn't receive thoughts. Just the essence of him, and that was both fascinating and repugnant
because his soul was really low on the gray tones—he was
hate without heat; ambition without limit; sex without
pleasure; night without light.

Dark-hearted. Yes, that fit.

And constantly hungry, too.

My sluggish progress through the ward must have
sounded an alarm for him, because I didn't receive any

images that would have given me a clue as to what he was seeing or doing in Merenwyn. Instead, he plunged me into a pitch-black cave that no amount of rapid blinking could bring bright light into.

Swirling head. Dizzy. Disoriented.

Goddess, he's blinded me.

My sense of direction disappeared. Was the end of the world off to my right elbow or my left? Had I been spun around in my confusion? *I can't see.* That abyss. That long, long plunge—to fall and never stop falling.

Don't move. Not until your head clears. Heart thudding in my chest, I hunched over my heels, trying not to twitch or even breathe, frightened that he'd soon find me, one toe in his thought stream and then . . . oh what would happen then? My knee began to shake against the trunk of his tree, tap, tap, tap, like a woodpecker on a tall pine.

"I see you now," he said softly.

Horror spiked through me as a fright-mask of a face suddenly sprang out at me from the gloom. Skin as pale as a ghost's, mouth set in a pitiless smile. And then . . . the Black Mage was on me. Around me. *In* me. A stab of pain, and a long cruel finger poked deep within me, scoring things that had never been touched.

I am dirty. I am bare.

"Close your mind!" my Fae cried. "Steel yourself!"

Too late. He was everywhere. Fondling things he should never touch.

Get him out.

His soiled fingers brushed against the Stronghold box—which I'd so carefully packed when I was standing in Trowbridge's bathroom, blithely considering murder. Inside it, the knowledge of those people precious to me. My Trowbridge, my Lexi, my Merry, and my Cordelia. Harry and Biggs and Ralph, too.

"And me!" shrieked my Fae.

No. He will not touch that which is mine.

With a banshee scream, I lifted my cudgel high and brought it down hard enough to feel the vibration of the

strike all the way up to my shoulder. I sensed a sharp re-
coil and, with it, the game turned—hello, avenging Valkyrie.

I rained blows upon his trunk.

Chips of bark flew, sap ran.

And you know what? For a bit I almost thought I could
just chop him down. Strike by strike. But then beneath me,
the black walnut began to sway. A whoosh of leaves to the
left. A protest of chafing branches to the right.

Trees shouldn't do that when you're blindly crouched in
them.

*That bastard's going to toss me soon and I'm going to
fall and never stop falling.*

Screw that.

Dumb luck met desperation—in the frenzy of blows
that followed that panic one of my strikes hit a bulbous
growth with enough force to crack it.

A loud, reptilian hiss . . . and the connection was broken.

The tree grew still. But I knew.

Evil was listening.

An elegant dismount was beyond me. I made a quick
prayer to the Goddess of GPS—*please let the abyss be on
my right*—and simply leaned far to my left.

I landed less than two seconds later on my tailbone—
ow—followed by my head bouncing on the ground—
double ow—and then I was lying prone on a crop of
rotting stone fruits. They smelled bad. Sweet and acid, a
little bit woody, too. *I'm lying on the seeds of evil. Move
away.* My ankle brushed against his trunk, and before the
Black Mage could snatch at me again with the hooks of his
agile, wicked mind, I painfully rolled past his reach.

Cored out, I lay near the foot of his tree, curled on my
side, my billy club clutched in my hand like a warrior's
sword. For a second I studied the scattered dark and wiz-
ened fruit, the new deadfall of twigs, leaves, and broken
branches that lay near the edge of the world—*good, I did
some damage to the bastard*—then I buried my head in
the crook of my arm.

And I tried really hard not to weep for my brother.

* * *

"Seek protection with the Old Mage!" urged my Fae. "Go! Now!"

My eyes shot open.

Crap. The tree's bark glistened with sweat. Right under my gaze, the shiny stuff sloughed off the trunk to pool on the soil, no longer shimmering, but widening in a dark wet stain. In less than half a second, that blot of ugly had gone from a puddle to a shape rising from the ground.

Something wicked this way comes.

I pushed myself shakily to my feet as the shape shifted into the ghostly outline of someone crouched, fingers spread and braced on the soil. *Was it the mage? Could he materialize here?* Heart in mouth, I was backtracking toward the ward as the shape changed and details were quickly added. Hair, short and roughly chopped. Clothing, loose and homespun. *Not the mage,* I realized. His feet would never be so small, so dirty.

The devil's spawn lifted his head.

This ten-year-old was the assailant who'd slunk along the bushes and lobbed fire at Mad-one? He was the person Lexi had called "the little mystwalking freak"?

Shame on both of them. He wasn't a spawn; he was a cub with a baby-soft mouth.

I pushed myself shakily to my feet.

The kid gaped at me then fumbled for the rough bark behind him. "It's not Tyrean," he babbled. "It is another!"

Who's planning on doing the slog march through the ward again. I edged close enough to feel the vibration of its doom message, while the Black Mage gave the problem a quick think. High up in the boughs of that wicked tree, a purple light flashed. Blip, blip.

The devil's spawn listened, mouth pulled down, before flicking me a searing glance. "Yes, her eyes are green." A pause then the kid's face twisted in a sly calculation. "But she has a stick, master," he wheedled.

Don't call him master.

A red mark bloomed on the boy's pale cheek. "I will do

it," he said sullenly before he lifted his hand. It was a small little paw, vividly red and swollen, at the end of a malnourished arm.

Puny muscles. I could take him.

The devil's spawn didn't use any words to call up his magic. The kid merely blinked, and a ball of fire burst into life above his soot-grimed finger. His personal incendiary device was softball-sized; blue toned versus orange, with the requisite tongues of yellow flame.

Shit.

"Get out!" he said, creeping toward me.

"You better hope you can outrun me," I said slowly. "I burn, you burn."

That would have been the moment he should have nailed me with it. When he didn't, I started speculating as to whether or not he could throw his great ball of fire while we were inside the Black Mage's ward. Even as I watched, the yellow heat licking the outside of his fireball sank low, almost disappearing into the bluish center.

It's a breath away from extinguishing on its own.

As he crept toward me, I asked, "You're responsible for all this destruction?"

He gave me an ugly, preening smile. "I am a myst-walker."

"Didn't anyone tell you that we're supposed to protect this realm, not destroy it?" I asked, gaze fixed on the sputtering sphere of flame. "What you've done here . . . doesn't it feel wrong?"

He made a dismissive noise that was a combination of a tsk and a huff.

Almost there. Come on, you little brat. Just another foot.

"I will burn you," he said.

"Uh-huh," I replied, then I puckered up my lips, leaned over, and blew. And, just as I suspected, his great ball of fire went out, leaving only a little, itty-bitty flame flickering above his ragged fingernail. Kind of like a Bic lighter, low on gas.

"You're out, buddy," I said.

What I'd counted on was for him to act like a kid. You know—get rattled, and then go home crying. Instead, he reignited his Bic finger and went for my hair. Swiftly, I intercepted his wrist. "Put it out!" When he didn't, I grabbed him in a one-armed bear hug then lifted him right off his feet. His feet bicycled as I blew out his flame. "Stop trying to light me on fire, you little guttersnipe—"

Snipes have teeth.

Faster than a pissed-off Pomeranian, he chomped down on my forearm. He must have had lots of practice at biting . . . he did it so very well.

Pain. Worse than stubbing your toe.

You little devil. I went to cuff him, hesitated—couldn't help the pause, he was a kid—and was rewarded for my sudden flare of ethics by him gouging my thigh with his sharp ragged nails.

Geeze Louise.

Automatically, I bent over, to move my legs out of the range of his claws, and when he slashed at them again, I feinted backward. And stepped right into the ward.

Sucking pressure. No air. Legs limp as overdone noodles.

Pomeranian hanging off my arm.

And . . . memories. It was like touching Mad-one all over again. I saw into the kid, and inadvertently discovered pieces of his history that I never wanted to know. And perhaps, in exchange, he discovered little pieces of mine. *Oh kid . . . oh sweet heavens . . . you poor little . . . oh kid . . .* I staggered out of that airless vacuum a whole lot faster than I shuffled through it the first time. Feeling sickened to my soul.

And hurting, too—when I emerged, the devil's spawn was still attached by his incisors.

"Stop biting!" I hissed.

If anything, he just bore down harder, seeming to want to connect with bone.

"I don't want to hurt you!" I yelled.

Half of a lie. You really do want to hurt someone when they bite you. But this kid, this brat, this little monster dubbed the devil's spawn—he'd already been hurt so. Sweet and trusting he'd been once . . .

Blood began leaking from the corner of his mouth.

My blood.

"You little vicious . . ." In frustration, I pinched his nose hard, sealing his nostrils tight. "One thousand, two thousand . . ." His eyes widened and I fancied I could see him mentally assessing how long he could last without air.

Not long, apparently.

The devil's spawn unhinged his jaw. "I'm going to tell him that you're the Shadow's sister," he said, before using his forearm to get rid of that inconvenient dribble of my blood on his chin. Just to make sure I was truly scared, he aimed another kick at my kneecap, then darted for the safety of the ward, and would have slipped into its veil had I not lunged, and reeled him back by his shirt collar at the last second.

"You don't have to go back to him!" I yelled.

It would have been easier to grab a wolverine by its tail. Little-boy ragged toenails jabbed for my shins, sharp feral teeth snapped for my fingers.

"Enough!" I yelled, giving him a shake. "Stop it, or I'll . . ." I lifted my cudgel in an empty threat and immediately he stilled, his eyes dead, his face set in a sullen expression, as if I'd just fulfilled every one of his expectations.

If I'd wanted to kill the Black Mage before, now I wanted to feed his entrails to a Cuisinart. Because I'd *seen* things as I backpedaled out of the ward with the mystwalker apprentice. Stuff I never wanted to know. Like the pants-wetting fear the devil's spawn felt about the dark, and how that anxiety spiked to bowel-loosening dread when the door to the room of magic was pushed open. The things that kid knew . . . no child should know that.

And now the sickening memory of it was in my head. Not like I'd read it in the newspaper, or watched it in a gritty documentary. It was as bad as that spring evening in the Trowbridge living room when all I'd smelled was blood, and all I'd known was that I was weaker than those who wished to hurt me. No escape. Just misery and endurance.

My life has been so easy.

Pity swelled. "It's wrong," I said shakily. "What's been done to—"

He actually cocked his head—and to this day, I'm not sure if it was because I'd reached him, or I'd shown a weakness he thought he could exploit. But suddenly, he saw something over my shoulder that made him go stiff as a mouse spotting the resident cat.

And that was about as much warning as I got.

I heard a sizzle, and out of the corner of my eye I saw an incoming flash of yellow and orange. Protective instincts, once prodded to life, are a bitch to ignore. I wrapped my arms around he-who-bites, and lunged for safety an instant before the burning fireball slammed into the ground not four feet from us, spraying moss, earth, and well . . . fire. Too damn close. Heat on my back, fear in my belly. I hunched protectively over the boy, and the flaming sphere bounced, once, and then began to roll toward the ward, frying moss as it did.

On contact with the Black Mage's shield, the incendiary device broke apart. Relatively softly, almost like when a bath bead finally pops in hot water. The oil within spread over the ward's invisible wall and burst into flames.

I spun around.

Chapter Twenty-four

Mad-one stood outside her foxhole, weaving slightly, her right hand lifted shoulder high. She grimaced, and another fireball burst into life above her sooty finger.

"Don't fire!" I yelled. "I've got it under control!"

As if the Mystwalker gave a damn——she saw her chance to remove two irritants and she planned to take it. With a deadly smile, she flicked her wrist backward. "Don't!" I screamed as I pushed the devil's spawn behind me.

The fireball arched through the air, and suddenly the stick in my hand was no longer a cudgel but a bat, and I wasn't a girl one hiccup away from being crispy-fried, I was Derek Jeter. Her meteor of hurt came in from high, and then curved downward.

Mouth pursed, I kept my eye on it, not on the kid, not on Mad-one.

For once in my life, I kept my eye on the ball.

My life has been easy.

I swung.

The tip of my improvised bat hit the fireball with a shower of sparks. I cringed, protecting my head, expecting to be doused in flaming oil. But instead of breaking apart, Mad-one's missile flew up in the air in a perfect arc, seemingly destined on a return trip to its origin, except out of nowhere, a strong, whistling gust of air caught it, and changed its trajectory. My mouth dropped open as my foul sailed sideways into the sky, brilliant orange and red, twisting and rotating.

Then it did the unthinkable.

No, no, no.

Spitting sparks, it hit the dry tinder of the Old Mage's wind-nibbled topmost branches—the ones flayed by wind and left splintered like an open book of matches—and the top right portion of his tree burst into flames. Just like that. As if someone had hit ignite on a gas barbecue.

Horror, gut-deep.

"Our mage!" cried my Fae.

She erupted inside me, and *took*.

Next thing I knew, I'd dropped my stick, and was streaking toward the disaster of my making, my Fae's anxiety fuel to my flying feet. Behind me came a shriek, agonized and awful. I flicked a glance over my shoulder.

Mad-one was following in my tracks, her face anguished, her blistered hand lifted skyward. "Storm!" she cried.

And holy cow, Batman. No sooner had she uttered the word, than it began to rain in Threall. Not a heavy downpour, but a barely there soft rainfall.

Let it be enough to put the fire out.

My Goddess must have heard my plea, because even as my Fae and I were reaching for that first handhold—a sturdy bough that led to an even sturdier one—the fire's horrible, popping, crackling noise died into a resentful hiss. Skirting the section that still smoked, I—no, *she*—starting moving up that tree faster than a squirrel in a race for the last nut of the season. Reaching for crook and vee and swollen knob, anything that could give me purchase up another foot, another inch, another hand's reach toward that soul light, high up in the tree.

"Master!" she screamed. "I am coming!"

Higher and higher, we climbed; my Fae keeping our eyes trained upward. Because the old man's soul—it called to her. She'd felt the tug of his presence since the moment

I'd opened my eyes last night in Threall. Hell, she'd been fan-girl over him ever since we'd begun dreaming of Merenwyn.

"Save me," he pleaded to her.

His soul ball glowed, so fierce, so bright. A distress beacon high in a mostly dead tree. Orange as a setting sun. And yes, even semimortal-me recognized the aching beauty of his dying soul. It was there in the glory of the golden light pouring from it. The summation of all the things thought before death—the loves you remember, the people you'll miss, all the moments you won't have in the future, all those sun-dappled days you spent in your past . . . when you die, that love, that wistful regret . . . it shines from within.

"I will save you, my liege," my Fae cried.

The tree's on fire. Let's stop and think—

No. There would be no thinking, no hesitating, no mulling of options. My Fae's reckless will pushed us higher, past fear of falling, past fear of losing. My hand slid off, met air, and then, miraculously, my knee met something immovable—I didn't even turn to see what it was. Up, up, toward that glowing orb of light. Four more forks, then just a stretch, an impossible stretch. Doable.

"I'm almost there!" I cried.

But here's the sad truth: if you're half dead, you're only half good.

Mad-one's well of water was not bottomless. The magic that fed her rain withered, and with that, her gentle rain softened to a light drizzle, which gave way to a damp fog. Which might have been okay; the fire had been doused and we were four fifths of the way toward our rescue victim.

Then Threall's wind stirred to life.

"Give me a break," I cursed.

The sweet-scented zephyr of air passed over me like a silk ribbon drawn over my skin then snaked to where tiny pockets of fire drowsed. With sinuous skill the wind breathed air into the mouth of dying embers. A puff here, a blow there, a gentle fan there.

Oh no.

I knew what to expect next; I'd seen what happened to a few dull gray coals after Dad had doused them in lighter fluid and sped things up with the blow dryer. *Hurry. Grab the soul ball and flee.* Frantically I jammed a foot into a crook, but even as I stretched for the bough above me, I heard the terrifying *whump* of a fire being reignited.

Crap.

Below me, a river of yellow wicked up the tree's spine, in search of that sun-bleached, bare-barked, gray *dead* wood in which I was perched.

"Master!" cried Mad-one.

Screw master, help me.

So high! How had we climbed so high? There was no soft landing, there was no simple way down. The trunk was aflame four feet below me and fire was running along each bough searching for more fuel. There remained one window of escape. We'd have to squirm down, perilously close to the branches that hung over the abyss. *Now.* We had to leave immediately, otherwise we'd both be Joan of Arc.

Our mage, she hissed.

She forced our gaze upward. Perhaps ten feet above me, the mage's cyreath swung with each breath of Threall's wind. Its ties to the realm precarious—the only thing that kept it tethered to the tree was the thin strand of umbilical cord looped through a spar of wood. Not enough time to climb for it. An image flashed. A man, silvered hair, gleaming robes, backlit by brilliant white light that gave him almost a godlike halo.

Our mage, breathed my Fae.

She surged up my arm, tore painfully through the narrow channel of my wrist then—without prodding or permission—streamed out of my fingers in a cable of green magic. A serpent of green. A Fae spirit, too long stifled, now unleashed in the Fae realm for which her nature had been formed. She sparkled. She glittered. She glowed.

"Our mage!"

My magic sped upward—beautiful and bright—and hit the Old Mage's withered soul light with her soft, open-mouthed kiss.

I'd touched one of Threall's soul balls before. Hell, I'd even carried it tucked under my arm. And as I'd done so, I'd felt a tenderness for the soul within. But this—oh, this blissful moment of unity when my Fae met mage—was totally different. She arched our back as old, deep-seated power, beyond any measure I ever owned or expected to, filled us.

It was a heroin fix for my Fae's deepest cravings.

"I am your servant," moaned my Fae to her mage.

Breathing? That got temporarily suspended. Using my knees to hug the limb? Almost forgot that, too. My Fae was larger than life, potent with promise, shivering with damn near orgasmic pleasure.

"Do you vow to be mine forever?" asked the mage. "My nalera?"

"Yes, forever," she answered with my voice.

Wait a minute—

Then, before I could tug the controls back to semimortal-me, he said, "Let it be so!"

"Yes," she said. Let it be so—joined to a mind far more brilliant than ours. Let it be so—earthly woes soothed, mortal worries vanished. Mmmmh, let it be so—this moment of bright white light, this moment of utter joy, this certainty that here, finally, was the job my Fae had been born to do. No longer the misfit among the animals. No longer hidden. No longer imprisoned.

Freedom.

She belonged here. In Threall.

With him.

My Fae's magic wound a tight coil over that fragile strand that tethered his soul to the flaming tree, then strained to pull it free. One more rush of wondrous heat, as his ball's tether stretched reed thin. Then it snapped—

There was the burst of a bright white light; a thousand klieg lights all turned on at once; and then—Goddess, *then*—he was ours.

Yeah, yeah, I know. *Hello. The tree's on fire.*

What was semimortal-me doing? Nothing much. Just experiencing secondhand a joy that transcended anything I'd ever felt before. Me, my Fae, and him might have just stayed there and fried, impervious to pain, in a disquieting mental climax that never ended, body shuddering, senses attuned only to the pleasure of belonging—such a communion, such a marriage of magic and mage—if a section of the burning tree hadn't suddenly broken with a loud, bliss-breaking crack.

My eyes flew open to hell.

The sizzling firebrand plunged toward the ground, taking with it weaker branches, all in a shower of sticks and branches and splinters of wood. And as it crashed through all that broken tinder, things aflame met things that weren't.

Tinder, they were.

With a loud whoosh, the entire bottom of the tree went up. Heat and smoke roiled toward us, bringing with it a searing agony, worse than any blistering payback throbbing heat. *Goddess, my feet! My hands!* Fire below us. Heat blistering the soles of my feet. Smoke everywhere. Stinging the eyes, clogging the throat.

I can't breathe.

"You must fly, nalera!" said the old man. "Bring us to safety!"

I haven't got wings!

"Fly! Leap from this tree, and fly!" he screamed.

It was my Fae—not me—who forced our legs from a crouch to a standing position. And it was she who put her faith in the magic of the soul ball we held in our arms.

She leaped but *we* flew.

Straight out into the sky we shot, out to where bluebirds fly, and dreams presumably come true. Not like a dust mote, but as a sprite with wings as light as a dragonfly's. So wonderful, so free, until semimortal-me looked down.

There was a whole bunch of blue-gray below me.

A few clouds.

And a lot more twilight blue.

Oh hell no. Me and Mr. Mage shot toward the clearing faster than a spitball blown through a shooter. The instant we passed the crumbling edge of the end of the world, and I saw ground below my trailing feet—mossy, firm, and solid—we lost altitude abruptly. I touched down with a knee-hurting jolt then bounced down the length of the clearing like a poorly piloted Cessna coming in on a wing and a prayer before finally staggering to a stop a scant ten inches from the graveyard of tree stumps.

Safe.

My legs went out, and I fell on my butt, his soul ball clasped in my arms.

Well, I'd always wanted to fly—why else would I have focused on the concept of flight to help my mind separate my soul from my mortal body—and now . . . well, I'd flown. Not drifted, flown. I'd had the ability to more or less navigate. *Son of a gun, I flew.* Part of me said "whoops." Part of me wanted to grin.

I coughed up some smoke. And then felt a bit sick, as remorse pushed aside "hey, I flew!" and retrospection kicked in. Fae Stars, what had my Fae done?

I stared at the ball clutched close to my heart. It had no heat, for such a powerful light. Its parchment-thin skin covering was sandpaper dry, and crisscrossed with wrinkles.

"Nalera" better not translate to "geriatric's fuck buddy."

My neck suddenly felt prickly the way it does when someone's staring at it and thinking of wringing things. Mad-one?

I twisted around to check behind me.

And there she was. Standing at the edge of the graveyard of tree stumps, staring at me like I was the new cheerleader who'd just hooked up with her old boyfriend. A stream of blue myst investigated a tear in her gown. Eyes still narrowed on moi, she gave her skirt a savage shake.

Okay, then.

Across the way, the devil's spawn wasn't looking much happier than me. He leaned against the trunk of the Black Mage's walnut, his face pressed to its fissured bark. "Yes, master. The Old Mage's tree is gone," he shouted over the hungry fire's pops and crackles. The kid's gaze flitted to me. "No, master. His soul lives. She holds him in her arms." His voice broke and the rest became a babble. "I couldn't help it, master. She used an enchantment! The cyreath floated straight to her!"

The wind had died, leaving the air feeling curiously heavy and expectant. A chill went down my spine as the walnut tree's leaves rustled.

The boy burst into sudden tears. "Yes, master. His light turned white."

Your "master" is evil, kid.

Don't wrap your arms around him and seek help.

"Master, I didn't know she had magic. I didn't know that she could be his nalera!" The devil's spawn began to weep in earnest now, tears and snot streaming, shoulders shaking. "I tried," he sobbed. "But she's stronger than me."

Oh kid.

The red-purple light in the Black Mage's soul ball flashed—horribly bright, its flare blinding. And the little mystwalker sprang back, horrified. "No," he wailed. "Please, master, I can learn. Please—"

The Black Mage's tree seemed to pull itself inward, coiling backward, and I suddenly realized that there was no failing allowed in the dark one's school. "Come here!" I screamed, surging to my feet. "Kid! Run to me!"

The Old Mage allowed me one step, and no farther.

That's the moment I discovered the fine print on the "chosen one" contract. Cruelly and firmly, the Old Mage threw a wall between my thoughts and the machine of my body and instantly I became a statue, ball clasped to chest, unable to flex a single large muscle. It was a far worse sensation than being caught in the glue of the ward—at least then I had something to wade through. *Oh sweet heaven, I can't move.* Claustrophobic panic squeezed the breath out of me—I was bound and helpless, inside a small tight casket that was being lowered into the ground.

"Please let me help him." I strained. "He's just a baby."

"It is kinder this way," I heard the mage murmur. "He is soiled."

"Are you *insane*?" I screamed. "Kid, come here!"

But the little cub didn't heed—he was cringing, his hands out as if to ward off a blow. There were other things I wanted to say to that little boy, mostly in the vein of "retreat," but the Old Mage had grown tired of listening to my pleas.

He sealed my mouth.

It would have been kinder to close my eyes so I didn't have to witness the rest.

The lowest bough of the black walnut tree became an arm—a heavy, brutish one—that swung back and then out. It swiped the sobbing boy right off his feet, and carried him right past land's end to an endless sky. Then the tree limb gave a hard downward shake, akin to emptying the contents of a dustpan into the trash.

The kid tried to wind his short legs around the bough.

He truly did.

But he had tiny mitts, and puny muscles. The tree gave a savage lurch to the left and he was thrown. A flash of his small body falling through the air with arms and legs flailing. Then, with a high trailing scream, the devil's spawn dropped from sight—a fledgling who'd never been granted wings.

The Old Mage loosened his mental hold on my legs and I sank to the damp ground. Disgust curled my nails into the sagging sheath of his soul ball. I wanted to rend it, or at least score the surface, but his skin was as difficult to pierce as a month-old helium balloon.

This world is wrong. This mission is over. Put the ball down and go home.

All I needed to do was swivel at the hips, and place the mage's soul on a bed of moss. Easy peasy. Except I couldn't do that, any more than I could slap on a pair of ice skates and perform a triple toe loop.

Put it down.

Veins throbbed in my forehead as I strained inwardly, but—oh Goddesss—I was stuck. Yes, I could breathe. I could even pant like a scream queen destined for the blade of the bad guy's axe. But I couldn't seem to force my arms to relinquish the burden they carried.

Fine. Forget the ball. Detach from this body.

Think of home.

Trowbridge. The bathroom with its eighties vanity and the lingering scent of Were. You're standing there. Trowbridge and Harry are talking by the door to the hall. You're standing there. The remnants of his dreadlocks are soft under your feet. You're in the bathroom in Creemore.

Imagine yourself there.

Standing.

There.

But no matter how many details I pulled up—the little tiny flowers on the wallpaper, the glob of shaving cream on the tap, the damp air sweetened by the scent of shampoo and Trowbridge—I couldn't force my body to pull away from the burden it held clawed in my arms.

Tears welled, then spilled in a thin hot rivulet down my cheek. And that's when I understood—profoundly so—that my choices were gone. The time for clicking my ruby slippers and wishing for home had passed. I wasn't going to detach from Threall, any more than I was going to place the Old Mage's soul ball beside me on the moss.

Not unless he let me.

I was going to sit cross-legged, arms quivering, holding a mage's soul ball for eternity.

I'm sorry, Lexi. A stream of blue myst wandered past us, curious to meet its cousin smoke. It wreathed upward, toward the heated pungent air where flames danced, and for a moment it was hard to tell the two apart as dark energy

swallowed blue. A second passed, and then another, before
the myst pulled itself free from the poisonous air. It darted
for the hawthorns, and sank into them, in a long thin spiral
of fright, seeking sanctuary with the green.

Would that running could be so easy.

Smoke in my nostrils; the taste of failure in my mouth.
The irony hadn't escaped me. No matter how long I stayed
captive here, I'd never be able to hurt the Black Mage's
soul—I was another mage's "nalera," which I was starting
to firmly believe was a synonym for one custom-ordered,
superbound mystwalker.

Well done, fool.

The ever-vigilant breeze stirred the trees and blew a
stream of thin air across the pitted ground, and with each
sweep of its breath, it kept cleaning the battlefield; rolling
a piece of moss, catching a fragment of torn vellum,
sweeping it all toward the abyss beyond the tree of fire.

I want to go home.

The air suddenly thinned, as if it were being sucked into
someone's lungs, and then a honeysuckle wind tore down
the clearing to buffet the smoking, blazing ruin of his citadel with the implacable intention of a housekeeper set on
finishing the job. Soil parted with a groan. A flash of dark
root tangle as the black walnut rolled onto its side. It held,
poised for one fragile second, trembling on the brink of an
abyss, then with a moan that sounded almost human, it
plummeted over the edge of the world.

Maybe he'll die when his tree dies.

Please, Goddess.

A moment of peace.

Then I heard the Old Mage speak. "Stand, nalera."

And I did.

Forgive me, Trowbridge.

Chapter Twenty-five

The hem of Mad-one's tattered dress snagged itself on a thin silver maple branch. It stretched to follow her, but of course it couldn't. Though the Mystwalker had summoned up enough magic to fly, she did so without her heretofore skill. Both her altitude and horsepower were unimpressive and she kept getting hooked up on irritations such as leggy shrubs that presumed to grow into bigger things.

Sad little sapling.

Fireballs had gone astray in the wild woods, and with them had come much splintering of aged wood, and searing of young bark. Mad-one's hem gave with a rip and the silver branch snapped back. It swayed, its leaves shivering a rebuke.

"Ah!" said Mad-one, who had paused. "Over there!"

She pointed deeper into the wild.

Why we were trudging through the wild woods, I hadn't quite figured out—the Mystwalker didn't appear to be setting a course so much as following a clue. Every so often she'd strive for some more elevation, where she'd bob, feet trailing, her gaze sweeping the tops of the trees.

I hated those moments because that's when I felt the intrusion of the Old Mage's curiosity the most strongly. He was defter at it than the Black Mage, but every so often— when he wasn't absorbed puzzling over some secret that vaguely vexed him——I could sense him trying to pry up the lid of my treasure box. What scared me was how often he'd managed to inch it open in the last five minutes. Sooner or later all my pretties would be exposed for his perusal.

Part of me wondered why I was still fighting it. The battle was lost.

Couldn't help it. I fought because that's what I do.

"I can see the glow," said Mad-one. "'Tis not far."

Then to my absolute horror, my mouth hinged open and the old wizard spoke, using my larynx, my tongue, and my lips to sound his words. "Her light is very strong."

"Yes," replied the Mystwalker. "But the glow of her cyreath is not that of a DeLoren."

Is that why we were traveling through these woods? To meet my soul ball? The mage was already squatting in my thoughts, ordering my vocal cords to work at his whim. A little de trop, no?

For the fifth time, I asked, "What is a nalera?"

As the mage considered whether to reply, I searched inside the edges of his control and discovered it strung like a net of spun magic over my self-will. Could I lift it? I tried. Too heavy. Could I slip under it? His rebuke was sharp—— "Stop!" he shouted. I cringed, and hurried away from its edges.

My heart slammed in my chest as I waited for what came next.

"Shhh, child."

I flinched as phantom fingers stroked my cheek. The caress was just like Mum's when Lexi had drifted off before me, and I was too frightened of sleep, worried that maybe I'd be pulled into a dream, into Threall——

"Stop trying to steal my memories," I said hollowly.

"You are beset," he replied.

Another stroke. This time, a rough pat—Dad's.

"Don't touch me like that," I said through my teeth.

"You are sad. Does this not comfort you?"

Being stroked like a pet?

"Calm yourself," he said mildly enough. "You will become accustomed to my presence soon."

"Says the puppeteer to his dummy as he walks to the incinerator."

I sensed his exasperation through my palms.

"To answer your original question, I must first explain that mages are born but rarely, thus the prospect of a mage's fade is frightening to the Court," he said with that faux paternal air that I so distrusted. "Jalo, King of the first Court, appealed to the stars, requesting that the life of his mage be extended. His plea was granted, and since that day, each mystwalker has been born with the kernel of desire to become the nalera to their wizard—the single mystwalker chosen among many to win the great honor of sharing the citadel of their soul with their mage."

Honor, my ass. However, it explained something that had been bothering me. "My Fae was just following her instincts."

"Yes," he said.

But Mad-one glanced over her shoulder at me, and I knew that reply was not the complete truth.

"You want to explain why we're taking this field trip?" I picked my way over the crumbling carcass of a long-dead elm.

"For the binding to be complete, my cyreath must be placed in the boughs of your citadel."

Oh sweet heavens. His soul ball hanging close to my soul ball.

"Not close," he said, reading my thoughts. "Our cyreaths must merge and become one."

"There!" said Mad-one as a flash of crimson briefly illuminated the sky, followed by a longer flare of frightened green.

The trees grew sparse, thinned, and then we reached the edge of a very small clearing.

"By all the stars in the heavens," the Mystwalker said, appalled.

In the middle of that barren patch of grass stood a single tree. Very much alone.

"That's me?" I said.

She nodded, her expression first sick, then oddly satisfied.

The black walnut tree was twisted and diseased. *That's me? I'm sick?* At eye level was a prime example of my citadel's decay—the remains of a stunted, now dead, lower limb. Where bark had been stripped, bare wood gleamed, bleached by the sun, raddled by beetles. Battered and somehow sad, the exhumed skull of a long-buried sinner.

"I'm a mage?" As I watched, a leaf dropped. "I'm an ugly, *dying* mage?"

"You are not a mage," he said flatly.

But I sure as hell am a goner. Look at that tree. There's too many broken branches. Too many see-through portions where the inner core has died, and all that's left is a shingle of worm-eaten bark and a hole exposing a deep cavity of crumbling wood.

My citadel's rotting from the inside out.

"The lights," whispered Mad-one. "Master, there are two—"

"I can see through her eyes." Though he'd chosen a flat voice, I could feel his dismay spilling inside me, foul as dirty water over the top of a levee.

Hah. The old guy had to be rethinking the "chosen one" concept. I let my stunned gaze wander, my lips puckering in gleeful schadenfreude. *Take that, Old Mage.* If I was going out, I was doing it in style. My inner fire wasn't going to be contained by the skin of my cyreath.

My light was *everywhere.*

In fact, a startling, flowing interplay of richly colored illumination wove around my tree's canopy—my own fuck-you version of the aurora borealis. Twisting and lovely, but a tad ethereal for my taste. I was more enchanted by the way my northern lights' reflection cast a patchwork of color on the ground—a dappled rectangle of red-violet here, some sapphire and royal-blue wavering squares over there.

My gaze swept the clearing.

Well, my, my. I was a veritable spectrum of hues. Jewels by my feet, and over there, where weak daylight still shone and grasses grew, another palette. Brighter. Wavering patches of gold, blurred blotches of vivid green, and small dapples of raspberry and blue—magic and love and open fields set to a whimsical poem of light.

Pretty, I thought, inexplicably drawn toward those.

Life—in the end, it all comes down to point of view, doesn't it? You see long lustrous hair hanging down the back of a jacket that owed a lot to the Edwardian period and you might think "girl," until you pass the person, and you change your opinion to "short, wannabe rock star."

And so it goes, even in a world made from dreams. From the edge of the small clearing, I had perceived one impressively massive and sadly dying black walnut. But four paces forward and five steps to the right changed my entire perspective.

Oh dear Goddess.

I would have covered my mouth in shock if my hands weren't full.

Not *one* tree stood in the clearing—but *two.*

Or, if you wanted to get really picky, whatever you call it when a walnut sinks a tiny filament of hope into the ground that takes root. The seedling develops into the beginnings of a tree, which in turn grows. Upward. Reaching for the sky like every other living thing. Then suddenly—for reasons only known to the Goddesses—the trunk of that tree decides it must split, and in one blind twist of fate, one black walnut becomes two.

Still joined at the same thick base.

Two trees, one root.

Twins.

Though comparatively speaking, my side of the black walnut—and that had to be mine, because what grew on the right above that split in the trunk was about a third the height and girth of my brother's—was doing better than

Lexi's. From what I could see, no canker spots befouled my foliage.

Not dying . . . at least not my portion of it.

My gaze swung upward, searching for the heart of me. It was easy enough to spot—I simply followed the path of the green-blue illumination, and found it lodged in the crotch of two wonderfully robust boughs. *Huh.* My cyreath was the same size and shape as everyone else's. Different color, though—the majority of the Fae had a sunnier undertone, whereas my gold had a greenish cast, with intermittent flickers of blue. Overall, it was relatively hale and hearty in appearance, other than one long, slanting brushstroke of raspberry staining its skin, and another patch roughened into a small and ugly scar.

For a second, I stared up at the gray blemish feeling bleak. The pain of Mum and Dad's loss reduced to a single ashen callus? It should have left a bigger blight.

But what about Lexi?

Mouth dry, I searched for my twin's soul in the other half of the conjoined tree. Leaf and limb had made an effort to disguise its location, but the spiraling heat of his self-destruction had seared away the green canopy above his cyreath. His true light spewed upward from the thinning thatch. Plum purple with hurt, bruised midnight blue with pain.

Oh, Lexi.

"What is his curse?" the mage demanded.

A sister who didn't wake him when the boogeyman crept in.

"No more of this foolishness! You will not guard your secrets!" the Old Mage roared. "Go to his citadel. Place your hand on it and show me his soul."

So my brother's soul—what was left of it—could be fingered by another mage? His memories picked through like bangles and bracelets at a flea market? Had Lexi cringed when the door to the room of magic was pushed open? Fearing the dark? Fearing the touch?

"No!" I set my teeth together.

Much good my bravado did me. A moment later, my foot jerkily lifted, lurched forward, and took me a step closer to the black walnut.

Do not yield to him. Sweat popped out on my upper lip as I bore down on that overwhelming need to shuffle toward the black walnut.

Do it for Lexi. Do it for yourself.

"You are trying my patience!" he shouted.

My toe hoed a furrow of resistance into the soil. My nails dug into his sagging cyreath. Small rebellions. But mine. *I will not cooperate. I never cooperate.*

That's when the pain came. A dull ache in my ear—*only an irritation*—that instantly grew hotter—*a tolerable burn*—and then it became a molten-hot knife held sizzling against the me of me—*hellfire, inside my head*—and yes, I did move.

Toward my unsuspecting brother. Toward my own self. Toward the obliteration of inner vows. Toward the rebreaking of us—because we were broken, we had been for quite some time, and now, we were going to be broken again.

Fae-me's scream was shrill and disbelieving.

Too late she understood the fate of those who were the chosen.

So we stumbled forward. Whimpering, sweating, stumbling. Our talent for obstruction defeated. Truth be told, if we could have shot to that conjoined tree, we would have.

And if we could have done it babbling, *"No, no, no,"* . . .

Well, we would have done that, too.

The wind, when it came, was a definite windfall in terms of my personal fortunes. It whipped down from the sky with a moan to shake our citadels. A blinding maelstrom of twigs and leaves and fluffs of moss flew about us. It sent Mad-one flying backward with a startled shriek. It forced me to huddle over his cyreath, eyes tearing, shoulders hunched.

And then, the hurting, digging blade stopped twisting itself inside my head.

I fell to one knee in absolute relief.

The hurricane eased to a light sighing breeze. The delicate scent of honeysuckle perfumed the air, a layer of sweet over the stench of the lingering smoke. After a count of three, I raised my head and straightened. I turned this way and that, my gaze darting from shadow to shadow.

Nothing.

I licked my dry lips. "I'll tell you what you want to know about my brother. You don't have to—"

A sharp crack from the woods made me flinch, but it was only Mad-one coming back through the hole she'd made between two tall saplings after the sudden gale had sent her hurtling toward the top of the tree line.

The hairs on the nape of my neck were damn tired of standing at attention but now they positively bristled as Mad-one studied me, head canted to the side. Graceful as a swan coming in for a soft landing, she readjusted her altitude—slowly sinking from her lofty tree-top hover, stopping only when the long, trailing hem of her gown stirred the waist-tall grasses in the clearing.

The Old Mage gave up on trying to appear paternal or even kind. "Close your eyes," he snapped. "And then open them, for we must meet."

"What do you mean?

"Close them!"

Doing that required faith that Mad-one wouldn't use it as an opportunity for attack. And there was something about the way she watched us—arms folded as if she were on the cusp of making a really bad decision—that had armed my alert system.

I sent a silent appeal toward my Goddess for a little heavenly protection, then closed my eyes. When I opened them, the mage stood beneath our tree. For all intents, fully corporeal, right down to the suggestion of a paunch. A patchwork of light dappled his ruddy cheek. Thinning, tousled white hair.

"Neat illusion," I said, glancing down at myself. My trembling arms were still occupied cradling the mage's soul ball and I was still on one bended knee. I rose stiffly. "It would have been a better one if I wasn't still here, holding your cyreath."

"Tell me about your brother," he demanded.

"Lexi's a liar and a thief—just like me. He's cruel, and merciless, and . . . so damn lost. He's what I could have been, if I'd gone to Merenwyn. He's probably what I'll be, after a few years as your unwilling soul mate . . . And yet . . ."

"And yet?"

"And yet, there is a piece of the real Lexi inside there still. But it's buried so far beneath his addiction that I can't even remem—"

"What is his addiction?" he asked sharply.

The urge to squeeze his cyreath until it popped like bubble wrap was overpowering. But I couldn't do that, any more than I could go over there and hit him, so I settled on giving him the facts coupled with a hard, accusing stare. "My twin needs a ration of sun potion every day, or he will die. Which is a real problem for him, because my world doesn't happen to have any."

The Old Mage's eyes turned to slits, the wrinkles fanning outward in sharp emphasis. "Then he must return to Merenwyn."

"He can't go back," I said, watching him stalk to the base of our citadels. "He's failed the Black Mage."

Don't touch Lexi's tree. When he didn't—he just gave the northern lights a glance of irritation before he began pacing beneath my twin's citadel—I realized that he couldn't. There were limitations to his illusion and touching the host of our souls was one of them.

"How long has he been taking the draught?" he asked.

"At least eighty or more Merenwyn winters."

He stopped, mid-stride, and slowly turned. "How many hours since his last dose?"

Hours? "About six."

"Is there no end to this!" he snarled.

I'm missing something here.

He spun around to glare at me. "He will be dead within hours."

"Lexi's got wolf blood in him. He can fight this."

"Can you not see with your own eyes?" The wizard drew in a seething breath through his teeth then jabbed at the black walnut. "There is no cure for what ails him in your world or mine. No elixir to swallow. He will die, and as your destiny is forever tied to his, you will shortly follow."

My stomach squeezed. "No."

"When he dies, you will feel a crack in your heart, a sudden, inexplicable pain. Shortly after that his citadel will fall, and when it does so, it will tear a wound in the trunk of your tree that will be irreparable. Within hours, your cyreath will drop to the ground, and you will complete your own fade." He ran agitated hands through his hair. "I need more time. Two days to travel to the castle. A few hours more to destroy the book."

Lexi goes, and—oh, too bad, so sad—I follow?

My mind spun then sharpened into a needle, silver bright. I jabbed its tip into the concept of my brother and me sharing fates, stared at that for a second with eroding disbelief, then—*oh Goddess, the prick of a sharp needle stings so terribly . . .*

"Trowbridge," I whispered.

"Who?" he asked testily.

"My mate."

He shrugged. "Yes, your lupine mate will die, as well."

Despair, a lead weight in my chest. "You could have saved yourself the termination speech. I've got it—okay? Lexi and I are toast. Trowbridge, too." I couldn't bear to look at him, or at Mad-one who was watching me with something akin to "what bug is this" interest, or at the purple-blue northern lights curling around Lexi's side of the black walnut, so I dropped my gaze.

The old wizard's soul ball glowed in my arms, his frustration as orange as the sun sinking angrily below the horizon. Ugly.

Don't cry.

I lifted my head to give him a cold stare. "Will you let me go home so I can tell my mate and brother the good news? Or are you going to make me stay here, holding your cyreath, until a new mystwalker shows up? Because if that's your plan, I should warn you that it won't go well."

"A mage can have only one nalera," he said with exquisite resentment. "Whether or not my cyreath joins yours, the agreement is sealed. We are bound—sharing fates, strengths, and enemies—until your final fade."

That made me happy in a bitter kind of way. Given Lexi's prospects, our association would be short-lived. I gave him my worst smile. "Wow, Karma got a two-for-one."

Four minutes ago (at least by my reckoning), the Old Mage had tapped the air and conjured up a chair. Now he sat slumped in it, worrying his chin. Six more leaves had dropped in that space of time.

"What did you need two days for?" I asked Mr. Mage.

"To save my world and yours from catastrophe," he said with a total lack of irony. When I rolled my eyes, his mouth pulled down. "It would be a conceit to pretend I am other than what I am. Mages are born but rarely, great ones even less frequently."

"And yet, the Great One managed to blow it." I flexed my fingers against a cramp. "Got himself forced into the Big Sleep."

He gave me a slit-eyed glance. "I had a daughter. Impetuous, and very often, foolish. She gave birth to a—"

"A half-breed like me."

"Elorna sought to hide his heritage before he reached the cusp of manhood as she greatly feared what would happen once his beast obeyed the moon's call." The Old Mage thoughtfully drummed his fingers on the curved armrest of his chair. "It was an interesting problem, but once I turned my attention to it, I did succeed in divining an elixir that allowed him to hide himself among us."

"Good job," I said dryly. "That potion destroyed my brother and led you right back here."

"It was an error in judgment," he admitted, looking, for a moment, honestly regretful. "And in the eyes of my Maker, but one of my crimes."

"Why does that not surprise me?" I rolled my neck, hoping to relieve the bite of pain nibbling between my shoulder blades.

He stared moodily at his outstretched foot. Scuffed toes, soft brown leather. One little brass buckle. "The first mage of the Court bade me to be wary of vanity and undue curiosity, but within six winters of his fade, I'd meddled with things best left to the stars. And to my eternal remorse, I recorded the results of my experiments, hoping to share my knowledge."

Bullshit. You wrote your Book of Spells to serve as a record of your brilliance.

He flicked me a look of dislike. "The day my sentence was handed to me, I fully understood the true measure of my vanity. I'd left the written sum of my knowledge to a mage who was unprepared, both in spirit and training, to receive it."

"Enter the Black Mage."

"Helzekiel," he corrected. "When my student reads the last page in my Book of Spells he will have the power to destroy worlds. And I very much fear that my Maker shall not grant me forgiveness when he does."

My shoulders began to throb in earnest; the weight of his soul ball, aching and heavy.

The wizard cast me a frown of irritation. "You shrug your shoulders, but it is very much your problem, too. Once the horror is unleashed, its misery will bleed into your world. Portals will drip with it."

I scanned the darkening sky. There were no birds in this world. "As far as I can see there's only one portal."

"There are more. You have seen very little of Threall."

Out of the corner of my eye, I saw Mad-one nod in agreement.

So, Aunt Lou and Trowbridge hadn't been wrong, there were indeed more portals. And soon—too soon—some very nasty Fae shit would begin dripping into a small fairy pond in Creemore. Then maybe the wind would carry it a few hundred feet to the Alpha of Creemore's house, where Trowbridge stood in the hall talking to Harry, and Cordelia puttered in the laundry room, and Biggs muttered in the . . . Oh Goddess . . . Merry and Ralph waited there, too.

None of them knowing that Armageddon was one drip away.

He shook his head. "I'd hoped that I'd been offered an opportunity for absolution. That my Maker had sent me one who would aid me in the destruction of the Book of Spells. But with my death, the wards I set to shield those pages will disintegrate and Helzekiel will learn the secrets held within the book. Now my soul shall never reach the Arcadian fields."

Well, boo-fucking-hoo. The old guy looked so aggrieved, sitting there in his slick silk robes—this arrogant mage who'd messed with the sun and produced the potion that was the key to everything in my life going up in flames.

"Hate to break it to you but that's a done deal," I said. "Dust to dust, right? You might have missed it what with all the drama, but your citadel is toast. Your wards are gone. By now, your boy Helzekiel is thumbing his way through your Book of Spells."

"My wards will hold until the death of my *cyreath*," he corrected, adjusting his sleeve. "Until that moment, they are invincible."

"Well, here's a newsflash for you, Old Mage—they were *invincible* to everyone but a Stronghold. Lexi's peeled half of your wards right off the page. Not only that . . . he told me that your hide spells were thinning—he could read right through some of them with his naked eye."

The old man turned sharply in his chair, his brow furrowed. "Your brother can see through magic?"

"He can steal it, too."

The wizard's eyes brightened like a kid with a bottle rocket and a pack of matches.

"Her twin is capable of seeing magic?" For a second I really thought he was going to rock in glee, but all he did was to observe in a tone of restrained awe, "Verily, it is a sign from my Maker. Salvation is at hand. How else could I choose a mystwalker with such a twin? Fate has been instructed to place us together so that I can undo—"

"Verily," I said. "You're dumber than a box of rocks if you're contemplating placing your trust in Karma. She's a vengeful—"

"What you call Karma is merely the stars seeking balance."

"She's still a bitch."

The Old Mage got out of his chair to stare upward at Lexi's citadel. "To save the world, I must save this creature's life." He fingered his lower lip thoughtfully. "How to cure him of the incurable?" Frowning, he spread his fingers then waved his hand crosswise through the air. The wind stirred, parting the greenery, and I caught a brief glimpse of my brother's amethyst-hued cyreath.

Mad-one drifted over to his shoulder.

"The cravings must be teased from his mind and body," he told her absently. "An almost impossible task, but it can be done."

The Mystwalker arched her neck then rose in the air until she was near level with the light streaming from the tree.

Stop looking at my twin like that, whackjob.

He turned to pace, his wizard robes snapping at his ankles. "It will require the most powerful magic in its most concentrated form to do so. Fortunately—" The old man stilled, mid-step, "Eureka!" written all over his face.

Hope started blipping in my chest as he lifted his chin to study the sky.

From where we were, deep inside the forest, the portal to Merenwyn was a distant coil above ragged treetops—a genie's tail streaking up into the sky. *I've already thought of that, Mr. Mage. First we'd have to get him past the Black Mage's archers. Then we'd have to find him some juice to tide him over until we got to the Pool of Life—*

"Bathing in the water will not lead to his cure," the mage said brusquely. "It would only increase his lust for sun potion."

I wish he'd stop listening to my internal thoughts.

"And I'd wish you would stop thinking," he snapped a tad peevishly. "Your endless chatter is an insufferable irritation."

Yeah? Can you read my thoughts now?

His eyes narrowed into squinty slits.

Chapter Twenty-six

I counted a slow and deliberate twelve "Mississippis" (which bugged the crap out of him in the most satisfying way) then asked, "Why won't the Pool of Life heal him?"

"Because sun potion was derived from the elements found within its sacred waters," he answered with forced patience. "Bathing in it will only inflame his cravings—precisely as one sip of spirits inevitably leads to a flagon of mead. His beast requires a different source of healing. One that must be derived from elemental magic."

Quite impervious to the way I'd stiffened at the B-word, he gazed at the portal with proud-papa pride. "Your twin will find healing in my passages."

"Your passages?"

"The portals are my creation," he said. "Perhaps my greatest achievement."

His creation, huh?

Bile rose in my throat. "So what did you tell those first few portal travelers? Psst, buddy, you want to see a door to another world? Go ahead, step right through it. Don't you fret, you won't end up in a dead end." Disgust laced my tone. "What were they? Fuel? Did their magic feed your portals?"

"They are immaterial. What is important is that each of my portals has a . . ." He paused to choose a word carefully. "A resting place. Created as a forethought for the possibility a mage might need—"

"A hiding spot."

Somewhat peevishly, he said, "Your brother will find healing there."

I gazed at the passage to Merenwyn for a moment, faint hope stirring despite my massive misgivings. Was there really a dead end that didn't lead to purgatory? One with a little cabinet fixed to that wall—inside that a small bottle of magic with a DRINK ME label? One sprint through the portal and he'll be healed?

"Not a sprint. It will take many days," said the mage. "He must remain there until such time as the demon is exorcised from his body and soul."

Days in that windy chute? Listening to those voices calling from the walls? Being buffeted by those winds? Did I have the courage? The stamina?

He'll be healed.

"You cannot lead him through the passages," he said, studying Lexi's cyreath.

"I beg your pardon?"

He turned to fix me with a penetrating gaze. "The addiction has woven itself around him so deeply that it has become a living fiend inside him which knows only that it wants to live. It knows you well, and will use every wile against you, playing on your fears and weaknesses." The Old Mage's eyes were hazel. Neither blue nor green. "Your brother's demon must not recognize the hand that wields the sword, else he will anticipate each feint and thrust. He must be attacked not from the outside, but from within."

From within?

A chill ran down my spine as comprehension rolled over me.

"You don't want my body anymore—you want Lexi's," I whispered, appalled. "You want to be inside *his* mind, not mine. Controlling his every move. Telling him where to go, what to say. Using his lips to form your words.

Giving his body commands that he must perform. Sit. Stand. Eat. Talk. Shit."

A quick death would be better than that.

"It's too late," I told him. "You've chosen your nalera."

"Nay," said Mad-one, moving toward the tall grass. "You share one root. It will suffice."

"One root but two trees!" I said. "Two!"

The Old Mage spread his hands, clearly perplexed by all the fuss. "Your brother's skills and physical strengths are far better suited for the task ahead."

I got a mental flash of Lexi creeping into that room with its arched window, and bottle-lined shelves, and a lectern on which sat one big, fat leather-bound book.

He'd be blamed for its destruction, unless—

"You ripe bastard," I hissed. "You've figured out how to have your cake and eat it, too, haven't you? You'll use Lexi to destroy your damn book, but when all is said and done, you'll stay in my brother's body and become the fourth mage to the Court."

I gazed at him, noting the softened jawline, the drooping eyelids and fatty pouches beneath them. "No one is going to recognize you for the old wizard they condemned to the Sleep of Forever, are they? How could they? You'll look and sound like Lexi. Goddess, the Black Mage will never see you coming."

"I need the use of your brother for naught but two days." Two blotches of outraged virtue rouged his cheeks. "I seek only to stop that which—"

"Save it," I said. "I've lived with a Fae. I know all about lies of omission."

Outraged virtue dissolved into simple outrage.

Here comes the pain, I thought, steeling myself.

But before his hot knife dug into my brain again, Mad-one dropped a bomb. "A cyreath can be parted from a nalera's," she said. "There is a very narrow window of opportunity—a few days, no more—but one does exist."

"You forget Simeon," the Old Mage threatened—his tone low and mean.

"I have never forgotten Simeon," she said fiercely. "But on this day you have lost your body in Merenwyn. You cannot rise from your Sleep Before Death. He is finally safe."

The mage made a quick flat sideways chop with his gnarled hand.

I saw no magic. But Mad-one suddenly gasped and pressed two knuckles against her left temple.

A small miscalculation on his part.

Whatever pain he'd sent her way was inferior to the venom that she'd kept hidden in her heart. Face twisted in pain, she said in a reckless rush, "Make him prostrate himself on his knees. Force him to pledge to his Maker that before the waning of the next full moon, his cyreath will be torn free from your brother's."

"Cease with your treason!" he shouted.

"There is no *treason* in this!" she screamed back.

He stabbed her again. Not with a real knife but with the hot blade of his anger. She buckled over with a keening cry, palms pressed hard to either temple. Grass swayed and snatched at her trailing hem.

"Our mage has deep fears over the quality of his life beyond this one," she said between ragged gasps of agony. "He will not break a sacred vow to his Maker, not if he is forced to mouth the words. That is but one of my mage's weaknesses—he *believes* that his Maker still listens."

"You dare!" he shouted, rising to his feet, his hand lifted like he had a spear and a clear shot at a target.

"Kill me, master, if you dare!" she shrieked. "But forget not who will place your cyreath in the boughs of his citadel!"

He stilled—no, the old guy froze.

"You need me," she said hoarsely. "You need me."

The wizard gazed at her for another beat. Then he lowered his invisible spear and stiffly walked back to his chair. To my amazement, he sat. Crossed his legs and strove for cultivated calm. But he watched her from beneath brows

set in a winged flare of repressed fury, with his fingers
steepled and his toe tapping like an angry cat's tail.

A thin ribbon of bright blood snaked down from her
ear. She painfully righted herself and used the edge of
her embellished sleeve to wipe her neck. With a slanted
glance toward the angry wizard, she said, "I bid you, Hedi
of Creemore, to perceive the opportunity if you have the
wit to seize it."

Always with the compliments. "Go on."

Gold and green lights played over her taut face. "Our
mage will not allow his cyreath to be melded to your
brother's before all battle risks are reduced. There could be
no site more suited to our mage's strengths than one of his
portals—that is where the war will begin. Their very walls
are permeated with his magic. Therein lies the fulcrum to
your opportunity. Use it well, mystwalker. For you will
never have another chance to negotiate with our mage."

"You lost me at fulcrum," I said flatly.

She sank to terra firma, then shoved her hair back over
her shoulder with more impatience than finesse. "The
magic *heals*. The moment your brother steps through the
gates, he will regain strength. And that is our mage's
conundrum—he needs your brother to be weak and the
timing perfect for his attack—"

"Attack?" I repeated, my voice raw. "How badly will
this hurt Lexi?"

"Would knowing the answer change your decision? If
so, we are doomed, for only the brave and the quick will
survive this test. Think beyond the moment, mystwalker."

Think beyond the moment? Just how well did that bitch
know me? She expected me to deduce his plan? Sniff out
the old bastard's motives? Figure out the side exit to all
this disaster? Good luck. My head hurt—threats hovered
over me like a cloud of hungry gnats.

"Do you not see your opportunity?" she demanded.

"No. I don't!" I shouted in frustration.

"Your brother must pose no threat of resistance—thus
he must be within the very moment of his death—and the

melding of their cyreaths *must* take place before Lexi crosses the gates. Someone with a vested interest in the outcome of this day—someone from your world—needs be ready to place his near-lifeless body through the gates."

And then, indeed, I saw beyond the moment.

With a sinking heart, I saw the portal with its hungry mouth. And my brother. And then—

"Me," I said in a hollow voice.

"You."

A blue myst wafted past me, indifferent to the fact that a girl stood like a statue in the middle of the small clearing.

Eventually, I lifted my gaze to study the Mystwalker of Threall. "Why would I believe that you suddenly wanted to help me? Not half an hour ago, you hurled a fireball at me and the kid."

Mouth pursed, she considered her answer. "Upon our first meeting, my wind blew you into the embrace of our mage's citadel."

Hard to forget that terror.

She plucked a shred of green from the folds of her blue skirt.

"It was not by happenstance. I have been forced to do so with each mystwalker who materialized in my realm since the day I said my final good-bye to those I loved in Merenwyn." The Mystwalker of Threall examined the filament of moss on her palm, then blew. Its flight was shallow and short. "Our mage tested their souls with the same callous indifference the King of the Court sampled sweet cakes. The stumps of those deemed not worthy of our mage's taste befoul the very ground I must walk on."

That's why she prefers to fly.

Mad-one lifted her gaze to mine. "I have observed his fade—limb by dying limb—and privately rejoiced. He is not the only person who dreams of walking the Arcardian fields with the sun warm on her face. I want this to end."

Her eyes were bleak and pained.

"I need this to end."

* * *

It had been all so much, you know? Finding myself bound. Discovering that my best-before date had been moved way up. Grieving for a life that wasn't going to happen, and then having an easy solution dangled in front of my desperate eyes.

If I took everything at face value, didn't look beyond the moment, then the decision was a lot easier. With one "aye," my job as wizard's grunt would be over and I'd get out of a no-win situation pretty much scot-free. I'd be able to go back home. Click my heels and find myself standing in the Alpha's bathroom, listening to the pack reorganize the house.

Arms free.

All I had to do was trust that everybody was going to do their jobs, and then nip back to do a bit of soul-tearing after the deed was done.

But there was the thing that could not be ignored: one root, two trees.

Come what may, twins forever.

And with that, a wash of rare clarity cleansed my mental eye. I saw the future like it was a long scroll that someone had just unrolled on the table. Oh Fae Stars, I could see it right to the end of its curling edge. There it lay with little flags pinned to it—one for the betrayal, two for the lies, three for the loss.

There were no words for the desolation that salted my despair.

Send Lexi into that world in my place. No free will at all. Look how well I'd tolerated it—after ten minutes my soul was screaming. But even as I tried to imagine the horror my brother would experience standing in my place, a craven part of me started wheedling. It would only be for two days, and then—

Stop it.

I wasn't a kid anymore, cowering in the cupboard, watching my brother being hauled off to another world. I could make a choice. I could take my bat and walk to the plate.

Merciful heavens, I'm not sure I'm strong enough for what's going to follow.

My mouth opened, and I heard myself say, "I have two terms before I agree."

"State them."

"You'll have two days in Merenwyn. Not a minute more. You will accept your final fade with good grace. Before the sun rises on the third day, I will personally remove your cyreath from Lexi's without any interference from you. You will leave not a trace of yourself inside him."

Take another look at the scroll. See the end of it? I swallowed down my fear.

"And I have to be there," I said. "Standing right beside my brother when he opens that book in Merenwyn."

His hiss of exasperation fed the roiling acid in my stomach. "Why?"

"Because Lexi's going to fight you, all the way, which will exhaust him. And because you're going to have to hurt him—"

"I have told you—I mean no harm to your brother!"

"But you will do it because he's just some half-bred wolf who's gotten in your way. We don't have much value to you." I felt my lips curve into a bleak smile. "But we're fighters, each and every one of us. Lexi will give you a brawl. And by the time you leave, both of you will be half mad with frustration."

My gaze flicked downward to where the Old Mage's cyreath glowed in my arms. *Oh, for the ability to tear you apart.* I watched a rivulet of red dribble down from the bite mark above my wrist, soaking the parchment of his soul's skin.

"You know what I think, Mr. Mage? You're the type of guy who doesn't give much thought to the messes he leaves behind—if you could leave that Book of Spells without pissing off your Maker, you would," I said. "And now you're feeling hard done by, so I'm pretty sure you don't give a shit about what happens after you've destroyed the Book of Spells."

The air grew still—not a breath of motion.

"But I do," I told him.

Silence from the old man.

"My twin won't be left standing there alone with a WTF look on his face when the Black Mage goes postal because his recipe book has been destroyed. So here's the final clause in the deal—you will pledge to me in front of your Maker that you will wait for me to join Lexi in Merenwyn before you attempt to destroy the book."

"You are a stubborn creature," he said with more than a hint of loathing.

Threall's wind found me again. It plucked at a tendril of my hair, and mercilessly tickled the sensitive inner whorls of my ears.

"You will add that to your vow, old man. Make sure there's no loophole in your wording, no omission of fact, no convenient misinterpretation of intent."

"It will be difficult to reconnoiter in Merenwyn."

"Pick a time and place," I said in a hard voice. "And let's be real clear. I know time passes differently in—"

"In my realm," he sniped. "Very well. I give you my solemn word, as Mage of the Highest Court, that you will be beside your brother as we destroy the Book of Spells. I vow to wait for you at Daniel's Rock before we proceed to the castle."

"I don't know where that is."

"You will," he said cryptically. "After you have sent your brother through the gates, wait one full day, then cross as the sun sets. We will meet at Daniel's Rock." His gaze raked over me. "My world is hard on one such as you. The weak and the soft die. Are you sure you wish to proceed with this childish desire to save your brother's life? He has chosen his path. The history he leaves in his wake is of his making."

"Don't talk to me about choices, mage. Vow that you will wait. Pledge that to me, word for word."

Anger twisted his face.

I listened carefully as he gave his oath to his Maker,

and then I swiveled to face Mad-one. "What do you want from this?

She looked surprised, then she inclined her head. "If only for one day, I want to know that I am living in my true body and that which I touch is truly there beneath my fingers."

"I'm not sure I can show you how to find your way back to Merenwyn. I'm not even sure I can return home."

Her gaze was steady and piercing. "And yet I believe you can."

"Don't confuse me for a hero, Tyrean."

"Nor I, Hedi of Creemore."

"Will Lexi die when I tear the Old Mage's cyreath from his?"

Mad-one lifted a shoulder. "That depends on your brother's will to live."

I looked away and watched the wizard walk back and forth beneath the citadel of my soul. Rage and frustration had stripped away his pretense of being a kindly old grandfather. His eyes were slits, the wrinkles fanning outward in sharp emphasis.

A current of air, sweet scented as honeysuckle, swirled around my waist.

"What changed your mind?" I found myself asking her. "You weren't going to help me at first."

She tossed her head as the same zephyr of air teased her hair. "You said that you distrusted him. It was the first thing you've said of significance in my hearing. It suggests that you might not be the knave that you appear—and it was the statement that changed the course of both our lives." Mad-one tilted her head. "Do not make me regret my choice. It would be wise to remember that I know the location of your citadel. I can touch it, and speak to you whenever I wish. With whatever voice I choose."

Then the Mystwalker of Threall drew in a long breath. "Now, pass me our mage's cyreath."

Once I had, she walked past the old wizard's illusion, head high. With a faint smile that had a definite gloating edge, she lowered herself to his chair. "I will keep my eyes trained on your brother's cyreath. When his light begins to dim, I shall touch his tree and yours. Thus I will know when to meld our mage's soul to your brother's."

She will know Lexi in ways I never will.

Me, too.

"There is no other way," she said quietly.

She was right.

So, I closed my eyes to the portal, to the blue myst, to the swaying trees, to the girl who looked young but felt old. To all of it. Every sickening bit of it.

Think of home. All you have to do is want it. Imagine Creemore. The pond, the gentle hills. The home where my brother lies dying. The room where my mate stands waiting. Think of Cordelia in the kitchen, humming to her Bobby McGee. Imagine Harry knocking on the door, a sheaf of papers in his hands. Shake your head at Biggs, always a day late and a dollar short.

Sound began to fade.

I wavered between this world and the other.

Home.

Chapter Twenty-seven

Returning home came with a hurting pain right in my solar plexus. Again a fist thumped my chest, just about where my heart was. Then a hard male mouth covered mine. I caught the sweet aromas of woods, and spice, and yum. *Trowbridge*. Two puffs of air were forced into my mouth, filling lungs that I hadn't realized were empty.

"Come on!" My mate gave me a good head-flopping shake. "Why did you do it? I told you never to go there," he shouted right in my sensitive half-breed ear. His voice was thick with grief. "You come back to me, you understand? You come back to me."

Home.

"Just hold me," I mumbled into his neck. "Don't let go."

He went rigid. "Hedi?"

There went my sense of gravity. Suddenly, the nice warm chest was gone and I was being supported by a hard arm. Fierce blue eyes examined me. "You came back." Trowbridge breathed. A vein throbbed at his temple.

"I really hope so," I said.

Was that my voice? That wobbly little voice?

A shaking hand cupped my face. "Don't you ever frighten me like that again," he said in a low, kind of menacing voice. "You promise me that you'll never do that again." Then, to my astonishment—okay, *you* add up the number of days we'd spent together and tell me if I should have been prepared——my mate sank back on his heels and rocked me in his arms like I was the most precious thing he'd ever held.

Back and forth. Holding me tight, as if I might fly away. I didn't deserve it but I sure melted into it.

The only thing that could have improved his passionate outpouring of affection was an "I love you." Just once before everything went to crap, I'd have liked to hear those three words one more time. But still, what he didn't say, I could smell in his scent. Relief, frustration——and here's a new one in connection with me——absolute joy, mixed with . . . what was that?

This was true love?

Trowbridge, you don't know the half of what's coming your way.

I turned my head and let my gaze roam the ring of faces. Cordelia stood closest, trying to look unmoved and falling well short. Biggs stood near the edge of the bed, chewing on his lower lip, hands deep in his pockets. Harry leaned against the door frame, one of his rare smiles creasing his age lines into deep seams.

Bad things will seep into this world.

Fae shit.

"Take me to the window," I told Trowbridge, knowing that my legs wouldn't hold me.

My mate didn't ask why; he simply gathered me up and brought me to it. Took him one breath and six long strides. He's a strong man, the Alpha of Creemore. I gazed out at the scene, my cheek resting on his muscled chest, my blistered paw curled loosely around Merry. Five cars parked along the long driveway. Freshly mown grass. Sweet. Fresh. Earthly. My mate's heart beat like an athlete's beneath my ear. Thump, thump. Beyond the cultivated edge of the property, where the wild began, pine trees swayed. Not a soul ball in them.

Home.

"That was quite a scare you gave us, Little Miss," observed Harry, dragging the easy chair over to the window.

Trowbridge sat down on the arm of it, me still a burden in his arms.

How much heavier am I than a soul ball?

"Well, I for one am getting heartily tired of these theatrics," snapped Cordelia. "I don't know anyone else who can hold their breath as long as you can. You have *got* to stop doing that."

Don't let go of me.

"Shh, Cordelia," Trowbridge murmured, smoothing my hair.

I'm going to miss this, I thought, letting him pet me. *Don't forget this—this perfect little slice of time.* When you're being held safe and sound, and people who care about you are flocked all around. Tucking your hair behind your ear. Clucking to hide their worry.

It wouldn't last. Karma had engineered it so that I had to push someone I loved through those same damn gates, which was going to require me lying like there's no tomorrow. And I knew what was going to follow that—I'd lose the family I didn't even know I had until this moment.

My forearm ached from the devil's spawn's bite.

It was the right thing to do, wasn't it? I needed to minimize their culpability in the eyes of the pack. Which meant that I was going to have to spin a fib for Trowbridge—for his own good—because I couldn't put him in the position of agreeing to release Lexi. My brother had stolen from the Alpha of Creemore. In front of *witnesses*. Urban gangs had nothing on Weres when it came to the subject of disrespect.

I'd have to lie to him.

And then I'd lose him.

Forever, this time.

Payback pain was beginning to make itself known. Which fell into the good-news category, right? Throbbing mitts meant the essence of my Fae wasn't floating in Threall

looking for a new home—she'd come back to Creemore
with me. Where was my Were? I probed and found her
back in her usual spot, giving me the stink eye.

So the troops were all together again.

One problem down. Ninety-nine to go.

I'd have to lie to him.

Concentrate on the other stuff.

How was I going to detach the people I cared about
from whatever finger-pointing would inevitably follow?
Think. I'd have to trick Harry into giving me the key to the
room in which my brother was caged. I'd have to send
Cordelia off on some trumped-up mission so that no one
could later turn the blame on her. I'd have to send Biggs on
a ferret hunt, just so that he looked innocent.

Nausea climbed up my throat.

"You went to Threall, didn't you?" Trowbridge asked.

I ached to tell him the truth. All about it. The fire, the
tree, the Old Mage—even the bit where I fucked up with
the Black Mage.

"You made a decision without me again," he said. "You
have to stop doing that."

Well, that would be one way to go.

"I need to know what happened up there," he asked.

What happened is that Karma wants a do-over, I
thought, staring at the trees. She was forcing me to reenact
the same scene—the portal, the lie, the push across the
threshold. Why? Had I missed some important lesson the
first time around?

I'm no hero. Neither is Lexi.

"She used magic," said Cordelia. "Her hand's a mess."

Trowbridge pressed a hard kiss on my temple.

I don't want to lose kisses.

It's not like I hadn't learned things in the last six
months. I'd figured out that there were times to run and
times to stand. Very recently—okay, *yesterday*—I'd come
to appreciate the fact that being an ostrich was only good
when the tide was out, the weather was balmy, and the

sand had not a single flea. Burying your head in the golden sand? It's just not practical.

Sooner or later, the tide of life will find you.

Fact is, no matter how hard you try to avoid making decisions (even if guilt and self-doubt are truly messing with your head), the sad reality is no one can get away in life without choosing between one thing and another. Even opting to ignore the existence of the choice was a choice. Living (and almost dying) among the pack had taught me that.

Threall had shown me the reverse side of the coin. Forget free will. Nobody really has it. Some things are just dumped on you by other people, courtesy of your connection to them, and you don't have the luxury of mulling over your choices. You end up opting for the best compromise and hoping it will be good enough.

The trick is learning to live with the result.

"Christ," hissed Trowbridge. "What bit you?"

I looked down at my arm. The devil's spawn's teeth marks were an oval of bruised purple on my pale skin. Blood welled from the imprint of each tooth, tiny beads, like black rubies on a pretender's crown. *You're going to leave a scar, aren't you, kid? You didn't have to. I'll remember you always.*

"Man, that looks bad," said Biggs.

It did. The teeth marks were actually kind of hideous on my pale white skin. Trowbridge cradled my arm and turned it toward the setting sun. "Who did this?" he growled.

"A kid in Threall." I stared at the devil's spawn's bite. What would have happened if the kid had come to me?

My mate's scent heated and clouded around us. Protective. Angry. Threatened. "Why did you go there?"

"To kill the Black Mage."

"Do tell us that you succeeded," drawled Cordelia.

Silently, I shook my head. Trowbridge's skin warmed my cheek.

His throat moved then he said, "I don't want you ever going there again."

But I will.

Merry rappelled up her chain to the open neck of my T-shirt. Trowbridge lifted his arm so that she could slide under the jersey and scoot down to position herself over my heart. Heat warmed my chest as she began the healing process.

My throat was so tight it hurt.

And there it was again. The road map of my life and choices open flat on a table again. Three entwined lifelines on it. Mine, Lexi's, and Trowbridge's. But now I saw other lines—fainter but no less important—woven loosely around my own.

They deserve more from me.

"I messed up, Trowbridge," I whispered.

"How?" he asked, his voice carefully neutral.

"Oh, it's huge." The trees outside were so beautiful. Just a few hardwoods and a swath of evergreens. "You'll want to tell the pack to leave the house and grounds. This is family business."

"Biggs," said the Alpha of Creemore, accepting the clean towel that Cordelia offered. "Do it."

No one talked while the grounds were cleared. Trowbridge wrapped the hand towel around my wrist and applied pressure. Cordelia busied herself sighing heavily and taking care of my mate's discarded dreads. Harry stood in the hall, hands in his back pockets, looking a little out of place.

The house turned funeral quiet. Was Lexi okay?

When Biggs returned, I told them everything. Every single terrible detail of what happened in Threall; all about Mad-one, the devil's cub, the Black and Old Mages, the pledges, the two trees with one trunk. I didn't gloss it over; I laid every one of my transgressions bare. My voice was flat—well, mostly; it did get kind of watery after telling about the kid. I finished by explaining that in sewing Trowbridge's life to mine, I'd tied him forever to the one man he hated among all others. After that, I'm not sure what I said. All I know is that I talked until I couldn't anymore. And then I sat there feeling empty and waiting for the moment Trowbridge dumped me on the broken seat of the easy chair.

Instead, he wrapped the end of my limp hair around his damaged finger, trying to set a curl in hair that resists suggestion. He slipped his digit free from the coil he'd made, and then gave a half smile as the strand twisted free.

A small head shake. "You are a lot of work, Hedi Peacock."

"Yeah, I am," I said evenly, listening to the steady beat of his heart.

Please don't dump me.

Trowbridge's arm tightened around me as he blew some air through his nose in one long stream of man-disbelief. "Just to recap: unless your brother is sent through the portal, you and I will die. Merenwyn will enter a dark age. Horror will seep—"

"Drip."

He nodded. "*Drip* into this world."

"It's a gift," said Cordelia wearily. "She's the only person I know who can tip our world toward disaster with one trip to the loo."

Harry cleared his throat. "Sounds to me like the disaster was already in the making. It's not all Little Miss's fault."

But some of it was. I had to own that.

My One True Love's chin ruffled the top of my head as he grimly shook his head. "I don't want you in Merenwyn."

"I know," I said softly, "but I'm going anyhow."

Don't cling, you fool. Get up. Stand on your own two feet. Resolutely, I slid off Trowbridge's knee and took a step to the window. I rested a shoulder against its frame and gazed outside. The mower had left lines in the grass.

"One way or the other, I've put each of you in a very difficult situation over the last six months," I said. "I can't

tell you how sorry I am for that." Merry shifted as I folded
my arms and tucked in my chin. I listened to a cardinal's
song for a few bars then nodded to myself. "So, it's probably best if I handle this on my own. If you can look the
other way while I bring Lexi to the portal, I'll do the rest.
That is, if you trust me." I swallowed. "And believe that I
told you everything that happened up there."

Someone had left a rake abandoned by the peony
bushes.

"You've forgotten some pretty important stuff," Trowbridge murmured.

My body stiffened. *He doesn't.* The Alpha of Creemore's scent reached for me and slid a tendril of him
around my throat. Was it threatening? No. A half second
later, I felt him—well, at least the heat of him—right beside me. So close. If I pulled my gaze from the peonies, if
I turned my chin just half an inch . . . No. I didn't want to
chance a look at him at the moment, because truth was, it
was taking everything I had to keep my lip from trembling.

His hand—one thumb, a pointer, and a middle finger—
curled around my shoulder. Into my ear he said softly,
"Did you forget what I said? Heart of my heart. Mate for
all my years. I offer you my life?"

Low blow. My nose burned in the way it did when it
was gearing up for a monumental boo-hoo. "Maybe the
mating vows didn't take and you still have a chance." I
rubbed my face and said wearily, "Maybe all we have between us is sex. Whenever I'm near you, I can't think
properly. Every time I see you, I keep thinking the same
thing over and over again, and it drowns out every rational
thought I ever—"

"Mine," he said.

My mouth fell open. I was thinking of a verb far less
profound.

"That's what I think when I see you. That's why I suffered nine years of blue balls. That's why I kept living
when it would have been easier to die. That's why I came
back and that's why I'm here now." He gave me a fierce

smile. "You are mine. I am yours. It's fucking simple. Don't make it complicated."

I gazed at the lawn, remembering the night I followed Stuart Scawens down to the pond.

"The vows took," he said. "I meant those words when I said them to you, mate."

No more lies.

"I tricked you," I whispered. "You thought you were saying the mating vows to Candy."

"Candy never smelled like wildflowers in the field."

"Sweet peas," I choked out. "My blood smells like sweet peas. Why don't you know that, Trowbridge?"

"It's a detail. I'm better on the big picture." The Alpha of Creemore turned me toward him. Blue-tailed comets spun in tired eyes, then his light—oh Goddess, his flare—it shone through his gaze.

Not painfully. Not hurtfully.

Mine, it said tenderly.

My flare—and oh sweet heavens, I was so far gone I didn't even feel its burn coming because my eyes had been blurred from the moment his scent had skimmed my flesh—burst forth. Mediterranean blue met brilliant green. Someone went "Aw" as turquoise light filled the bedroom.

"You are my mate who smells like tiny flowers." He cupped my face with his two large hands and tilted my face toward him. And that was that. His lips brushed mine. Once, twice. Not landing, just for a fly-by warning. His breath mingled with mine as he nuzzled the corner of my lips. "Don't ever forget that again."

Things have happened since he said those words.

But still, I've never forgotten him saying them.

Someone blew their nose then flushed the toilet. "What I want to know is how we're going to call the portal when it's time to go fetch brother dearest from the clutches of the Black Mage?" drawled Cordelia as she emerged from the bathroom.

We.

"You're not going," said Trowbridge. "Too many people crossing the gates at the same time is just going to increase the chances of getting caught. I can get Hedi to cover quicker if there's just the two of us."

We.

Cordelia's eyes narrowed.

Before she could put thought to word, I said, "Casperella can do it." Trowbridge lifted an eyebrow so I elaborated. "There's a Fae ghost in your cemetery who knows the words to the song." I felt my cheeks flush. "She's the one who called the portal last night. I couldn't remember the words."

"There's a ghost in the cemetery," Trowbridge repeated.

"There're three."

"I knew it," Biggs said.

Trowbridge's breath was warm, his heart solid. "If there was a ghost in the cemetery who knew the song, then why did you wait six months before telling her to summon the gates?"

Shame bit me. "I didn't know she was a Fae. And besides, Casperella was mute until she got her mitts on my magic."

"You shared your magic with a ghost?"

The emptiness—that searching feeling I'd felt without my talent—it didn't bear thinking about. "Not willingly," I said quietly. "And I got it back eventually." I lifted a shoulder, then let it drop. "Casperella would probably be willing to make a trade. She wants to go home. Back to Merenwyn. I could loan her my magic if she summoned the portal for us. The trickiest part would be to make her to give me back *all* of my green sparkling bits before she slipped across the portal."

"Sweetheart," he said. "A warrior never gives up his weapons. Ever."

A weapon? Was that how he saw my magic?

"We won't need the ghost," said Trowbridge. "The ghost didn't call the portal—your brother did. It started to materialize up on the hill within three bars of the song."

I thought back. Who had really called the portal? Casperella? My twin? Or had Fate suddenly decided to inter-
cede? Had she watched, unseen, until the precise moment
all three of us so desperately needed an intervention? Was
something larger than all of us guiding our destinies?

Trowbridge ran a soothing hand down my back. He
murmured, "Your brother knows the song, let him sing it."

And just how would I get Lexi to call the portal? Without giving him false hope?

My head hurt.

Ralph flashed a "hey, over here!" as Merry emerged
from my neckline. "Ralph needs to be fed. Merry, too." I
smoothed the dark hair on Trowbridge's arm. It was soft
and silky.

Harry cleared his throat. "There's a shrub or two that I
can pull out from the mess out back if he needs something
fast."

"There will be no shrubs in the bedrooms," said Cordelia. She'd used the brush. Her hair was a nice smooth sheet.

I got a flash of her last night—hair askew, mouth twisted
in pain.

Harry and Biggs, too.

"You guys should leave when the portal is summoned.
The pack will smell the magic of the portal—they'll come
to watch." I thought of those jiggling asses. "But they're
afraid of the gates so they'll keep their distance. It would
create a diversion. You could use it to slip out of Creemore. With any luck you can be on the highway before
anyone notices you're gone."

"That's true," said Cordelia. "They'll smell the magic
and come running."

Nod and let her go.

My friend's face twisted into her full diva scowl.
"Damn. We'll have to think around that—it will make getting her brother through the portal a lot harder."

Harry did a man-sigh as he scrubbed his mouth. "If
Bridge doesn't take immediate action against her brother,
he'll look weak. We've got to factor that in, too."

We.

Suddenly, Biggs spoke up. "She should let the old guy keep her brother's soul." His expression grew haunted as an awful silence fell and stretched. "What? I'm only saying what everyone else is thinking. Her brother might have been a good guy back in the day but he's a bit of a douche now."

Trowbridge's arms tightened around me.

"Not the time to bring this up," Cordelia said, her voice very low.

"Well, when is?" Biggs was already leaning on the wall. But he upped his homage to James Dean by crossing his arms and flattening one foot behind him. "Someone needs to give her a wake-up call. We all earned the right when we stood by her—"

"A man doesn't bring that stuff up," growled Harry. "Now get your damn foot off the wallpaper."

Biggs did, if a little slowly. "Well, someone still needs to tell her that she should just let the old guy take over her brother's body." He flicked a wary glance toward his Alpha. "The old dude will take better care of it than her brother ever did. And with all that magic shit he's got going on, he might live forever." He dug his hands into his jeans pockets, his expression mulish.

Harry looked neutral. Cordelia played with her earlobe, her gaze slanted from my searching one.

And Trowbridge?

He played absently with a strand of my hair while he stared at the floorboards in deep thought. "The Black Mage is a cruel bastard but I'm told that compared to the Old Mage, his magic skills are . . ." Brows furrowed, he groped for the right word. "Pedestrian. He's never going to come up with the end of the world on his own."

Biggs muttered, "I don't care if the Fae world blows up."

"Well, you sure as hell should. Because it wouldn't surprise me if things did 'drip' down from the passages. I've seen stuff in Merenwyn. Stuff that . . ." A long pause grew, which was never filled with words, but somehow managed to swell with misery.

The Alpha of Creemore said very quietly, "So if you want to worry about something a little more home-based, you think about that." He lifted his head and his gaze swept the room, touching on each one of them—the family that was not my family and yet somehow had become my family. "The old guy's chances of succeeding on his own are bad. Forget his magic skills—he'll use a lot of that to carry him past any guards the Black Mage has left by the gates. Then he has two days of terrain to cover before he reaches the castle, and he'll be wearing the Shadow's face the entire time he dodges the Royal Guards and the Raha'ells.

"My mate did the right thing," he told them. "The Old Mage will need backup—that will be me and her. And when it's done, his cyreath has got to be taken from her brother's."

Burning pressure behind my eyes again—either pent-up tears or a simmering flare.

He lifted my chin so that he could gaze into my eyes. "You did exactly what I would have done."

"You shouldn't be coming to Merenwyn," I whispered. "You've got a kill-me sticker slapped on your head."

"Small sticker." He smiled. "Even smaller print."

"Lovely." Cordelia stomped over to the dresser. "Just lovely." She opened the dresser's second drawer, from which she pulled out a folded white T-shirt. This, she tossed to Bridge. "Before we challenge Armageddon, can we focus on tonight? How are we going to do this under the pack's nose without screwing the pooch?"

Face grim, my mate shook out the cotton with two quick snaps. His voice grew muffled as he pulled the garment over his head. "We can't hide it from them."

"This is going to be a mistake," muttered Biggs.

The Alpha brooded. "Your brother has to be near death when he goes through the portal—the mage was right about that. So, we'll turn that into something we can use.

I'll summon the pack. Then we're going to have to make it
look like an execution."

That sick feeling came back.

"After the pack witnesses your participation, they'll
never doubt you again."

I don't care if they doubt me.

I closed my eyes. But I couldn't seal my ears, so I heard
the rest. "There's enough sun potion in Knox's bottle to
put Lexi into a coma. Once the Shadow calls the portal,
we'll force him to drink it."

I flinched.

Trowbridge said, "He'd just go to sleep, sweetheart."

Knowing I'd betrayed him.

An angry sun was setting over the tree line. I shivered.
Trowbridge wrapped an arm around me and drew me close.
We stood near the edge of the cliff, overlooking the pond,
under the very same oak tree where a teenage Trowbridge
had once strummed his guitar.

"Are you cold?" he asked.

"Not really," I said quietly. But I was, right down to the
bones, and I was beginning to worry that it was the type of
chill that was never going to get better.

Cordelia peeled off her tasteful beige sweater. "She's
lying through her teeth." My ex-roomie looked worn out,
but then again, age, worry, and fatigue are hard to hide
when a woman hasn't had a chance to trowel on a thick layer
of foundation. "Here, put this on," she said gruffly, holding
it out so that I could thread my arms into it.

"I don't need it," I said, shaking my head.

Let me be cold. Let me be numb.

But Trowbridge gently turned me around so I faced him
and helped me thread first one arm, and then the other,
into the sleeves. Hard to do with the bulky bandage I wore
above my wrist. Cordelia fussed over how the cardigan sat
on my shoulders. "I told them to get some of your clothing
from the laundry basket on the chair in my bedroom," she

fumed as she rolled the sleeves. "Instead they rummaged through my bag for Goodwill. So bloody lazy."

You can't fix me, my Cordelia. Even if you feel a powerful need to fix something in the face of all this wrong. Trust me on that.

"We'll get some new clothes tomorrow," Trowbridge said dismissively. He began to do the buttons up, with more adeptness than I thought he'd manage considering the pearl closures were small and slippery. When the last button was done, he pulled my hair free of the neckline and used two fingers to rake its length so that it spread over my shoulders. "You hanging in there?"

I gave him a dumb nod.

"It will be over, soon," he murmured. "Stay strong."

Seriously, he was saying that to a Stronghold?

I wanted to tell him—this wasn't near over; this was only the beginning. Because I knew what lay ahead—I could see that string of nights where I would wake up and lie there, unable to fall back to sleep because I'd had a nightmare about my brother being trapped inside the portal's walls for eternity. But why share with my mate the things that will haunt my soul?

We both bore scars already, didn't we? Some of them hardly scabbed over.

If he could silently bear the pulling pain of his healing wounds, I could bear the sharp slicing pain of mine.

Besides. It was a little late to start wringing my hands in dismay and whining doubt. I'd put my trust in a wily old goat. And yes, when it all came down to it, I'd wagered my twin's life on the slim odds and a brief nod toward higher principles—which had to have Karma bent over in a belly laugh. What follows now . . . oh Goddess, what follows now?

Karma. Please. If I'm wrong, take it out on me.

Not the people I love.

A quack from the pond below the cliff turned my head. The water looked dark and brown but a ray of a fading sun had fallen across the pond in a streak of golden light. It played on the beaks of the duck family, gilding them with vibrant green highlights. I watched them paddle single file. Daddy led—at least I assumed the pretty one was the father—then made a sharp turn at the edge of some bull-rushes. The entire raft uniformly turned at exactly the same spot, though the third mallard in the string waggled his tail feathers at the apex of the curve.

Seems even duck families have their Biggs.

They should leave before the wind turns frigid and the pond ices over.

I slid my hand into my pocket. The small glass bottle resting inside it had already been heated to my body temperature. What if my mate was wrong? What if the contents sent Lexi into a final sleep, not just a coma?

Trowbridge whispered in my ear, "They're coming."

Harry nodded and picked up the stick he'd leaned against a nearby tree. "I'll be off to the cemetery to wrangle a ghost, then." When I'd voiced a concern that Casper-ella might try to snatch some of my magic from the air, he said, "Ghosts don't scare me. I'll take care of it."

I watched him leave, his spine erect, his long white silver hair strangely riveting in the dying light. Though—perhaps not so strange. We instinctively search for light in the gathering dark, don't we?

Make it be over soon. The air in my chest stayed there—heavy and hurting—until I saw that first flash of my brother's light gray shirt through the dark shadows of the pines.

Chapter Twenty-eight

Lexi had to have known the pack was waiting for him long before he stepped into the clearing. His nose would have warned him. But smelling danger and seeing it are two very different things.

He entered the clearing with a bit of a fanfare, stumbling into Biggs's back hard enough to send the smaller Were tripping into a shrub. Whether Lexi meant to do that or it was a consequence of the fact that his hands were tied behind his back and the symptoms of his withdrawal had turned his balance to crap, I couldn't be sure.

But still, his feet faltered as he saw the gathered pack.

Perhaps he'd forgotten how many of them there were.

I knew what that felt like. Walking into a field with your arms pinned behind your back, smelling the pack's excitement and the pond. Hearing those murmurs drop to hushed anticipation.

The Stronghold in me resented the ropes, but I couldn't completely blame Biggs. His upper lip was swollen and that shirt he loved so much was never going to be wearable again.

Score one for my brother, I thought.

He looked so foreign and Fae, with his high boots and his tight pants.

One of the pack escorts gave my brother's back a hard,

motivational push that sent Lexi staggering for a few steps.
But ever graceful—yet another gene he'd swiped from me
in the great placenta divide—he grimly turned what could
have been a face-planting sprawl into a dancer's run.

His gaze bounced from the pack, to me and Trowbridge,
then to the small path beyond us—the one that led down the
Trowbridge ridge to the pond and then wound back up to
the Stronghold property. That he gave brief consideration.

A bead of sweat rolled down my back.

Finally, he was before us. Sandwiched between two of
the taller pack guys, with Biggs in the rear. The setting sun
made the wolf tattooed above his ear seem almost alive.

Lexi didn't look at the Alpha of Creemore. Just at me.

His brows rose in a silent question.

I should have said something soothing along the lines
of "it will be all right." But I—that girl who could spin a
lie faster than the truth—came up empty. Treachery had
formed a knot in the middle of my throat and I couldn't
push a word past it. So, I gave him my very best I'm-no-
betrayer smile instead.

But we were twins.

Lexi's expression turned to stone. My eyes burned as he
took a deep breath and lifted his chin—exactly the way he
had back in grade two when Sean Edwards had called him
the son of a whore. "Am I on trial?" he drawled. "Or is this
my execution?"

I can't do this.

"Neither, Shadow," said Trowbridge truthfully.

"So you're full pack now, Hell?" Three dark vees of
sweat soaked Lexi's shirt—one for each armpit and another below his pecs. "Do you have a leash hanging from a
hook somewhere?"

"She is your sister and my mate," Trowbridge grated.
"Show her your respect."

My twin shook his head with slow insult. "All I see is a
wolf's bitch."

Trowbridge's fist caught Lexi's chin hard enough to snap
my twin's head back. But my twin was a Stronghold, too,

wasn't he? Again, he didn't fall—probably because he must have counted on a blow coming his way the instant he used the B-word and, accordingly, had braced himself. An appalled hush came from the spectators as Lexi shook his head like a boxer.

Then, in an impressive display of insolence, my brother rolled his neck and firmed his mouth. I read the intent behind his glittering eyes.

"Don't, Lexi!" I said in a low voice. "Don't force him to hurt you."

Blood welled from Lexi's split lip. "Still the mouse afraid of a raised fist, Hell?"

Hedi, the mouse-hearted.

Hedi, the betrayer.

"Idiot. You were brought here to summon the portal." I forced that stiff smile back on my liar's face. "Not to die."

My twin's mask fell. Very, very briefly. Almost immediately he covered up his response with an overlay of gloating triumph, but I saw quick unguarded reaction and for once—Karma still had her claws in at that point—I could read a facial expression without having to consult a manual to figure out what it meant.

Restored faith. That's what I saw.

"You did it," he said in the softest whisper. "You talked him into letting me go."

I gave him a dumb nod for which he favored me with a large smile—one of his real ones—too wide, white teeth gleaming. "Are you coming with me?"

"No, she's not," said Trowbridge.

Lexi's gaze clung to mine for another beat or two then he nodded. "That's all right," he said. Just like he did the afternoon I didn't want to try using that flimsy rope to swing over the pond. "I'm going to have to move fast once I go through the other side, anyhow. You never were that good in a footrace, Hell."

You won't be running when you get to other side, brother-mine. You'll be shambling on your feet. Tossing your head in agony.

I can't do this.

Misreading my expression, my twin gave me a quick grin. "Don't worry, runt. I've got a trick or two up my sleeve. I'll get through."

I searched his face. "You're sure?"

"Do you think I'd have come here without a backup plan?" He looked around. "Where's my bag?"

Cordelia held it up by the straps. "I have it."

My twin stared at it then gave me a frustrated smile. "You're going to have to tell them to undo these ropes. I can't go through the passage tied up."

Trowbridge answered for me. "You lose those after you call the gates."

"Alpha to the end, Son of Lukynae?" mocked Lexi.

"Mate to the end, Shadow," replied Trowbridge.

I wanted to cry again but I figured I hadn't earned the right.

See it through.

Then cry.

The pack remained wary of the woo-woo. They'd moved back in the clearing—far enough that they could scoot into the woods if any Fae came slithering through the gates when we called them. But close enough to watch.

To stare.

Back at the house, when all this had been theory and planning, I'd told Trowbridge that I'd need a minute or two for just me and Lexi.

"He'll be easier to handle that way," I'd said.

A few moments ago, Trowbridge had taken my silent cue. As had Cordelia and Biggs, who'd taken a few steps back.

So here we were. Ninety seconds and counting for alone-time. *And I had thought the right words for good-bye would come to me.* My twin and I stood at the edge of the cliff, gazing at my trailer on the opposite ridge. From the Trowbridge property it really did look like a silver bug.

"Tell them to tow it away," he said. "Mum would have hated it."

"I will."

He tapped his toe, once, twice. "I was beginning to think you were going to leave me there in that room . . . I thought . . ." His voice drifted off and he shrugged. "Never mind what I thought. In the end, you came through." Then he gave me a rogue's wink. "For you, runt, I'm giving a one-time, special performance."

Lexi's long fall of hair rippled down his back as he tilted back his head and closed his eyes.

I don't think I can stand to listen to him sing—not like this.

Back when we'd been very small, Lexi had liked singing. Little tunes as he waited for his turn at the sink. Small little-boy ditties as he helped shell the peas. His voice had been girlish high. Fluting even. But when we hit school, one of our classmates had chosen the purity of his tone as a good tool for mockery and had hit him over the head with it, over and over again. "Celine Dion"—that's what the boys of St. Hubert of Liege called my brother.

I never heard him sing again. Yeah, I'd listened to him making *ch-ch-ch* sounds for guns in his bedroom. I'd rolled my eyes as he hummed to pop songs played on the car radio. But after Brad Mosbergen taunted him in the halls after Miss Fitzgerald's Christmas pageant, he'd never truly sung again. Not once.

And now I knew why he refused.

His true singing voice had never really broken. It was still pure and high as a choirboy's. A clean falsetto. No slur, no funny trills. It was as if the sweetness of my brother had been distilled and saved for song. Kept shielded from all the ugly, completely untainted.

Does the portal retain the essence of those trapped Fae souls? Do they hear the music? Appreciate it? Value one voice over another? I'm not sure. All I know is that it took my aunt Lou over five minutes to lure the portal to her call and it only took my brother a few bars of song. Almost immediately, Fae magic started sweetening the soup of pond smells. As his voice rose, the air began to swirl over the pond, clockwise. Next the myst began to show, pink-white, at first, then circling, circling. My brother sang all the way to the end—even that high and hard bit—eyes closed, head thrown back, and as he did, I saw the Weres straining to listen.

It was utterly beautiful.

When Lexi finished, the portal floated in midair some six feet below the crumbling edge of the ridge. Merenwyn beckoned through its hobbit-round window.

"I'll love you forever, Lexi," I said, staring at it. "Don't ever forget that, okay?"

"Hey." He gave me a shoulder bump. "Don't get all sentimental on me. It's a portal. I can come back." Green eyes, two shades darker than mine. Winning and for once guileless. Bloodshot, though. "Matter of fact, I *will* come back. To check on—" His head rotated. "I can't find her among them. Is she here?"

"No," I said. "We thought it best Anu stayed low for a bit."

Another lie. Anu had wanted to come and I'd put my foot down. She may not have known that Lexi was her father but I did.

That piece of information hit him hard—why, I couldn't fathom. He'd barely looked at her. Never publicly claimed her. But the fact that she wasn't there, watching him cross the portal? It hurt him. I could read his deep unhappiness by the very fact that his expression grew shuttered and remote.

Lexi, you complicated man. "Can I tell her about you later?"

A tiny shoulder lift as he gazed at Merenwyn. "I don't know what you'd say."

That once you were a good brother and a loved son.

"It's time for me to go," he said. "Which of the amulets do I get?"

"Someone needs to cut these ropes off my brother," I said sharply.

A pause. Then I heard Trowbridge say, "Do it."

Lexi slanted his head as Biggs came up behind him with a knife. "Easy, little guy," he said insouciantly. "Don't pinch." When the knots were sliced and Biggs had stepped away, Lexi flexed his hands. He gave me his big-brother look, ruined somewhat by the fact that his face was a sheen of sweat and a nerve was tugging at the corner of his eye.

Give me strength, Goddess, so I can do what must be done.

"I'll be back," he lied.

I opened my mouth because it was time—hell, it was *beyond* time. The second hand was sweeping us toward the point of no return. Once that line was crossed? Even if I won—the Book of Spells destroyed, the Old Mage bested, my brother's soul restored—I was going to lose.

Trust is an exquisitely valued thing to someone who's had near every particle of it wrung from them. If you break it? There's nothing left.

Suddenly, my brother said in a hard, flat voice, "I became a father because I was piss drunk."

"What?"

"Listen, okay?" He swallowed, hard, giving me his profile. "I'd been taking potion all night and had topped that off with several glasses of mead. I'd left the table—just to get some air—because I'd suddenly felt like . . ." He knuckled the blood from his lip, his gaze downcast and unseeing. "Sometimes it was hard to breathe in that room. On the way out, I stopped to let a Kuskador servant refill my cup because I was out of the juice."

"You don't have to tell me this," I said, reaching for him.

He twisted away from my touch. "I only want to say this once, so listen. My mage was making a toast—he's always such an asshole with the toasts, they go on forever—and . . . I'm a good mimic, do you remember that?"

"I remember everything."

"That's what did it. I mimicked the Black Mage." My twin shook his head, his face bleak. "The timing couldn't have been worse. The room had fallen quiet and everyone heard me. They were still laughing as I was being dragged by my heels out of the Great Hall."

Absently, he went to push back his hat. But it was missing, like his natty suspenders—both stripped from him before he'd been locked in the room in the basement. Instead he raked his fingers through his hair, from brow to nape, roughly twisting its length into a golden tail that he pulled over his shoulder.

His fist dropped. Tapped against his thigh twice.

"I spent a few days in prison. Then I was brought to the Spectacle field and thrown into the pen with the Kuskador servant who'd served me the wine."

Lexi inside that pen, with the wolves in the field.

"I'd lived in the Royal Court long enough to forget that I really didn't belong there," he said. "You start believing that as long you're careful and smarter than most of them . . . But that night I looked up at the spectators and saw the women I'd slept with, and the men I'd gamed with, making bets on how long I'd last."

All expression left his face. "They'd given the Kuskador her ration of sun potion—so she couldn't change—but hadn't given me a drop in four days. I changed to my beast, half crazed from withdrawal, contained in that cage with no one but a small, terrified girl to fight me off . . ."

My hand went to my mouth.

"After my appetite had been satisfied, they dropped the sides of the pen and the Raha'ells moved in. You know what saved me? I flared. For the first time in my miserable existence, I flared." His shoulders lifted in a huff of disbelief. "Saved by the Raha'ells' prophecy—that one day the Son of Lukynae would come for them and they'd know him by his flare. I ended up fucking one of their bitches right under the viewing stand, a few feet from all my fine royal friends."

"Was that Anu's mother?"

"Yes, that was her mother," he replied. "The Black Mage 'forgave' me the next day though he gave me something to remember my 'error.' "

A paw print, forever inked upon his skin.

"When I found out that the Raha'ell carried my seed, I went down to the birthing stalls to kill her. But I was a day late. The bitch had whelped my by-blow the night before and died early that morning. The baby still lived . . . She had your eyes, Hell." A muscle flexed in his cheek. "No one has eyes like yours—so clear."

His chest lifted as he drew in a long, slow breath.

"Anyhow, you tell her what you want from that."

My twin pursed his lips as he stared at the shimmering gates to the world he'd so recently left. "Now give me some of your magic, Hell. I'll bring it closer."

My hand tightened on the glass bottle.

"Let me," said Trowbridge, moving to my side.

Hedi, the mouse-hearted.

I clenched my teeth and shook my head. "No." That was part of the deal—I'd told Trowbridge that if I were the one who passed Lexi the potion, I'd look more badass to the pack. And if my mate smelled my lie, he chose not to call me on it in front of the others.

The thing is, something had birthed inside me as I'd listened to the plans being drawn and redrawn in the Trowbridge master bedroom. As epiphanies go, it was simple—I couldn't stand the thought of hiding behind people anymore. Which, as personal awakenings go, was stunningly poorly timed. Because, *come on.* The nastiness unspooling was definitely one instance where it would have been preferable to hide in the shadow of the Alpha of Creemore, mouthing, "It's his fault."

Let Trowbridge give him the potion.

But I couldn't . . . I just couldn't. First of all, it wasn't Trowbridge's fault. None of it was. And secondly . . . it felt wrong. Cowardly, somehow. This was *my* brother. If a proverbial gun was going to be fired, it had to be me pulling the trigger. I don't know why or how to explain how I became convinced of that.

But I knew it. Soul deep.

It was agony to pull my paw from my jeans pocket. But

I found some kernel of strength—for once both my Fae
and inner-bitch were leaning on the oars. Then I drew in a
long breath and extended my fist toward my brother, fingers still curled around the vial of sun potion.

"Hell?" asked Lexi.

*Open your hand. Show him what you have hidden there.
Go on. Do it.*

I forced myself to uncurl my fingers to expose the bottle
lying on my palm. "You have to drink this, Lexi."

"That's unexpected." He stared at it—*one thousand,
two thousand, three*—his tongue wet his lips—*four thousand, five thousand*—then he took it from my palm. His
smile was as shaky as his fingers as he unscrewed the cap.
"But I'll think better and move faster after a hit, so bottoms
up." My twin took a small sip. This he savored briefly, rolling it in his mouth. Then with a look of utter bliss, he swallowed a measure.

A discreet shudder.

He replaced the cap and began to twist it closed.

That's when Trowbridge said softly, "No, Shadow. You
need to drink all of it."

"All?" Lexi's brows pulled together. "That's too much,
Hell. I can't—"

"It's the only way," I told him. "You have to finish the
entire bottle, Lexi."

Some things can't be swallowed as quickly as sun potion. Things like betrayal. Reversals of fortune. Over-
doses. Murder.

Pain swelled in me as I watched him fight against it.
But the full realization of my deceit came, anyhow.

It had to. Didn't it?

His face twisted into something ugly.

"I should have known—you're not wearing Mum's amulet. When I saw it around the Son of Lukynae's throat, I
figured he was going to pass it to you at the last minute.
But he didn't want me tearing that thing from your little
neck, did he?" His shoulders lifted in a fuck-me huff. "So,
what's the plan, sis?" Venom laced his voice. "Oh, forget it.

You're just his little fuck toy, aren't you? You don't the know the plan." He turned to Trowbridge. "*This* is how you're going to appease the Black Mage? You stupid piece of shit—he doesn't give a damn whether or not I come back dead or alive. Sending my body across won't stop him from coming here if he wants to."

"Trust me," I whispered.

His glance was quick and scathing. "Trust the Son of Lukynae's whore? I don't think so. You want me to finish this bottle? Well, then, your *mate*'s going to have to force it down my throat."

"No problem," said Trowbridge.

Faes.

We tend to behave predictably in certain situations. When faced with ruin, my aunt Lou had vindictively chucked Ralph into the pond. When faced with the task of infuriating the Alpha of Creemore, my twin chose the same option.

He twisted for the pond.

Trowbridge lunged—they grappled on the edge. I saw disaster in the making, since Weres can't swim, so I threw myself into the fray. My hand scrabbled for the bottle. Lexi swung a fist at Trowbridge.

It connected with my arm.

And I screamed in pain.

Lexi froze—both of them did—at the sound of that single, sharp, shrill cry of hurt.

It shouldn't have burned so much. It was just a glancing blow. But it had landed dead-square on my bandage, and it reopened the pain of the bite like I was back in Threall, on the retreat from evil with a kid hanging off my arm, his incisors chewing through my flesh.

I swear. It so felt like the kid all over again.

And thus, I screamed and immediately felt terrible for doing so.

Hedi, the mouse-hearted. Hedi, the weak.

Trowbridge sank to his knees, the Shadow all forgotten. "Hedi?"

I bit down on my lip, trying to quell its tremor.

"I'm good," I said huskily.

The bottle of sun potion had been dropped in the scuffle. It had landed, improbably, in a tuft of crabgrass. It hadn't broken; it hadn't even fallen over on its side. It stood, looking pristine and poisonous, upright in the weed's tough blades.

Behold the Stronghold soap opera.

Did I reach for it? Pass it silently back to my brother? *No.*

My anger came spewing up. "Why couldn't you resist it?" I screamed at my brother, frustration frothing up. "You knew it was dangerous and yet you took it anyhow! Why couldn't you have just held off? Accepted your wolf? You stupid, stupid . . . *stupid* man. You turned into a fucking junkie . . . You've ruined everything."

Yeah. I heard myself somewhere in there.

But my mouth was a runaway horse. It was running on in terror. Bad things were behind it. Safety was just . . . there. Somewhere up ahead.

No—not *here*.

Not here, where once the boy of my dreams strummed the guitar.

Not here, where a broken girl sat on her ass in a bed of crabgrass.

Words dried up. And in truth, I don't exactly know all I said before they dribbled off. But eventually there was silence. Not even a cricket had the balls to chirrup. My chest heaved. I counted to seven. Then I yanked my gaze from that bottle and painfully forced my repentant eyes upward.

"Forgive me." That's what I wanted my eyes to say to Lexi.

"I'm sorry," too.

But Lexi wasn't looking at me—or, for that matter, the sun potion. He was staring at the bandage above my wrist. Blood—sweet-pea scented and bright red—had soaked through the bandage.

"He hurt you?" he asked, his voice throbbing.

Oh Goddess, could this awesomely terrible comedy of hurt get any worse?

"No, Lexi," I said. "Trowbridge wouldn't hurt me. He'd *never* hurt me."

But abused people? They can't believe that. There is no such thing as a safe harbor. There are only people who have hurt them and people who will hurt them.

There's nothing in between.

"Give me it," he said roughly to Trowbridge.

My mate didn't hesitate. He passed the vial of sun potion to him, his arm curved protectively around my shoulders.

Lexi looked at it for a moment. Self-acknowledgment, bitter fruit. "I shouldn't have come back. You are right. I am a selfish prick who fucked it all up." He drew in another deep breath. Tilted his head back and took two long swallows.

"Hell, I know you think you've found a life of happiness here with these wolves," he said. "But I don't think you'll get it." Another swallow. His mouth curved in a gruesome smile. "At least now I won't have to fight against my wolf anymore. "

Then his face hardened. His gaze drifted to Trowbridge and paused there for a long moment. What they said to each other with their eyes, I'll never know.

Then—because he was Lexi, who never knew the meaning of humility—he brought the vial to his lips and tossed back the rest in three quick gulps. When he'd drained the bottle, he wiped his mouth. Gave Trowbridge a glittering smile. "See?" he said. "It's not going to be that easy. I've drunk gallons of this stuff. You're going to have to sit around watching me for hours. I couldn't . . ." His brows drew together. Slowly, clumsily. "I couldn't . . ."

My brother's head turned slowly in my direction. "Hell?"

Then his eyes rolled up and he finally—*oh Goddess, curse me—finally,* he fell.

I couldn't catch him. He outweighed me by at least seventy pounds. But I managed to catch his head before it hit

the ground, and that I eased tenderly down onto the bed of
grass. Then I stared at his bruised, slack face and knew a
measure of self-hatred and remorse that took me to a level
of misery I'd never sunk to before.

"I don't want him lying here, like this. Not in front . . ."
My gaze flicked to the pack. "Please, Trowbridge."

Cordelia. She could move so fast sometimes. I knew—
peripherally—that she was over there somewhere. Yet,
suddenly, she was right beside me. Her bony knee grazing
mine.

"We'll carry him to the tree," she said. "Would that be
good?"

I nodded.

They were sweet to me. Later, I'd recognize that.

But in the seconds that followed the collapse of my
twin all I knew was anger. Deep and festering. I felt the
pack watching us—*when will they stop doing that?*—eyes
wide, mouths agape.

Lexi was carried back to the tree. When they went to put
him down, I caught Trowbridge's sleeve. "I need to hold
him," I said, scuttling between my brother and the trunk of
the tree.

"He's a deadweight," warned Cordelia.

And she was right. An unconscious person is heavier
than a lead weight. My shoulders bowed, cradling him.
Trowbridge crouched beside me. "Are you okay?" he asked.
His scent wove around both of us.

I nodded and pressed my chin on top of Lexi's head.

This is Karma's price.

Chapter Twenty-nine

Yes, I was wonderfully calm for about fifteen seconds.

Then the panic started to squeeze my stomach. I had nothing to give comfort to my brother. A blanket—he wouldn't feel it. Privacy—the house was too far and the pack needed to witness every anguished moment of the Stronghold brat's fall. All of them—the Danvers bitch and Rachel Scawens. Probably Brad Mosbergen, too.

No, no, no.

I should have talked to my brother first. Pulled him aside. Warned him about wily old goats. It was stupid not to have let him know . . . What if the Old Mage had other plans?

Oh Goddess. I've made a mistake.

Was he afraid? Did he feel alone? How long before his breath rattled in his throat? Minutes? Oh sweet heavens, hours? What does a "rattle" even sound like anyway?

I might wait too long.

Mad-one might wait too long.

Was there a place in heaven for broken men?

Fae Stars. Was there a place for Trowbridge and me?

I squeezed my eyes shut. And in the roiling darkness of my mind, all I could see was Lexi when he was twelve: too thin, too much fire, too much want and desire, mind sly. My

ally in those painful, early years. Sending thought pictures
to comfort me. Leading me on charges through the woods.
Bravely swinging from his pirate rock to the rescue of
damsels in distress.

The rest of the stuff . . . The lies. The hatred I'd seen
gleaming from his green eyes. The sour scent of the sun
potion leaking from his skin. The wolves' eyes tatted
above his ear. The blood on his hands. The ugly stains on
his soul . . . Those I didn't recall.

My heart was open—it flowed with hurt and love.

There was just one sacred thing left between us.

Please, Goddess, I'll pay whatever you want.

I sent my twin a nudge.

Lexi?

Nothing.

Someone coughed. *Go away. Leave us alone.*

I could smell his blood, sweet scented like mine.

Lexi? Please, *Lexi.*

I was on the brink of pulling back and then—I felt him.
A faint shadow on the edge of my mind. My brother, my
twin. Warmth flooded me.

A "yes" if ever I knew one.

A slip. A slide.

And then I was with my twin's mind once more.

In his dreams, Lexi sat under the leafy canopy of a very
old tree.

It was a tall, single-trunk maple. Fissured bark. Roots
so thick they lay like thick-muscled arms atop the soil. My
twin's back was braced against its trunk, one wrist rested
on his raised knee. No hat—and no wolfish tattoo or
shaved skull, either. Hair uniformly long, one side draped
in tangled disorder across his shoulder. He wearily lifted
his head; his eyes were sleepy.

"Sit," he said, giving a faint head toss toward the little
hollow between two roots in the dirt beside him.

I did. Close enough that my shoulder could brush his.

We sat on a gentle hill. Words unspoken between us, an

invisible barrier. A summer sun shone above, brilliant in a clear sky. Below us lay the Pool of Life, a couple of miles away, or perhaps more. Blue. Not the hue of Trowbridge's eyes. Bluer.

"It's beautiful," I said in awe.

"Yes," he said, his voice so tired.

Virgin forests, untouched by man. Supersaturated colors. So many greens. Apple and kelly; pistachio and lime. Yellows, too—drifts of tiny starburst daisies nodding in Merenwyn's wind. Beyond the Pool of Life the landscape climbed, hills dipping into valleys, and then rising again, rolling upward toward distant mountains.

"Have you ever seen the Pool of Life up close?" I asked.

"Once I swam in it," my brother said. "I thought it might cure me."

I drew in a sharp breath and then realized that I had a sense of smell—something I never possessed in my own dreams. *Oh Lexi.* Here in the world of my brother's fantasy, where there was only truth as he knew it, my twin carried the scent of the wolf. Woods and the wild, with the faintest trace of summer flowers.

Remember his scent.

"The Pool of Life's water is cold," he said drowsily. "Like the creek used to be in spring. You have to pick your way carefully because the bottom's all shale. But there are no weeds or eels . . . I hate eels."

Lexi's hand lay limp by his hip, fingers half curled.

"I remember." I stared at his bluing nails.

You're cold.

With a silent prayer, I reached for his hand.

The odds were heavily weighted that he'd withdraw from my touch. I waited, knowing he had the absolute right to do so. But, no. Lexi didn't resist or stiffen. He allowed me to curl my fingers around his icy ones so that I could warm them with my heat.

"The water is really clear; you can see right to the bottom." He made a low, wistful hum. "The deeper you go, the rougher the ground gets."

"With rocks," I said, thinking of Trowbridge. "Some of them are slippery."

A slow nod. "So you know."

Yes, I know. So many things I know too late.

"I'm tired, Hell," he said heavily.

A dark bird flew overhead. A hawk? A raven? Some bird of prey, winging its way back to its nest with something small and limp hanging from its beak.

"I can't remember what Dad looked like anymore." Quiet misery a dragging weight to each word. "The only things I can remember well are his hands. He had big hands."

"Yes, he did." Very much like the one I clasped.

"I wish I could remember his face."

The tree line blurred and I took a ragged breath. "I can show you if you want."

"Yeah?"

"You bet." I riffled through my memories and chose my favorite.

"Ah," he breathed as he received it.

It was a simple thought picture. Mundane even. The four of us—Dad and Mum, Lexi and I—sitting at our pine table under the golden light of the old brass lamp. The kitchen's old faded red-checked curtains pulled tight against the dark of the night. A heaping platter of roast beef down at the boy's end of the table. A bowl of maple syrup in front of me. Mum's honey-laden spoon close to her parted red lips. Dad's head thrown back, his dark eyes twinkling as he laughed at something Lexi had said.

"We were so young," he marveled.

"Yes."

Lexi's eyelids drooped. "You were right. Dad would have hated what I've become."

Twin, forgive me for the hurt I have caused.

"Lexi, I was talking trash. You have to believe this— Dad would *never* have hated you." A breeze, pine fragrant, without the slightest trace of honeysuckle, stirred the leaves overhead. "He would have raged over every blow that you received. He would have mourned for every choice taken from you. You survived, Lexi. Dad would have been so happy that you did."

"I had a few choices, Hell," he said. "But I always chose life instead."

As I have for you, Lexi.

I pulled a wisp of hair free from his eyelashes. "Believe that, okay?" I coaxed. "He'd never have stopped loving you."

He needs proof.

So, I brought up one last thought picture. It had been seared into my memory; my covetous eyes had snapped it in a moment of pique. The two of them as seen by me from the back steps of our old home. Dad stood, both hands in the back pockets of his jeans, looking out over the pond. His thick dark hair cut short so his tanned neck was visible. At his elbow, a young Lexi. Same haircut. His shoulders sparrow thin. His hands thrust into his pockets.

Two wolves inspecting their territory.

The picture had always stirred my jealousy, but now, I blessed it. Pleasure, sweet and pure, softened my brother's face.

"I miss him," he said huskily.

The urge to tell him, to offer him hope, was so strong. *Silence is the price, Hedi of the mouse heart.*

"I'm tired," he said. "So tired."

"You can leave, Lexi." I rested my head on the hard rounded swell of his shoulder. "If you have to go, you can."

"I will soon." He sighed. "It's nice like this, isn't it?"

"Yes," I said simply.

The bird of prey lifted off from his perch with a fast flutter of strong wings. A peregrine? Yes, probably. I watched the falcon beat his way high into the clear blue sky, searching for a thermal current, finding it, then spreading his feathers wide. Lazily, he glided on it. Slipping from airstream to airstream. Thieving power from the wind. With a harsh cry, he turned away from the Pool of Life. Another beat of wings. Upward to another current. He used it to soar toward the hills. Free. Beautiful.

Lexi said something too low to catch, under his breath.

"What did you say?" I asked, watching the bird.

"My daughter will never have to drink sun potion." Satisfaction in his voice.

Will I ever really understand him?

"No," I swore. "She'll never have to do that."

"You'll raise her as pack?"

"Yes." The bird was but a distant speck in the sky.

"School's going to be hard. Keep an eye out, okay?"

My throat tightened. "I promise."

"I love you, Hell."

Dark brown eyelashes, thick and stubby, fluttered closed.

"I love you, too, Lexi," I whispered, stroking his jaw.

He murmured, "I'm really sleepy now, Hell."

"You rest." I combed his tangled skein of hair flat. "I'll stay with you until you fall asleep."

Chapter Thirty

Things followed after that.

Simple things, if you examined each action separately. I waited until I could count to twenty between each breath and then I pressed a final kiss on Lexi's brow. After that, it took no effort of will at all to detach from my brother's dream—the connection between us had dimmed as his world had darkened.

All I had to do was open my eyes and there was Creemore.

My brother lay in my arms. His hair was spiked and sour smelling. Something glittered, caught between two strands of wheat. I teased the thing free.

A Fae tear.

"Now?" Trowbridge asked softly.

I slid the tear into my brother's palm then gave him a nod. Cordelia and Biggs helped us stand.

Then, I called to my magic. My Fae's essence flowed upward, but this time—for the first time—it followed the pathway of my arteries and veins with a solemnity that bordered on respectful. Once at the ends of my fingertips, my magic waited patiently, and when I gave it leave, it streamed to the portal and found an anchor hidden in the depths of that fog-wreathed floor.

I felt the tug of those floating gates all the way up to my shoulder.

Just like Lexi had done the night before, I wrapped my cable of magic around my fist, over and over again. Slowly, bit by bit, the stately castle of dreams and myst rose to the edge of the crumbling cliff. One last twist of my bandaged wrist. There. Now it was just one easy step from one world's soil to another world's gates.

Trowbridge went down on one knee to pick up my brother, and with a gentleness that made the knot in my throat swell, lifted my twin in his arms.

Please, Mad-one. Do it now.

Cordelia gestured to Lexi's bag, and asked, "Should this go, too?"

I spared the black satchel a quick glance. Leather bulged and flexed. "Yes, but take out the ferret."

"Dibs," said Biggs in a low voice.

"Hurry," I told them as Lexi's squirming pet was extricated.

"Shit!" cursed Biggs as the ferret turned unexpectedly feral. "I'm trying to help you, little—"

An ache gnawed at my shoulders. "The portal's heavier than I expected, you really, really need to hurry." Lexi had made reeling in the portal look easy. That, plus my own arrogance, had made me believe that the Gates of Merenwyn were as light as the vapor they resembled.

But in truth, the portal was a lead weight.

Trowbridge turned to me, a question in his eyes.

"I will hold," I said. "That's what we do."

A muscle tightened in Trowbridge's jaw. He turned toward the portal and stared at the columns of myst, the round hobbit window with its view of Merenwyn. Then he drew in his breath and stepped onto the floor.

Tyrean, if you can hear my thoughts . . . Here is my vow: whatever it takes, I'll show you the way home.

Do it now.

No answer in my head. Trowbridge laid Lexi on the myst-covered floor.

Cordelia stepped across the gap, her chin lifted in its most obstinate tilt. She sank to her haunches, reaching with her big-knuckled hand to pick up Lexi's fisted one. Then she lowered her voice to a whisper that perhaps she thought I couldn't hear. "The Fae will lose the bag and the Fae tear the moment the wind catches him."

"He'll revive in there," said Trowbridge grimly. "Just slip the strap through his arm."

Once she had done so, my mate turned to me, waiting for me to give him leave.

Why was this harder than sending Trowbridge? Was it because I'd seen the gray that swallowed white hope? The dark that waited to pounce on those with too bright dreams?

I nodded to Trowbridge.

Be strong, Lexi. Get well.

"Now," I said.

My mate slid my brother through the mouth of the gates. A wind tugged my twin upward and teasingly held him for my inspection, his head slumped, his body upright, caught in the embrace of her cold and cruel current of air.

I've made a mistake. I've put my faith in—

Suddenly, my brother gasped. His back arched. His eyes shot open.

Honeysuckle sweet, she whisked him away.

I listened hard—was there a scream? An echo of a cry? But all I heard was the distant chime of bells.

I'll see you soon, my twin.

My wrist throbbed.

Breath held, I watched for the surface of the gates' window to Merenwyn to ripple like water does when a pebble is tossed into it, but it remained flat. Placid. The pastoral scene beyond the gates unmoved and unchanged by the events from this world. The same grasses sighing. The same patch of yellow flowers gently bobbing to Merenwyn's fragrant breeze.

So, I'd done my job. I'd fed my brother to the beast.

It had swallowed him, and for the moment, my part was done.

Face set in her trademark scowl, Cordelia walked away from the portal as if it were her stage. Back straight, hips swaying, head lifted.

Trowbridge turned to the pack. The columns of pink fairy myst were an unlikely background for a man who'd seen hell and come back from it.

"It's done," he told them. "We have sent a message back to the Fae. Do not come here, hoping to take that which is ours."

"Oh yeah!" shouted someone from the back.

Rachel Scawens pivoted and said, "Shut your mouth."

And he did. They all did.

"It comes down to this," said Trowbridge. "We stand united or we don't stand at all."

An Alpha's light sparked in his eyes.

"We are the Werewolves of Creemore. This is our land. Our lives. We will stand for what we have. We will protect what we own. We will handle each threat delivered to us with the same speed and ruthlessness—be it from the Fae or some asshole from the Council who wants to squeeze us for some more tithes."

His flare carried across the field and painted each one of their faces with his own tint of Trowbridge blue.

A girl moaned.

Then he said simply, "Now go home to your families."

With that, they left the field. Quietly. Hats were pulled from back pockets and replaced on bowed heads. Arms were crossed against the fall chill. They left, not really looking like a feral pack of wolves, but more like a group of everyday people who'd suddenly seen their world picked up, shaken, and put back down again—the townsfolk streaming out of the high school following the big vote; the church group heading to their cars after a service that had shaken them to their core.

Harry touched Cordelia's arm, and she smacked Biggs's shoulder.

They left, too.

And still I held the damn gates.

"Tink, let it go," Trowbridge said softly.

"I will in a second."

"He's not coming through," he said. "You need to close the gates."

"You took a long time to come through the other side. I watched and I watched and then just when I thought you hadn't made it, Cordelia said that I had to wait a little longer—"

"I'm sorry I took so long, sweetheart." His scent touched me, tentatively.

"What if Mad-one didn't place the Old Mage's soul in our tree and Lexi's lost in a hook-back?"

"There's no way of knowing that until I bring you to Daniel's Rock."

"What if the Black Mage gets him when he crosses into Merenwyn?"

"Then we'll rescue him."

I tore my gaze from the hobbit window to look at my mate. "How can you have so much faith? I went to Threall thinking that I could solve things, and I only made it worse."

"You didn't make it worse. You just made it different."

"Why would you rescue the man who ordered your back flayed?"

"Because he's part of you." His gaze locked on mine. There was no shield, no mask. "And you are part of me. I'm not letting anything come between us again."

"How can you promise that?"

"I can't but I can promise that I'll die trying to keep us together. And that I will protect and love you for as long as we have left." Trowbridge's scent licked my trembling arm. "Come on, sweetheart, say the word to close the gates."

I looked through the Gates of Merenwyn. Saw the grass

swaying in its wind. The wedge of blue in the valley. A bird circled the trees, looking for its nest.

Karma—this is it. No more lessons from you.

The next person through that round window will be me.

Did she hear me? I don't know. Truth be told, I no longer cared.

We were done.

I'd never be her bitch to torture again.

"Sy'ehella."

Epilogue

The kitchen smelled of soap and candles. To Cordelia's baleful dismay, the power had inexplicably gone off just after we straggled back to the house. "I'll get the utility company out here first thing in the morning," Harry had said grimly, just before he'd gone to pick up the barbecued chicken order from the Swiss Chalet in Collingwood. In the interim, the pack had brought every type of candle and votive you could imagine, until Cordelia taped a note to the door advising them that our needs had been met. She and Biggs had chosen the best from the collection set on the front porch and placed them here and there. Candlelight flickered and scents mingled—cinnamon, pumpkin, and vanilla. Not a floral tone among them. But then again, they'd been brought by Weres.

With wolves it's all about the things that speak to the stomach.

And perhaps, for some, the heart.

I studied Trowbridge. Dark hair, less than a quarter inch long. Blue eyes the color of the Mediterranean, now downcast, fixed on his task. A streak of dirt highlighting sharp cheekbones. Shoulders wide with a hollow right there, below his collarbone—warm and ready for my head. Muscles strong enough to carry a whole pack's burdens.

Wearing Ralph and the T-shirt I'd worn last night to bed.
Faded jeans tight, top button undone.

Bare feet.

Nice feet.

Mine.

My Trowbridge wrung out the tea cloth, and resumed his
ministrations. Dab. Press. Dab. The bite wound on my forearm was worrying him. He hadn't said anything, but the
deep furrow of his brow was telegraphing his uneasiness.

If I thought he'd believe me, I'd have told him that the
sweet Fae blood that kept oozing from one of the deeper
tooth marks wasn't a big deal. Merry had done her best.
Sooner or later, I'd heal; I always did, one way or the other.
Besides, we'd dodged a bullet. We weren't dead yet. While
my twin was in—

No. Stop it.

Yet, it was impossible not to think of him. Someone
had recovered Lexi's hat from the floor and placed it on
top of the refrigerator. Probably Biggs. He would have
seen it, and thought "hat" instead of what it was; my twin's
bowler, with a single strand of long blond hair curled on its
brim. I drew in a ragged breath and Trowbridge's head
sharply lifted. "You didn't hurt me," I said softly. "I was
just thinking about our assault on Merenwyn."

"You think too much," he murmured.

"Ditto." With a sigh, I tugged his makeshift compress
free from his hand. "That dirt on your face is driving me
crazy. Let me get it."

And . . . I felt it. The instant I placed the cloth tenderly
to his cheek, a faint tremor went straight through his body.
I glanced up. His jaw was hard, his gaze hooded. Someone
less observant than me might not have noticed he'd just
vibrated like a tuning fork. Though they might have cued
into the fact that the air between us was becoming decid-
edly musk-toned.

"I feel it, too," I told him with my eyes. "And I'm no
longer frightened by the strength of my desire for you."

Whether he got that, I don't know. But one of us had to

change the subject before my knees started knocking, so I asked, "What are you going to tell the pack when we come back from our secret mission?"

He gave me a real, true-life Trowbridge grin—devil winking from glimmering blue eyes, teeth flashing. "I'll cross that bridge when I have to."

Despite myself, I smiled back. "You really shouldn't use that phrase, Trowbridge."

Gravel crunched as Harry's truck pulled up at the back.

"Dinner!" called Cordelia. She placed a glass by Trowbridge's seat—the tall Windsor chair with the armrests had to be his. The others didn't have a nice strip of wood to balance your elbows on. Or, for that matter, come with a relatively new seat cushion. I still don't know where Cordelia found that ruffled gem.

"I'm starved." Biggs walked into the kitchen with the ferret draped over his arm—evidently a truce had been called. The animal's small head tilted toward me, its expressive face so human, I couldn't shake the feeling that Lexi's pet had something to say but not the language skills to say it.

Ferret, I'm going to bring him back, even if I have to club a few mages to do it.

Cold fall air chilled the room as Harry shouldered through the door, his arms burdened. A second later Anu ghosted into the room. She stood near the doorway, her posture set on preflight, her eyes fixed hungrily on the food that Cordelia was pulling out of the sacks. Trowbridge pulled out a chair at the other end of the table and said something to her in Merenwynian. With a coy sideways glance toward me, she dropped into the chair.

Forget about it, niece. He's mine.

Cordelia fussed, taking time to discard the containers and rearrange the food on serving platters. Meanwhile, Harry tore open a white plastic bag, pulled out a bottle of Grade A maple syrup, and set it in front of me with a "There you go, Little Miss. Your main course."

Then he winked and pulled out a medium paper bag from the recesses of his coat jacket—the type you got from Deidre's Bakery on Wellington Street. "She saw me passing and sent these to you. Compliments of the shop."

I inhaled. "White chocolate chip with macadamia nuts."

"Your favorite," Cordelia said. "Try not to eat more than four at one sitting."

The rest of the family's meal was set on the table.

I would say that they fell on it like wolves, but they didn't. Everybody politely (and somewhat impatiently) waited for Trowbridge to choose the first piece. He requisitioned a whole chicken, *then* they fell on the platter like the wild creatures they truly were.

Hiding my smile, I twisted the cap off the bottle of syrup and poured a good measure into the bottom of a bowl. Then—I *promised*, okay?—I slid the happy meal to my niece. For a moment Anu's gaze stared at it. Then, she half stood, leaned over, and filched a piece of chicken off Biggs's plate.

"She just . . ." Biggs's head swung back and forth. "She just . . ."

Trowbridge grinned—which made him look about ten years younger and three times handsomer. Then he picked up his fork with his left hand, and searched for my hand with his right. He rested our entwined hands on his strong thigh.

I stroked his thumb with mine.

We could grow together, if time and fate let us.

Get stronger over time.

Suddenly, that desperate race I'd envisioned in my future—me plodding heavily around the track, sides burning, feet whimpering, all in grim hope of catching up to Trowbridge—seemed enormously stupid. He was here with me, right now. Not ahead of me.

Beside me. Holding my hand.

How simple was that?

Tonight, no one at this table expected me to be anything other than what I was.

I picked up my spoon.

I am Hedi Peacock-Stronghold.

And I am loved.